CROSSING THE LINE

LUCIUS TOOK A LONG TIME choosing his words. "You are a puzzle to me, Jessica," he finally said. "A mystery. But at least I am open to the possibility of exploring that which I don't understand."

The dim light glimmered in his black eyes, and we were so close that I could see the faint shadow of stubble on his cheeks. Most guys I knew still seemed more like boys than men. Did Jake even shave? But Lucius . . . he had crossed that line. And I was sitting on a bed with him. Alone. In a darkened room. Talking about "exploring" my so-called "mysteries." I edged away.

"What would happen, anyway, if we didn't get married?" I asked, trying to change the subject. Distancing us again. "How bad could it be?"

Jessica's Guide to Dating on the DARK SIDE

BETH FANTASKEY

GRAPHIA

HOUGHTON MIFFLIN HARCOURT

Boston New York

All rights reserved. Published in the United States by Graphia, an imprint of Houghton
Mifflin Harcourt Publishing Company. Originally published in hardcover in the United
States by Harcourt Children's Books, an imprint of Houghton Mifflin Harcourt Publishing
Company, 2009.

For information about permission to reproduce selections from this book, write to
Permissions, Houghton Mifflin Harcourt Publishing Company, 215 Park Avenue South,
New York, New York 10003.

Graphia and the Graphia logo are registered trademarks of Houghton Mifflin Harcourt
Publishing Company.

www.hmhbooks.com

The Library of Congress had cataloged the harcdover edition as follows:
Fantaskey, Beth.
Jessica's guide to dating on the dark side/Beth Fantaskey.
p. cm.
Summary: Seventeen-year-old Jessica, adopted and raised in Pennsylvania, learns
that she is descended from a royal line of Romanian vampires and that she is betrothed
to a vampire prince, who poses as a foreign exchange student while courting her.
[1. Vampires—Fiction. 2. Dating (Social customs)—Fiction. 3. High schools—Fiction.
4. Schools—Fiction. 5. Arranged marriage—Fiction. 6. Identity—Fiction. 7. Kings,
queens, rulers, etc.—Fiction. 8. Pennsylvania—Fiction. 9. Romania—Fiction.] I. Title.
PZ7.F222285Jes   2008
[Fic]—dc22   2007049002
ISBN 978-0-15-206384-9
ISBN 978-0-547-25940-6 pb

Text set in Garamond
Designed by April Ward

Printed in the United States of America
DOM 10 9 8 7 6 5 4 3 2 1

For my parents,
Donald and Marjorie Fantaskey

"Just remember, girls: The young male vampire is a predator by nature. Some boys may look at you not only as a romantic interest, but as prey . . ."

Chapter 1, "On the Verge of Adult Vampiredom," *in* Growing Up Undead: A Teen Vampire's Guide to Dating, Health, and Emotions

Jessica's Guide
to *Dating* on the
DARK SIDE

Chapter 1

THE FIRST TIME I saw him, a heavy, gray fog clung to the cornfields, tails of mist slithering between the dying stalks. It was a dreary early morning right after Labor Day, and I was waiting for the school bus, just minding my own business, standing at the end of the dirt lane that connected my family's farmhouse to the main road into town.

I was thinking about how many times I'd probably waited for that bus over the course of a dozen years, killing time like any mathlete would, by doing calculations in my head, when I noticed him.

And suddenly that familiar stretch of blacktop seemed awfully desolate.

He was standing under a massive beech tree across the road from me, his arms crossed over his chest. The tree's low, gnarled branches twisted down around him, nearly concealing him in limbs and leaves and shadows. But it was obvious that he was tall and wearing a long, dark coat, almost like a cloak.

My chest clenched, and I swallowed hard. *Who stands*

under a tree at the crack of dawn, in the middle of nowhere, wearing a black cloak?

He must have realized I'd spotted him, because he shifted a little, like he was deciding whether to leave. Or maybe cross the road.

It had never struck me how vulnerable I'd been all those mornings I'd waited out there alone, but the realization hit me hard then.

I glanced down the road, heart thudding. *Where is the stupid bus? And why did my dad have to be so big on mass transit, anyhow? Why couldn't I own a car, like practically every other senior? But no, I had to "share the ride" to save the environment. When I'm abducted by the menacing guy under the tree, Dad will probably insist my face only appear on recycled milk cartons. . . .*

In the precious split second I wasted being angry at my father, the stranger really did move in my direction, stepping out from under the tree, and I could have sworn—just as the bus, thank god, crested the rise about fifty yards down the road—I could have sworn I heard him say, "Antanasia."

My old name . . . The name I'd been given at birth, in Eastern Europe, before I'd been adopted and brought to America, rechristened Jessica Packwood. . . .

Or maybe I was hearing things, because the word was drowned out by the sound of tires hissing on wet pavement, grinding gears, and the whoosh of the doors as the driver, old Mr. Dilly, swung them open for me. *Wonderful, wonderful bus number 23.* I'd never been so happy to climb on board.

With his usual grunted "Mornin', Jess," Mr. Dilly put the bus in gear, and I stumbled down the aisle, searching for an empty seat or a friendly face among the half-groggy riders. It sucked sometimes, living in rural Pennsylvania. The town kids were probably still sleeping, safe and sound in their beds.

Locating a spot at the very back of the bus, I plopped down with a rush of relief. Maybe I'd overreacted. Maybe my imagination had run wild, or too many episodes of *America's Most Wanted* had messed with my head. Or maybe the stranger really had meant me harm. . . . Twisting around, I peered out the rear window, and my heart sank.

He was still there, but in the road now, booted feet planted on either side of the double yellow line, arms still crossed, watching the bus drive away. Watching me.

"Antanasia . . ."

Had I really heard him call me by that long-forgotten name?

And if he knew *that* obscure fact, what else did the dark stranger, receding in the mist, know about my past?

More to the point, what did he want with me in the present?

Chapter 2

"SO THAT PRETTY MUCH sums up my summer at camp." My best friend Melinda Sue Stankowicz sighed, pulling open the heavy glass door to Woodrow Wilson High School. "Homesick kids, sunburn, poison ivy, and big spiders in the showers."

"Sounds like being a counselor was awful." I sympathized as we entered the familiar hallway, which smelled of cleanser and fresh floor wax. "If it helps, I gained at least five pounds waitressing at the diner. I just kept eating pie every time I got a break."

"You look great." Mindy waved off my complaint. "Although I'm not sure about your hair . . ."

"Hey!" I protested, smoothing down my unruly curls, which did seem to be rebelling in the late-summer humidity. "I'll have you know I spent an hour with a hair dryer and this 'straightening balm' that cost me a week's tips . . ." I trailed off, realizing that Mindy was distracted, not listening to me. I followed her gaze down the hall and toward the lockers.

"And speaking of looking great," she said.

Jake Zinn, who lived on a farm near my family's place, was struggling with his new locker combination. Frowning at a scrap of paper in his hand, he spun the lock and rattled the handle. An obviously brand-new white T-shirt made his summer tan look especially deep. The sleeves hugged tight around bulging biceps.

"Jake looks *amazing*," Mindy whispered as we approached my neighbor. "He must have joined a gym or something. And did he get *highlights*?"

"He lugged hay bales all summer in the sun, Min," I whispered back. "He doesn't need a gym—or bleach in his hair."

Jake glanced up as we walked past, and smiled when he saw me. "Hey, Jess."

"Hey," I replied. Then my mind went blank.

Mindy chimed in, preventing an awkward silence. "Looks like they gave you the wrong combination," she noted, nodding at Jake's still-closed locker. "Did you try kicking it?"

Jake ignored the suggestion. "You didn't work last night, huh, Jess?"

"No, I'm done at the diner," I said. "It was just a summer job."

Jake looked a little disappointed. "Oh. Well, I guess I'll have to catch up with you around school, then."

"Yeah. I'm sure we'll have some classes together," I said, feeling my cheeks get warm. "See ya." I sort of dragged Mindy along with me down the hall.

"What was *that* all about?" she demanded when we were out of earshot. She glanced over her shoulder at Jake.

My face grew warmer. "What was *what* all about?"

"Jake looking all sad that you quit the diner. You turning bright red—"

"It's nothing," I advised her. "He came in a few times near the end of my shift and gave me a ride home. We hung out a little . . . And I am *not* red."

"Really?" Mindy's smile was smug. "You and Jake, huh?"

"It was no big deal," I insisted.

The gleam in Mindy's eyes told me she knew I wasn't being completely honest. "This is going to be a very interesting year," she predicted.

"And speaking of interesting . . ." I started to tell my best friend about the scary stranger at the bus stop. But the moment I thought of him, the hair on the back of my neck prickled, almost like I was being watched.

"Antanasia . . ."

The low, deep voice echoed in my brain, like a half-remembered nightmare.

5

I rubbed the back of my neck. Maybe I would tell Mindy the story later. Or maybe the whole thing would just blow over and I'd never even think about the guy again.

That was probably what would happen.

Yet the prickly sensation didn't go away.

Chapter 3

"THIS IS GOING to be such an exciting class," Mrs. Wilhelm promised, bubbling over with enthusiasm as she handed out the reading list for Senior English Literature: Shakespeare to Stoker. "You are all going to love the classics I've selected. Prepare yourselves for a year of epic quests, heart-stopping romances, and the clashes of great armies. All without ever leaving Woodrow Wilson High School."

Apparently not everybody was as ecstatic about clashing armies and thumping hearts as Mrs. Wilhelm, because I heard a lot of groans as the reading list circulated through the class. I accepted my copy from my longtime tormentor Frank Dormand, who'd plopped into the seat in front of me like a massive, gooey spitball, and did a quick survey. *Oh, no. Not* Ivanhoe. *And* Moby Dick . . . *who had time for* Moby Dick? This was supposed to be the year I had a social life. Not to mention Dracula . . . *please.* If there was one thing I hated, it was spooky fairy tales with no basis in reality or logic. That was my parents' territory, and I had no interest in going there.

Stealing a quick look across the aisle at Mindy, I saw panic and misery in her eyes, too, as she whispered, "What does 'wuthering' mean?"

6

"No idea," I whispered back. "We'll look it up."

"I also want you to pass around this seating chart," Mrs. Wilhelm continued, squishing around on her sensible shoes. "The desk you've selected will be your assigned seat for the year. I see some new faces out there, and I want to get to know you all as quickly as possible, so *do not move*."

I slouched in my seat. *Great.* I was destined for a whole year of Frank Dormand's moronic, but mean, comments, which I was certain he'd spew every time he turned to hand something back down the aisle. And legendarily bitchy cheerleader Faith Crosse had claimed the seat directly behind me. I was sandwiched between two of the school's nastiest people. At least Mindy was across from me. And—I looked back to my left—Jake had found a desk near mine. He grinned when I met his eyes. It could have been worse, I guess. But not much.

Frank slid around in his chair to toss the seating chart at me. "Here you go, Packrat," he sneered, using the name he'd bestowed on me in kindergarten. "Put *that* on the chart." Yup. Moronic and mean, just like I'd predicted. And only 180 school days to go.

"At least I can spell my name," I hissed at him. *Jerk.*

Dormand squirmed back around, scowling, and I dug into my backpack for my pen. When I went to write my name, though, my ballpoint was bone dry, probably because it had lingered uncapped in my pack all summer. I gave the pen a shake and tried again. Nothing.

I started to turn to my left, thinking maybe Jake could loan me one of his pens. Before I could ask him, though, I felt a tap on my right shoulder. *Not now . . . Not now . . .* I considered ignoring it, but the tapper struck me lightly again.

"Excuse me, but are you in need of a writing instrument?"

The deep voice with the unusual Euro accent came from close behind me. I had no choice but to turn around.

No.

It was him. The guy from the bus stop. I would have recognized the strange outfit—the long coat, the boots—not to mention his imposing *height* anywhere. Only this time, he was just a few feet away. Close enough for me to see his eyes. They were so dark as to appear black and were boring into me with a cool, somehow unnerving, intelligence. I swallowed thickly, frozen in my seat.

Had he been in class all along? And if so, how could I have failed to notice him?

Maybe because he was sitting sort of apart from the rest of us. Or maybe it was because the very air in his particular corner seemed murky, the fluorescent light directly above his desk snuffed out. But it was more than that. It was almost like he *created* the darkness. *That's ridiculous, Jess. . . . He's a person, not a black hole. . . .*

"You require a writing instrument, yes?" he repeated, stretching his arm up the aisle—a long, muscular arm—to offer me a shiny gold pen. Not the plastic Bics that most people used. A real gold pen. You could tell just by the way it glittered that it was expensive. When I hesitated, a look of annoyance crossed his aristocratic face, and he shook the pen at me. "You do recognize a pen, right? This *is* a familiar tool, yes?"

I didn't appreciate the sarcasm, or the way he'd crept up on me twice in one day, and I kept staring, stupidly, until Faith

Crosse reached forward and pinched my arm. Hard. "Just sign the chart, *Jenn*, all right?"

"Hey!" I rubbed what would be a bruise, wishing I had the nerve to tell Faith off, both for pinching me and calling me by the wrong name. But the last person who'd tangled with Faith Crosse had ended up transferring to Saint Monica's, the local Catholic school. Faith had made her life at Woodrow Wilson that miserable.

"Hurry it up, *Jenn*," Faith snapped again.

"Okay, okay." Reluctantly reaching out to the stranger, I accepted the heavy pen from his hand, and as our fingers touched, I felt the most bizarre sensation ever. Like déjà vu crashing into a premonition. The past colliding with the future.

He smiled then, revealing the most perfect set of even, white teeth I'd ever seen. They actually gleamed, like well-tended weaponry. Above him, the fluorescent light sizzled to life for a second, flickering like lightning.

Okay, that was weird.

I slid back around, and my hand shook a little as I wrote my name on the seating chart. It was stupid to be freaked out. He was just another student. Obviously a new guy. Maybe he lived somewhere near our farm. He'd probably been waiting for the bus, just like me, and missed getting on somehow. His somewhat mysterious appearance in English class—a few feet from me—probably wasn't cause for alarm, either.

I looked to Mindy for her opinion. She'd obviously been waiting to make contact. Eyes wide, she jabbed her thumb in the guy's direction, mouthing a very exaggerated, *"He's so hot!"*

Hot? "You're crazy," I whispered. Yes, the guy was technically good-looking. But he was also totally terrifying with his cloak and boots and ability to materialize near me seemingly out of nowhere.

"The chart already," Faith growled behind me.

"Here." I passed the seating chart over my shoulder, getting a deep, razor-thin cut as impatient Faith snatched the paper from my hand. "Ouch!"

I shook the stinging, bleeding finger, then jabbed it into my mouth, tasting salt on my tongue, before I twisted back around to return the pen. *The faster, the better . . .* "Here. Thanks."

The guy who generated his own gloom stared at my fingers, and I realized that I was dripping blood on his expensive pen. "Um, sorry," I said, wiping the pen on my leg, for lack of a tissue. *Ugh. And will that stain come out of my jeans?*

His gaze followed my fingers, and I thought maybe he was revolted by the fact that I was bleeding. Yet I swore I saw something quite different than disgust in those black eyes. . . . And then he ran his tongue slowly across his lower lip.

What the hell was that?

Tossing the pen at him, I spun around in my seat. *I could change schools, like that girl who messed with Faith. Go to Saint Monica's. That's the answer. It's not too late. . . .*

The seating chart made its way back to Mrs. Wilhelm, and she read through the names, then glanced up with a smile that was directed just past my desk. "Let's take a moment to welcome our new foreign exchange student, Lucius . . ." Frowning, she referred back to her chart. "Vlades . . . cooo. Did I say that correctly?"

Most students would have just muttered, "Yeah, whatever." I mean, who really cared about a name?

My early-morning stalker, that's who.

"No," he intoned. "No, that is not correct."

Behind me, I heard the scrape of a chair against linoleum, and then a shadow loomed over my shoulder. My neck prickled again.

"Oh." Mrs. Wilhelm looked slightly alarmed as a tall teenager in a black velvet coat advanced up the aisle toward her. She raised a cautionary finger, like she was about to tell him to sit down, but he strode right past her.

Grabbing up a marker from the tray beneath the whiteboard, he flipped off the cap with authority and scrawled the word *Vladescu* in a flowing script.

"My name is Lucius Vladescu," he announced, pointing to the word. "Vla-DES-cu. Emphasis on the middle syllable, please."

Locking his hands behind his back, he began pacing, as though he was the teacher. One by one, he made eye contact with each student in the room, obviously summing us up. I sensed from the look on his face that we were found wanting somehow.

"The Vladescu name is rather revered in Eastern Europe," he lectured. "A noble name." He paused in his pacing and locked onto *my* eyes. "A *royal* name."

I had no idea what he was talking about.

"Does it not 'ring a bell,' as you Americans say?" he asked the class in general. But he was still staring at me.

God, his eyes were black.

I flinched away, looking to Mindy, who was actually fanning herself, totally oblivious to me. It was like she was under a spell. Everyone was. No one was fidgeting, or whispering, or doodling.

Almost against my will, I returned my attention to the teenager who'd hijacked English lit. It really was almost impossible not to watch him. Lucius Vladescu's longish glossy black hair was out of place in Lebanon County, Pennsylvania, but he would have fit right in with the European models in Mindy's *Cosmopolitan* magazines. He was muscular and lean like a model, too, with high cheekbones, a straight nose, and a strong jaw. And those eyes . . .

Why wouldn't he quit staring at me?

"Would you care to tell us anything else about yourself?" Mrs. Wilhelm finally suggested.

Lucius Vladescu spun on his booted heel to face her and capped the pen with a firm snap. "Not particularly. No." The answer wasn't rude . . . but he didn't address Mrs. Wilhelm like a student, either.

More like an equal.

"I'm sure we'd love to hear more about your heritage," Mrs. Wilhelm prompted, admitting, "It *does* sound interesting."

But Lucius Vladescu had returned his attention me.

I slunk down in my seat. *Is everyone noticing this?*

"You shall learn more about me in due time," Lucius said. There was a hint of frustration in his voice, and I had no idea why. But it scared me again. "That is a promise," he added, boring into my eyes. "A promise."

Yet it sounded more like a threat.

Chapter 4

"DID YOU SEE how the foreign guy was looking at you in English lit?" Mindy cried when we met up after school. "He's gorgeous, and he is so into you! And he's *royal.*"

I squeezed her wrist, trying to calm her down. "Min . . . before you buy a gift for our 'royal' wedding, I have to tell you something scary about the so-called gorgeous guy."

My friend crossed her arms, skeptical. I could tell that Mindy had already made up her mind about Lucius Vladescu, basing her opinion entirely on broad shoulders and a strong jaw. "What could you know about him that's scary? We just met him."

"Actually, I saw him earlier this morning," I said. "That guy—Lucius—was at the bus stop. Staring at me."

"That's *it*?" Mindy rolled her eyes. "Maybe he takes the bus."

"He didn't get on."

"So he missed the bus." She shrugged. "That's stupid, but not scary."

Mindy wasn't getting it at all. "It's weirder than that," I insisted. "I . . . I thought I heard him say my name. Just as the bus pulled up."

Mindy looked puzzled.

"My *old* name," I clarified.

My best friend sucked in her breath. "Okay. That could be a little weird."

"Nobody knows that name. Nobody."

In fact, I hadn't even shared much of my past with Mindy. The story of my adoption was my closely guarded secret. If it ever got out . . . people would think I'm a freak. I *felt* like a freak every time I thought about the story. My adoptive mother, a cultural anthropologist, had been studying an off-the-wall underground cult in central Romania. She'd been there with my dad to observe their rituals, in hopes of writing one of her groundbreaking insider journal articles about unique subcultures. However, things had gone wrong over in Eastern Europe. The cult had been a little *too* strange, a little too off-beat, and some Romanian villagers had banded together, intent on putting an end to the whole group. By force.

Just before the mob attacked, my birth parents had entrusted me, an infant, to the visiting American researchers, begging them to take me to the United States, where I would be safe.

I hated that story. Hated the fact that my birth parents had been ignorant, superstitious people duped into joining a cult. I didn't even want to know what the rituals were. I knew the kind of things my mom studied. Animal sacrifices, tree worship, virgins tossed into volcanoes . . . maybe my birth parents had been involved in some sort of deviant sexual stuff. Maybe that's why they had been murdered.

Who knew? Who *wanted* to know?

I didn't ask for details, and my adoptive parents never pressed the issue. I was just happy to be Jessica Packwood, American. Antanasia Dragomir didn't exist, as far as I was concerned.

"Are you *sure* he knew your name?" Mindy asked.

"No," I admitted. "But I thought I heard it."

"Oh, Jess." Mindy sighed. "Nobody knows that name. You probably just imagined the whole thing. Or else he said a word that sounds like Antanasia."

I looked at Mindy crosswise. "What word sounds like Antanasia?"

"I don't know. How about 'nice to meetcha'?"

"Yeah, right." But that did kind of make me laugh. We walked toward the street to wait for my mom to come pick me up. I had called at lunch to tell her I was *not* taking the bus home.

Mindy added her last two cents. "I'm just saying maybe you should at least give this Lucius a chance."

"Why?"

"Because . . . because he's so *tall*," Mindy explained, like height was proof of good character. "And did I mention European?"

My mom's rusty old VW van rattled up to the curb, and I waved to her. "Yes. It's so much better to be stalked by a tall European than an American of average height."

"Well, at least Lucius is paying attention to you." Mindy sniffed. "Nobody ever pays attention to me."

We reached the van, and I opened the door. Before I could even say hi, Mindy shoved me aside, leaned in, and blurted, "Jess has a boyfriend, Dr. Packwood!"

Mom looked puzzled. "Is that true, Jessica?"

It was my turn to shove Mindy out of the way. I climbed in and slammed the door, shutting my friend safely on the other side. Mindy waved, laughing, as Mom and I pulled away from the curb.

"A boyfriend, Jessica?" Mom asked again. "On the first day of school?"

"He's *not* my boyfriend," I grumbled, clicking on my seat belt. "He's a creepy foreign exchange student who's stalking me."

"Jessica, I'm sure you're exaggerating," Mom said. "Male adolescents are frequently socially awkward. You're probably misinterpreting innocent behaviors."

Like all cultural anthropologists, Mom believed she knew everything about human social interactions.

"You didn't see him at the bus stop this morning," I argued. "He was standing there in this big black cloak . . . And then when my finger bled, he licked his lip . . ."

When I said that, Mom hit the brakes so hard that my head nearly smacked the dashboard. A car behind us honked angrily.

"Mom! What was *that* about?"

"Sorry, Jessica," she said, looking a little pale. She stepped on the gas again. "It was just something you said . . . about getting cut."

"I cut my finger, and he practically drooled over it, like it was a ketchup-covered French fry," I shuddered. "It was so gross."

Mom grew even paler, and I knew something was up.

"Who . . . who is this boy?" she asked as we pulled up to a stop sign near Grantley College, where my mom taught. "What's his name?"

I could tell she was trying hard to sound unconcerned, and that made me more nervous.

"His name is . . ." Before I could say Lucius, though, I spotted him. Sitting on the low wall that surrounded the campus.

And he was watching me. Again. Sweat broke out on my forehead. But this time, I was pissed. *Enough is enough, already.* "He's right there," I cried, jabbing my finger at the window. "He's staring at me again!" It was not "socially awkward behavior." It was *stalking.* "I want him to leave me alone!"

Then my mom did something unexpected. She pulled over to the curb, right next to where Lucius waited, watching. "What is his name, Jess?" she asked again as she unbuckled her seat belt.

I figured Mom was going to confront him, so I grabbed her arm. "Mom, no. He's, like, unbalanced or something."

But my mother gently peeled my fingers from her arm. "His name, Jess."

"Lucius," I answered. "Lucius Vladescu."

"Oh, goodness," Mom muttered, looking past me at my stalker. "I suppose this really was inevitable . . ." She had a queer, distant look in her eyes.

"Mom?" *What was inevitable?*

"Wait here," she said, still not looking at me. "Do not move." She sounded so serious that I didn't protest. Without another word, Mom climbed out of the van and strode directly toward the menacing guy who'd tailed me all day. Was she crazy? Would he try to run away? Go berserk and hurt her? But no, he slipped gracefully off the wall and bowed—a real bow, at the waist—to my mother. *What the . . . ?*

I rolled down the window, but they spoke so softly I couldn't hear what they were saying. The conversation went on for what seemed like eons. And then my mother shook his hand.

Lucius Vladescu turned to go, and Mom got back in the van and turned the key.

"What was that all about?" I asked, dumbfounded.

My mother looked me straight in the eye and said, "You, your father, and I need to talk. Tonight."

"About what?" I demanded, a prickly feeling in the pit of my stomach. A bad prickle. "Do you *know* that guy?"

"We'll explain later. We have so, so much to tell you. And we need to do it before Lucius arrives for dinner."

My jaw was still on the floor when Mom patted my hand and pulled out into traffic.

Chapter 5

MY PARENTS NEVER got a chance to explain what was happening, though. When we got home, my dad was in the middle of teaching his tantric yoga class for oversexed, over-the-hill hippies, out in the studio behind the house, so Mom told me to go ahead with my chores.

And then Lucius arrived early for dinner.

I was in the barn mucking out stalls when, out of the corner of my eye, I saw a shadow cross the open barn door.

"Who's there?" I called nervously, still jumpy from the day's events.

When there was no answer, I got the bad feeling my visitor was our dinner guest. *Mom invited him,* I reminded myself as, sure enough, a tall European exchange student strode across the dusty riding ring. *He can't be that dangerous.*

Mom's endorsement aside, I kept a firm hold on my pitch-fork. "What are you doing here?" I demanded as he approached.

"Manners, manners," Lucius complained in his snooty accent, kicking up little puffs of dust with each long stride. He arrived within a few feet of me, and I was struck again by his height. "A lady doesn't bellow across barns," he continued. "And what sort of salutation was that?"

Is the guy who spied on me all day lecturing me *on etiquette?* "I asked you why you're here," I repeated, clutching the pitch-fork a little tighter.

"To become acquainted, of course," he said, continuing to appraise me, actually circling me, staring at my clothes. I spun around, trying to keep him in view, and caught him wrinkling his nose. "Surely you're eager to get to know me, too."

Not really . . . I had no idea what he was talking about, but the head-to-toe survey of my person was not cool. "Why are you staring at me like that?"

He stopped circling. "Are you *cleaning* stalls? Is that *feces* on your shoes?"

"Yeah," I said, confused by his tone. *Why did he care what is on my shoes?* "I muck the stalls every night."

"*You?*" He seemed baffled—and appalled.

"Somebody has to do it," I said. *Why does he think this is his business?*

"Yes, well, we have people for that, where I come from. Hired help." He sniffed. "You—a lady of your stature—should never do such a menial chore. It's offensive."

When he said that, my fingers tightened again on the pitchfork—and not out of fear. Lucius Vladescu wasn't just intimidating. He was *infuriating.* "Look, I've about had it with you creeping up on me, and your attitude," I snapped. "Who do you think you are, anyhow? And why are you following me?"

Anger and disbelief flickered in Lucius's black eyes. "Your mother still hasn't informed you, has she?" He shook his head. "Dr. Packwood vowed that she would tell you everything. Your parents are not so good at keeping promises."

"We . . . we're supposed to talk later," I stammered, my outrage fading a little in the face of his obvious anger. "Dad's teaching yoga . . ."

"Yoga?" Lucius gave a harsh laugh. "Contorting his frame into a series of ridiculous configurations is more important than informing his daughter about the pact? And what manner of man practices such a pacifist pastime? Men should train for war, not waste their time chanting 'om' and blathering about inner peace."

Forget the yoga and the blathering. "Pact? What pact?"

But Lucius was staring at the beamed ceiling of the barn, pacing around, hands clasped behind his back, muttering to himself. "This is not going well. Not going well at all. I advised the Elders that you should have been summoned back to Romania years ago, that you would never be a suitable bride . . ."

Whoa, there. "Bride?"

Lucius paused, turning on his heel to face me. "I grow weary of your ignorance." He moved closer to me, leaning down and peering into my eyes. "Because your parents refuse to inform you, I will deliver the news myself, and I shall make this simple for you." He pointed to his chest and announced, as though talking to a child, "I am a vampire." He pointed to my chest. "You are a vampire. And we are to be married, the moment you come of age. This has been decreed since our births."

I couldn't even process the "getting married" part, or the thing about "decreed." He'd lost me at "vampire."

Nuts. Lucius Vladescu is completely nuts. And I'm alone with him, in an empty barn.

So I did what any sane person would do. I jammed the pitchfork in the general direction of his foot and ran like hell for the house, ignoring his yowl of pain.

Chapter 6

"I AM *SO* not undead," I wailed.

But of course, no one paid attention. My parents were too focused on Lucius Vladescu's injured foot.

"Lucius, sit down," Mom ordered, looking none too happy with either of us.

"I prefer to stand," Lucius replied.

Mom pointed firmly at the ring of chairs around the kitchen table. "Sit. *Now.*"

Our injured visitor hesitated like he was going to disobey, then, muttering under his breath, took a chair. Mom yanked off his boot, which bore the visible imprint of a pitchfork tine, while my dad puttered about the kitchen, searching under the sink for the first aid kit while he waited for the herbal tea to brew.

"It's just bruised," Mom announced.

"Oh, good." Dad crawled out from under the sink. "I can't find the bandages, anyway. But we can still have tea."

The lanky self-proclaimed bloodsucker who had commandeered *my* seat at the kitchen table glared at me. "You are very lucky that my cobbler uses only the finest leather. You could have impaled me. And you do *not* want to impale a vampire. More to the point, is that any way to greet your future husband—or any guest, for that matter? With a pitchfork?"

"Lucius," my mother interrupted. "You did catch Jessica off guard. As I explained to you earlier, her father and I wanted to speak to her first."

"Yes, well, you certainly lingered over the task—for seventeen years. Someone had to take charge." Lucius pulled his foot from Mom's grasp and stood up, limping around the kitchen with one boot on, like a restless king in his castle. He picked up the container of chamomile, sniffed the contents, and frowned. "You *drink* this?"

"You'll like it," Dad promised. He poured four mugs. "It's very soothing in a stressful time like this."

"Enough with the tea. Just tell me what's going on," I begged, sitting down to reclaim my chair from Lucius. It wasn't warm at all. Almost like no one had been there just moments before. "Anybody. Please. Fill me in."

"As your parents wish, I will relinquish that duty to them," Lucius conceded. He lifted his steaming mug to his lips, sipped, and shuddered. "Good god, that's foul."

Ignoring Lucius, Mom shared a knowing glance with my dad, like they had a secret. "Ned . . . what do you think?"

Apparently he understood what she was hinting at, because Dad nodded and said, "I'll get the scroll," then left the kitchen.

"Scroll?" *Scrolls. Pacts. Brides. Why is everyone talking in code?* "What scroll?"

"Oh, dear." Mom sat in the chair next to mine and cradled my hands. "This is rather complicated."

"Try," I urged.

"You've always known that you are adopted from Romania," Mom began. "And that your birth parents were killed in a village conflict."

"Murdered by peasants," Lucius scowled. "Superstitious people, given to forming vicious hordes." He unscrewed the lid on Dad's organic peanut butter, tested it, and wiped his finger on his pants, which were black and hugged his long legs, almost like riding breeches. "Please tell me there's *something* palatable in this house."

Mom turned to address Lucius. "I'm going to ask you to stay quiet for a few minutes while I tell the story."

Lucius bowed slightly, his glossy blue-black hair gleaming under the kitchen lamp. "Of course. Continue."

Mom returned her attention to me. "But we didn't tell you the whole story, because the topic seemed to upset you so much."

"Now might be a good time," I suggested. "I couldn't get much more upset."

Mom sipped her tea and swallowed. "Yes, well, the truth is, your birth parents were destroyed by an angry mob trying to rid their village of vampires."

"Vampires?" Surely she was joking.

"Yes," Mom confirmed. "Vampires. Your parents were among the vampires I was studying at the time."

Okay, now it was not uncommon to hear words like *fairy* or *earth spirit* or even *troll* in my house. I mean, folk culture and

23

legends were my mom's research interest, and my dad had been known to host the occasional "angel communication" seminar in his yoga studio. But surely even my flaky parents didn't believe in Hollywood *movie monsters*. They couldn't have honestly believed that my birth parents had turned into bats, or dissolved in sunlight, or grew big fangs. *Could they?*

"You said you were studying some sort of cult," I countered. "A subculture that had some unusual rituals . . . but you never said anything about *vampires*."

"You have always been very logical, Jessica," Mom said. "You do not like things that cannot be explained by math or science. Your father and I were afraid the truth about your birth parents might deeply disturb you. So we kept things . . . vague."

"You're saying my birth parents actually thought they were vampires?" I sort of yelped.

Mom nodded. "Well . . . yes."

"They didn't just *think* they were vampires," Lucius grumbled. He'd retrieved his boot and was hopping around on one foot, attempting to pull it on. "They *were* vampires."

As I gawked at our guest in disbelief, the most disgusting thought in the world crossed my mind. Those rituals my mom had alluded to, related to my birth parents . . . "They didn't . . . actually *drink blood* . . ."

The expression on Mom's face said it all, and I thought I might pass out. My birth parents: deviant, disturbed blood drinkers.

"Tasty, tasty, stuff," Lucius commented. "You wouldn't, perchance, have any here, in lieu of this tea—"

Mom shot him a look.

Lucius frowned. "No. I suppose not."

"People do not drink blood," I insisted, my voice spiking kind of high. "And vampires do not exist!"

Lucius crossed his arms, glowering. "Excuse me. I'm right here."

"Lucius, please," Mom said in the calm but serious tone she reserved for hard-to-control students. "Give Jess time to process. She has an analytical bent that makes her resistant to the paranormal."

"I'm resistant to the *impossible*," I cried. "The *unreal*."

At this low point, Dad returned with a mildewed scroll cradled in his hands. "Historically, a lot of people are resistant to the idea of the undead," Dad noted, carefully placing the document on the table. "And the late 1980s were an especially lousy time for vampires in Romania. Big purges every few months. Lots of very nice vampires eliminated."

"Your birth parents—who were quite powerful within their subculture—realized that they were likely marked for destruction and entrusted you to us before they were killed, hoping we could keep you safe in the United States," Mom added.

"People don't drink blood," I repeated. "They don't. You didn't *see* my parents act like vampires, did you?" I challenged. "You never saw them grow fangs and bite necks? I know you didn't. Because it didn't happen."

"No," Mom admitted, taking my hands again. "We were not allowed that kind of access."

"Because it didn't happen," I repeated.

"No," Lucius interjected. "Because biting is very private,

very intimate. You don't just invite people to watch. Vampires are a sensual race but not given to exhibitionism, for god's sake. We're discreet."

"But we have no reason to believe anyone lied to us about drinking blood," Mom added. "And it's nothing to be upset about, Jess. It was quite normal to them. Had you grown up in Romania in that subculture, it would have seemed ordinary to you, too."

I yanked my hands away. "I really don't think so."

With a deep sigh, Lucius resumed pacing. "Honestly, I can't stand this going around anymore. The story is quite simple. You, Antanasia, are the last of a long line of powerful vampires. The Dragomirs. Vampire royalty."

Now that made me laugh, a squeaky, kind of hysterical laugh. "Vampire royalty. Right."

"Yes. Royalty. And that is the last part of the story, which your parents still seem reluctant to relate." Lucius leaned over the table across from me, bracing his arms, staring me down. "You are a vampire princess—the heir to the Dragomir leadership. I am a vampire prince. The heir to an equally powerful clan, the Vladescus. More powerful, I would say, but that's not the point. We were pledged to each other in an engagement ceremony shortly after our births."

I looked to my mom for help, but all she said was, "The ceremony was quite dramatic, very elaborate."

"In an enormous cave in the Carpathians," Dad added. "With candles everywhere." He gazed at my mom with loving admiration. "No other outsider ever had such access."

I glared at them. "You were *there*? At this ceremony?"

"Oh, we met lots of vampires on that trip and saw so many interesting cultural events." Mom smiled a little, remembering. "You should read my research summary in the *Journal of Eastern European Folk Culture*. It was rather landmark insider work, if I do say so myself."

"Let me finish, please," Lucius grumbled.

"Easy there," Dad chided gently. "In this little democracy, everybody gets a chance to speak."

From the disdainful look Lucius shot my dad, I could tell he didn't care much for democracy. The delusional Dracula wannabe resumed pacing. "The betrothal ceremony sealed our destinies, Antanasia. We are to be married soon after you come of age. Our bloodlines united, consolidating our clans' strength and ending years of rivalry and warfare." His black eyes gleamed, and his gaze drifted far away. "It shall be a glorious moment in our history, when we ascend to power. Five million vampires—your family, my family combined—all under our rule." My so-called betrothed snapped back to reality and glanced at me, sniffing, "I'll do all the 'heavy lifting,' of course, leadership-wise."

"You're all insane," I declared, staring from one face to the next. "This is crazy."

Moving closer to me, Lucius crouched so we were face to face. For the first time, I saw curiosity, not disdain or mockery or raw power, in his dark eyes. "Would it be so repugnant, really, Antanasia? To be with me?"

I wasn't sure what he meant, but I thought he was talking about . . . the two of us together, not in a bid for political power, but in a romantic way.

I didn't say anything. Did Lucius Vladescu really think I would fall for him, just because he had a handsome face? A killer body? That I would care that he smelled like the sexiest, spiciest cologne I'd ever sniffed . . .

"Let's show her the scroll," Dad interrupted, breaking the moment.

"Yes, it's time," Mom agreed.

I had almost forgotten the musty paper, but now Dad sat down and carefully unrolled the scroll on the kitchen table. The brittle paper crackled as he smoothed it with gentle fingers. The words—Romanian, presumably—were unintelligible to me, but it looked like some sort of legal document, with lots of signatures at the bottom. I shifted my gaze, refusing to look any closer at a bunch of nonsense.

"I shall translate," Lucius volunteered, standing up. "Unless, of course, Antanasia's studied her Romanian?"

"It's next on my to-do list," I said through gritted teeth. *Multilingual show-off.*

"You would be wise to start learning, my future bride," Lucius replied, edging even closer and leaning over my shoulder to read. I could feel his breath on my cheek. It was unnaturally cool, sweet. Against my better judgment, I kept inhaling that unusual cologne, too, drawing it deep into my lungs. Lucius was so close that my curly dark hair brushed his jaw, and he absently swept the stray locks away, the back of his fingers grazing my cheek. I jolted at the touch. The sensation hit me, right in the pit of my stomach.

If Lucius felt the same shock I did, he didn't betray it as he focused intently on the document. *Am I getting dizzy from sniffing cologne? Imagining things?*

I shifted slightly in my chair, trying not to touch him again, as our arrogant visitor ran his finger beneath the first line of the scroll. "This declares that you, Antanasia Dragomir, are promised in marriage to me, Lucius Vladescu, shortly after the achievement of your maturity at the age of eighteen, and that all parties in witness agree to this covenant. And upon the marriage, our clans shall be united and at peace." He leaned back. "As I said, it's quite simple, really. And see: your adoptive father's signature. And your mother's."

I couldn't resist glancing when he said that, and sure enough, Mom and Dad's scrawled signatures were on the document, amid dozens of unfamiliar Romanian names. *Traitors.* Shoving the scroll away, I crossed my arms and glared at my parents. "How could you promise me away like . . . like . . . a prize cow?"

"We didn't 'promise you away,' Jessica," Mom soothed. "You weren't our daughter then. We were merely there to witness a unique ritual, in the interest of my research. This was weeks before the purge, weeks before we adopted you. We had no idea what the future held for any of us."

"Besides, no one promises cows," Lucius scoffed. "Who would promise cattle? You are a vampire princess. Your destiny is not entirely your own."

Princess . . . He honestly thinks I'm a vampire princess. . . . The strange, almost pleasurable, sensation I'd felt when he'd brushed my cheek was forgotten as reality hit me again. Lucius Vladescu was a lunatic.

"If I were a vampire, I'd want to bite someone. I'd be thirsty for blood," I said in a last ditch attempt to interject reason into a discussion that had devolved into the absurd.

"You will come into your true nature," Lucius promised. "You are coming of age right now. And when I bite you for the first time, *then* you will be a vampire. I've brought you a book—a guide, so to speak—which will explain everything—"

I stood up so fast my chair tipped over, smashing to the floor. "He is not going to bite me," I interrupted, pointing a shaky finger at Lucius. "And I'm not going to Romania and marrying him! I don't care what kind of 'betrothal ceremony' they had!"

"You will all honor the pact," Lucius growled. It wasn't a suggestion.

"Now don't get dictatorial on us, Lucius," Dad urged, kicking back in his chair and stroking his beard. "I told you. This is a democracy. Let's just all just take a deep breath. Like Ghandi said, 'We must become the change we want to see.'"

Lucius had clearly never grappled with a master of passive resistance before, because he seemed genuinely caught off-balance by Dad's firm, yet mellow, and totally off-kilter, assessment of the situation. "What does that even mean?" he finally asked.

"No one's making any decisions today," Mom translated. "It's late, and we're all tired and a little overwhelmed. Besides, Lucius, Jessica is not ready to contemplate marriage. She hasn't even kissed a boy yet, for goodness' sake."

Lucius smirked at me, raising one eyebrow. "Really? No suitors? How shocking. I would have thought your pitchfork skills would be attractive to certain bachelors here in farm country."

I wanted to die. Die right there. I wanted to run to the knife drawer, grab the biggest blade I could find, and plunge it into my heart. To be exposed as never even being kissed . . . it was almost worse than being a vampire princess. The vampire thing was a ridiculous fantasy, but my total lack of experience . . . that was real. "Mom! That is so embarrassing! Did you have to tell him that?"

"Well, Jessica, it's true. I don't want Lucius thinking you're some sort of experienced young woman, ready for marriage."

"I shan't take advantage," Lucius promised seriously. "And she can't be forced into a marriage, of course. It is a new century. Unfortunately. But I am afraid that I am compelled to pursue this courtship until Antanasia realizes her place at my side. As she will."

"I will not."

Lucius totally brushed this off. "The linkage of our clans is mandated by the oldest, most powerful members: the Elders of the Vladescu and Dragomir families. And the Elders always get their way."

Mom stood. "It will be Jessica's decision, Lucius."

"Of course." The condescending half-smile on Lucius's face said otherwise, though. "Now where shall I stay?"

"Stay?" Dad blinked, confused.

"Yes. Sleep," Lucius clarified. "I've had a long journey, endured my first stultifying day at the so-called public school here, and I am weary."

"You're not going back to school," I objected, panicking. I'd forgotten about school. "You just can't!"

"Of course I shall attend school," Lucius replied.

"How *did* you enroll?" Mom asked.

"I'm here on what's called a 'student visa,'" Lucius explained. "The Elders thought it would be difficult to explain my extended presence here otherwise. Vampires don't like to raise suspicions, as you can imagine. We like to blend in."

Blend in? In a velvet topcoat in summer? In Lebanon County,
Pennsylvania? The conservative, bologna-making heart of the state's
farm country, where sturdy people of Germanic descent still think
pierced ears are radical and possibly portals to hell?

"You're really a foreign exchange student?" Dad was frowning.

"Yes. *Your* foreign exchange student, to be exact," Lucius clarified.

Mom raised a cautionary hand. "We never agreed to that."

"Yeah," Dad added. "Wouldn't we have to sign something? Isn't there paperwork?"

Lucius laughed. "Oh, paperwork. A small detail worked out in Romania. No one with any good sense turns down a request from the Vladescu clan. It's just bad form. And the consequences of refusing us a favor . . . well, let's just say that people everywhere tend to *stick their necks out* for us."

"Lucius, you should have consulted with us first," Mom objected.

Lucius's shoulders slumped, but just slightly. "Yes. Well, perhaps we did overstep our bounds there. But you must admit, you are honor bound to welcome me. You knew this day—and I—would arrive."

Dad cleared his throat and looked at Mom. "We did promise the Dragomirs years ago that when the time came—"

"Oh, Ned, I don't know. We need to consider Jessica's feelings . . ."

"You made an oath to my family," Lucius reminded them again. "Besides, I have nowhere else to go. I will *not* return to the so-called country inn downtown where I slept last night.

The room had a pig theme, for god's sake. Pig wallpaper, pig tchotchkes everywhere. And a Vladescu does *not* slumber with swine."

Mom sighed, laying her hands on my shoulders reassuringly. "I suppose for now, Lucius can stay in the guest apartment above the garage while we figure things out. Okay, Jessie? It's just temporary, I'm sure."

"Hey, it's your farm," I mumbled, knowing I was defeated. My parents always took in strays. Nasty cats, nippy dogs . . . if it was homeless, it could live on our farm, even if it threatened to bite you.

And that is how a teenager who claimed to be a vampire came to reside in our garage at the start of my once-in-a-lifetime senior year. And not just any vampire. My arrogant, overbearing vampire *betrothed.* The last person in hell—or *from* hell—I wanted to share a ride to school with, even, let alone be bound to for eternity.

I lay awake half the night thinking about my ruined life. My birth parents: cult members who swore they drank blood—and whom I'd try never, ever to think of again. There was nothing I could do about them now except put them out of my mind. Their story could—and would—remain hidden in the past.

But the future . . . all I'd wanted was a chance to go out with Jake Zinn, a normal guy, and instead I'd gotten a freakish fiancé, right in my garage. As if everyone at school didn't already think my family was bizarre enough, with Dad's yoga and his unproductive, organic, anti-meat farm, and my mom being the breadwinner, studying make-believe mumbo jumbo. Now . . . now I would really be a pariah. The high school girl engaged to the ghoul.

And what a ghoul.

Lying in bed, I couldn't stop recalling the smell of Lucius's cologne, as he'd leaned close to me. The power he'd exuded striding around my English lit class. The touch of his fingers against my cheek. His assertion that one day, he would *sink his teeth* into me.

God, what a psycho.

Tossing back the covers, I sat up and pushed aside the curtain, looking out the window toward the garage. A light still burned in the second-floor apartment. Lucius was awake out there. Doing what?

Swallowing hard, I fell back on my pillow and pulled the covers up tightly around my throat—my tender, vulnerable, as yet un-kissed throat—half wishing for and half dreading the morning.

Chapter 7

DEAR UNCLE VASILE,

I write to you from my "loft" above the Packwoods' rundown garage, where I am housed, not unlike some sort of unwanted automobile or forgotten piece of luggage, no doubt breathing in stale vehicle exhaust day and night.

Although here only a few weeks, how I mourn the rugged splendor of the Carpathians, the way the wolves howl in the night, chilling and beautiful. Only when one is in a place that completely lacks danger or mystery can one understand how profoundly the dark places of the world can be missed.

Here, one worries only about colliding on the narrow lanes with a wagon overloaded with hay (and people say Romania is backward!) or whether there will be a "good show" on the television at night. (The Packwoods have been kind enough to supply me with a TV out here in my backyard exile, to which I can only reply with the Americanism "Whoopee.")

But of course I realize that I am here not for the entertainment, the arts, or the architecture. (Can I ever again be happy in our soaring Gothic castle after walking the halls of Woodrow Wilson High School, a literal ode to linoleum?) Nor should I be focused on the cuisine. (Really, Vasile—vegans?) Or the scintillating conversation of my fellow students. (The word like has become completely unlikable.)

But I digress.

The girl, Vasile. The girl. Imagine my shock at finding my future wife—my "princess"—knee-deep in animal waste, barking at me from across a barn and then attempting to stab me in the foot with a farm implement, like a demented stable hand. I will not address the fact that the horse excrement seemed permanently encrusted on her man-boots; it is probably bad manners even to bring it up.

Regardless. She is rude. She is uncooperative. She lacks any appreciation of her culture—and certainly of her duty, her destiny, the rare opportunity being afforded to her by the simple fact of her birth.

In sum, Jessica Packwood is not a vampire. Living in America seems to have cleansed our future princess of all traces of the royal blood that we know must have coursed through her veins at birth. She has undergone a terrible cultural dialysis, so to speak.

Blessed with the black, curling hair that makes Romanian women so distinctive, she tugs and greases it into submission in a vain attempt to look like every other American teenager. But why be someone else?

And her fashion sense . . . How many manifestations of denim can there be? And the T-shirts with the horses and the arithmetic-related "puns" . . . Is it really "Hip2B^2"? Would it hurt to wear a dress now and then?

To smile?

Vasile, I realize that I am honor bound to form a relationship with this young woman, but really, can she lead our legions? And as for the two of us sharing any sort of physical intimacy . . . Well, any details you can provide regarding my responsibilities toward that end would be greatly appreciated.

You know I am always willing to "take one for the team"— a new expression I've learned here; rather like that one—but honestly, this all seems a bit out of hand. Perhaps we'd be wiser to call the whole thing off and just hope for the best. Are we really certain there would be an all-out war between the clans if the contract is not fulfilled? If we're talking only a few minor clashes, with minimal losses, I say let's think about this marriage pact. But, of course, your opinion must prevail.

In the meantime, I shall continue my thus far fruitless efforts to educate and engage this impossible American female, in that order. But please, Vasile—do consider my concerns.

Your nephew, duty bound,

Lucius Vladescu

P.S. I've been recruited for basketball. The coach thinks I might start!

Chapter 8

"I CAN'T DO IT," Mindy complained, scratching out yet another wrong answer.

"These problems are not that hard," I said, glad that this was the last year I'd have to tutor Mindy in math. Calculus was totally stumping her, and we were getting on each other's nerves. It probably didn't help that my bedroom was insanely hot. No matter how much I begged, Dad refused to install air-conditioning, saying it wasted energy. I picked up the textbook and began reading. "'Two men are traveling by trains, which leave the station—'"

"Nobody uses trains anymore," Mindy nitpicked. "Why do we always have to talk about trains? Why not planes?"

I glanced up from the book. "You are impossible to teach."

Mindy snapped her notebook shut. "Speaking of teaching, how about Lucius in class today? Mrs. Wilhelm about had an orgasm when he stood up and gave that big talk on *Hamlet*." She paused. "He *did* make it almost interesting, for a play about Denmark."

"Getting back to the problem . . ."

"Where is Lukey, anyway?" Mindy abandoned calculus entirely, hopping on my bed to look out the open window. She pulled the curtains aside. "Looo-cious," she cooed. "Come out and play . . . Mindy wants to see you . . ."

"Please don't summon him," I requested, meaning it.

"Just a little peek at those sexy black eyes . . ." Mindy

leaned way out the window. "Hey, somebody's coming. There's a truck on your road."

"Who is it?" I asked, not really caring. It was probably one of Dad's yoga students, early for class. I heard the sound of tires on gravel, then an engine cutting off.

My best friend spun around, dropping the curtain. "Jake. It's Jake's blue truck. He pulled in next to the horse barn."

Jake?

I tried to act nonchalant. "Oh, that's just our hay delivery. We buy from Jake's farm. He'll unload it and be gone in a few minutes."

"Oh." Mindy processed this, then whirled back around, stuck her head out the window, and hollered, "Hey, Jake! We're coming down!"

No, she did not just do that. "Mindy! I'm wearing a T-shirt with a hole in it. I don't have any makeup on!"

"You look gorgeous." She overrode my protests, tugging me by the arm. "Besides, I told him we were coming."

Reluctantly I let her drag me downstairs and outside. "I am *so* going to kill you."

Mindy ignored me. "He's shirtless," she whispered, hauling me across the yard toward Jake's truck. He was standing in the back, tossing bales to the ground. "Look at those muscles!"

I wrung her arm. "Mindy, shut up!"

"Ow!" She wrested free, frowning at me.

"What are you guys up to?" Jake smiled, pausing in his work. He pulled a red bandanna from the pocket of his worn jeans and wiped the sweat from his forehead. His bicep bowed and a complete six-pack of abs flexed, glistening slickly in the setting sun.

"We're just studying calculus," I said, shifting my arm to hide the hole in my T-shirt. The hole that was positioned right over my stomach, which still bulged from my summer of diner pie.

"You want to come in for a drink when you're done?" Mindy offered like it was her house.

"Yeah, sure," Jake agreed with a grin. "Just let me finish unloading before the sun sets."

Mindy yanked on my wrist, signaling that we should go inside to wait. "We'll change your shirt," she muttered in my ear.

"See you in a few minutes," I told Jake, sneaking one final look at his pecs. *Not bad.*

But as I turned to head for the house, I caught a glimpse of a Romanian foreign exchange student leaning against the side of the garage, arms crossed over his chest.

Maybe it was a trick of the slanting, fading light, which cast harsh shadows on his angular face, but he did not look pleased.

Chapter 9

"TOMORROW YOU ARE on your own, no matter what Mom says about helping you adjust," I warned Lucius, who was trailing me through the lunch line, dismissing every offering. "You know the system by now."

"Oh, yes," he said, pushing his tray along with one finger like it was toxic. "Line people up like cattle in a chute, present them with food *fit* for livestock, and force them to consume it hunched over, shoulder to shoulder, at troughlike tables."

"Just get something," I groaned, taking a sandwich for myself. "These sloppy joes aren't bad."

Lucius stayed my hand, and his fingers on my wrist were strong. And so cool. "Jessica . . . is that *meat*? But your parents' prohibition . . ."

"What Mom and Dad don't know about school won't hurt them," I warned, shaking off his hand and shoving my tray along. I rubbed my wrist, warming it. "So don't say anything."

"How insubordinate and seditious of you." Lucius smiled, appreciation in his voice. "I wholly approve."

"Really, I don't care about your approval."

"Of course not." Lucius skipped the sloppy joes but picked up some French fries. "*Cartofi pai*. At least we have these in Romania."

"By the way, where'd you get the drink?" I asked, pointing to his tray, which held a huge plastic cup emblazoned with the logo ORANGE JULIUS. "You're not allowed to go off campus, you know."

"Ahh, the terrors of detention." Lucius sighed, lifting the cup to sip through the fat straw. Red, clotted liquid advanced upward. He swallowed with satisfaction. "Not enough to deter me from the pleasures of a 'Strawberry Julius.' I fear I'm addicted."

"You should toss that out," I said, reaching for the cup. "Seriously, if you get caught . . ."

Lucius swiped the drink away before I could touch it. "I think not. And I strongly urge you not to spill this."

I glanced up at his face, not sure what he meant. His black eyes were mischievous.

"Come on," I said, taking some lime Jell-O. "We're holding up the line. Let's go pay if you don't want anything else."

We carried our trays to the cash register, and as I dug into my pockets, Lucius whipped out his wallet and flipped it open. "My—dubious—treat."

"No way." I located a few dollars wadded in my pocket, but Lucius was faster. He handed the cafeteria lady a twenty-dollar bill.

"Keep the change." He smiled at her, folding his wallet and lifting both our trays.

"But—," she started to protest.

"He's not used to our money yet," I explained, turning to Lucius. "Our lunch only cost, like, six dollars."

Lucius frowned. "Jessica, do you not think I'm familiar with the valuations of numerous world currencies—especially the American dollar, which is the universal standard? I live in Romania, not a sealed box."

The cafeteria lady was still holding out the change, looking uncertain. "I'll give it to him later," I said, accepting the cash.

"Look, there's Melinda," Lucius noted, carrying both our trays, "waving at us somewhat hysterically. She is rather . . . effervescent, isn't she?"

"I suppose you're eating with us." I sighed, following as he glided through the maze of tables, headed toward Mindy. Some of the other students glanced up, or edged away even, as the tall teenager in the crisp white shirt, black pants, and polished boots passed by. Lucius didn't seem the least bothered by the attention. On the contrary, I got the sense that he felt he deserved nothing less.

"Hey, Jess." Mindy grinned when we reached the table. She blushed. "Hi, Lucius."

"Melinda, so nice to see you," Lucius said, sliding our trays onto the table. "You look stunning today."

My best friend flushed with pleasure. "Why, thank you. Must be my new shirt. It's Abercrombie, from an outlet." She pointed to Lucius's fitted black trousers. "And speaking of clothes, those pants rock. Does everybody in Rome dress like you? Or just the other royal kids?"

"Romania," I corrected. "Not Rome."

"Oh, it's all European." Mindy waved me off, still staring at Lucius in a way that could only be described as raptly. "Either way, the pants are supercool."

Lucius smiled. "I'll tell my tailor his work is 'rockin' and 'supercool.' I'm sure he'll be gratified to learn that he can compete with the Gap."

He moved to pull out a chair for me, but it was my turn to grab his hand. "I'll get it."

"As you wish," he said, stepping back.

"Oh, I wish I lived in Romania." Mindy sighed, propping her chin in her chubby hands. "Your manners are so . . ."

"Impeccable." Lucius supplied the word for her.

"Oh, great," I muttered, searching my tray. "I forgot a spoon."

"I will be right back," Lucius offered, rising.

"No, I'll get it," I insisted, standing up, too.

Lucius moved behind my chair, clasped my shoulders in those powerful hands, and gently but firmly guided me back into my seat. He leaned over me, speaking softly, still holding my upper arms. His cool breath grazed my ear, and I got that traitorous, ticklish feeling in my stomach again.

"Jessica. For god's sake," he said. "Allow me to do at least one common courtesy for you. In spite of what 'women's lib' teaches you, chivalry does not imply that women are powerless. On the contrary, chivalry is an admission of women's superiority. An acknowledgment of *your* power over *us*. This is the only form of servitude a Vladescu ever practices, and I perform it gladly for you. You, in turn, are obligated to accept graciously."

Lucius released my shoulders and strode off before I could reply.

"I have no idea what that meant, but it was, like, the hottest thing anyone ever said." Mindy followed Lucius with her eyes. "How did you get so lucky? Why don't my parents ever get exchange students?"

"I wish he *was* your problem," I said. *Oh, do I ever wish it.* If only Mindy knew how crazy Lucius Vladescu was. What he claimed to be. "Why does he have to act like that? I just want him to leave me alone."

Mindy jabbed a straw into her carton of chocolate milk. "I don't get you, Jess. When we were five, all we ever did was dress up like princesses. Now a real-life Prince Charming wants to wait on you hand and foot and you complain!"

"Oh, Min . . . just don't encourage him, okay?"

"You're just too hung up on Jake Zinn to see that real, honest-to-goodness European royalty is hitting on you, Jess. You are going to waste your time on a guy who milks cows for fun—"

"Jake's family doesn't even have cows," I protested. "They grow crops. And I thought you liked Jake. You were just drooling over his muscles!"

"Oh, hey, Lucius," Mindy chirped, giving me a kick under the table. "You're back quick."

"I didn't want the Jell-O to grow even less palatable by sitting out," Lucius said from behind me, leaning over my shoulder again, arranging my silverware on the tray. Fork to the left of my sloppy joe. Knife and spoon to the right. "This is the American way, too, yes?"

"So what do you do in Romania besides going to, like, the world's best etiquette school?" Mindy inquired as Lucius sat down.

He leaned back in the metal folding chair and stretched his long legs out into the aisle, pushing aside his uneaten French fries. "Well, my education is rather rigorous, although I am privately tutored. I enjoy frequent travel to Bucharest and Vienna, when the mood strikes. Hunting is popular in the Carpathians. And riding."

"Hey, you and Jess have something in common!" Mindy cried.

I shot her a warning look.

"Well, you do!"

Lucius arched his eyebrows at me, intrigued. "Really, Jessica? I thought your equine activity was confined to mucking stalls," he teased. "I had no idea you were familiar with the view from atop a horse, too. You've kept this a secret."

"Because I didn't want you lurking around the barn, spooking my horse," I said, taking a bite of my forbidden sloppy joe.

"Jess is jumping in the 4-H show this fall," Mindy added.

Lucius smiled approval. "You know, I am known as quite the rider in my hometown of Sighişoara. Perhaps I could help with your seat—"

"No!" I cried, louder than I'd meant to. I lowered my voice. "I don't need help, okay?"

"Are you sure? I was All-Romanian National Amateur Polo Team captain, outdoor and arena rules."

"Oh, for crying out loud," I moaned, scooping a big glob of lime gelatin into my mouth.

"Better ease up on the Jell-O, Packrat," someone called. "You already shake like a bowl full."

Oh, no . . . I glanced over to see pudgy Frank Dormand, flanked by Faith Crosse and her jock boyfriend, Ethan Strausser, walking by our table, laughing.

"You're one to talk, Dormand," I advised him. "At least all my fat's not in my head."

But they were already shambling off, laughing together.

"Ingrates." Lucius sat upright, disbelief in his voice. "Did he just *taunt* you, Jessica?"

He started to rise from his seat, and I clutched his arm. "Lucius, let it go. I handled it. Like I always do."

Lucius paused, half standing, to stare at me, incredulous. "I'm to allow that . . . that . . . half-wit to mock you?"

I held firm to his sleeve, feeling his taut muscles even

through the fabric. "It's just Frank Dormand being a jerk, as usual," I said. "Don't start a fight over it."

For a moment, Lucius seemed to forget Frank, thank god, as he sank back down, searching my face, clearly baffled. "Jessica . . . I don't understand. You, of all people, to endure mockery . . ."

"Stop it, Lucius," I warned, silently begged him, locking on to his dark eyes. *Please don't mention vampires, or betrothals, or anything about me, of all people, being a princess. Not with Mindy here. Not ever.* "I know how to handle it."

Lucius conceded but with clear reluctance. "As you wish. But I will acquiesce only once. Such behavior by imbeciles— toward *you*, Jessica—will not go unanswered again."

He leaned back again in his seat, crossing his arms, watching the door through which Frank, Faith, and Ethan had departed—watching it intently, as if he wished they would return and test him. As if he was plotting, strategizing, living the fight in his imagination. His gaze was so coolly scary that even Mindy grew quiet, for once in her life.

We finished lunch in silence. Lucius never ate a thing, just picked up his Strawberry Julius now and then, absently, as he watched the door. As we left the cafeteria, he tossed the cup into the garbage can, and it clattered hollowly against the side, empty.

"I hope he kicks Frank's ass someday," Mindy whispered to me, dumping her tray. "It would be, like, no contest. Lucius looked like he was ready to *kill* for you."

The way Mindy said it, the words almost sounded romantic. But I'd seen the look in Lucius's eyes, too, and felt his anger, barely contained in the tensed muscles beneath my hand.

No, the prospect of Lucius Vladescu fulfilling any vendetta on my behalf didn't seem romantic at all. On the contrary, it just filled me with an unease that bordered on dread. Indeed, the more I thought about it, Ethan, Frank, Faith, Lucius—and I—seemed like a combination that could lead only to disaster.

Chapter 10

DEAR UNCLE VASILE,

The lentil is perhaps the world's most versatile, indestructible food.

One can eat the lentil unadorned; marry it off to its first cousin, the oafish "bulgur"; or attempt to drown it in harsh vinegar for a "vegan salad." But the lentil, alas, will always survive. Indeed, at the Packwood house, the tenacious little legume will forcibly resurrect, as free of anything resembling taste as ever, and insinuate its indefatigable, pelletlike self onto yet another dinner plate, expecting to be eaten. Again, and again, and again.

And do not even speak to me of "Jell-O" and "sloppy joes."

FOR GOD'S SAKE, VASILE.

How much must I endure in the interest of peace between the clans? Am I to sacrifice myself as the first prisoner in a war that has not even started yet?

Honestly, Vasile, it's not just the food, either. (Or what the Packwoods and the Pennsylvania Department of Education insist is food.)

American high schools should be outlawed under the rules of the Geneva Convention. The unspeakable cruelties I endure would astonish even you, an expert at cruelty!

As you know, I have always been curious about our immortality . . . how it will feel to live on and on through time (assuming one avoids the stake, as I intend). I need speculate no longer. I have sampled eternity in Miss Campbell's fifth period "social studies" class. Three days on the concept of "manifest destiny," Vasile. THREE DAYS. I yearned to stand up, rip her lecture notes from her pallid hands, and scream, "Yes, America expanded westward! Is that not logical, given that Europeans settled on the eastern shore? What else were they to do? Advance vainly into the sea?"

But I must not rant. It would be bad form to lose my composure. I must endure, fighting the temptation simply to become slack-jawed, like most of my school "peers" (they wish!), who will themselves into a collective, vacant, trancelike state for the duration of each class. (Although I sometimes secretly envy their ability to empty their minds completely for a full fifty minutes, reanimating only at the sound of a bell, like Pavlov's dogs. At which point they bark and yip about the hallways until classes start again. . . .)

However, you are no doubt more intrigued by news of the courtship than my so-called education. And so I will turn to my progress with Antanasia.

I am happy to report that my future princess sometimes shows hints of tremendous spirit. Unfortunately, all of Antanasia's considerable force of will, her "spunk," (to use the American word, which sounds like something one should scrape off the bottom of one's shoe, as opposed to an admirable quality), is completely concentrated upon rejecting me.

Truly, she shows single-minded devotion to this endeavor.

Meanwhile, I get the sense that Antanasia harbors an ill-advised attraction to a hay-baling farm lad (A peasant! And a short one at that!) who is so unremarkable in appearance and demeanor that, although he occupies a desk near mine in English lit (I have largely taken over the instruction in that class—perhaps I'll earn "tenure"!), I can never manage to recall his name. Justin? Jason? (Sadly, those are both good guesses. We seem to have a glut of each, here at Woodrow Wilson.)

The point is, I seem to have "competition," Vasile. Competition from a peasant, whose crude courting strategies include showing up at the Packwood farm, unnecessarily shirtless, to "flex" in front of her! Preening like a puffed-up pheasant! And if you could see her batting her eyes at the lout . . .

Does this reflect poorly upon Antanasia—or upon me, whom she shuns?

And if the Dragomirs have developed a penchant for breeding with peasants, could we not just allow their bloodline to diminish naturally, as opposed to uniting with them?

I jest.

Of course I shall prevail. (A Vladescu against a rustic laborer . . . I could win Antanasia with one hand tied behind my back and perhaps wearing a blindfold.) But the whole situation is disheartening, to say the least. To think that Antanasia even considers a bumpkin, when a prince shows an interest . . . When a Vladescu shows an interest! I blame the lentils. Can a nobleman accustomed to meat be expected to function at full capacity on soggy grains?

Meanwhile, I was recently further disheartened to witness Antanasia disparaged by one of Woodrow Wilson High School's most tedious characters, a boy with the unfortunate name Frank Dormand. (No wonder he's bitter!) But imagine: a common simpleton insulting a vampire princess. I sat there, dumbfounded, like an oaf myself, unable to believe my eyes and ears. That shall not happen again. I am cognizant that I must follow the local rules of conduct (sadly, there are strict sanctions against heads rolling in streets here), but another insult from a "Dormand" will not be endured. My future bride—however temporarily peasant-inclined—will not suffer insubordination.

More than the insult itself disturbs me, Vasile. I ask you: How can Antanasia understand her true worth, raised under such circumstances? Do we wonder that she considers consorting with a peasant? Had she been raised in Romania, brought up as a ruler, Antanasia would never have accepted an insult from a commoner. She would have ordered the offender put down like the sick mongrel he is. Here, all she could do was strike back with her own (crude but encouragingly cutting) wit—a weapon, yes, but a princess should have real power at her fingertips.

I am concerned by this, Vasile. Rulers are not just born, as you know. They are forged. Antanasia knows nothing of wielding power. What will that mean for her, for the clans she will lead, when she takes the throne?

Getting to the main point of my missive, though. Could you please release, say, an additional 23,000 lei—equivalent to about 10,000 American dollars—from my trust? I am interested in making a small purchase, related, of course, to my courtship of Antanasia. Although I may use a minor portion to buy a small store of red meat.

Thank you in advance for your generosity.

Your nephew,

Lucius

P.S. Basketball practice will soon begin. Perhaps you would like to fly over and attend a game?

Perhaps not.

Chapter 11

"WHY DOESN'T LUCIUS have to help with the dishes?" I complained, handing Mom a dripping plate. "He eats with us. He could help clean up. And I'm tired of doing his laundry, too. He always whines about the starch. Who even uses starch?"

"I understand your frustration, Jessica." Mom swiped the plate with a towel. "But your father and I have discussed this, and we both think Lucius is having enough difficulty adjusting to life in the United States without giving him chores, too."

"He's adjusted just fine. Too fine, if you ask me."

"Don't mistake Lucius's swagger for happiness," Mom said. "His life is altered dramatically enough without forcing him to do extra work that would be done by servants in his home."

"Or so he claims."

Mom laughed. "Regardless of what you think about Lucius's . . . er, vampireness—"

"I think it's a bunch of bull—" I caught myself. "I mean, garbage."

"Regardless, Lucius does come from a very wealthy, privileged background."

I swished around in the soapy water, feeling for sunken silverware. "How privileged? Honestly? Because sometimes I wonder about the polo ponies and the trips to Vienna."

"Oh, I wouldn't be surprised, Jessica," Mom said. "The Vladescu family lives on quite an impressive estate. It's a castle, really. High in the Carpathian Mountains."

"A castle?" Nobody lives in castles except in Disney movies. "And you've seen this 'castle'?"

"Only the exterior, which was imposing enough," Mom said. "We weren't allowed inside. The Vladescus were not the most accessible of vampires . . ." It seemed as if she was going to expand on that but changed her mind. "The Dragomirs were more welcoming."

We were veering too close to a discussion of my birth parents. "What did it look like? The castle?"

Mom smiled. "This is the first time I've sensed that you're intrigued by anything related to Lucius."

I rinsed some knives. "Just by his house."

Mom tossed the towel over her shoulder and leaned against the counter. "Not by Lucius? Even a little bit?"

I recognized the subtle suggestion in her voice. "Mom! No."

"Jessica . . . you must admit, Lucius is a physically attractive young man, and he's clearly interested in you. It would only be natural if you evinced *some* interest in return. It wouldn't be anything to be ashamed of."

Dunking a casserole dish, I scrubbed at some lentils that had fused to the sides during baking. "He thinks he's a vampire, Mom."

"That doesn't change the fact that Lucius Vladescu is a charming, powerful, wealthy, good-looking boy."

I recalled the feel of Lucius's strong hand brushing against my cheek the night we'd met. That fluttery feeling in the pit of my stomach. And the fact that he had actually voiced his intention to bite my neck. "Have you ever seen me look at Lucius with anything but disgust? Seriously?"

Mom smiled. "You'd be surprised how often disgust turns to lust." There was a knowing look in her eyes. As if she had just read my mind as I'd recalled Lucius touching my face.

I blushed. "That sounds like alchemy. Which is about as real as vampires."

"Oh, Jessica." Mom sighed. "What is love if not a form of alchemy? There are forces in this universe that we just can't explain."

Yes. Forces like the time-twisting gravity of a black hole. And the endless string of pi zooming out across the universe. Those were *true* forces and realities. Mysterious, sure. But also measurable and perhaps understandable if we applied math and science and physics. Why couldn't my parents ever get that? Why did they have to look at the world and see magic and the supernatural where I saw numbers and elements?

"I don't like Lucius, Mom, so you can just forget about alchemy, disgust, and especially lust," I promised, rinsing the casserole dish.

Mom didn't seem convinced as she dried the last of our

dishes. "Well, if your feelings should change, you can talk to me. I get the sense that Lucius is a very experienced young man. I wouldn't want you to get in over your head . . ."

"Is Jessica 'in over her head,' somehow? Can I be of assistance?"

Mom and I both turned to see Lucius standing in the doorway to the kitchen. *How long had he been there? How much had he heard? "Disgust turns to lust"?*

If Mom was embarrassed to be caught talking about Lucius behind his back, it didn't show on her face. "Jess will be fine, Lucius. But thank you for asking. What brings you in from the garage?"

"A craving for that delicious carob 'tofu ice cream' you keep in the freezer," Lucius said. He moved to the fridge and swung open the top door. "Would either of you care to join me?"

"Actually, I'm headed to the barn to see some kittens your father found," Mom said to me. "I suppose there's room for one more litter, but I like to put up token resistance. If I encourage him too much, we'll be overrun." She patted our exchange student's shoulder on her way out of the kitchen. "Good night, Lucius."

"Have a pleasant evening, Dr. Packwood." Lucius set the mock ice cream on the counter and took two bowls from the cupboard, holding them up. "Jessica? Can I tempt you?"

"Thanks, but I'm sort of avoiding dessert."

"Why?" Lucius seemed genuinely puzzled. "I know carob isn't the most enticing flavor, but dessert is one of life's greatest pleasures, don't you think? I rarely forgo it—aside from the time your father attempted that eggless, creamless pumpkin pie. It hardly seemed worth the effort of lifting the fork to one's mouth."

I pulled the plug on the sink, releasing the now-cold dishwater. "Yeah, well, you're not fat. You can eat dessert."

When I looked up from the swirling suds, Lucius was frowning at me. Staring me up and down.

"What?" I glanced down at my tank top and shorts. "Is there something on me?"

"Surely you don't think you're *overweight*, Jessica?" he said, disbelief in his eyes. "You don't believe that *imbecile* who taunted you in the cafeteria . . . I knew I should have silenced him—"

"This has nothing to do with Dormand—who is my problem, not yours," I said. "I just need to lose a pound or two, that's all. So calm down."

Lucius pried open the container, shaking his head. "American women. Why do you all want to be nearly invisible? Why not have a *physical presence* in the world? Women should have *curves*, not angles. Not points." With the mock shudder he usually reserved for Dad's cooking, he added, "American women are too *pointy*. All jutting hip bones and shoulder blades."

"It's fashionable to be thin," I advised him. "It looks good."

"One should never confuse fashionable with beautiful," Lucius corrected. "Trust me, men don't care what fashion magazines say. They don't think skeletal women look 'good.' The great majority of men prefer curves." He dug a spoon into the frozen tofu and advanced toward me, holding it out, in my face. "Eat. Be happy to have curves. A *presence*."

I smiled slightly, but still pushed his hand away. I fully intended to lose five pounds. "No, thanks."

Lucius gave an exasperated sigh and jabbed the spoon back into the container. "Antanasia, embrace who you are. A woman who wields the power you will enjoy doesn't need to follow fashion—or be swayed by the malicious ridicule of inferiors."

"Don't start with that royalty crap again," I begged, slapping the dishrag into the sink. Any small warmth I'd felt toward Lucius vanished. I felt angry, suddenly. "And don't call me by that name!"

"Oh, Jessica. I didn't mean to upset you," he said, setting the container on the counter. His voice softened. "I was only trying to—"

"I know what you're trying to do," I said. "You try every day."

We had squared off, facing each other. Lucius started to reach out to me, then apparently thought the better of it. His hand fell to his side.

"Look, we need to have a serious talk," I said. "About this whole 'pact' thing. This whole 'courtship.'"

Lucius paused, considering this. And then, to my surprise, he agreed. "Yes. I suppose we should."

"Now."

"No," he said, reaching for the fake ice cream again. "Tomorrow night. In my apartment. I have something to show you."

"What?"

"I prefer surprises. Another of life's greatest pleasures. Most of the time. Well, some of the time."

I didn't like the sound of a surprise. I'd had enough surprises lately. But I agreed anyhow. I didn't care if Lucius presented me with the deed to his castle, a herd of sheep—or whatever they used for dowries in Romania—and a diamond ring. I was going to persuade him once and for all that our "engagement" was off.

"I'll see you tomorrow night," I said, wiping down the countertop. "And wash out your dish when you're done."

"Good night, Jessica."

I knew I'd find that bowl in the sink at breakfast.

Later that night I drifted off to sleep thinking about my mom's assertion that disgust could turn to lust. Surely that didn't happen, did it? Nobody believed in alchemy anymore. You couldn't create gold from rocks or lead.

But as I slept, I had a dream about Lucius. We were standing in my parents' kitchen, and he held that spoon up to my face. Only it wasn't full of frozen tofu anymore. It was smothered with the richest, most decadent chocolate sauce imaginable.

"Eat it," Lucius urged, lightly pressing the spoon against my lips. "Chocolate is one of life's greatest pleasures." His black eyes gleamed. "*One* of them, at least."

I wanted to protest. *I'm too fat . . . too fat. . . .* But he kept holding out that spoon, and the chocolate, starting to drip, was too tempting for any mortal to resist, and in the end, I ate it all. It was like silk on my tongue. I swore I could taste it in my sleep. I clasped and clung to Lucius's hand, steadying it and closing my eyes as I finished the last of the imagined sweet elixir. When I was done, and I opened my eyes again, the spoon had disappeared, as things do in dreams, and it was just me and Lucius, my fingers entwined in his, my soft chest—my curves—pressed against his hard frame.

He smiled at me, revealing those amazing, surreally white teeth. "You didn't regret that, did you?" he asked, and started to nuzzle my neck. My throat. "It was perfect, wasn't it?" he whispered in my ear. Then Lucius wrapped his powerful arms completely around me, embracing me, engulfing me . . .

And I woke up, flat on my back.

It was dawn, and the sunlight was streaming in my windows. I was breathing hard. *Wow.*

I rolled to my side, curling up, and was reclaiming reality when the sunlight glinted off something shiny on the floor near my closed door. A silver bookmark, poking out of a book. A thin volume.

The book hadn't been there when I'd gone to sleep. Someone had obviously slipped it under the door.

Crawling out from under the covers, I picked it up, turning it over to read the title: *Growing Up Undead: A Teen Vampire's Guide to Dating, Health, and Emotions.* The top of the bookmark was engraved with an LV, in bold script.

Oh, god, no. The guide Lucius had referenced on the first day we'd met. I vaguely recalled him mentioning it—right after he'd announced his plans to bite me.

I sank to the floor, staring at the unwanted gift.

Then, against my better judgment, I flipped to the marked pages, reading the chapter heading, "Your Changing Body." *Oh, for crying out loud . . .* There was a passage underlined, too, in red ink. It read, "Young ladies will naturally feel confused, even ambivalent, as their bodies change. But don't be ashamed!

Developing your curves is a natural part of becoming a womanly vampire."

I resisted the urge to scream. *I do not need Lucius Vladescu's advice on becoming "womanly," especially a "womanly vampire." And who printed this stuff, anyhow? Who would publish a sex ed book for mythical beings? It would only fuel delusional people's lunacy. . . .*

Before I hurled the thing in my wastebasket, where it belonged, I took a quick peek inside the cover, looking for the publisher. A handwritten note caught my eye first, though.

Dearest Jessica,

Of course I never required advice on any of these topics—really, "emotions"?—but I thought perhaps you, as a "newcomer," so to speak, might find the guide helpful. In spite of the gratingly frothy tone, it's really quite respected among our race.

Enjoy—and do consult me if you have questions. I consider myself quite an expert. Except on the "emotions."

Yours,

L.

P.S. Did you know you snore? Pleasant dreams!

He just didn't give up.

As I slammed the cover shut, I noticed that there was something tucked in the back of the book, too. An envelope. I started to slip it from between the pages. The little packet was waxy and nearly transparent, and I drew a sharp breath as I realized it contained a photograph. Even through the paper, I could make out the indistinct image of a woman.

No.

I knew without looking whose picture I held. *My birth mother . . .*

I shoved the photo back inside the pages. Lucius would not manipulate me, would not force the past upon me. He couldn't make me look at the long-deceased, disturbed woman who'd given me away.

Fighting back anger—at Lucius, at the sad, embarrassing secrets of my past—I tossed the book under my bed. I didn't want my mom to find it accidentally if she emptied my waste-basket. I could tear it up and bury it deep in the compost pile later.

As the slender volume spun across the hardwood to land amid the dust bunnies, it struck me: Had Lucius been standing outside my door as I'd dreamed about him? Shame washed over me. Why had I had that late-night fantasy? And what had Lucius meant by "pleasant dreams"? Why had he written that?

I hoped desperately that, along with snoring—which I did *not* do—I didn't talk in my sleep. And I recalled, with more than a little misgiving, my agreement to meet with Lucius alone in his apartment later that night.

Chapter 12

"WELCOME," LUCIUS SAID, swinging open the door to his apartment. He stepped back to usher me inside. "You're my first guest."

"Holy shit."

Lucius closed the door behind us. "Well, that's a pleasant reaction. Very ladylike."

I gasped. "What did you *do* here?" As my eyes adjusted to the dim light, I noticed more and more details in the room. "Wow." The apartment, once decorated with flea market junk that was vaguely "country," had been overhauled in the fashion of what I assumed was a Romanian castle. A bloodred velvet blanket covered the bed, a tastefully worn Persian rug overlaid the beige carpet remnant, and the walls had been painted a deep blue-gray. The color of old stone. My survey came to an abrupt halt at a wall-mounted display of what appeared to be antique weaponry. Sharp things. Spiky things. "Um . . . what happened to Mom's collection of indigenous, fair-trade folk dolls of the world?"

"They've repatriated."

From the grimly pleased look on Lucius's face, I had a feeling the dolls' exile was permanent.

"Mom and Dad are going to kill you when they see this."

"Impossible." He laughed. "Besides, it's all cosmetic. Easily reversed. Although why anyone would prefer gingham to this . . ." He gestured around the room. "How about you, Jessica? Do you like what I've achieved?"

"It's . . . interesting," I hedged. "But when did you have time to do this? Without anyone seeing?"

"You might say I'm a night person."

As my astonishment faded, my anger with Lucius resurfaced. "Speaking of your late-night activities, I didn't like the book," I advised him. "Or the way you delivered it."

Lucius shrugged. "Perhaps in time you will find it useful."

"Sure. I'll keep it on my shelf right next to *The Idiot's Guide to Becoming a Mythical Creature.*"

Lucius actually laughed. "Very funny. I didn't know you made jokes."

"I'm a funny person," I defended myself. "And by the way—I don't snore."

"You *do* snore. And you mumble, too."

My blood froze. *The dream . . .* "What? What did you hear?"

"Nothing *too* intelligible. But it must have been a rather pleasant dream. You sounded *ecstatic.*"

"Don't lurk around my room," I ordered him. "I mean that."

"As you wish, of course." Lucius lowered the volume on an old record player, which spun a warped vinyl disk that wailed unfamiliar music, scratchy and whiny, like cats fighting. Or a coffin with rusty hinges opening and closing over and over again in a deserted mausoleum. "Do you like Croatian folk?" he asked, seeing my interest. "It reminds me of home."

"I prefer *normal* music."

"Ah, yes, your MTV with all the bumping and grinding. Like a shot of raging adolescent hormones administered via television. I'm not averse." He gestured to a chair, which definitely hadn't belonged to my parents. They didn't buy leather. "Sit, please. Tell me why you've called this meeting."

I sank down, and the chair nearly swallowed me. It was buttery soft. "Lucius, you have to stop following me around. And you need to go home."

"You are direct. I like that about you, Anta—Jessica."

"I've made up my mind." I plunged ahead. "The 'marriage' is officially off. I don't care what the scroll says. I don't care what the Old Country old people—"

"The Elders."

"The Elders expect. It's not happening. I'm telling you now so you don't waste any more time. I'm sure you want to return to a *real* castle . . ."

Lucius shook his head. "No. We must learn to coexist, Jessica. I have no choice in this matter—and neither do you. So I suggest that you at least try to work with me here, to use the popular expression."

"No."

Lucius smiled a little. "You do have a will of your own." The smile faded. "This is not the time to use it." He began pacing, like he'd done in Mrs. Wilhelm's class. "Not to honor the pact . . . it would not only result in a political crisis, it would dishonor the memory of our parents. *They* wished this, in the interest of peace."

I looked at Lucius with a little surprise. "What happened to your parents?"

"They were destroyed in the purge like yours. What did you think?"

"Sorry. I . . . I didn't know."

Lucius sat down on the bed, leaning forward, lacing his fingers together. "But unlike you, Jessica, I was raised within our race, with proper role models."

"The so-called Elders?" I guessed.

"Yes. I was sent to live with my uncles. And if you knew them—as you should—you would not have that smirk in your voice." He ground his palms together, clearly masking some sudden frustration. "They are fearsome."

I frowned. "And living with fearsome Elders was a good thing?"

"It was a proper thing," Lucius said. "I was taught discipline. Honor." He rubbed his jaw. "By force, when they deemed it necessary."

My anger at him was forgotten. "You mean your uncles *hit* you?"

"Of course they hit me," Lucius said very matter-of-factly. "Time and again. They were making a warrior. Forming a ruler. Kings are not created with sweets and hugs and kisses on Mommy's knee. Kings bear scars. No one wipes your tears when you sit on a throne. It's best not to be raised expecting it."

"That's . . . that's just wrong," I objected, thinking of my parents, who couldn't bear to exterminate the termites that were gradually chewing away the barn, let alone hit a child. "How could they hurt you?"

Lucius waved away the sympathy. "I did not speak of the Elders' strict discipline to generate your pity. I was a wayward child. Strong-willed. Difficult to control. My uncles needed to groom me for leadership. And they did." He looked pointedly at me. "I learned to accept my destiny."

I groaned. We were back to square one. "Lucius, it's not happening. The cult or whatever it was or is . . . it's not for me. I'm not joining."

Lucius stood up and started pacing again, raking his long fingers through his shiny black hair. "You're not listening."

"*You're* not listening," I shot back.

Lucius rubbed his eyes. "Damn, you are infuriating. I told the Elders long ago that it was insane to raise you outside of the culture. That you would never be a suitable bride. A suitable princess. But everyone, both clans, were insistent that you were too valuable to risk your life by keeping you in Romania—"

"I'm not a princess!"

"Yes, you are," Lucius insisted. "You are an invaluable woman. Royalty. Had you been raised properly, you would be fully aware of that already. Ready to rule." He jabbed a finger at his chest. "To rule at my side. But as it is, you remain an unschooled *girl*." He nearly spat the word. "I've been paired for eternity with a child!"

A little shiver zipped down my spine. "You really are crazy."

He moved to the bookshelves, reaching high. "And you are impossible."

I popped out of my chair. "What are you doing? What are you getting?"

"A book. The item I wanted to show you." Lucius dragged a massive, shiny, leather-bound volume off the top shelf and hoisted it onto the mattress, where it sank into the plush blanket. He pointed. "Sit here. Please."

"I'll stand, thanks."

Lucius arched his brows, mocking, and sat down, patting the spot next to him. "Are you afraid of me? Afraid of *vampires*?"

"No." I joined him on the bed. He edged even closer, until our legs were almost touching, and opened the book over both our laps. This time, I recognized Romanian script on the pages, and the branching lines of a genealogy. "Your family?"

"All the vampire families. The nobles, at least."

The parchment crackled as he searched through the pages, smoothing two open. "This is us. Where we connect." He tapped his finger at the juncture of two lines. "Lucius Vladescu and Antanasia Dragomir."

Not again. "I saw all this before, remember? I read the smelly old scroll."

He shifted slightly to meet my eyes. "And you will see it again. And again. Until you stop saying flippant things like 'smelly old scroll' and understand *who you are.*"

For once, I didn't shoot back with a quick retort. Something in his expression stopped me.

After a long silence, Lucius returned his attention to the book. I realized I needed to breathe, having stopped for a few seconds. *Dammit.* My stomach felt like it held squirming kittens again, too. I ignored the genealogy for a moment and watched Lucius in profile. A shock of his ebony hair fell over his high forehead, and a muscle twitched in his jaw. A small scar ran right along the jaw line where he'd rubbed his face.

Honor. Discipline. Force. What did these Elders do to him?

I was used to men like my dad and the other fathers I knew. Nice guys. Guys who wore Dockers and played kickball with their kids and put on funny ties at Christmas. Lucius was as different from those men as his weapons collection was from Mom's dolls. He was undeniably charming when he wanted to be, his manners were smooth, but there was a roughness just below the surface.

"Those are your parents," Lucius continued, his voice very quiet. I returned my attention to the genealogy as he ran his fingers over the names Mihaela and Ladislau, just above my own.

My birth mother. And biological father. Their death dates were scrawled there, too.

I stifled a groan of frustration and anger. *Why do we have to keep returning to my birth parents?* This was supposed to be a happy year for me. A carefree time. But Lucius had arrived, and with him my past. He didn't just drag me down with a nonsensical story about vampires and weddings, but he kept trying to lasso me with my *real* past, too. To loop a noose around my neck and drag me through a graveyard. Lucius's presence was a constant reminder of who I might have been in Romania. A reminder of not just vampires but ghosts. The ghosts of Mihaela and Ladislau Dragomir.

They were strangers, really . . . I wouldn't grieve them . . . And yet I felt sad.

His own sorrow made Lucius's voice even softer. He traced the unfamiliar words *Valeriu* and *Reveka*. "And these were my parents."

I wanted to say something. The right thing. But I didn't know what that might be, for either of us. "Lucius . . ."

"See this date," he continued, not looking at me. "Under our names? That marks our betrothal ceremony. Our parents wrote that date. At least, one of them did." A whisper of a wistful smile played upon his lips. "That was a great day for the Vladescus and Dragomirs. Our two warring clans at peace. Prepared to join together. So much power in one place. How many times have I heard that story?"

"But that's what it is . . . a story."

"It's an edict." Lucius slammed the book shut with a thud. "We are meant to be together. Regardless of how we feel about each other. Irrespective of how much you *despise* me."

"I don't despise you . . ."

"No?" His eyebrows arched, and his mouth twisted into a wry smile. "You could have fooled me."

I turned the tables. "You talk a lot about obligation and duty and chivalry, but I don't get the sense you really like me that much, either. You can't tell me *you* want to marry *me*. You just called me a child!"

Lucius took a long time choosing his words. "You are a puzzle to me, Jessica," he finally said. "A mystery. But at least I am open to the possibility of exploring that which I don't understand."

The dim light glimmered in his black eyes, and we were so close that I could see the faint shadow of stubble on his cheeks. Most guys I knew still seemed more like boys than men. Did Jake even shave? But Lucius . . . he had crossed that line. And I was sitting on a bed with him. Alone. In a darkened room. Talking about "exploring" my so-called "mysteries." I edged away.

"What would happen, anyway, if we didn't get married?" I asked, trying to change the subject. Distancing us again. "How bad could it be?"

Lucius moved away, too, reclining back on the bed, propped on his elbows. "Most likely a full-scale war, your family against mine, some five million vampires struggling to fill the power vacuum, building coalitions, leaders rising and falling, destruction and bloodshed on a massive scale. And when vampires war . . . well, as the old adage says, 'an army travels on its stomach.'"

68

I wasn't familiar with the saying, so—against my better judgment—I asked, "And that means . . . ?"

"Armies need to eat," Lucius clarified. "So the streets will run with human blood, too. There will be chaos. Countless loss of lives." Lucius paused, shrugging. "Or maybe nothing would happen. Vampires are a very capricious people. It's one of our best—and worst—traits. But really, it's probably not wise to risk it."

"Why do Vladescus and Dragomirs supposedly hate each other so much?"

Lucius shrugged. "Why do all powerful nations and cultures and religions clash? For control of territory. For the simple lust for dominance. It has always been so between our two clans—until the pact secured a tentative promise of peace through unification, as equals. If we fail to complete the bargain—you and I—the blood is on our hands."

Images of blood-drenched streets—my fault—kept flashing in my brain like a movie scene being replayed over and over, so I stood, shaking my head. "That's the stupidest story I've ever heard."

"Really?" Lucius's eyes were now inscrutable, which was somehow scarier than his anger. He rose, too. "How shall I make you believe this 'story'?"

"You can't." I backed up a little. "Because vampires don't exist."

"I exist. You exist."

"I'm not a vampire," I insisted. "That genealogy means nothing."

Anger flashed in Lucius's eyes. "The genealogy means *everything*. It is the only possession I prize."

I retreated a few more paces. He seemed to loom taller than ever. "I have to go now," I told him.

But with each step, Lucius advanced toward me, slowly, and I found myself halting, spellbound by those black eyes, mesmerized. The shiver down my spine came stronger, rooting me to the floor like an electric shock.

"I don't believe in vampires," I whispered, but with less conviction.

"You will believe."

"No. It's not rational."

Lucius was inches from me now, and he leaned down, the better to see eye-to-eye. And then he bared his teeth. Only they weren't just teeth anymore. They were fangs. Two fangs, to be precise. Two sharp, seductive, gleaming fangs. They were the most awful, perfect, unbelievable things I had ever seen.

I wanted to scream. Scream as loud as humanly possible. Or maybe feel Lucius clasp my shoulders, pull me tightly to himself, feel the authority in his hands, the touch of his lips, those teeth on my throat . . . *Oh, god.* What was wrong with me? What was wrong with *him*? He was a freaking vampire. He really was. *No.* It was a magic trick. An illusion.

I closed my eyes, rubbing them, cursing myself for falling for the fakery and yet half expecting the sensation of razorlike incisors slicing into my jugular. "Please . . . don't!"

There was a moment of silence that stretched on forever. A moment when I honestly believed that he might hurt me. And then, suddenly, Lucius really did grab my arms and pull me close, enfolding me against his chest, just as he'd done in my dream. Firmly, but gently.

"Antanasia," he murmured, and his voice was soft again. He smoothed my curls with his hand, and I allowed him to soothe me, too relieved to object. "I'm sorry . . . that was cruel to scare you," he said. "I should not have done that, that way. Please, forgive me."

Tentatively, I wrapped my arms around Lucius's narrow waist, not even sure why I did it, and he squeezed me even closer, resting his chin on the top of my head. His hand covered the entire small of my back, which he stroked softly. We stood that way for about a full minute. I could feel his heart beat against my cheek. Very softly. Very slowly. Almost impercep- tibly. Mine was pounding, and I knew he could feel that, too.

Finally I pulled back, and he let me go.

"Don't ever do that stupid trick again," I said, surprised to find that my voice was shaky. "Never. It's not funny."

The crazy Croatian music spun on the turntable, eerie and penetrating. Lucius took my arm, and I hated that a part of me welcomed his touch again. Hated that it had been hard to pull away. *He's a lunatic, Jess.*

"Please, Jessica. Sit." Lucius gestured to the bed. "You look a little pale."

Sit . . . and then what will happen?

"I . . . I have to go," I said.

Lucius didn't try to stop me, and I left him standing there, in the middle of that dark room. I tripped down the steps, and when I reached our yard, I ran, not stopping until I'd locked the door in my own room, breathless, flushed, and incredibly, in- credibly confused. Because what I'd felt hadn't just been fear. It had been something like the sensations I'd had in my dream about Lucius. *Disgust turned to fear turned to lust* . . . alchemy. Insanity. It was all mixed up in my brain suddenly. And it was so, so wrong.

Chapter 13

"TODAY WE'RE GOING to discuss the concept of transcendental numbers," our math team coach, Mr. Jaegerman, announced, rubbing his hands together with arithmetic glee.

All five of us mathletes leaned over our notebooks, pens poised.

"A transcendental number is any number that is non-algebraic—not the root of any integer polynomial," Mr. Jaegerman began.

Mike Danneker's hand shot up. "Like pi."

"Yes," Mr. Jaegerman cried, jabbing chalk at the board, writing the symbol for pi. "Exactly." He was already sweating a little. Mr. Jaegerman was bald, and slightly overweight, and wore polyester, but he had an admirable enthusiasm for numbers.

I wrote the symbol π in my notebook, wishing we weren't wasting time on theoretical concepts. I preferred to practice with practical problems, as opposed to dealing with abstract ideas.

"Pi is an excellent example of a transcendental number," our teacher continued. "The ratio of the circumference of a circle to its diameter. We're all familiar with pi. But we usually just stop at 3.14 when we use it. As we all know, though, pi is actually much longer. And although we humans have figured out pi to roughly the trillionth digit, there is no end in sight. It is infinite, 'unsolvable.' And—this is the mind-blowing part—the numbers form no pattern."

He scribbled on the board. *3.1415926535897932 . . .* "It goes on and on, randomly. Forever."

We all paused, drinking this in. Of course, as students interested in math, we'd all thought about pi before. But the idea of those numbers streaming across galaxies, across time . . . it was very confusing. Unnerving, almost. Impossible to grasp.

"And of course"—Mr. Jaegerman broke our reverie—"a transcendental number like pi is, by definition, *irrational.*"

He paused to let us catch up, and I carefully printed the word in my notebook. *Irrational.*

The word seemed to stare back at me off the page. In the back of my mind, I heard my mother saying, *"Jessica, there are things in the world that you can't explain . . ."*

But you can *explain them,* my brain objected. *Even pi is explainable. Sort of. Numbers are solid. Real.*

Except numbers that snaked their way to eternity. *Eternity.* Now there was another concept I couldn't grasp.

Souls linked for eternity. Lucius had said that one time when he'd brought up the betrothal ceremony. Lucius, the least rational person I knew. *Vampires and pacts, they are irrationals. Like pi?*

"Miss Packwood?"

My name jolted me back to reality. Or what I thought was reality. Why did it all seem so uncertain suddenly? "Yes, Mr. Jaegerman?"

"You seemed a little daydream-y." He smiled. "I thought I should bring you back to reality."

"Sorry," I said. *Reality.* Mr. Jaegerman obviously believed in it. He certainly wouldn't believe in unreal things. Like vampires. Or eternal destinies. Or "disgust turned to lust."

Reality was the taste of my plastic pen in my mouth. The sight of the hideous design on Mr. Jaegerman's tie. The feel of the smooth desk under my fingertips.

Yes. Reality. It was good to be back. It was where I needed to stay.

When I focused back on my notes, though, I realized that I had doodled a rough sketch of a very sharp set of fangs in the margin of my notes. I hadn't even realized I'd done it.

Clutching my pen, I scribbled out the drawing, smothering it in ink, until every line was completely obliterated.

Chapter 14

DEAR UNCLE VASILE,

I write to thank you for releasing the money from my trust, as requested, and for so expeditiously shipping my weapons collection and other miscellaneous furnishings, carpets, etc. I fear I couldn't have endured one more day with those doe-eyed "folk" dolls staring at me from every cheerful, plaid-covered corner of this room. It was like being surrounded by a multicultural army of midgets, all waiting to attack some night as I slept.

I have done the Packwoods the favor of disposing of the entire collection, with the assistance of the medieval maul you were so kind to include. A pair of salt and pepper shakers shaped like dogs wearing chefs' toques have, alas, met their doom, too. Some day the Packwoods will no doubt come to their senses and thank me.

On to the bad news. I fear I've made a slight misstep, having introduced Antanasia to the concept of vampiric transformation rather abruptly last night. Her reaction was raw fear, followed by denial. Honestly, Vasile, she dismissed my fangs as some sort of parlor trick. Can you imagine? One of nature's most compelling metamorphoses disclaimed as a magic act? God, the girl irks me. So resistant. So rational.

In short, I have taken no steps forward, and two steps backward.

I will gladly shoulder the blame for my mistake (I should have anticipated Antanasia's reaction—my pedagogy was less than subtle), but did I not predict all of this difficulty years ago?

Lying awake in the garage, I often ponder how different things could have been had Antanasia been raised as a true vampire. Not to sound arrogant, Vasile, but I know from past experience that I do not repulse women. (Is the Bucharest debutante season underway? Heavy sigh.) And Antanasia, for all her faults (T-shirts rank at the top of that list) . . . well, I can sometimes see flashes of who she could have been. Of what we could have been.

Indeed, Antanasia's most vexing quality—her aforementioned will—is the very thing that would serve her so well as a ruler. She stands up to me, Vasile. How many are willing to do that? There is great intelligence in her eyes, too. And a certain mocking laughter—a hallmark of our kind. She is beautiful, too, Vasile. Or she would be if she did not try so hard to hide it. If she only believed she is beautiful.

At times, it is not impossible to imagine Antanasia in our castle, at my side—provided she cultivated better manners, acquiesced to the concept of women's clothes, and straightened that spine. (No one in America exhibits the slightest interest in posture. Standing upright seems to be something of a lost art, like fencing.)

In the wished-for reality that I sometimes envision, our courtship consists of excursions to the opera in Vienna, riding in the Carpathians (she does ride!), and conversing as we linger over meals that actually consist of food. That is how I have always approached—and succeeded with!—the fairer sex in Romania.

But of course daydreams and wishing are wasted, idle exercises that may amuse more effectively than the available television programs (an entire network devoted to the game "poker"—need I say more?) but do nothing to alter reality. No amount of horrified shuddering on my part will change the fact that Antanasia is an American girl who apparently requires an American approach. Now I must determine exactly what that means. Some activity involving a "burger and fries," no doubt.

At any rate, that, "in a nutshell"—to use yet another quaint Americanism (is there no end to them?)—is the situation here in "our little democracy," as my faux father figure Ned is so fond of repeatedly calling this ridiculous farm where virtually no agriculture is practiced. Honestly, if ever a place needed the firm hand of a tyrant . . . Fewer beasts in the yard, more in the oven: That would be my first decree. But again, wishes change nothing.

Your nephew,

Lucius

P.S. At the risk of testing your patience, I have one more request. I have nearly depleted my supply of Type A. (Basketball practice does make me thirsty. Go team.) Are you familiar with a good domestic source I might tap?

76

Chapter 15

"YOUR HOROSCOPE SAYS 'today is a good day to take a risk,'" Mindy read, leaning against the lockers, nose buried in her new copy of *Cosmo*.

"I can't believe you read that." I laughed, rummaging around for the books I needed to take home. "I mean, do you really need to know '75 Sex Tricks to Drive Him Wild'? Wouldn't twenty or so be enough for anybody?"

Mindy surfaced from the pages, a grin on her face. "They might all come in handy someday. Don't you want to be prepared in the event that you want to 'drive him wild'?"

I flushed, recalling my mom's talk, the dream I'd had about Lucius, the feelings I'd had that night in his apartment when he'd done that stupid trick with his teeth. And Jake, shirtless, standing on the back of that truck . . . "Well, sure. I guess so. But it's not like I'll get to use any 'tricks' soon."

"Hey, you never know." Mindy pointed behind me. "Look who's here."

I turned around, half expecting to see Lucius amid the crowd of students getting ready to go home. Mindy's crush was getting out of control, and if she talked about sex, a mention of Lucius couldn't be far behind. But no, it was Jake, pulling his leather-armed wrestling jacket from his locker. I spun back around, feigning an even greater interest in the contents of my own locker.

"You should go talk to him," Mindy advised, a little too loudly. "Unless you've finally realized that Lucius is the better choice . . ."

"Lucius is not better, and he's not a 'choice,'" I said.

"Well then, this is your chance to ask Jake to the fall carnival," Mindy said. She held up *Cosmo*. "Listen to your horoscope. Take a risk."

"I know you *read* it, but you don't really *believe* that 'guided by the stars' stuff, do you?" I pulled out of my locker, cradling my pile of books.

"Of course," Mindy said.

Not you, too, Mindy. . . . Is there not one rational person left in the universe?

"Jake was obviously into you that night at your house," she added. "I mean, he hardly talked to me."

"Really?"

"Jess, I was, like, invisible. Go. Ask him to the carnival. Unless, of course, you're having second thoughts about Lucius . . ."

"No, I'm not," I assured her.

"Then ask Jake."

I glanced down at my outfit. Why had I worn my filthy old Chuck Taylors? I hadn't lost those five pounds, either. "Oh, I don't think so . . . I look terrible, and . . . well, shouldn't Jake ask me?"

"It's not the Middle Ages," Mindy pointed out. "Girls ask guys out. It happens all the time, which you'd know if you read *Cosmo*."

Mindy had a point there. If there was one thing I was sick of, it was having one Chuck-clad foot stuck in the Middle Ages. I wondered what Mindy would think if she knew I supposedly had no choice when it came to my husband, let alone my date for the Woodrow Wilson High School fall carnival. Still, I wasn't convinced that asking Jake was a good plan. "I could go without a date."

"But it's cooler to have a date. And you'd better hurry, because he's leaving."

I turned around again to see Jake slamming his locker door shut. Mindy gave me a little shove. "Go!" Her second thrust gave me no choice. Especially since Jake was walking in our direction.

"Hey." He smiled as I practically crashed into him. "Thanks for the drink the other night."

"Sure." *Brilliant, Jess.* I looked around for Mindy, for support, but she and her *Cosmo* and her 75 Sex Tricks had disappeared.

"I was just talking about you," Jake said. "I hear you're odds-on to win a top spot at 4-H this year."

"Really?"

"Yeah. Faith says your Appaloosa can really jump."

"Faith Crosse said that? Are you sure?" Even though Faith boarded her thoroughbred at my parents' farm, she managed to act like I didn't exist. Like Lucius, she seemed to mistake me for some sort of stable hand. I certainly didn't think she'd ever bothered to watch me ride.

"Yeah. She thinks you're her best competition."

"I'll never beat Faith's thoroughbred," I said. "Not on an Appaloosa. Even one as good as Belle."

"I'm sure you'll do great." Jake hesitated. "Maybe someday I could come watch you ride."

"Really? I mean, that would be great." I smiled, meeting Jake's beautifully bland gaze. His blue eyes were so blessedly . . .

simple. Not dark and terrifying and changeable. And his teeth . . . so wonderfully average. So un-fanglike. Jake blinked. There was a briefly uncomfortable silence. It was now or never. I took a deep breath. "Jake?"

"Yeah?"

"Are you going to the carnival?" My heart was thudding so hard that I was afraid I wouldn't catch his answer. "Because I was thinking maybe we could . . . you know, go together."

He paused. "Well, I really wasn't sure—"

Oh, no. Even half deaf, I heard the hesitation in his voice. He was turning me down. I knew it. *It's the Chucks. It has to be the Chucks. Or the five pounds . . .* "Oh, I understand," I interrupted, cheeks on fire. "It's no big deal."

"No, wait—"

"Hey, Packrat!" A heavy arm thumped down around my shoulders, and I found myself cheek-to-cheek with Frank Dormand, who was hanging on me, a slimy grin on his fat face. Horrified, I tried to slip free, but Frank held tight, giving me a little shake. "Did I just hear you asking Jake here to the carnival? What's up with *that*?"

"Stop it, Frank," I begged, clutching my books to my chest. "This is none of your business."

"Yeah, Frank," Jake said. "Leave it alone."

Frank rumpled my curls. "Oh, you crazy kids."

I tried to push his hand away and smooth my hair, but I was so flustered that I dropped my books from my hot, wet hands. My homework crashed to the floor, my papers scattering everywhere. "Get lost, Frank," I pleaded, furious. *It was one thing to call out a quick taunt in the cafeteria, but he went too far this time. . . .*

Frank winked at Jake. "So what's it gonna be, Jake? Are you going to take the Packrat? Because rumor has it that she's getting it on with that foreign undertaker who lives in her garage. You *are* boffing him, right, Jess?"

I twisted under Dormand's arm, trying again to pull away, when suddenly I was liberated. Because Frank was pinned against a locker, his throat in the grip of a calm but very determined Romanian exchange student.

Frank's heels banged metal. "Hey!"

But Lucius only hoisted Frank a little higher. "Gentlemen don't ask women impertinent questions about delicate subjects." His voice was even, almost bored. "And they never, ever use crude expressions in mixed company. Not unless they're ready to face the consequences."

"Lucius, no!" I cried.

"Let go," Frank sputtered, his face turning as red as mine. He clawed futilely at Lucius's grip as a crowd gathered in the hall. "You're choking me, man."

"Let him go, Lucius," I begged, watching Frank turn from red to blue. "He's suffocating!"

Lucius eased his grip, allowing Frank to touch the floor with his toes but keeping him firmly contained. "Tell me what you want me do with him, Jessica," Lucius urged, over his shoulder. "Name the punishment. I shall deliver it."

"Nothing, Lucius!" I said, face flaming even brighter. *He isn't my bodyguard.* "It's not your fight!"

"No," Lucius agreed. "It is my *pleasure.*" He turned his attention back to Frank, who had ceased struggling and remained flattened, motionless, against the locker, eyes bulging. "You will pick up the young lady's books, hand them to her nicely, and apologize," Lucius ordered. "Then we will go outside and conclude *our* business."

He dropped Frank, who slumped forward, gasping for air.

"I'm not fighting you." Frank wheezed, rubbing his neck.

"It will be a lesson, not a fight," Lucius promised. "And when I am finished, you *will not* bother Jessica again."

I shared a worried glance with Jake, who stood by, silent, wary.

"We were just goofing around," Frank complained.

Lucius glared, drawn up to his full six-foot-plus height. He seemed to fill the hallway. "Where I come from, causing a woman distress isn't amusing. I should have made that clear the other day. I will not miss another opportunity."

"Where *do* you come from?" Frank challenged, puffing his chest, a little bolder now that he could breathe. "Some of us are starting to wonder."

"I come from civilization," Lucius retorted. "You wouldn't be familiar with the territory. Now pick up the books."

Frank must have heard the final warning in Lucius's low snarl, because he bent and did as he was told, muttering the whole time. He shoved the books into my hands and started to slink away. Lucius grabbed him again. "You forgot to apologize."

"I'm sorry," Frank said through gritted teeth.

Lucius gave Dormand a little shove. "Now let's go outside."

"Lucius," I said, grabbing his arm. The muscles were rigid beneath my fingers. He'd *destroy* flabby Dormand, who couldn't do ten push-ups if his life depended on it. "Stop it. Now."

Lucius stared down at me. "You are worth this, Jessica. He will not disrespect you. Not in my presence."

"You can't do that here . . . not like that," I warned. "This isn't Romania." *This isn't your family, with whatever brutal rules they enforced.* "You've taken it too far."

We stared at each other for a long moment. Then Lucius glanced at Frank. "Get out of here. And feel fortunate that you have a reprieve. Because you won't get another, no matter what Jessica wishes."

"Freak," Frank muttered. But he hurried into the crowd, which melted away behind him, leaving only Lucius, Jake, and me. Jake started to backpedal, too, but Lucius wasn't quite finished.

"I believe you two were engaged in conversation. Please. Finish."

"We're done," I promised, pushing Lucius away. He held his ground, without taking his eyes off Jake.

"Is that true?" Lucius asked Jake. "Were you finished?"

"I . . . we were talking about . . ." Jake shuffled, glancing at his feet. "Look, Jess, I'll talk to you later."

"It's okay, Jake, I understand. Please—you don't have to say anything else." The tears that had been forming in my eyes for about five minutes started to spill over.

"Why is she crying?" Lucius demanded. "Did you say something to her?"

Jake put up his hands. "No. I swear."

"Just go, Lucius," I insisted.

Lucius hesitated.

"Please."

He met my eyes. I saw sympathy in his gaze, and that was probably the worst part of the whole day. A total outcast feeling sorry for me. "As you wish," he said, and stepped back. But not before adding, "I'm watching you, too, Zinn."

"Hey," Jake soothed when Lucius was out of earshot. "That was intense, huh?"

I sniffled, wiping at my eyes. "Which part? When Lucius nearly killed Frank or threatened you?"

"The whole thing."

"I'm really sorry."

"No, it's okay. Frank's a jerk. He deserved it."

"The whole thing is so embarrassing."

"Yeah. It kind of was."

"Don't worry about the carnival," I said. "It was stupid of me to ask."

"No, I was going to say yes." Jake stared down the hallway in the direction Lucius had departed. "Unless you guys are . . . together or something. I mean, that's the rumor. And Lucius seemed sort of . . . possessive, right there."

"No," I kind of barked. "Lucius is *not* my boyfriend. More like a . . . an overprotective big brother."

"Well, he wouldn't try to plaster *me* against a locker if we go, would he? Because I could take him, but having seen him in action, I think it would be a hell of a fight," Jake said, only half joking, it seemed.

"No, Lucius is harmless," I fibbed. *If you don't count the fact that he thinks he's a warrior prince representing a semi-cannibalistic race of undead bat people.*

"Then I'll call you, okay?" Jake promised.

"Great." I smiled then, almost forgetting that I'd just been crying.

Jake started to walk away, then hesitated. "Jess?"

"Yeah?"

"I'm glad you asked me."

"Me, too," I said, silently thanking Mindy and her faith in *Cosmo* and horoscopes as I turned away, grinning.

Lucius was waiting for me outside the school, sitting on a low brick wall near the entrance. When he saw me, he hopped down and held out his hands for my books like he always did when he managed to track me down after school.

"We missed the bus," Lucius pointed out. He didn't sound disappointed.

"We can walk to Mom's office. She'll give us a ride." Grantley College was just a few minutes from the school.

"Excellent idea." Lucius fell in step with me, and we headed toward the campus in the cool mid-autumn late afternoon. After a few moments of silence, he pulled a crisp linen monogrammed handkerchief from an inner pocket in his coat, handing it to me. "Your face is tearstained."

"Thanks," I said, accepting the handkerchief. I wiped at my cheeks and blew my nose. "Here," I said, handing it back.

Lucius held up a hand, cringing. "You keep it. I beg you. I have others."

"Thanks." I wadded up the handkerchief, trying to stuff it in my pocket.

"My pleasure, Jessica." Lucius's gaze was trained far-off, his tone distracted. About a block later, he advanced slightly ahead of me, walking backward, bent over, searching my face. "That *boy* . . . that squatty Zinn . . ."

"What about Jake?" It was my turn to look away, focusing down the oak-lined street.

"He's . . . he's someone you're *honestly* attracted to?"

I crossed my arms over my chest, shrugging, kicking at a fallen acorn. "Oh, I don't know. I mean . . ."

"Well, you're accompanying him to this gala everyone's talking about—"

"It's a carnival. Like a party in the gym. Not a 'gala.' Nobody says 'gala.' At least nobody at Woodrow Wilson."

Lucius frowned. "Gala, carnival . . . regardless. You're courting?"

Is that hurt in Lucius's eyes? Or just the usual darkness? "It's just one date, but yeah, I guess so," I admitted, not sure why I suddenly felt guilty. I had no reason to feel guilty. Just because Lucius believed we were engaged didn't make me a cheater, for crying out loud. But he kept staring, so I added lamely, "I hope that's not a problem. What with the *pact* and all."

"I just find it hard to understand."

"What?" This I had to hear. "I thought you knew everything."

"He didn't even defend you." Lucius rubbed his chin, genuinely confused.

I got a little defensive myself, on Jake's behalf. "Here, women defend themselves. Men don't have to fight for us. I told you—I can handle Dormand."

"Not the way *I* can on your behalf. Not the way Zinn *should have.* Like it or not, you are bound by gender. You can swat at the fly, but I could crush him. Any *honorable* male would have stepped up."

"Hey," I protested. "Jake has honor."

"Not enough to protect you."

"Oh, Lucius," I groaned. "Jake thinks you went totally overboard—and he's right."

Lucius shook his head. "Then he didn't see your face."

I didn't quite know what to say to that.

We resumed walking in silence, Lucius reining in his big stride to match mine. He seemed even more distracted than before, a big frown on his face.

We passed through the gates to the Grantley campus, heading toward Schreyer Hall, where Mom's office was. Suddenly Lucius brightened. "You do drive, don't you? Have a license?"

"Well, yeah, sure. Why? Where do you want to go?" *The blood bank?*

"I think I would like to buy some jeans," Lucius announced. "Perhaps a T-shirt. And they're very rigid about wearing certain shoes in the gym. My Romanian soles break some sort of rule. Apparently I need shoes with a 'swoosh' on the side if I'm to continue playing basketball."

I stopped in my tracks. "You want to buy *regular* clothes?"

"No, I want to update my wardrobe in line with cultural norms," he corrected. "You do know how to get to these famous 'outlets' I hear so much about, right?"

I gasped, jamming one finger against Lucius's chest. "Wait right here. Don't move. I'll ask Mom if we can borrow the van." *This I have to see.*

What in the world would Lucius Vladescu deem normal? And more importantly, how would a tall, imperious Romanian accustomed to wearing tailor-made black pants look in a pair of jeans?

Chapter 16

"HONESTLY, I DON'T KNOW how some of these stories got started," Lucius complained, adjusting the van's radio, probably looking for Croatian folk music but settling for classical on the public station. "Hollywood, I suppose."

I flipped to a pop station, just to irritate him. "So you don't think you can change into a bat?"

Lucius turned down the music and shot me a look that said he was insulted. "Please. A bat? What self-respecting vampire would transfigure into a flying rodent? Would you become a skunk, even if you had the ability?"

"No, I guess not." I braked for a traffic light. "Maybe once, just to see what it was like."

"Well, vampires cannot transform into anything."

"How about garlic? Does it repulse you?"

"Only on someone's breath."

"And stakes? Can you be killed with a stake?"

"Anyone can be killed with a stake. But yes—that one is true. In fact, a stake through the heart is the only effective way to destroy a vampire."

"Uh, yeah. Sure."

"To save you time, I will add that we do not sleep in coffins. We do not sleep upside down. We, quite obviously, don't disintegrate in sunlight. How could one live a practical, useful life that way?"

"So far, being a vampire sounds pretty dull if you ask me."

"At the risk of raising a bad subject—and again, my apologies—you didn't seem to think my fangs were dull the other evening. In fact, you reacted quite strongly to their *sharpness*."

And to the feel of his hands, his body . . . Don't go there, Jess. "How *did* you do that? Did you have, like, a set of plastic teeth in your mouth?"

Lucius shot me an incredulous look. "Plastic teeth? Did they look plastic?"

"No," I admitted. "But dentures look real."

"Dentures." He snorted. "Don't be absurd. Those were—are—my teeth. That is what vampires do. We grow fangs."

"Do it now then." I steered the van onto Route 30, navigating traffic.

"Oh, Jessica . . . I don't think that's wise while you're driving on a busy road. You quite panicked the other night."

"You can't do it, can you?" I challenged. "Because it was a stupid trick, and you don't have your props."

"Don't provoke me, Jessica. Not unless you really want me to do as you ask. Because I can, and I will."

"Do it."

"As you wish." Lucius turned toward me, bared his teeth, and I nearly ran off the road. Lucius grabbed the wheel, swerving us back into place.

"Holy shit." He'd done it again. He really had. I slid my gaze over, cautiously. The pointy teeth were gone. *It's a trick. A trick.* I wouldn't fall for it. Teeth were covered with enamel, one of the hardest substances in the body. Enamel couldn't shift or change. It was impossible, at the molecular level.

"You really must get used to that," Lucius chided.

"Do you buy the trick at, like, a magic shop?"

"It's not a *trick*. Please stop using that word." Lucius drummed his fingers on the VW's vinyl passenger seat. I could tell he was getting frustrated again. "Vampiric transformation is a *phenomenon*. If you'd read the book I provided—"

I groaned. "Oh, god, that thing." My unwanted copy of *Growing Up Undead* was still under my bed. I kept meaning to throw it out but somehow never got around to it. I didn't want to think about why.

"Yes, 'that thing,'" Lucius said. "If you'd read the guide as you should you would know that male vampires gain the ability to grow fangs at puberty. It happens when we're exceedingly angry. Or . . . aroused."

"So you're saying 'fangs' are like an—" I started to say "erection" like I said it every day of my life. But the truth was, I had never said that word out loud, and discovered that I couldn't do it then. But Lucius understood.

"Yes. That. Precisely. Often kind of a tandem effect, if you understand my meaning. But it gets easy to control with practice. And women can grow fangs, too, of course."

"So why can't I do it if I'm supposedly such a big-time vampire?" Sooner or later, I would confound him with logic.

But Lucius shot right back, "Women have to be bitten first. *I* need to bite you. It's a great privilege for a man to be his betrothed's first bite."

"Don't start that betrothal talk again," I said seriously. Spotting the first entrance to the outlet mall, I made a quick turn. "Not even joking. We're done with that."

Lucius tilted his head. "Are we done with it?"

"Yes."

I pulled into a parking spot. "How about mirrors? When you try on clothes, will you be able to see yourself in a mirror?"

Lucius rubbed his temples. "Have you taken basic science at Woodrow Wilson High School? Do you know the principles behind reflectivity?"

"Of course I do. I'm the one who actually believes in science, remember? I was just joking." I yanked the keys out of the ignition. "So let's recap. You can't change into a bat, you don't dissolve in sunlight, and you're visible in mirrors. What *can* vampires do? Why's it so awesome to be one, then?"

"What would be so wonderful about dissolving in sunlight? Or not being able to look in a mirror and judge if you've dressed yourself properly?"

"You know what I mean. You keep saying vampires are so great. I just want to know why."

Lucius's head dropped back against the seat. He stared at the shag carpet on the ceiling of the van as though begging for patience or guidance. "We are only the most powerful race of superhumans. We are physically gifted with grace and strength. We are a people of ritual and tradition. We have heightened mental powers: the ability to communicate without speech when necessary. We rule the dark side of nature. Is that 'awesome' enough for you?"

I grabbed the door latch. "So why drink blood?"

Lucius sighed deeply, opening his own door. "Why is everyone so obsessed with the blood? There's so much more."

I dropped the subject. I'd sort of became distracted, anyhow, now that we were about to go shopping. "So where do you want to go first?"

Lucius came around the front of the van and placed his hands on my shoulders, pointing me toward the Levi's outlet. "There."

Five stores and about five hundred dollars later, Lucius Vladescu looked almost like an American teenager. And, I had to admit, a hot American teenager. He wore a pair of 501s even better than his black pants. And when he put on a loose white untucked oxford shirt—having decided that a T-shirt would be a bit too *Real World/Road Rules Challenge* for Romanian royalty—well, the effect was pretty nice. It didn't seem embarrassing to be with him. Not at all. Mindy would probably pass out, literally, when she saw him.

"So how about getting rid of the velvet coat?" I asked.

"Never," he replied.

So much for not being embarrassing.

We were walking toward the car, juggling all our shopping bags, when Lucius stopped short and grabbed my arm, dropping a bag.

I turned. "What?"

He was looking in the window of a store called Boulevard St. Michel, an upscale boutique with very, very expensive clothes. The kind of clothes that rich women wear to cocktail parties. I'd never been inside. For one thing, my dad didn't believe in dry cleaning, because of the "perc emissions" that messed up the environment. And for another, I couldn't afford one shoe from Boulevard St. Michel, even at outlet prices. Not even after a whole summer slinging burgers at the diner.

"What are you doing?" I followed his gaze.

Lucius kept staring at the window. "That dress—the one with the flowers scattered across the bodice—"

"Did you just say 'bodice'?"

"Yes, and skirt—"

"The dress with the V-neck?"

"Yes. That one. You would look lovely in something like that."

Lucius had officially fallen off his already cracked rocker. Not only did he think he was a vampire, but now he believed I was some sort of thirty-year-old cocktail-party attendee. I laughed out loud. "You really are crazy. That's designed—and priced—for women who do things like go to, I don't know, symphonies or something."

He shot me a look. "What's wrong with the symphony?"

"Nothing. Except that I don't go. I mean, can you see me in that at 4-H? I bet it costs a mint, too."

"Try the dress on."

I pulled back. "No way. I am one hundred percent sure that they don't like teenagers in there."

Lucius scoffed. "They like anyone with enough money."

"Then they won't like me. I don't have enough money even to look."

"I do."

"Lucius . . ." But I'll admit, I was kind of intrigued. It *was* a beautiful dress. I'd never even tried on anything like it. It was so . . . sophisticated. It was the color of fresh cream, with tiny, black, embroidered flowers scattered here and there across the whole thing, not really in any kind of pattern, but that only made it prettier somehow. It reminded me of chaos theory: random but beautiful in its simplicity. The neckline was more daring than anything I'd ever worn. You could see the swell of the mannequin's plastic breasts peeking out above the fabric. The *expensive* fabric. I tugged Lucius's arm. "Come on. Let's go."

Lucius pulled back, and of course he was stronger. "Just look. Every woman needs beautiful things."

"I don't need *that*."

"Of course you do. You could wear it to, say, this 'carnival' you're attending with Squatty Boy. It would be perfectly suitable for affairs like that."

"He's not squatty."

"Try on the dress."

"I have plenty of clothes," I insisted.

"Yes. And you should throw them all out. Especially the T-shirt with the white horse, the heart, and the letter *I* on the front. What is the purpose?"

"To show that I love Arabians," I said.

"I love rare steak, but I don't sport the image of raw beef on my chest."

"I already picked out an outfit."

Lucius scowled. "Something shiny from 'the mall,' I suppose?"

I flushed. I hated when Lucius was right.

"Believe me," he said. "If you wear that dress, you won't regret it. That was made for you."

I narrowed my eyes. "How do you know about dressing girls?"

"I don't know about dressing girls. I know about dressing women." Lucius smiled archly. "Now come along. Indulge me."

Lucius led the way into the store, and I had to follow. As I'd predicted, the sales lady looked less than thrilled to see two high school students in her showroom. But Lucius was oblivious. "That dress in the window, with the embroidery." He pointed to me. "She'd like to try that." Crossing his arms and leaning back slightly, he mentally measured my body, head to toe. "Size eight?"

"Ten," I mumbled.

"The ten is in the window on the mannequin," the saleswoman noted. She jammed her skinny, red-fingernailed hands on her hips. "It's very troublesome to bring it down. If you're not serious about it . . ."

Uh-oh. There wasn't much that I understood about Lucius Vladescu, but I knew for a fact that the saleslady's tone would not sit well with him.

Lucius arched an eyebrow. "Did I not sound serious?" He leaned forward, reading the woman's name tag. "Leigh Ann?"

"Come on, Lucius . . ." I started for the door.

"We're in rather a hurry, so if you could get it now, please," Lucius said, holding his ground. It was suddenly very easy to imagine him ordering around servants in a castle.

The saleswoman narrowed her eyes, assessing Lucius. Apparently she sniffed at least a hint of money in his cologne, heard it in his accent, or saw it in his swagger. "Fine," she huffed. "If you insist." She crawled up into the window and came back out a few minutes later with the dress. "Here," she said, draping it across my arms. "The dressing rooms are in the rear."

"Thank you," Lucius said.

"Whatever." Leigh Ann moved behind the counter, proceeding to ignore us.

Lucius followed me back toward the dressing rooms. I stopped him at the entrance with a firm hand on the chest. "You wait here."

"Let me see, though."

In the privacy of the dressing room, I kicked off my Chucks, wriggled out of my jeans and T-shirt, and slipped on the dress, wishing I was wearing a nicer bra. A bra that would do the dress justice.

Although it looked delicate, the fabric was heavier and softer than anything I'd ever owned. I zipped up the back as far as I could, the dress fell into place around me, and suddenly all the places I hated most on my body transformed into my best assets. My breasts filled out the bodice even better than the mannequin's angular, skimpy little peaks. Looking at myself in the mirror, I remembered what Lucius had said about "pointy" girls and the benefits of having curves. In that dress, I understood what he meant. The hem swirled around my knees, and I twirled a little, staring at my front. My back. The fabric swept close to my full hips and draped perfectly across my butt. Lucius had been right. I looked *good*. It was like a magic dress.

"Well?" Lucius called from outside the dressing room. "How is it?"

"It's pretty," I admitted, understating how I really felt. Which was *beautiful*.

"Come out, then."

"Oh, I don't know . . ." I was kind of embarrassed to show him. I glanced down at my chest. Skin usually covered by shirts was peeking out. The swell of my breasts—breasts I usually tried to de-emphasize—was visible for the world to see. For

Lucius to see. It wasn't obscene, by any standard. But it was revealing for me.

"Jessica, you promised."

"Oh . . . okay." I tried to pull up the bodice a little but to no avail. My curves refused to hide. "Don't laugh or anything. Or stare."

"I will not laugh," Lucius promised. "There will be no *reason* to laugh. But I might stare."

Taking a deep breath, I shoved aside the curtain.

Lucius was lounging in the chair set out for bored husbands, his long legs stretched in front of him. But when he saw me, he shot straight up. Like I'd jolted him. And I swore I saw appreciation in his black eyes.

"Well?" I resisted the urge to cross my arms over my chest as I spun to look in the mirror. "What do you think?"

"You—you look amazing." Lucius stood, coming up behind me, never taking his eyes off me.

"Really?"

"Beautiful, Antanasia," he murmured. "Beautiful."

Before I could remind him not to call me by that name, Lucius stepped even closer to me, slipped his hand under my long, unruly hair, and pulled the zipper all the way up. "Women always need help with the last few inches."

I swallowed hard. *How experienced* was *he?* "Um, thank you."

"My pleasure." Then, to my intense surprise, Lucius snaked his fingers into my curls and gathered them up into a big, loose twist on top of my head. Suddenly, my neck looked very long. "Now that's how a Romanian princess should look," he said, drawing down to whisper in my ear. "Don't ever again say that you are not 'valuable,' Antanasia. Or not beautiful. Or, for god's sake, 'fat.' When you get the urge to indulge in such ridiculous, misplaced self-criticism, remember yourself at this moment."

No one had ever paid me a compliment like that.

For a minute, we stood there admiring me. I met Lucius's eyes in the mirror. In that split second, I could almost picture us . . . together.

Then he released my hair. It tumbled down my back, and the spell was broken. I glanced down at the price tag. "Oh my gosh. I have got to take this off. Right now. Before I sweat on it or something."

Lucius rolled his eyes. "If you must refer to 'sweat' in reference to yourself—and I strongly discourage it—use the word *perspire*."

"I'm serious, Lucius. I'm about to start *perspiring* over the price."

Lucius bent to read the number on the tag and shrugged.

I hurried back to the dressing room, yanking on my jeans and lacing up my battered Chucks. The princess effect was definitely gone. Reluctantly, I handed the dress to the saleslady, who was waiting, holding a beautiful black cashmere wrap. "I'll box these up for you."

I glanced around for Lucius and found him standing at the sales counter, tapping a credit card against the glass countertop.

"It's too much," I whispered, hurrying over.

"Consider it a thank-you for your shopping guidance today. My gift for your gala."

I searched for irony or sarcasm in his eyes, saw none. *What does that mean?* That Lucius Vladescu was giving up his courtship of me? Doubtful. *Maybe?* "Thanks," I said uncertainly.

Leigh Ann carefully packaged the dress and the wrap in two boxes and handed them to me. "Enjoy." She had warmed considerably after the credit card had been approved.

"Have a nice day, Leigh Ann." Lucius placed a hand on the small of my back, guiding me out of the store.

"I really don't know what to say," I stammered when we were outside. "It's such a huge gift. The dress alone cost a fortune, and the wrap is cashmere."

"It will no doubt be cool at night, and you can't wear a 'jean jacket' with that dress."

"Well, thank you."

"I told you. Every woman deserves beautiful things," Lucius said. "I just hope Squatty Boy appreciates you in this." He paused outside, scanning the storefronts. "Couldn't you go for a Strawberry Julius about now?"

Chapter 17

"SO, JAKE, HOW WAS the hay crop this year?" Dad asked, trying to make conversation.

"Good, I guess." Jake seemed uncertain about even that simple answer, probably because he was on the spot, under inspection by my parents.

"I'd be happy to show you some of the chemical-free pest control methods we use, if you're interested—"

"Dad," I interrupted. "You promised. No environmental lectures."

Why had my parents been so intent on having dinner with Jake, anyway? They were all about personal space and learning autonomy—until it came to me actually going out with a guy. Then suddenly they'd gone all *Seventh Heaven* on me, insisting that Jake have dinner with us—even though he'd grown up just down the road and delivered hay to our house every few weeks. It was totally awkward. And the fact that Lucius was in a nasty mood wasn't helping.

"More soy milk?" Mom offered.

Jake held up a hand, a little too quickly. "No thanks."

"It's kind of an acquired taste," I sympathized.

"Uh, yeah. I guess I'm used to the regular kind of milk."

"Which exploits cows," Dad added, jabbing a fork in Jake's general direction. "Poor animals, lined up in a row, their teats attached to cold metal—"

Teats? "Dad, please. Don't say that word—"

"What?" My dad tossed up his hands, all innocence. "Jake lives on a farm. I'm sure he is familiar with a cow's teats."

Every drop of blood in my body rushed to my face. Leave it to Dad to bring up a cow's personal anatomy during my first dinner with Jake and then accuse him of being "familiar" with the bovine equivalent of breasts. Like Jake went to second base with livestock or something. I glanced at Lucius, expecting him to smirk, but he simply picked at his salad, examining one of Dad's prized cherry tomatoes like it was a mucus-filled alien life-form that had somehow become stuck on the end of his fork.

"Ned," Mom intervened. "Perhaps we *could* change the

topic." I experienced one brief moment of relief, until my mom turned to Jake and noted, "I understand you're reading *Moby Dick* in your literature class."

"Um. Yeah."

"I loved that book when I was your age," Mom said. "The whole idea of adventure at sea. And so thought provoking. What are we to make of the white whale? What, ultimately, does it symbolize?" she mused, still addressing Jake. "God, nature, evil—or is it simply a symbol of Ahab's very straight-forward, very human pride?"

There was a moment of silence while poor Jake tried to think of a response to my mom's question, which, from the look on his face, was about as digestible as the soy milk. "Um . . . all of those things?" he finally ventured.

"We're only reading the abridged version," I pointed out stupidly. I was used to living with a professor—there was usu-ally some sort of quiz at dinner—but did Mom have to tor-ment Jake? "Maybe they cut out some of the metaphors—"

"The whale represents the hidden forces of destruction that long to break through the surface of a complacent world," Lu-cius broke in, speaking for the first time, causing all heads to swivel in his direction.

"Huh?" Jake blurted out, clearly baffled. Then he caught himself and shot me a sheepish glance.

"I like the whale," Lucius added glumly, still staring at his plate. "And Ahab. They understood persistence. They under-stood how to bide their time." He lifted his black eyes and gave me a look as pointed as his "fangs." "And they accepted their *mutual destiny,* however grim."

No. My stomach clenched. *If Lucius starts talking about the betrothal, Jake will run for the hills. And why is Lucius referring to a destiny with me as "grim," anyway? Is he implying that being married to me would be as bad as being strapped to a dying whale?*

"Hey, Lucius. How was basketball practice?" I asked, trying desperately to harpoon the conversation and bring it under control.

"I've seen you in the gym, man," Jake noted. "You're, like, NBA-bound. You could take the team to states with that jump shot. You nailed every one in drills."

"Ah, yes, drills," Lucius said, clearly bored.

"Drills build skills," Jake offered. "You gotta do the drills."

"Drills are dull," Lucius countered, not really looking at Jake. "I prefer competition."

"You're a wrestler, right, Jake?" Dad asked, passing Jake more *saag*. My parents were in an Indian food phase. The evening's entrée consisted of limp spinach. God forbid we'd throw a few burgers on the grill and just have a barbecue when guests came over.

Jake gave the bright green, mushy contents a wary glance but accepted the bowl. "Yeah. I wrestle. I'm captain this year."

"How Greco-Roman of you," Lucius said dryly, lifting a glob of spinach and letting it drip, slowly, from his fork. "Grappling about on mats."

Jake shot me a confused look. I shrugged an ignore-the-moody-exchange-student shrug.

Mom slapped her napkin onto the table. "Lucius, may I see you in the kitchen?" Except it wasn't really a question.

Oh, thank god. I made a mental note to clean my room or do an extra load of laundry. Even Lucius's boxer shorts. I owed her one.

Lucius slunk out behind my mother. There was an uncomfortable lull in the conversation at the table, during which we all pretended like we didn't hear the phrases "take part in polite conversation," "feeble-minded nincompoop," and "remove yourself," coming from the kitchen in stage-whispered tones.

A few minutes later, the kitchen door slammed shut. Mom came back alone. "Who wants more flatbread?" she asked, smiling grimly, not offering an explanation for the loss of one very irritable Romanian teenager.

Across the table, Lucius's *saag* congealed on his abandoned plate.

After Jake left, I wandered out to the garage. Lucius was shooting foul shots, using a rusted old hoop that the rest of us had forgotten even existed. Dribble, aim, swish. I watched him make about ten in a row before I interrupted him. "Hey."

He turned around, tucking the ball under his arm, looking incredibly like an average American high school student in the Grantley College sweatshirt Mom had bought for him. Until he spoke. "Good evening, Jessica. To what do I owe this visit? Aren't you *entertaining* this evening?"

"Jake had to go."

"What a shame." Lucius tossed the ball over his shoulder. It dropped through the rim.

"What was wrong with you tonight? You know we could hear you insulting him in the kitchen."

"Really?" Lucius looked a little crestfallen. "I didn't intend that. That's just boorish."

I crossed my arms. "Do you have something to say about me and Jake? Because if you do, just say it to my face. Don't give a cryptic dinner table lecture about whales and destiny."

"What could I have to say? You've made yourself quite clear."

"I don't know what you're getting at," I said honestly. "When you bought me the dress, I thought that was your way of saying you didn't care if I went out with Jake."

The ball rolled near Lucius's feet, and he bent to scoop it up, then traced the worn seams with his thumb, avoiding my eyes. "Yes. I did think that . . . but this evening, when I saw him *looking* at you . . ."

"What?" Was Lucius actually *jealous*?

"I just don't like him, Jessica," Lucius finally said. "He's not good enough for you. Regardless of how you feel about our tenuous relationship at this point, don't sell yourself short with any man. Any *boy*."

"You don't know Jake," I said, growing angry. "You didn't even try to get to know him. He tried to be nice to you at dinner."

Lucius shrugged. "I see him in school, struggling to understand basic concepts in English literature. That's very telling, don't you think?"

"So Jake doesn't like *Moby Dick*. Who cares? I don't like it, either."

Lucius looked disappointed with me. Or sad about something. Or both. "I find that I'm in a very unusual mood tonight, Jessica," he said, avoiding my eyes again. "I'm not the best company. Perhaps you'll excuse me—leave me to my solitary pursuits."

"Lucius—"

"Please, Jessica." He turned his back on me and launched the ball with a flick of his wrist. It swooped through the hoop without touching the rim.

"Fine. I'll go."

Lucius was still shooting hoops when I went to check on him an hour later. It was dark outside, and he played in a small circle of light from a floodlight mounted on the garage. He'd switched to layups. I started to call out a greeting then changed my mind. Something about the single-minded way he was drilling shot after shot after shot, never missing, rising over the rim with ease to slam the ball through the hoop, like he was punishing the ball, sort of freaked me out.

Chapter 18

DEAR UNCLE VASILE,

Best wishes as we approach All Hallows' Eve. You would so enjoy the universally naïve but ubiquitous depictions of vampires the Americans somewhat compulsively display at this time of year. One would think our entire race consisted of pale, middle-aged men with a genetic tendency toward "widow's peaks" and a penchant for the overapplication of hair gel.

But getting to the point. I am loath to admit that I increasingly see the situation here slipping from my control.

As per my last correspondence, I have tried numerous "American" strategies to at least build a rapport with Antanasia—including donning "jeans" (quite comfortable, actually) and, as I've mentioned, playing basketball, a sport for "popular kids." (Just call me "Number 23.")

Thus far, Antanasia seems less than impressed with my best efforts, though. She is actually getting "involved with" the peasant. (Vasile, if you heard him attempt to make conversation . . . it's unendurable, really. I would rather have our omnipresent lentils shoved into my ears than listen to him for more than two minutes.)

Honestly, Antanasia quite baffles me. Just the other day, I thought we had experienced a significant breakthrough. I purchased for her the most magnificent dress—really, if you had seen her in it, you would have judged her nearly ready to take the throne. . . . For the briefest moment, I thought we had made progress. The look in her own eyes as she watched herself in the mirror . . . She was altered, Vasile. And altered toward me . . . I could have sworn it.

And yet the peasant clings on like a parasite. A leech or a tick that cannot be dislodged. What does Antanasia see in him? And why does she persist in seeing it? I could offer her so much more. In particular, conversation. Repartee. Not to mention leadership of two powerful clans. A castle. Servants. Anything she desired. Things she deserves, Vasile.

Damn. I'm blathering.

The point is, I quite fear that you will be disappointed with me if I fail to convince Antanasia to honor the pact and accept me as her husband. And, in all candor, your disappointment is a rather formidable prospect. Thus I feel compelled to keep you updated on the situation as it unfolds. I certainly wouldn't want to present you with an unanticipated failure. I would much rather prepare you for the worst eventuality—even as I fully intend to continue my efforts.

Your nephew, most humbly,

Lucius

P.S. If anyone offers you "saag," decline if at all possible to do so without breaking the rules of polite society. Is there any chance the cook might ship a frozen hare or two this way?

P.P.S. The investment I've made with your advance on my trust will arrive soon. I am rather looking forward to it.

P.P.P.S. The peasant doesn't understand the symbolism of the whale in Moby Dick, Vasile. It's true. Concepts literally pummeled into my brain (recall my half-Gypsy tutor, Bogdana, whose grasp of literary devices was exceeded only by her grip on the switch?) during preadolescence remain beyond his grasp. Is he feeble-minded? Or just obtuse?

Parasite.

Chapter 19

"HEY, BELLE." I grinned, giving my Appaloosa's muscular neck a firm pat. "Ready for a workout? Only a few more practice sessions before the show." My grin quickly faded, though. The 4-H show, just a few weeks away, had seemed like a good idea when I'd signed up, but now I was suffering from some serious attacks of nerves.

Well, it was too late to back out. Or was it?

As I reached for Belle's bridle, lifting it from a nail in the wall, I heard a truck pull up outside the barn. A door slammed, and I glanced toward the barn door to see a stranger walking toward me. A stocky man in dirty coveralls, holding a clipboard.

"Can I help you?" I offered.

"You know a . . ." He glanced at the clipboard. "A Lou Vlad . . . here." He extended the roster. "I can't make out that name."

"Oh, no." My heart sank. I didn't even have to look. "Vladescu. What did he do now? Did he order something?"

"Yeah. And he needs to take delivery of this monster that's kicking my trailer all to hell. I want that thing out of there now."

"Monster?"

"You're looking for me?" As if on cue at the word *monster,* Lucius appeared from out of the shadows, accepted the clipboard and a pen, and signed.

"I hope you know what you're doing," the delivery man said, shaking his head.

"Oh, I'm sure I do."

I followed as Lucius and the man strode through the indoor riding ring, headed toward the door. "Lucius? What did you buy?"

The delivery man called over his shoulder, answering on Lucius's behalf. "Your friend bought a murderous horse. Thing oughta be put down."

"Lucius?" We all passed through the barn door and arrived at the dirt drive, where I saw a horse trailer. Rocking. Thudding sounds were coming from inside.

"You get her out, kid," the man insisted. "I'm not touching that thing again."

Without hesitation, Lucius approached the rear of the trailer, unlatched it, and opened the door.

"Um . . . Lucius? Should you go in there?"

"Kid's dead meat," the delivery man noted.

There was the sound of a scuffle, then I heard Lucius's voice calming the animal, and hooves against metal. Then silence. A long silence. And finally Lucius emerged, leading a very skittish, very powerful horse. The blackest horse I had ever seen. It had to stand a full nineteen hands high. Its eyes rolled wildly, showing whites against its ebony face. I stepped back as it passed by, but it shied, then nipped at me.

"Easy, there," Lucius soothed. He called back to me, "Sorry, she's a tad excitable."

The delivery man took off, muttering about broken skulls, and I followed Lucius, who was persuading his new mount to enter a stall. Right next to Belle's.

"I want them to be neighbors." Lucius smiled.

It was my turn to roll my eyes. "Great."

"Easy," Lucius told the mare again as she snapped at his fingers. He clapped his hand across her muzzle, struggling with her as he hooked her halter to both sides of the stall. When she was contained, he released her, and she took one last lunge at him, clipping his forearm with her teeth. "Dammit!" He shook out his arm.

I planted my feet and crossed my arms. "You bought a horse? *That* horse?"

"Yes," Lucius said, rubbing the bite. "I recall a while back that you said—and I quote—that we 'have nothing in common.'" He jerked a thumb toward his hell horse. "This is something we can share. An activity. A way for us to spend time together."

"You're not joining 4-H," I told him.

"My commemorative club jacket is being embroidered as we speak." He grinned. "I do so look forward to wearing that blue corduroy. You do know that 'corduroy' means 'fabric of kings,' right? Appropriate, I think."

"But I thought you had sort of given up . . ."

Lucius frowned, stroking his horse's muzzle. This time she flinched but didn't snap. "You thought I'd forgotten a pact that I have been prepared to fulfill since childhood just because I endure Squatty Boy's crude advances toward you? I think not."

"Stop calling him squatty and stop insinuating that he's stupid. Jake is a very nice guy."

"Nice. Now that's an overrated quality." Lucius unhitched one side of the ropes restraining his horse, and she half reared. He patted the mare's neck. "Isn't nice overrated?" He paused, turning to me. "What should I name her?" he mused. "She needs a name if I'm to enter her in the jumper class."

"You can't," I cried. "I'm competing in that."

"I know. I thought we could practice together."

"I already told you, I don't want your help."

"You're not afraid of a little friendly competition, are you?"

I stamped my foot. In part because, no, I didn't want to compete with him. He was a natural athlete. A Romanian all-star polo player. I also didn't want him to start skulking around the barn. "I told you I don't want to ride with you."

"You are completely overreacting."

"And you are a stupid . . . stupid . . . vampire! You never listen to me. I specifically told you not to interfere in this part of my life. We live together, go to school together . . . This is one place where I don't have you bugging me all the time."

"A vampire?" The voice came from close behind us.

Uh-oh.

Lucius and I both swung around to see a very curious, somewhat bemused Faith Crosse watching our argument. Her lightly tanned arms were crossed over her tight cheerleading-camp T-shirt, and her blond ponytail bobbed, gleaming in the dim light, as she cocked her head. "Did you just call him a *vampire*?"

I stammered, grasping for an explanation. "He's . . . he's sucking the life out of me today," I finally said.

"Jessica's full of pet names for me." Lucius smiled, nonplussed. He extended his hand. "So nice to see you outside of the classroom, Faith."

Oh, brother.

Faith seemed a little surprised, but extended her hand, too. "Um . . . you too, Lucius."

Lucius didn't shake. He grazed her knuckles with his lips. "Charmed, as always."

"Oh. Wow. That was different." Faith withdrew her hand, addressing me, the stable hand, as an afterthought. "Hey, Jenn."

"It's Jess."

"Right." But Faith's attention had shifted again, to the unnamed horse. "What a beautiful mare. I saw you bringing her in. She looks dangerous, though."

Lucius unhooked the other lead, freeing his new perilous pet. "I find that horses, like people, are boring if completely broken. I prefer a little spirit." The animal jerked its head, but Lucius soothed her. "Calm down now." He addressed Faith and me. "She's been treated hard, poor beast. Unpleasant childhood."

"Unpleasant?" Faith cocked her head.

"Don't ever come near her with a crop or a whip," Lucius advised. "That's what the previous owner strongly suggested. Apparently her first master had a quite heavy hand."

Raised under the whip. I thought of Lucius's own admission that he'd been hit by his uncles. Again and again. I wondered if he had deliberately chosen the mare for the cruel connection they shared. It seemed like something he would do.

Faith and I both stepped back, dodging quickly, as Lucius led the mare out of the stall.

"You're not going to ride her, are you?" I asked, incredulous.

Lucius frowned. "That's what one does with horses, right?"

"I have a spare saddle," Faith offered.

I glared at Faith. "No! Are you serious?" Normally Faith wasn't the type of person whose actions you questioned, but I couldn't believe she thought Lucius should make any attempt to ride the mare with the diabolical look in her eyes and the snapping jaws. "Lucius, don't even think about it."

"Oh, I don't think she'd like a saddle," he said. "Not yet. I'll let her get used to carrying just me first."

I shook my head. "You're going to get killed."

Lucius shot me a conspiratorial look. "You, of all people, should know that's unlikely. Animals can't use tools."

Without further hesitation, he swept to the horse's side and leapt onto her back, with the same ease he demonstrated doing layups on the basketball court. The mare immediately whinnied and wheeled, but Lucius lived up to his boasts. Within seconds, he brought her under control, and the two—madman and mad animal—proceeded into the center of the ring at a brisk but controlled clip, Lucius guiding with his knees and the halter. Every few steps, the horse shied or twisted back to nip at Lucius's legs. But the two kept a steady, if edgy, partnership. "We'll be jumping in no time," Lucius called, grinning.

He was doing it. Riding the meanest-looking mare I'd ever seen. My relief was short-lived as I realized exactly what his survival meant for me. When it came time for the 4-H show, I'd be competing with both Faith Crosse and a Romanian all-star on a devil horse.

Lucius urged his mount into a trot. Then a canter. It was half dance, half barroom brawl.

"Wow." Faith watched with appreciation. "Lucius must have, like, some kind of magic. I really thought he'd get killed."

"Give him time," I replied under my breath. "Just give him time. Someone'll kill him yet."

Chapter 20

"THANKS FOR WINNING me the plush hot dog." I squeezed the big stuffed wiener Jake had won by throwing two softballs through a clown's mouth. "I had a great time at the carnival."

"Sorry I couldn't get the bear."

"Well, a hot dog's nice. It's different, you know?"

We were sitting in Jake's big Chevy 4x4, idling in front of the farm, trying to figure out how to say good night. Was I supposed to just hop out of the truck at this point? Would he get out, too?

"Did I tell you that you look really great in that dress?" Jake asked.

He hadn't, but I'd seen the look in his eyes when he'd come to the door to pick me up. The same admiration that I'd seen in Lucius's eyes back in the boutique. All night long, I'd caught guys checking me out. At first I'd felt a little self-conscious. But it was easy to get used to that kind of attention.

"I like your hair up like that, too," Jake added.

I twisted one of the tendrils that straggled out of my updo. I'd done my best to mimic the effect Lucius had achieved just by twining his fingers in my hair. "Thanks."

"I'm glad you asked me to go with you. I had a great time."

There was a long pause.

"I guess I'll get going," I finally said, resting my hand on the door handle.

"Oh . . . uh, yeah. I'll get the door." Jake shut off the engine and jumped out, coming around to my side. He opened my door, and I tried to climb down, almost falling in my heels.

"Crap!" *Classy, Jess.*

As I stumbled, though, Jake caught me, and suddenly we were very close to each other. Face to face.

That's when he kissed me. Really kissed me. His lips were softer than I expected, and a little wet. My lips parted slightly, like I'd seen on TV and in the movies for years and years. It seemed so natural as it was happening—and then our tongues met. Jake kind of squashed his tongue against mine. *So this is what it's like. . . .* The feeling wasn't electric, but I felt a thrill of happiness. Jake wrapped his arms around me, a bearlike embrace. A wrestler's hug. Our tongues twisted around and around and Jake stroked the small of my back. *Nice.* And it would no doubt get better with practice. Maybe I would borrow Mindy's article on "75 Sex Tricks to Drive Him Wild."

Jake pulled away first. "I gotta get going, or I'll break curfew. I'll call you, okay?"

I realized I was still clutching the stuffed toy. "Yeah. Sure."

He leaned in to kiss me again. A light, sweet touch on the lips. "Later."

"Bye." I stood there watching as the truck pulled away.

When the taillights had almost disappeared into the darkness, I walked toward the porch, swishing the hem of my dress against my knees. *My first real kiss.*

"Well, how was it?"

The deep voice coming from the darkness startled me, stopping me short. I peered into the gloom. "Lucius?"

"I'm right here."

I followed his voice to the front porch steps, where he sat in the shadows next to a dimly flickering jack-o'-lantern. I walked closer. "You were spying on me."

Lucius held out a bowl. "I'm on candy duty. Want some? I think it's mostly soy nuts left. The children were *not* happy with the selection."

I accepted a pack and sat down next to him on the step.

"We don't get many trick-or-treaters out here. Nobody lives within a mile."

"Oh." Lucius shrugged. "I guess it was me that hated the soy nuts." He pulled the stuffed hot dog from my arms. "Your parents won't like this in the house. Meat toys. Did Squatty win that with some feat of physical prowess?" He tossed the wiener over his shoulder, onto a chair on the porch.

I ignored the taunt. "You were waiting for me, weren't you?"

Lucius stared into the dark distance. "How was it?"

"How was what?"

"He kissed you. How was it?"

I smiled, remembering. "Nice."

"Nice?" Lucius gave a short, derisive snort. "I repeat one more time: Nice is overrated."

"Please, don't go there," I urged. *Don't ruin this.*

"When you kiss the right person, it will be a hell of a lot better than nice," Lucius grumbled.

"You have no right to say that." I stood to go inside, smoothing my dress. He would *not* spoil this moment for me. It would not happen.

To my surprise, Lucius relented. "You are right. That was rude. I had no right." He patted the step. "Please. Keep me company. I find that I'm melancholy this evening."

"You should have gone to the carnival," I said, sitting back down.

Lucius took a deep breath, exhaled. "There's nothing there for me."

"It was kind of fun. There were games, and we—"

116

"Do you ever, for one minute, look at my life from my perspective?" Lucius interrupted, a bit sharply. "Think about how I might feel?" He turned to face me, his eyes glowing dimly, like the jack-o'-lantern's. "Do you ever look beyond yourself?"

"What? Are you . . . homesick or something?"

"Something like that, yes." The glimmer flickered to life. "For god's sake. I live in a garage, away from everything I've ever known. I'm sent here to court a woman who dismisses me in favor of a peasant—"

"Jake is a perfectly nice guy, Lucius."

Lucius snorted again. "Is that what you want out of life? Nice? Must everything be *nice*?"

"Nice is . . . nice," I protested.

Lucius shook his head. "Oh, Antanasia. I could show you things so far beyond nice, they'd spin your lovely head."

His voice had changed suddenly. Grown even lower and more throaty. There was a quality in it I'd never heard before but instinctively recognized. *Sexual power. Lust. Desire.* An edgy, angry, frustrated desire.

"Lucius . . . maybe we should go inside."

But he only edged nearer, spoke more softly, yet still with that hint of barely suppressed frustration. "I could show you things that would make you forget everything you know here, in your safe little life . . ."

I swallowed hard. *What can he show me? What kind of not-nice things? Do I want to know?*

Yes. No. Maybe.

"Lucius . . ."

"Antanasia." He leaned even closer to me, and I found that

he was breathing hard, and so was I. Inhaling the power he always exuded, sharing his rarified air. "Don't you *ever* wonder about that part of you? The part that is Antanasia?"

"Antanasia is just a name . . ."

"No. Antanasia is a person. A part of you." Then Lucius caressed my cheek, tracing it with his thumb, and I found myself closing my eyes, sort of swaying, like I was a cobra under the spell of a snake charmer. I knew I should stop whatever was happening, but I just sat there, swaying.

"That other half of you. That half would not settle for 'nice,'" Lucius said softly. He cupped my chin, and I could feel his breath on my mouth now. Cool and close. "I finally saw it, that part of your being, your spirit, when you put on that dress . . . You look so beautiful in that dress. It transforms you . . ."

My dress . . . I'd started to enjoy a sense of power when guys had watched me at the carnival. But with Lucius, I felt that power slip out of my control and into his hands. He took the reins as surely as he did with his half-wild horse. And that was terrifying. I licked my lips, stomach taut with that queer mix of hunger and loathing and fear that I'd felt that first time he'd bared those teeth up in his room.

Will he do that again? Will he? Should he?

"Antanasia." His lips barely touched mine, and a craving ripped through me, like the craving in my dream for that decadent, irresistible, forbidden chocolate. *No . . . I just kissed Jake. . . . I don't want to want Lucius. . . .* He was everything I *didn't* want. He thought he was a goddamn vampire. And yet I felt myself pressing against him, felt my hand reaching up of its own accord to stroke his jaw, where the scar was, a jagged path of smooth skin tracing through the rough stubble. *The violence in his childhood . . . it had made him hard. Dangerous, even? Maybe?*

Lucius's arm slipped around my back, and he brushed my lips again, less gently this time. Even his mouth was hard. But I wanted to taste more. "Like this, Antanasia," he murmured. "This is how it should be . . . not *nice . . .*"

He was *tempting* me to want more. The image of him zipping up my dress, assured, knowing, flashed through my brain. *Experienced . . .* Mom had warned me. *Don't get in over your head, Jess. . . .*

Lucius slid his hand up to my neck, circling the nape with his fingers, his thumb stroking the hollow of my throat. "Let me kiss you, Antanasia . . . *really* kiss you . . . as you should be kissed."

"Please, Lucius . . ." Was I begging or protesting?

"You belong with me," he said softly. "With *our* kind . . . You know you do . . . Stop fighting it . . . Stop fighting *me . . .*"

No!

I must have cried out loud, because Lucius pulled back abruptly. "No?" His voice was incredulous, his eyes filled with shock and uncertainty.

My mouth was moving, but no sound was coming out. *Yes? No?* "I just . . . I just kissed Jake," I finally stuttered. "A few minutes ago." Wasn't it wrong to mess around with two guys on one night? Wasn't that sort of . . . slutty? What the hell was this dress making me do? And that thing he'd said about "*our* kind . . ."

No.

Lucius yanked his hand from my throat and leaned forward on the steps, doubling himself over, digging his hands into his long, black hair with a sound that was half groan, half growl.

"Lucius, I'm sorry . . ."

"Don't say that."

"But I am sorry . . ." Yet I didn't quite know what I was sorry for. For kissing Jake? For almost kissing Lucius? For making us stop?

"Go inside, Jessica." Lucius was still bent over his knees, fingers laced in his hair. "Now. Please."

And then the front door opened. "I thought I heard voices out here," Dad said, pretending to be oblivious to the obvious tension.

"Dad," I squeaked, popping up. "I just got home. Lucius and I were talking."

"It's getting late," Dad said, pulling me to his side. "And Lucius, I think it's safe to say trick or treat is over. You should probably head up to bed."

"Of course, sir." Lucius slowly unfolded himself and rose to his feet, too. He seemed weary as he handed the bowl to my dad. "Happy All Hallows' Eve."

"Yeah, good night," I said. Then I tore inside, ran upstairs, and yanked off my dress, tossing it to the back of my closet. I tugged at my hair until it tumbled back down around my shoulders. All back in place and normal. After pulling on a T-shirt and sweats to sleep in, I crept to the window and looked out at the garage. But Lucius's light was off. He'd gone to bed. Or perhaps he'd gone out into the night.

Mom knocked on my door. "Jessica? Are you all right?"

"Fine, Mom," I lied.

"Do you want to talk?"

"No." I just kept watching Lucius's window, not sure what I was looking for. "I just want to sleep."

"Well, then . . . good night, honey."

Mom's footsteps receded down the hall and I climbed into bed, shutting my eyes tight. I would not—would not—wonder what would draw Lucius into the darkness. Given the mood I'd left him in, I honestly feared it might be something "not nice."

Chapter 21

DEAR VASILE,

What a mess here. What a mess. This would be so much easier to express if you'd just try e-mail. It's available everywhere these days. Do consider it, please, for the duration.

Until then, I have the difficult task of informing you via post that the entire pact seems to stagger, endlessly and irrevocably, toward oblivion.

This evening . . . where to begin? What to say?

If that was not the moment, then I don't know what more I can do. If Antanasia did not feel as I felt at that instant in time, if she had the presence of mind to pull back, actually to cry out "No!" to me when I will admit I was too far lost to her . . . I honestly don't know what more I can do.

I am sure you can infer, from the lines above, what passed between us, in a general sense. I will not disgrace myself—or dishonor Antanasia—by elaborating with details. To do so would be not only humiliating but ungentlemanly. And surely you understand.

Have I really been bested by a peasant? A squatty, obtuse, parasitical peasant?

Perhaps in the morning, the situation will appear less grim. One can only hope.

In the meantime, I don't suppose you might offer me some insights into the punishment I will face in the event of failure on my part? I should like to begin preparing myself mentally. Especially if I face the worst. I have always preferred to confront fate with shoulders back and head high, as you taught me. And one can best do that if one has the opportunity to steel oneself.

Yours in doubt and with no small measure of confusion and concern,

Lucius

Chapter 22

"YOU'RE GOING TO do fine, dear," Mom promised, pinning my number on the back of my riding jacket.

"I'm going to throw up," I said. "Why did I sign up for this?"

"Because we grow by challenging ourselves," my mom replied.

"If you say so." In a few minutes, my turn would come. I would ride Belle into the 4-H ring, and we would jump a series of obstacles.

The whole thing would last about three minutes, tops.

So why was I so terrified?

Because you might fall. Belle might balk. You're not an athlete; you're a mathlete. . . .

"I should have just raised a calf, like last summer," I said, groaning. "All you have to do is walk into the ring and wait to see if you won a ribbon."

"Jessica, you are a fine horsewoman," Mom insisted, spinning me around by the shoulders to look into my eyes. "And it's not as though you've never competed in front of people before . . ."

"But that's math," I protested. "I'm good at math."

"You're a good rider, too."

I thought of Faith and Lucius. "But not the best."

"Then today is an excellent time to push your boundaries. Risk a second or even third place."

I glanced across the field, where Lucius was cantering on his horse, which he'd named "Hell's Belle." *Ha-ha.*

"Risks aren't always so great," I said, watching Lucius work to control the still half-wild animal. Lucius was the only one who could touch her. He insisted that she was misunderstood, but I thought the mare was just plain evil.

"That's a little *too* risky," Mom conceded, following my gaze. She sighed. "I hope he's going to be all right."

The way she said it, I got the weird feeling that she wasn't just talking about the jumper class competition.

"He needs his number, too," Mom added. She shaded her eyes, waving to Lucius.

He raised a hand, acknowledging, and trotted over, dropping from his mount and looping the reins around a fence post.

123

Hell's Belle would never be the kind of horse that could wait without a tether.

Lucius bowed slightly. "Dr. Packwood. Jessica."

I gave a small, uncomfortable wave. "Hey, Lucius."

He turned around, and my mom pinned on his number. To my surprise, Mom then spun Lucius around, just like she'd done with me—and hugged him. Surprise blew up to shock when Lucius actually hugged back. *When did those two bond?* Sometime since Halloween, I guessed. Lucius and I had given each other a wide berth since our weird moment on the porch.

"Good luck," my mother said, brushing imaginary lint off Lucius's impeccable, perfectly fitted show coat. "And wear your helmet," she added. "It's mandatory."

"Yes, yes, safety first," Lucius said, voice dripping sarcasm. "I'll go find it." He looked at me, eyes neutral. "Good luck."

"You, too."

Lucius untied his horse and led her off. Mom watched him, face tense.

"He'll be fine," I promised her.

"I hope."

"I'm second, right?" I asked.

"Yes. After Faith."

Great. The toughest act I could possibly follow. Faith didn't just compete in the annual 4-H show. She did bigger horse shows on her expensive gelding. My stomach clenched again.

"You'll do great," Mom promised. She hugged me, too.

The intercom blared, and it was time.

"Let's go."

Of course, Faith completed a flawless run on her thoroughbred, Moon Dance. She dominated the course, her horse's fleet, fine-boned legs launching them both over every fence, even the fifth, which loomed like a tower, impossibly high from where I was waiting on the sidelines.

I really needed to pee, a nervous pee, but there was no time. I mounted up as Moon Dance's hooves pounded by, run completed.

"Next up, Jessica Packwood, Woodrow Wilson High School, riding Belle, a five-year-old Appaloosa."

They'd said my name.

I took a deep breath, catching sight of Jake, who watched from the bleachers. He grinned, giving me an okay sign. I forced myself to smile back.

Lucius was also in the arena, watching, leaning against the fence. *Dammit.* Like I needed his hypercritical eyes on me, judging me.

I glanced over my shoulder, wondering what would happen if my horse and I just sort of backed out. . . . But it was too late. There was no turning back.

Taking a deep breath, I dug in my heels. Belle's hooves thudded quietly in the thick dirt of the nearly silent arena. Feeling my horse's power, her familiar steps beneath me, I began to focus. The first obstacle approached. A hedge. We cantered, jumped, and cleared it. *You're just jumping with Belle. Just like at home.* We cleared the next low rails, and the nerves faded, replaced by exultation. All of those people were watching us, and we were doing it.

Belle cleared the next two fences, hooves not even nipping at the rails.

The fifth, highest fence loomed, and my heart thudded. But Belle lifted, soared, and we were past.

A perfect round. No faults. In the end, we'd completed a perfect round. A huge, victorious smile broke across my face. *Take that, Romanian all-star.*

As I cantered toward the exit, I waved to my parents, who were cheering, and to Jake, who had both fingers jammed in his mouth, whistling. Seeking out Lucius, I saw that he was clapping heartily, hands raised, and he mouthed "Good show." Whatever had broken between us, it had just been fixed a little.

I returned from cooling down Belle just in time to see Lucius's round.

He sat easily, regally, on Hell's Belle, as if he'd been born there. The midnight black horse seemed strangely calm, too. Nudging her flanks, Lucius urged her to a canter, rising close to a full gallop. The pace was insane for the small course, but Lucius didn't seem to notice. There was a small smile on his lips as he approached the first fence. Hell's Belle flew over, landing smoothly, and I realized this was a horse born to jump. They seemed fused together, horse and rider, tearing up the course, Hell's Belle reaching twice as high as she needed to clear, and all at once the spectators were cheering. Gasping and cheering.

It was reckless. Too reckless. I glanced at my parents in the stands. They looked terrified, and suddenly I was, too.

As Lucius soared over the fifth fence, a hand clamped down on my wrist, causing me to jump. "Look at him go," Faith Crosse whispered to no one in particular. I was pretty sure she hadn't even realized who she touched, she was watching Lucius that intently. Faith tapped her riding crop absently against her calf, in time to the hoofbeats. I tugged my arm away.

"Sorry," Faith murmured, without removing her gaze from Lucius.

Hell's Belle cleared the last fence, and the announcer called a new 4-H record for time.

Lucius and the horse pulled up in front of the gate, and Lucius slipped down, coolly peeling off his riding gloves like he'd just been on a trail ride through a park, seemingly oblivious to the applause.

Always the show-off.

"I'm going to congratulate him," Faith said.

I caught a peculiar look in the future prom queen's eyes.

Faith disappeared into the crowd, headed for the exit, following Lucius out behind the ring. That's when I thought about the riding crop. Hell's Belle would not like the crop. Lucius had even posted a warning sign in the barn—a sign I saw almost every day. "Faith, wait," I called, following.

But I was too slow. By the time I caught up with her behind the barn, Faith had reached Lucius and Hell's Belle, and was waving the crop, calling for Lucius's attention. The crop nipped the horse's flank, and Hell's Belle spun around in a fury, backing away, nearly ripping the reins from Lucius's hands before he realized what was happening.

I heard him order Faith to drop the crop, but it was too late.

The mare reared, pawing the air, too close to Faith. I screamed, seeing what was about to happen, as Lucius pushed Faith away, putting himself in front of the flailing hooves, falling under them.

There was a sickening, audible crack as the force of Hell's Belle's hooves, driven by a full ton of sinew and muscle, collided with Lucius's legs and ribs. It was all over in seconds, before I could even scream again, and Lucius was lying, his tall body folded, broken, on the grass. There was blood on his white shirt, blood seeping from his high leather boot and staining his fawn-colored riding breeches.

"Lucius!" I finally found my voice, crying out, running over, dropping beside him. I was so scared for him that I completely forgot about the dangerous beast looming over my shoulder, still loose.

"Catch her," Lucius insisted through clenched teeth, trying to roll over, gesturing toward the horse, which stood, flanks heaving, scared but still wary. "You can do it. Before she—"

Faith began crying, abruptly and loudly as reality sank in, but no one heard us out behind the barn. Everyone was inside now, watching the competition. Hell's Belle stood, head low, snorting like a furious sentinel over Lucius. I could feel her hot breath on my own neck, and then I got scared for me, too. *No sudden moves . . .*

"She needs to be tied up, Jess," Lucius begged, wincing with the effort of the words.

I nodded mutely, knowing he was right. Standing very slowly, as slowly as possible, I turned.

"Easy, girl," I whispered, extending my hands, palms up.

The horse flinched, and so did I. *Just stay calm, Jess. . . .*

I edged closer. Hell's Belle's eyes spun more wildly, but she didn't run. Didn't lash out.

She seemed to understand that something had gone horribly wrong. With shaking hands, I reached for her loose reins, dangling from her bridle. "Easy, girl." Keeping my eyes on the horse's, I located the reins with my fingertips. Her breath kept coming heavy and fast, but still she didn't move. Lucius groaned. I had to work more quickly. Moving with more assurance, but trembling fingers, I fumbled to tie the reins to a post.

Thank god. She was secure.

I hurried back to Lucius, who was clutching his ribs through his bloody shirt. Kneeling, I grabbed his free hand. "It's okay," I promised. But I couldn't help glancing at his leg. The break had happened at midcalf, the leather boot actually bent. "Get help," I called to Faith, who seemed paralyzed, wailing over and over, "It was an accident."

"Get someone!" I yelled at her again. "Now!"

This woke her up, and Faith turned to run.

"No," Lucius barked, louder than I would have thought possible, given the twisted state of his body. But something in his tone caught Faith up short, and she spun around. "Get Jessica's parents. No one else."

Faith hesitated, panicked, puzzled, unsure. She looked to me.

"Get the paramedics," I begged Faith. What was Lucius doing? He needed an ambulance.

"Jessica's parents only," Lucius said, speaking right over me, in his most commanding tone. He clutched my hand so I couldn't go.

"I . . . I . . ." Faith started to say something.

"Go," Lucius ordered.

Faith ran. I prayed that she would get the paramedics.

"Damn this hurts." Lucius groaned, face twisting as a wave of pain shot through him. He squeezed my hand. "Just stay here, would you?"

"I'm not going anywhere," I said, willing my voice not to quiver. I was terrified and struggling not to let Lucius see my fear. A trickle of blood seeped from his mouth, and I stifled the urge to cry out. That couldn't be good. That could mean internal bleeding. I wiped the crimson liquid away with shaky fingers, and a tear fell on his cheek. I hadn't even realized I was crying.

"Please, don't do that." Lucius gasped, meeting my eyes. "Don't fall apart on me. Remember: You're royalty."

I squeezed his hand tighter. "I'm not crying. Just hang in there."

He shifted a little, winced. "You know . . . this can't kill a . . ."

God, was he still going to do that vampire shtick now? I didn't believe for a second that he couldn't die. "Lie still." *And hope that Faith ignores your commands.*

"This leg . . . Dammit." His chest heaved, and he coughed. More blood. A lot of blood. Too much blood. It was coming from his lungs. Probably a puncture. I had taken enough first aid training at school to know a little bit about accidents. I swiped his lips with my sleeve, but that only smeared more blood on both of us. "Help's coming," I promised. *But will it be too little, too late?*

On instinct I smoothed Lucius's dark hair with my free hand. His face relaxed just a shade; his breathing calmed slightly. So I kept my hand there, resting on his forehead.

"Jess?" He searched my face with his eyes.

"Don't talk."

"I . . . I think you deserve . . . a ribbon."

In spite of myself, I laughed, a ragged, clenching laugh, and bent to kiss his forehead. It just happened. It just felt like the right thing to do. "So do you."

His eyes closed. I sensed his consciousness was slipping away. "And Jess?"

"Be quiet."

"Don't let them do anything . . . to my horse," he managed, through difficult breaths. "She didn't mean . . . any harm. It was just the crop, you know . . ."

"I'll try, Lucius," I promised. But I knew I wouldn't succeed. Hell's Belle's reprieve was over.

"Thank you, Antanasia . . ." His voice was almost inaudible.

From around the side of the barn I heard car tires on grass. I exhaled with a small measure of relief. Faith had gone for the ambulance.

But no. When the vehicle spun around the corner, it was a beat-up VW van with Ned Packwood at the wheel. My parents jumped out, fear on their faces, and pushed me out of the way. "Take me to your home," Lucius begged, coming around a little. "You understand . . ."

Mom spun around to face me. "Open the back of the van," she ordered.

"Mom—he needs an ambulance!"

"Do it, Jessica."

I started to cry again then, because I didn't understand what was happening, and I didn't want to take part in killing Lucius. But I did as I was told.

My parents lifted Lucius into the van as gently as they could, but he still moaned, even though he was now fully unconscious, the pain so bad that it must have ripped through even his insensate brain. I started to crawl in after him, but Dad stopped me with a firm hand on my shoulder. Mom climbed in instead, crouching next to Lucius.

"You stay here and explain what happened," Dad said. "Tell them . . . tell them we took Lucius to the hospital."

I saw the lie in my father's face, and my eyes widened. "You *are* taking him there, aren't you?"

"Just tell everyone he's okay," Dad said, not quite answering my question. "Then take care of the horse."

It was too much, what they were asking. What if they really didn't take him to the hospital and Lucius died? They would be responsible. Maybe accused of negligence, or some sort of *murder*. Faith had seen that Lucius wasn't okay. She knew he needed a doctor. And 4-H would check to see that he'd been hospitalized. Liability issues and all that. What the hell were my parents doing? They could go to *jail*. And for what? It made no sense to keep Lucius away from a hospital.

But there was no time to protest, no time to ask for guidance. Lucius needed to get somewhere warm, at least. Hopefully someplace where people knew how to handle broken bones and bleeding lungs. As long as it wasn't our kitchen, where Dad might attempt some herbal cure . . .

My chest seized again with dread. If my parents were going to try some sort of "natural healing" on Lucius—they were so far out of their league. All of these things spun through my mind as I followed on foot behind the old van, staring helplessly as it bumped out of the grassy area and bounced through the gravel parking lot, as fast as Dad could drive without, presumably, arousing suspicion or jostling Lucius too much.

I was still standing there watching a cloud of receding, drifting dust, when Faith reappeared at my side, more composed. Her eyes were rimmed red, but her shoulders were stiffly at attention again. Still, her voice caught, just a hitch, when she asked, "Do you think he's going to . . . to be . . . ?"

"He'll be fine," I promised, lying more smoothly than I'd thought possible. But I had to sound convincing. My whole family's survival, not just Lucius's, was at stake. "I don't think his injuries were as bad as we thought at first," I added.

"No?" Faith shot me a skeptical look. But it was a hopeful look, too. I realized she wanted to believe the lie. After all, she didn't want to be responsible for Lucius's injury—or death.

"He sat up a little," I told her, forcing myself to meet Faith's ocean blue eyes. "And made a joke."

The tension in Faith's face eased, and I knew she had willed herself to believe me. She was so desperate to be absolved. "It must have just looked bad at first because it happened so fast . . ."

"Yeah, probably," I agreed. "It was definitely scary, at first."

Faith's gaze drifted off toward the parking lot, as if she expected to still see the van driving away. I noticed then that she continued to hold the crop, and tapped it idly against her boot. I would have tossed that thing in the trash, ground it into dust. *How could she have not seen the sign in our barn?*

The answer was so easy it was almost laughable. Because Faith Crosse didn't see anything beyond her own small sphere of concern. That's why.

"Even if he wasn't as bad off as we thought, why didn't he want the paramedics?" she wondered aloud.

I wasn't quite sure myself, but I had a feeling it had something to do with Lucius's delusions about being a vampire. That definitely wasn't a suitable answer for Faith, though, so I ventured, "I think he's too proud. Too brave to be carried off with a bunch of sirens and people watching." Actually, knowing Lucius, that might have been true, too.

Faith smiled a little at that, still gazing off in the distance. The crop beat a steady rhythm on her boot. She was completely calm now, almost at ease. "Yes," she said, more to herself than to me. "Lucius Vladescu does not seem like he's afraid of anything. And he does know what he wants, doesn't he?"

You have no idea, I wanted to tell her. But by then, a whole crowd of 4-H officials was marching in our direction, and I turned to face them, ready to tell more lies.

Chapter 23

IT WAS DARK by the time I got home, riding Belle the back way, cutting through empty cornfields and avoiding the roads as much as possible, almost like I was afraid I was being followed. I certainly hadn't wanted to catch a ride home with any of the people who'd offered: Faith or the 4-H leaders. Especially the 4-H leaders, whose questions I'd already answered at least fifty times. They'd just keep harping on why none of the local hospitals seemed to know anything about a boy who'd been injured by a horse. And then they'd want to talk to my parents, at which point they might just walk into our farmhouse to find Lucius Vladescu near dead—or dead, even—on our couch, my father trying to resuscitate him with herbs and infusions.

I spurred Belle a little more quickly at the thought.

Could Lucius really be dead? How would I feel if he was? Would I mourn him? Grieve? Guilt tugged at me. *Would I be relieved on some level?*

And was I worried more for Lucius or for my parents' role in this disaster?

All of these questions roiled around in my mind like a stinking stew made from spoiled odds and ends as Belle and I picked our way home, stuck at a horse's pace when I longed for a jet. Our progress seemed ridiculously slow. *Einstein had explained that feeling, hadn't he? Relativity. One's perception of time was relative to one's desire for its passage. Right?*

Time. Relativity. Science.

I tried to focus on those concepts instead of pointless worrying, but my mind kept wandering back to the blood on Lucius's shirt. The blood spurting from his mouth. The red, red blood. By the time I reached the end of our lane, I had Belle at a recklessly full gallop, and I dropped the reins, sliding from her back, as I caught sight of my parents' van parked in front of the house. There was another car, too. An unfamiliar but equally decrepit sedan. The house was mainly dark, but a few muted lights glowed from deep inside.

Abandoning poor Belle, knowing I should cool her down and put her in her stall, I stomped up the steps and ran inside.

"Mom!" I hollered at the top of my lungs, slamming the door behind me.

My mother emerged from the dining room, shushing me with a finger to the lips. "Jessica, please. Keep your voice down."

"What happened? How is he?" I pushed past her toward the dining room, but Mom caught my arm.

"No, Jessica . . . not right now."

I searched her face. "Mom?"

"It's serious, but we have reason to believe he'll pull through. He's getting good care. The best care we could give him, safely," she added cryptically.

"What do you mean 'safely'?" Safe care came from *hospitals*. "And whose car is out there?"

"We called Dr. Zsoldos—"

"No, Mom!" Not Dr. Zsoldos. The crazy Hungarian quack who'd lost his medical license for using controversial folk "remedies" from the old country, right here in the United States, where people had the good sense to believe in real medicine. I should have recognized the car. Long after the rest of the county had shunned him, old Zsoldos and my parents had remained friends, huddling around the kitchen table and gabbing into the night about fools who didn't trust "alternative therapies." "He'll kill Lucius!"

"Dr. Zsoldos understands Lucius and his people," Mom said, taking me by the shoulders. "He can be trusted."

When my mom said "trusted," I got the sense that she wasn't just talking about whether the quack should have a license. "Trusted with *what*?"

"Discretion."

"Why? Why do we have to be discreet? Did you see the blood coming from his mouth? His smashed leg?"

"Lucius is special," Mom said, shaking my shoulders a little, like I should have realized this fact a million years ago. "Accept it, Jessica. He would not be safe in a hospital."

"And he's safe here? In our dining room?"

Mom released my shoulders and rubbed her eyes. I realized how tired she must be. "Yes, Jessica. Safer."

"But he's bleeding inside. Even I can tell that. He probably needs blood."

My mom looked at me strangely, like perhaps I'd finally just grasped some important truth. "Yes, Jess. He needs blood."

"Then take him to a hospital, please!"

Mom stared at me for a long moment. "Jessica, there are things about Lucius that most doctors wouldn't understand. We can talk about this later, but right now, I need to return to him. Please, go upstairs and try to be patient. I'll tell you as soon as I have news on his progress."

Turning her back on me, Mom opened the door to the dining room, and I heard soft voices come from inside the darkened room. My father's voice. Dr. Zsoldos's. Mom slipped in to join their secret cabal, and the door clicked shut.

Furious, scared and frustrated, I ran upstairs, forgetting poor Belle entirely. I'm ashamed to admit that she spent the whole night in the November cold, wandering around the barns and the paddock, her saddle still on her back. I was too unhinged to think about the horse that had carried me to a measure of personal glory just a few hours earlier. Instead, I climbed onto my bed and stared out the window, trying to figure out what to do.

As I debated calling a real doctor myself, I caught sight of my father slipping out the door and hurrying across the yard toward the garage. The light went on in Lucius's apartment, but only for a few moments. It snapped off again, and seconds later, Dad was back, striding across the lawn. I could see, in the moonlight, that he carried something in his hands. Something about the size of shoe box but with rounded corners. Like a paper-wrapped parcel.

I waited until Dad's footsteps passed through the house and the dining room door snicked shut before creeping downstairs, avoiding all the squeaky spots that might give me away. I practically crawled up to the dining room door and turned the knob, opening the door just a crack. Just enough to see inside.

The fire in the fireplace had nearly guttered out, and the dimmer switch on the iron chandelier had been spun to its lowest setting, but I was able to make out the scene.

Lucius was laid out on our long plank dining table, the one we used only for big occasions. He was bare-chested, the bloodstained clothes gone—cut away, I supposed—and his lower half was covered with a white sheet. His face was completely placid. Eyes closed, mouth composed.

He looked like death. Like a corpse. I'd never been to a funeral before, but if someone could look more dead than Lucius did at that moment . . . Well, I couldn't imagine how they'd manage it.

Is he dead?

I stared at his chest, willing it to rise, but if his lungs pumped, it was too weakly for me to discern in the darkened room. *Please, Lucius. Breathe.*

When Lucius's chest still didn't move, something cracked

open deep inside me, and my entire body felt like a vast cave with a frozen wind surging through the empty spaces. *No . . . he can't be gone. I can't let him go.* I struggled to calm myself. If Lucius was dead, they wouldn't be hovering over him, caring for him. They'd stop treating him. Cover his face.

My mother paced near the fireplace, one hand over her mouth, watching as my father and Dr. Zsoldos conferred in hushed tones over the package that Dad had retrieved from the garage.

Some decision must have been reached, because Dr. Zsoldos retrieved a knife—a scalpel?—from a black bag. *Is he going to operate on Lucius? On our table?*

I almost turned away, too sickened to watch, but no, the Hungarian quack didn't slice into Lucius. He simply cut the strings that bound the package and tore open the paper. He lifted out the contents, cradling it as if he was delivering a baby—a wobbly, slippery baby that almost escaped his grasp. *What in the world?*

I leaned closer, pressing my face against the crack and fighting to control my breathing so I wouldn't be caught. No one was focused on the door, though. Mom, Dad, and Dr. Zsoldos were all staring at that . . . thing in Dr. Zsoldos's hands. It looked like . . . what? Some sort of pouch? Made of a material I couldn't identify. Something pliable, though, because the package slipped around in Dr. Zsoldos's grasp, like Jell-O in a plastic bag.

"We should have realized he'd have this, hidden," Dr. Zsoldos whispered, nodding so his white beard bobbed. "Of course he would."

"Yes," Mom agreed, moving forward now, toward Lucius. "Of course. We should have known." At a nod from Dad, they both slid their forearms under Lucius's shoulders and gently lifted him, almost to a seated position. Lucius made a sound then, half a moan of pain, half the roar of an angry, injured lion. My damp fingers slipped off the doorknob at that sound. It wasn't quite human and not quite animal. But it was completely chilling, reverberating off the walls.

I wiped my hands on my riding breeches, squinting harder at the scene in front of me.

Dr. Zsoldos leaned close to his patient, holding out the pouch like an offering in front of Lucius's face. The firelight glinted off the doctor's half-moon eyeglasses, and he smiled a little as he urged, softly, "Drink, Lucius. Drink."

The patient didn't respond. Lucius's head lolled sideways, and Dad shifted to catch him, steadying him.

Dr. Zsoldos hesitated, then grasped the scalpel again, using it to pierce the pouch, right under Lucius's nose. The eyes that I feared had been extinguished fluttered open, and I yelped then.

Lucius's eyes, always dark, were pure black now. Deep, deep ebony, as though the pupils had consumed the irises and most of the whites, too. I'd never seen eyes like that before. You couldn't look away from them.

He opened his mouth and his teeth . . . they'd changed again, too.

My parents must have heard my cry, but it was too late. What was happening was happening, and they, too, were transfixed as Lucius tilted his head, sinking his fangs into that pouch, drinking wearily but with obvious hunger. A bit of liquid dribbled down his chin and ran across his chest. Dark liquid. Thick liquid. I'd seen liquid just like that before, not too many hours ago, staining that same chest.

NO.

I closed my eyes, disbelieving. Shaking my head, I tried to think straight. To banish the image of what I thought I'd seen. What I was fairly sure I'd seen.

There was a smell, too. A pungent odor that I'd never smelled before. Well, I'd smelled it faintly before, but now . . . now it was so strong. And getting stronger. I opened my eyes and forced myself to watch again. That aroma—it wasn't like I was even sensing it with my nose. I *felt* it, somewhere deep in the pit of my stomach, or in the farthest reaches of that primitive part of the brain that we'd talked about in biology class. The part that controlled sex and aggression and . . . pleasure?

Lucius pulled himself more upright, supporting himself on one elbow, still drinking lustily, like he couldn't get enough. Finally, though, there was nothing left. The bag was empty. Lucius sort of fell back with a moan that managed, somehow, to convey both raw agony and pure satisfaction, and Dad grabbed his bare shoulders just in time, easing him onto his back again.

"Rest, Lucius," Dad urged. Mom stepped in with a cloth to wipe his chest, where the blood had spilled on him. . . .

Blood. He was drinking blood.

I squeezed my eyes shut again, more tightly this time. Something strange happened then, because I was obviously crouched on a solid, wooden floor, which could not move, and yet it started pitching and whirling under my feet. The whole house was heaving around me, and even when I opened my eyes, trying to get my bearings, it was only to feel my eyes spin of their own accord toward the ceiling, which faded away like a movie screen at the end of the film.

I awoke later that same night in my own bed, dressed in my flannel pajamas, but confused and disoriented, as if I'd suddenly found myself in a foreign country, as opposed to my own bedroom. It was still dark. I lay as still as possible, eyes open, just in case the room started lurching and the ceiling started to fade again.

The house didn't shift, though, even as I replayed, in vivid detail, everything I'd seen. Everything I'd felt.

I'd seen Lucius drink blood. Or had I? I had been woozy. Confused. And that smell . . . Maybe Dr. Zsoldos had dosed Lucius with some sort of heady Romanian liquor or potion or something. Maybe I'd misunderstood, in my panic and my fear.

But the one thing I couldn't explain away was what I'd felt when I'd actually believed Lucius was dead.

Grief. The deepest grief I could imagine. Like a jagged hole ripped in my soul.

That . . . that was the part that really had me freaked. So freaked, in fact, that I slipped downstairs again in the middle of the night, creeping into the dining room. The fire had been stoked back up, and Lucius was still on his back on the table, but there was a pillow under his head now. A warmer blanket had been placed over the sheet, too, covering him from shoulders to toes. My dad was still in the room, dozing in the rocking chair, snoring lightly, but Mom was gone, and Dr. Zsoldos was gone, and his bag, and the pouch I'd probably dreamed. . . .

I stole up close to Lucius's face. There were no traces of red on his lips, no stain down his chin, no hint of a change in his mouth. Just a pale, injured, now-familiar face. As I watched him, he must have sensed a presence, or maybe he dreamed, because he shifted slightly, and his hand dropped off the table. The position looked uncomfortable, so after waiting a moment to see if he would move again, I gently grasped his wrist and replaced it on the table. In spite of the blanket and the fire crackling just a few feet away, his skin was so cool to the touch . . . cold, actually. He was always so cold. My fingers slipped down, lacing with Lucius's for just a moment, to offer him some comfort or warmth.

He was alive.

I started weeping then, as soundlessly as possible, desperate not to wake Dad. I just let the tears run down my face, dripping onto our clasped hands. Lucius drove me insane. He *was* insane. But no matter. I didn't want to feel that sense of profound loss again. Never.

I hiccuped a sob, unable to hold it back. At the sound, Dad grunted, the huge snort of someone trying to sleep in a hard chair, and I was afraid he might wake up, so I released Lucius's hand, wiped my face with my sleeve, and returned to my room again. It was almost dawn by then, anyway.

Chapter 24

DEAR UNCLE VASILE,

It is with profound regret—and no small measure of apprehension regarding your reaction—that I write to inform you that

I have encountered a small accident with a horse I purchased "online."

Oh, how you would have appreciated Hell's Belle. Such a terrible, awesome, feral creature. Black from her forelock to her hooves and, needless to say, the very core of her being. Would I have desired anything less?

Returning to the narrative, though. My deliciously vicious mare dealt me an admirable thrashing—for which I absolve her completely. The result was a broken leg, a few cracked ribs, bit of a gaping hole in one lung. Nothing I haven't survived before at the hands of family. But of course, I'm afraid I shall be on my back for at least a week or so.

I write less in hopes of gaining your sympathy . . . (Oh, that's a rich thought, isn't it? You, Vasile, getting weepy over someone's well-being. I really would laugh out loud at that, if doing so wouldn't make me cough up more blood.) No, I put pen to paper more in the interest of giving the Packwoods their just due, as I have certainly never been spare with them in terms of criticism. (Recall my missive following that first lentil casserole? I cringe a bit, to recall. There's never really a need to resort to expletives.)

In this crisis, however, much to their credit, Ned and Dara rose to the occasion, immediately grasping the fact that taking an undead individual to the hospital would have been a decidedly unfortunate move. (How many of our modern brethren have been inconveniently lodged in basement morgues for days—and even stone mausoleums for years—due to a lack of what humans call "vital signs"?)

But as usual, my musings wander. Returning to my point, perhaps we have been unjustly harsh regarding the Packwoods.

They showed great insight, and, more importantly, risked themselves for me. I almost wish that I could replace their hideous folk dolls, as a gesture of my gratitude. Could you, perhaps, have one of the local women fashion some crude poppet out of, say, a wooden spool and some scraps of wool? Nothing fancy. Aesthetic standards for this particular collection were not high, believe me. "Ugly" and "ill-crafted" seem to have been the key criteria.

As for Antanasia . . . Vasile, what can I say? She responded to my accident with the valor, will, and fearlessness of a true vampire princess. And yet, a princess possessed of a kind heart. What, we must ask ourselves, would this mean for her in our world?

Vasile, few are the times when I would claim to have greater experience than you, regarding any subject. You know that I am humbled before your authority. But I will risk addressing you with some authority here, myself, as one who has spent considerable time now in intimate contact with humans.

(No doubt you already grow angry at my impertinence—believe me, I can feel the sting of your hand across my face, even several thousand miles away—but I must continue.)

Living as you have in our castle, isolated high in the Carpathians, you have had little contact with those outside our race. You know only the vampire way—the Vladescu way. The way of blood and violence and the harsh scrabble for survival. The endless fight for dominance.

You have never seen Ned Packwood crouched above a box full of squirming kittens, nourishing them with an eyedropper, for god's sake—when our people would have thrown the shivering strays out into the cold, watched them carried off by the circling birds of prey, with no regret. Nay, with a sense of satisfaction for the hawk that would not go hungry that night.

You have never felt Dara Packwood's trembling hand searching for your pulse as you lay prostrate—*vulnerable!*—half naked, injured, on a plank table.

What would one of our kind have done, Vasile? If Dara had been a Dragomir, not a Packwood, would she not have been tempted, at least, to take down the rival prince in that opportune moment? Yet she feared for my life.

This—this is how Antanasia was raised. She is not just an American, but a Packwood. Not a Dragomir. She has been coddled with kittens and kindness and soft touches. Nourished with pale, limp "tofu" in lieu of the blood-soaked spoils of a slaughter.

And you didn't hear her cry, Vasile. You didn't feel her grief, as I did, when she thought I was destroyed. . . . It was palpable to me, Vasile. It tore through her.

Antanasia—no, Jessica—is soft, Vasile. Soft. Her heart is so tender that she could not help but mourn even me—a man whom she can barely abide.

Her enemies—and we know, as a princess, she would have them, even in peacetime—would smell that weakness, just as I sensed her grief. At some point, another female would rise up, thirsty for power, hungry to take Jessica's place. Is that not the way of our world? And when confronted, at the moment of truth, Jessica would falter, just for a split second, not sure if she could bear to waste a life—and she would be lost. Even I could not protect her at all times.

In the past, I fear that I have considered Jessica superficially. I (we?) have been guilty of believing that a change of clothes, lessons on etiquette, a deep and satisfying thrust of fangs to the throat could make her vampire royalty.

But you didn't hear her cry, Vasile. You didn't feel her tears fall on your face, your hand.

Perhaps vampiredom could survive Antanasia—but could Antanasia survive vampiredom? She shows promise, Vasile, but that promise is years from maturation. In the meantime, she would be doomed.

Maybe it is the medication speaking. Honestly, Vasile, the Packwoods have the most wonderful Hungarian healer, very loose with dispensation, if you get my meaning. Yes, perhaps it is the plethora of potions coursing through my veins and saturating my brain, but I ponder these things as I lie here—missing, I might add, the first basketball "scrimmage" of the season, against the rival "Palmyra Cougars." (As if I haven't slain those before, and would have done so again on the court.)

Getting back to Jessica, though. We vampires are soulless, yes. But we do not betray our own, do we? We do not destroy wantonly, correct? And I fear that vampiredom would, indeed, destroy Jessica.

Should we not consider setting her free to be a normal, human teenager? And leave the problems of our world where they belong: in our world, as opposed to on the shoulders of an innocent American girl who longs only to ride her horse, giggle with her best friend (I've developed a somewhat twisted liking for the deliriously sex-crazed Melinda), and share "nice" kisses with a simple farmer?

I look forward to your thoughts, even as I already anticipate your phenomenally negative response. But you raised me to be

not just ruthless but honorable, Vasile, and I felt honor bound to
bring these issues to light.

Yours, recovering,

Lucius

P.S. Regarding the doll: Request button eyes if possible. That
seemed to be a "theme."

Chapter 25

"MOM, I WANT you to tell me what happened that night."

My mother was in her home office, glasses perched on her nose, poring over her latest delivery of academic journals by the pale glow of her desk lamp. At the sound of my voice, she glanced up. "I was hoping you'd come to talk soon, Jess."

She motioned to the lumpy, cast-off La-Z-Boy that served as a guest chair next to her desk. I sank in, pulling the musty Peruvian wool blanket over my legs.

Mom spun her chair toward me, sliding her glasses up into her hair, giving me her full attention. "Where should we start? With what happened between you and Lucius on the porch?"

I flushed, looking away. "No. I don't want to talk about that. I want to talk about two nights ago. When you brought Lucius here. Why? Why not to a hospital?"

"I told you, Jessica. Lucius is special. He's *different.*"

"Different *how?*"

"Lucius is a vampire, Jessica. A doctor trained in an American medical school would not understand how to treat him."

"He's just a guy, Mom," I insisted.

"Is he? Is that what you *still* believe? Even after what you saw, crouched by the door?"

Staring down at my hands, I twisted a loose thread around my finger and tore it out of the blanket. "It's so confusing, Mom."

"Jessica?"

"Hmm?" I glanced up.

"You've touched Lucius, too."

"Mom, please . . ." We weren't going *there* again, were we?

Mom gave me a level stare. "Your father and I aren't blind. Your father caught the tail end of your . . . moment . . . with Lucius on Halloween night."

I was glad the desk lamp barely cast a puddle of light on the desk, because my cheeks were blazing. "It was just a kiss. Not even that, really."

"And when you touch Lucius, you don't notice anything . . . unusual?"

His coolness. I knew immediately what she meant, but for some reason, I hedged. "I don't know. Maybe."

Mom realized I wasn't being completely honest, and she had little patience with people who got intellectually lazy when faced with a difficult concept. She pulled her glasses back onto her nose. I knew I was being dismissed. "I want you to think about what you saw back in the dining room. What you've felt. What you *believe*."

"I want to *believe* what is *real*," I whined. "I want to understand the *truth*. Remember the Enlightenment? Geometric order replacing superstition? Sir Isaac Newton? Who unlocked the 'mystery' of gravity? And who once said, 'My greatest friend is *truth.*' How can a vampire be 'true'?"

My mom stared at me for a long moment. I could hear the clock on her desk ticking as she marshaled her considerable store of knowledge.

"Isaac Newton," Mom finally said, "retained a lifelong faith in astrology. Did you know that about your so-called rational scientist?"

"Um, no," I admitted. "I did not know that."

"And remember Albert Einstein?" Mom noted, smugly. "Who unlocked the *atom*? Something we could barely conceive of just a century or so ago? Einstein once said, 'The most beautiful thing we can experience is the mysterious.'" She paused. "If atoms can exist, hidden and yet everywhere, for millennia . . . why not a vampire?"

Damn. She was good.

"Mom . . ."

"Yes, Jessica?"

"I saw Lucius drink blood. And I saw his teeth. Again."

Mom took my hand and squeezed it. "Welcome to the world of the mysterious, Jessica." A shadow crossed her face. "Please be careful there. It's very, very tricky territory. Completely untamed. The mysterious can be beautiful—and dangerous."

I knew what she meant. Lucius. "I'll be careful, Mom."

"The Vladescu family has a certain reputation for ruthlessness," she added, more directly. "You know your father and I like Lucius very much, and he is charming, but we must also keep in mind that his upbringing was no doubt very different from yours. And not just in terms of material possessions."

"I know, Mom. He's told me a little bit. Besides, I keep telling you—I don't feel like that about him."

Liar.

"Well, just so you know, I'm always here to talk. So is your father."

"Thanks, Mom." I tossed aside the blanket and stood to go, kissing her cheek. "For now, I just need to think."

"Of course." Mom spun back around to her journals. "I love you, Jessica," she added over her shoulder as I pulled her door shut. In spite of her warnings, in spite of her obvious concerns for me, I swore I heard the faintest hint of a smile in her voice.

Chapter 26

DEAR VASILE,

I continue to await your response to my concerns regarding Jessica's near-certain fate, should she take the throne. Have you nothing to say?

What am I to read from your silence?

Honestly, Vasile, I tire of navigating this situation with little guidance, thousands of miles from home. I am fatigued by competing, unsuccessfully, with a peasant. I am drained by bodily injury. I grow impatient for . . . for what? Something I cannot even name. I grow weary of my own nature, my own thoughts, my past, and my future, lying here.

In the absence of constructive comment, I will proceed as my instinct currently dictates regarding Antanasia. I doubt that you will agree with my course of action, but I feel, of late, frustrated and restive and recklessly willful. I chafe at the bit you've kept in my mouth for so long.

Yours,
Lucius

Chapter 27

"WELL, YOU'RE FINALLY out of the garage like you wanted," I teased.

"I can't believe you live like this," Lucius smirked, propped against my pink satin pillows. In my bedroom. Mom had insisted Lucius move inside until his leg healed. His cast was propped up on the oversized stuffed hot dog. "It's like living in a frothy cocoon of cotton candy." He made a face. "So much pink."

"I like pink."

Lucius sniffed. "It's just red's sorry, weak cousin."

"Well, it's not forever. You'll be back in your gloomy dungeon with your rusty weapons before long." I glanced around my room. "Have you seen my iPod?"

"This?" Lucius located my MP3 player in a jumble of sheets and held it up.

"Yes." I held out my hand. "Give."

"Oh, can't I keep it? It's so boring being confined here, and I'm enjoying exploring your musical preferences."

Here we go. "Why don't you buy your own?"

"But yours is already loaded with the Black Eyed Peas." He was mocking me.

"Don't be a jerk."

"I like them. Honestly." A devilish grin crossed his face. "My humps, my humps! What's not to like?"

I swiped the iPod from his hands and he laughed. I grinned, too. "If you weren't already broken all to pieces . . ."

"What?" He grabbed my wrist with lightning speed for someone with broken ribs. "You'd beat me into submission? Right. In your dreams."

Yes. Sometimes, lately. In my dreams. I mean, I wasn't dreaming about beating him up. But lately, Lucius had been making more guest appearances in my sleep. At weddings. In dark caves. By flickering candlelight.

He released me, growing serious. "Jessica, I've consumed so many pain medications. I really can't thank your local physician, Dr. Zsoldos, enough. Why suffer?"

"You're rambling."

"Oh, yes. Well, I've never properly thanked you." He pushed himself up a little straighter, wincing as his ribs shifted. "Catching Hell's Belle, staying with me. You were very brave."

I shifted my weight, trying not to jostle his leg. "I'm sorry they put her down."

Lucius looked out the window, mouth drawn down. "You did your best. But some things are just too dangerous to live, I suppose."

"You tried to tame her," I added lamely. "It worked for a while."

"It wasn't in her nature to be tamed. In the end, we are all true to our natures. Our upbringings."

We sat in silence for a second, and I wondered what Lucius was thinking about. The horse—or himself?

"Congratulations on second place," he finally said.

I followed his gaze to the corkboard on my wall, where I'd hung my red ribbon next to a bunch of blue ones I'd won for math competitions. Of course, Faith Crosse had won the blue ribbon. My performance had been good, but not good enough. "You deserved the blue," I told Lucius, meaning it.

"How odd that I received a 'lifetime ban' from 4-H, then," he noted wryly. "They created a whole new rule, you know. Just for me. 'Prohibition against knowingly bringing a vicious animal to a public event.' I was the first violator, retroactively. A pioneer in lawlessness, so to speak." He laughed, coughed sharply, and clutched his ribs. "Damn."

"Are you okay?"

"Yes, I just *slay* myself, at times." He smiled. "Literally."

I fidgeted with my iPod. "Lucius?"

"Yes, Jessica?"

I met his black eyes. "I was there. That night."

"I know."

"You do?"

"You came to me late at night. Took my hand."

I resumed my study of my iPod, embarrassed. "Oh . . . I thought you were asleep."

"Don't fidget while conversing." Lucius plucked the MP3 player from my fingers. "Of course I knew you were there. I'm a light sleeper. Especially when every inch of my body is wracked with pain."

"Sorry." I smiled weakly. "I didn't mean to disturb you."

"No . . . on the contrary, I was quite touched," Lucius said. His eyes softened, all of the imperiousness fading away. "You wept for my distress. No one has ever wept to see me suffer before. I shall not forget that kindness, Jessica."

"It was just how I felt then. I couldn't help crying."

"No, of course not." The admission seemed to pain him, somehow. "Still, when I return to my life in Romania, no one will cry to see Lucius Vladescu broken. And when I suffer—as is inevitable—I shall remember your gesture with fondness and appreciation."

"I won't forget that night, either," I promised. I wiped my palms on my legs. They'd grown sweaty. "Lucius . . . I saw you drink the blood."

"Ahh, the blood." He didn't seem surprised by my confession. "I hope you were not unduly upset. Not *too* disgusted. I hadn't judged you ready to see *that*. It can be rather *off-putting* for those not used to it."

"I sort of passed out."

Lucius smiled sadly and stared out the window. "Even insensate on a table, I manage to sicken you. Quite a talent I have."

"No. It wasn't just seeing the blood. I . . . I smelled it, too."

Lucius turned his head slowly to look at me, as if he couldn't quite believe what he'd heard. There was a small spark in his eyes. "You did?"

"Yes."

"And what, exactly, did it smell like?"

"It was strong. Almost overpowering."

"Yes. So it is. So it becomes."

"That's what you keep in that Orange Julius cup, isn't it?"

Lucius smiled wryly. "Did I really seem like a man who would drink strawberry froth from a kiosk at the mall? Have I not expressed my feelings toward pink things?"

"Yeah. I guess I should have known." A question had been burning in my mind. A question I wasn't sure I wanted answered. But I had to ask. "Lucius, where do you *get* it?" Visions from old movies, of terrified women in gauzy nightgowns cowering before fanged attackers, loomed in my mind. "Is it . . . violent?"

"Oh, Jessica . . . vampires have ways. It is not as rapacious now as it was in the past. Much is maintained in collections, like wine. One need not always stomp a grape to drink champagne, you know."

Moving carefully to protect his ribs, Lucius laced his fingers behind his head, sinking into the pillow, gazing at the ceiling. His deep voice grew wistful. "Our cellar in Romania . . . it is the best in the world, some say. Vintages dating back to the 1700s. One can just summon a servant with a snap of the fingers, name one's poison—to use one of my favorite colloquialisms—and indulge."

Half disgusted and more than a little bit unsettlingly thrilled, I let him talk on, watching him fall deeper into a reverie.

"And then, of course, when two vampires marry—unite for eternity—they have each other. That is said to be the finest vintage. The purest source." Lucius grew even more introspective, more distant. "Male to female. Woman to man. Blood comingled. Could there be a stronger bond between two beings?"

A smile flitted across his lips. "Intercourse is a fleeting pleasure, indeed. Undeniably an intimate act. Not to be dismissed—or missed, for that matter. Indeed, crucial for procreation, beyond its other obvious virtues."

The smile faded. "But sharing one's *blood* with another: exposing one's most vulnerable place, where the pulse beats just below the skin, and trusting your partner to satisfy without subduing . . . It makes sex seem almost insignificant by comparison. An unequal act—male *to* female. But blood . . . blood can be shared as true equals."

He seemed to have forgotten me perched by his side. I listened to him, mesmerized. Mesmerized and . . . more.

Or maybe Lucius hadn't forgotten my presence. His gaze flicked to me. "But of course you think I am delusional, that I ramble about impossibilities, irrational acts. And you are right: The existence of a vampire *is* irrational. We are a study in impossibilities."

Vintage blood. Fangs piercing pulse points. It did still sound crazy. But not impossible anymore. Or even undesirable, the way Lucius described it. No, not in the least. "Lucius, I saw you drink the blood. It's not impossible."

"Ahh, Jessica." He unlaced his hands from behind his head. "Why now? Why so damnably late in the goddamn game—as the perennially profane Coach Ferrin would say on the basketball court?"

"What do you mean? Late in the game?" It seemed early in the game to me. I was just starting to understand. Just starting to believe. As difficult as it was for me to wrap my brain around, I couldn't deny it any longer. I believed Lucius Vladescu was a vampire. And that I could, at the very least, smell the blood, too. Respond to it. There was so much more to understand . . . to figure out. "Why is it late?"

Lucius leaned wearily into his hands, rubbing his eyes. "Why did I just tell you all that romantic claptrap? I allowed myself to get carried away. Damn, I am irresponsible sometimes. I had so wanted you to understand, and now the timing is so wrong. I had longed to tell you all that before. To share it with you. Thus, when you finally showed interest, I just couldn't shut the hell up."

"It didn't sound like 'claptrap,' " I assured him. On the contrary, everything he'd said had been intriguing, in an admittedly disconcerting way. "And why not now?"

But before Lucius could respond, my dad knocked on the half-open bedroom door. "Lucius, you have a visitor."

Propping himself up straighter again, Lucius arched his brows. "Me? A guest?"

I was surprised, too. To my knowledge, Lucius hadn't cultivated many friends in America.

Before I could hazard a guess, though, Dad stepped away, the door swung wider, and a pert little nose—attached to a stunning face topped by a curtain of hair so fair it practically glowed—poked tentatively into the room. "Hey, Lucius."

Lucius stared toward the door. Stared very hard, almost as though he'd never seen Faith Crosse before.

I assumed he was furious with her for nearly killing him. But suddenly his face broke into a smile. A strange smile. Kind of like he'd had a revelation. "Welcome, Faith," he said. "Do come in. This *is* a pleasant surprise. I'm sorry I can't rise to greet you."

"No, I'm the one who has to apologize," Faith said, entering my room with an exaggerated pout. "It seems like my fault you're stuck here." She surveyed the room. "I mean, it's just awful."

I narrowed my eyes at her. *Does she mean Lucius's injuries? Or my decor?*

"My mare and I were on a collision course from the outset," Lucius reassured her. "I courted inevitability; you merely performed the marriage ceremony."

Faith cocked her head, as if she wasn't sure if he was blaming her or not. "Well, I hope you're feeling better." She rummaged in her purse and pulled out an iPod. "And I brought you a get-well gift."

She handed the MP3 player to Lucius, who smiled up at her. "Why, thank you, Faith. That was very thoughtful." He shot me a look. "I guess I won't need yours after all, Jessica."

"I thought you might be bored, stuck in bed," added Faith, who still hadn't acknowledged my existence. "It's the latest, and you can load it up with whatever you want."

"He likes Croatian folk," I noted. Not that anyone had asked for my input.

Lucius raised a finger. "And the Black Eyed Peas. And don't forget Hoobastank. Can any of us forget Hoobastank?"

"Really?" Faith squealed, clapping her hands together. "I love Hoobastank, too!"

Lucius gestured to the bed. "Please, have a seat, Faith."

Three would definitely be a crowd on my narrow twin mattress—especially with a six-foot vampire sprawled there—so I stood. I wasn't really excited to hang out with a rude, egotistical cheerleader, anyway. "I guess I'll get going."

"See you, Jenn." Faith dismissed me, taking my spot next to Lucius. She thumped down on the bed, and he winced, almost imperceptibly.

"Watch his leg," I advised, thinking what a self-absorbed witch she was.

"Jessica," Lucius called me back as I headed for the door. "Wait."

I turned around. "What? Do you need something?"

"No. I have something for you." He felt around behind the pillow and withdrew a book. I sucked in my breath, recognizing my copy of *Growing Up Undead: A Teen Vampire's Guide to Dating, Health, and Emotions.*

"You abandoned this under your bed." Lucius held it out to me, keeping his hand strategically positioned over the title. "Forgotten amid the considerable dust. And after all the thought I put into the inscription."

I accepted the manual from him, folding it against my chest, hiding it from Faith. "Uh . . . thanks."

"I think you'll find chapter seven helpful," he noted. "I'm sorry I can't offer you more guidance than that. But the book should answer most of your questions."

"I thought this was your area of expertise," I joked obliquely, referring to his inscription.

"To be honest," he said, "I suggest you satisfy any curiosity you might have, and then discard the guide. Permanently. It's really much ado about nothing."

My eyes snapped open. "What?" Since when did Lucius Vladescu think anything related to vampires was "much ado about nothing"? I'd just heard him wax poetic about blood ties. . . .

160

I tried to read his expression, but Lucius was already focusing back on Faith. "I am rude, though, to speak of private concerns when I have a guest. Please forgive me, Faith."

"No problem, Lucius. I've got lots of time." Faith smiled at me and repeated, "See ya."

"Yes, good-bye, Jessica." Lucius dismissed me, too. A little abruptly, I thought.

"Um . . . see you," I said.

But they didn't even notice me. Faith had already scooted in closer to Lucius, demonstrating all the features on his new iPod. Their heads were bent over the little screen, and they were laughing.

I glanced one more time at my stupid second-place ribbon, wishing I had never hung it on the corkboard. Faith was sitting practically right under it. The ribbon in her room was blue. And bigger. A winner's ribbon. My red ribbon was technically brighter, bolder, gleaming in the sunlit room, eye-catching as an exotic bird. And yet, the crimson slip of silk was really just blue's weak, sorry cousin.

"Bye," I repeated. They still didn't answer, already too deep in their conversation, so I left, taking my book.

Pausing at the foot of the staircase, I flipped to chapter seven. It was entitled, "So You Smell Blood? Congratulations!"

I skimmed the opening paragraph, not once but four or five times, reading, "A heightened olfactory awareness—sometimes approaching sexual stimulation—when you are in the presence of blood is a sign that your vampire nature is blossoming!"

My vampire nature.

A few paragraphs later, the guide advised, "Soon you will thirst for blood, especially when emotions run high!"

Above me, I heard Lucius laughing with Faith Crosse. Laughing loud and hard, as if they already shared some long-standing joke.

Chapter 28

"MINDY, WHAT ARE YOU doing here?" I asked, picking my way through the bleachers to where she was perched.

"I could ask you that same thing," she countered, motioning for me to sit next to her.

I dropped my backpack and sat down. "Jake invited me to watch wrestling practice." I caught Jake's eye and waved. He winked up at me, his muscles bulging almost cartoonishly, barely contained by his tight spandex unitard. "So I repeat: What are *you* doing here?"

"Oh, I don't know." Mindy smiled. "I stop by sometimes, just to watch the practices."

The gym was sectioned off to allow teams with overlapping seasons to share the space. The wrestling mats were unrolled in one corner, the cheerleaders bounced around next to the wrestlers, and the basketball team hogged a full half of the shiny hardwood floor. The air was filled with grunts and cheerleading cries, the squeak of rubber shoes, and the smell of sweat.

A whistle blew sharply. "Vladescu! Front and center, dammit!" Coach Ferrin's booming voice rang out above the din. "You've been at the goddamn water fountain for a damn hour! Get your loitering ass back in the drill!"

I sat up a little straighter, watching as, sure enough, a tall, dark-haired Romanian loped out from near the boys' locker room and onto the court. "Lucius is *playing*?"

"Is he *ever*." Mindy sighed dreamily.

"Mindy, is *Lucius* why you come here?"

"It's not, like, an addiction," she protested. "Maybe just once or twice a week. But I mean, look at him!"

As we watched, Lucius snatched a ball hurled at his chest, took a few aggressive strides toward the hoop, rose seemingly without effort—and crushed the ball through the rim.

"But he hasn't even been back in class yet."

"Yeah, I saw him in the hall before practice," Mindy said. "He said he's coming back to classes tomorrow." She gave me a curious look. "I thought you said his leg was *broken*?"

"It was hurt . . ." Oh, hell. I'd given up trying to explain the mysteries of Lucius Vladescu. "I guess it's better now."

"I'll say."

"Mindy!"

"Well, look at him in shorts, Jess. Some guys—you wish they'd keep their clothes on. But Lucius makes you wish he'd peel off another layer, even. I mean, wouldn't you like to know what's *under* there?"

Indeed, there was a reason that Lucius looked so good in clothes. The body beneath them was just about flawless—with the exception of another scar, a wide, serrated mark that sliced across his bowed right bicep. *How did he earn that? And did he have more on other body parts?* His left leg, which *had* been snapped, bore a large black bruise, the only sign that he was still injured. Aside from those minor imperfections, there just wasn't anything to criticize. Okay, even the scars were sexy.

Lucius also stood a good head taller than most of the other players, his leg muscles were more defined, and his shoulders were broader, more masculine, without bulging. . . .

I cast a guilty glance at Jake, feeling I'd betrayed him.

Mindy followed my gaze. "Oh, hey, look, your boyfriend is grappling away."

"I don't know if he's my *boyfriend* . . ."

"Come on, Jess. You guys are together. You were out twice last week, you eat lunch together almost every day, and you're here, aren't you?"

I watched Jake spinning around on the mat, grunting. "Can you keep a secret, Mindy?"

"Hey, we've been friends since preschool," Mindy said. "Have I ever spilled your secrets?"

"No. Never." Mindy was a lot of things—flighty, impulsive, sex-obsessed—but she was never disloyal.

"So? Talk."

"I'm not sure if Jake and I are a great match."

Mindy's eyes, rimmed by a thick layer of Cover Girl charcoal eyeliner, widened. "What? I thought you really liked him!"

"He's . . . nice," I said, flinching a little at my use of Lucius's despised adjective. "But I don't know if there's a real spark there. Not like I thought there would be."

"Hmm. Well, Jake is no Lukey," Mindy concurred, her gaze wandering back over to the basketball court. "I told you that from the beginning."

"Yes, they are very different," I agreed. If only she knew how different . . . maybe she wouldn't be so keen on her Lukey. Mindy had gotten queasy when we'd dissected worms in sixth grade. She wasn't a blood-drinking-type girl. "Not that I'd be dropping Jake for Lucius," I added. "I'm just saying that I'm not sure about Jake and me."

"And I'm saying you should finally come to your senses and choose Lucius, before he gets sick of chasing you," Mindy observed. "Face it, Jess. Lucius has charisma," she added, nodding toward the cheerleaders. "Look at the way even Faith is staring at him. Lukey just draws your attention."

Sure enough, when I looked across the gym, Faith Crosse was climbing high atop a pyramid of cheerleaders—walking all over people, as usual—but her face was turned toward the basketball court, where Lucius was deep in conference with his coach. The way Lucius stood, hands on narrow hips, towering over Coach Ferrin, it looked like the starting center was the one in charge. I glanced back at Faith. She was atop her people pile but still watching the discussion at midcourt.

"By the way," Mindy interrupted my thoughts. "You look really good today. Is that a new outfit?"

I tore my gaze away from Lucius and Faith and smoothed my crinkled skirt over my knees. "Yeah, do you like it?"

"Definitely. Purple is a good color on you. And the V-neck—very sexy."

"Too sexy?"

"No. Just right. You should wear stuff like that more often. You look . . . exotic. Like a gypsy or something." She stared at my head. "And did you do something to your hair?"

I rumpled my curls. "I used this 'curl polisher,' instead of trying to flatten my hair down every day. I guess I'm tired of fighting nature."

"Looks great." Mindy nodded, assessing me. "Shiny. And different from what everybody else is doing. Kind of cool."

A sharp cry rang out, and I looked to its source just in time to see Faith Crosse topple toward the ground, taking down the entire pyramid. Her squad fell one by one like shrieking dominoes beneath her.

Pretty much everyone on the gym floor ran over to gawk or help. And the first person at the scene of the accident, extending his hand to help Faith to her feet, was none other than Lucius Vladescu.

One by one, the other cheerleaders scrambled up and checked themselves for injuries. Although like everyone else, Faith seemed to be okay, Lucius held her arm and walked her toward the locker room, where they paused, talking.

"Well, well, well." Mindy observed. "If you *are* dumping Jakey for Lukey, you'd better act fast, because it looks like you just might have competition. Look at her—getting him to play white knight to her damsel in distress!"

I nearly laughed at that. For one thing, Faith had been with football player Ethan Strausser for as long as anybody could remember. More importantly, Lucius would never abandon me for another girl, no matter how skinny her butt looked in her flippy cheerleader skirt. He liked women with curves. And he was pledged to me.

But as I watched, Faith and Lucius laughed loudly, as they had in my bedroom. Then she gave him a flirtatious little shove, and he grinned down at her, looking less burdened somehow than he had in the past. More relaxed in his posture. More . . . free.

"Yup." Mindy chuckled. "If you want Lukey, I'd get a move on. Faith's drooling over him like he's a Prada bag that somehow turned up in a sale bin at Wal-Mart. Discount priced and ready to move—right onto her arm."

"No, that's crazy," I protested.

But then again, I'd thought vampires were a crazy concept just a week or so ago.

What did Lucius mean when he said, "late in the game"?

As I watched Lucius and Faith talking, joking together, an unfamiliar sensation like hot pins—jealousy—started to prick at my heart. Another feeling welled inside me, too. A possessive feeling. A strong, proprietary sense that bordered on anger. A sense of ownership. Of my *right* to Lucius.

My fingers curled around the bleacher seat, squeezing.

And suddenly, for the first time ever, I got thirsty.

Really, really thirsty.

For something I'd never craved before. Just like my vampire sex guide had warned me.

Chapter 29

"I'M TOTALLY BEAT." Mike Danneker yawned, gathering up his books and snapping his laptop's screen shut. "I can't take any more math."

"Just a few more problems," I urged him, opening one of my more challenging calculus texts. "We could do these sample word problems . . ."

"No way," Mike said. "And you should go home, too, Jess.

You're gonna burn out, studying this hard. The competition is still a few weeks away."

"Which is exactly why we need to practice."

Mike stood, shouldering his laptop case. "See you, Jess. Get some rest."

He strolled off through the aisles, leaving me alone deep in the heart of Woodrow Wilson's library. I turned a page in my notebook, trying to focus. Maybe I *was* tired: The whole idea of numbers seemed difficult. I was having a hard time training my mind on the problems. Maybe because I couldn't stop thinking about how I'd just recently been in the gym, thirsting for blood.

As I stared at my book, my mind once again drifting far away from limits, derivatives, and integrals, I heard voices and footsteps in the maze of stacks.

"We should just buy papers off the Internet."

Frank Dormand.

"No way. Three guys got caught last year, and two of them lost their football scholarships. They missed a whole year of college ball."

Ethan Strausser.

"So what, we're supposed to find a bunch of books on the League of Nations?" Dormand asked. "Like I give a shit?"

I heard volumes being pulled off shelves.

"Why don't you just get Faith to write 'em for us?" Dormand added. "She's smart."

My ears pricked at Faith's name.

"She's been a total bitch lately," Ethan said. "I don't know what the hell is wrong with her."

"She's hanging out with *Vladescu*," Frank said, spitting out Lucius's name like it was a gnat that had flown into his mouth. "He's probably rubbing off on her, the bastard."

How much are Lucius and Faith hanging out? How often? And what are they doing? Possessiveness and jealousy rippled through me again. I tried to remember: When was the last time Lucius had mentioned the pact? Courtship? It struck me that I wasn't really sure. *How can I not be sure?*

"That freak thinks he owns the damn school because he can make a few shots from center court," Ethan groused.

"There's something wrong with that guy," Dormand noted. "He's not normal."

I sat frozen in my seat, intent upon my eavesdropping. Frank and Ethan couldn't really *know* anything about Lucius, but it bothered me to think that two of the school's biggest morons were starting to discuss the fact that Lucius was different. I wasn't sure *why* it bothered me—two stupid goons certainly couldn't be a threat to someone as self-possessed and physically strong as Lucius—but I was unnerved a little.

"You're just pissed because he smacked you down in front of everybody, banging your thick head on a locker," Ethan noted.

"Yeah. And if he'd just about strangled you, you'd still be pissed, too." Dormand paused. "I'm telling you. There's something different about him. When he grabbed me . . . I don't know . . . it felt weird."

"What, did you get hot for him?" Ethan joked. "What the hell do you mean, it felt *weird*?"

I expected a macho jerk like Dormand to go berserk over

what Ethan was implying. For once, though, Frank seemed almost thoughtful. "Shut up, man," he said. "You didn't feel it."

I heard the sound of books being slammed back onto the shelves. "Let's get the hell out of here," Ethan said. "I'll get somebody else to write the paper."

As they walked away, I heard Dormand add, "Vladescu—someday that guy's gonna get what he deserves. He is not *right*. And one of these days, I'll put my finger on it . . ."

Dormand's voice trailed off as they left the library.

I stared into space, trying to tell myself that the vague unease I felt was totally unjustified. But for some reason, I didn't really believe that. Frank Dormand was a relentless bully, as surely as Lucius was a vampire. I'd been the object of Frank's taunting for as long as I could remember. I knew how he could latch on to a target, refusing to let go. . . .

What if Frank starts looking into Lucius's life? His past? What he is? Can Dormand find out anything?

No.

The notion was almost silly. Frank Dormand couldn't even find a book on the League of Nations in a high school library. He'd never figure out that Lucius was a vampire. Never in a million years.

And even if he did, what was the worst that could happen? Lebanon County wasn't Romania. It was a civilized place. People didn't form mobs and murder their neighbors with stakes, for god's sake. The idea was laughable. Lucius would be fine.

So why didn't I feel better as I closed my books, giving up on math—slamming the cover on logic and reason—for the night?

Chapter 30

DEAR VASILE,

December in Lebanon County, Pennsylvania, would quite "blow your mind," to use the expression I have determined to be my favorite of all those I've acquired during my extended stay. Is it a good thing to have one's mind "blown"? Or a bad thing? Even in context, it is sometimes difficult to tell—although I quite enjoy trying to conjure the visual imagery. Heads exploding. Exposed brains on tables, caressed by the breeze from electric fans. That sort of thing.

Remaining on the subject of visual stimulation: December is celebrated quite heartily here in the United States. Aggressively, one might say. Every conceivable surface is corseted with strands of twinkle lights, buildings are smothered beneath greenery, and a mass mania for erecting oversized, inflatable, waving "snowmen" in front of homes erupts amid the populace. It's quite a hysteria—and the evergreen trees are not just a myth, Vasile. People really do purchase them, in abundance. They are for sale everywhere. Imagine paying for the privilege of dragging a filthy piece of the forest into your living area for the purpose of bedecking it with glass balls and staring at it.

Why a tree? If one needed to display glass balls—and I highly discourage it—why not just a case of some sort? A rack?

Honestly, I've expended so much energy defending vampires against charges of "irrationality." Had I known about the ubiquity of the temporary in-house evergreen, I would have said, merely, "Yes, perhaps I am irrational. But I keep my trees where they belong. Out-of-doors. You tell me, who is the sane one?"

But enough about "the holidays." (Ho-ho-hold my head under water until I drown and am freed from yet another round of "Jingle Bells"!) I write primarily to report that I have very little to report. I seem to be healed, and I have mastered the art of sleeping in "social studies" class. (Drone on, Miss Campbell! I have circumvented your nefarious attempt to make tedious World War I one of Earth's most dramatic conflicts: mustard gas! Trenches! The obliteration of no less than four empires!)

Oh, yes. You might be interested—or perhaps not—to know that I have also made a friend. A quite iniquitous girl, Vasile. I feel rather confident that the "jolly old elf" St. Nick has inked her firmly on his "naughty" list. (A reference too obscure for you, no doubt. Just trust me: She is rather a fascinating creature.) Her name is Faith Crosse. While often "cross," she is as "faithless" as one can imagine. You know I love irony.

I suppose that is all from "stateside."

I would wish you a "merry Christmas," but really, I feel certain that the only thing you would like less than the holiday would be the state of "merriness."

You nephew,

Lucius

P.S. Rest assured that, although I have not addressed it in the body of my letter, I received your thunderous, if belated, response to my suggestion that we release Antanasia from her vampiric responsibilities. Nor did I fail to comprehend your wrath at my assertion that I "chafe at the bit." Indeed, your meaning was very clear when you wrote in your reply that you would "make me miss the bit when the whip was applied." Equine imagery is so vivid. All points are taken under careful consideration. But do I comply with your directive to continue my aggressive pursuit of Antanasia? It is difficult to tell from Romania, isn't it? The distance rather "blows one's mind," does it not?

Chapter 31

"JESSICA, IS THAT YOU?" Lucius asked. I heard the door to the garage apartment close, followed by the sound of snow being stomped off feet.

"Hey." I peeked out from the kitchenette. "You're here early."

"And you're here . . . at all." He tossed his coat on the leather chair. "I thought we had permanently resumed our traditional residences."

"We did." I popped back into the kitchenette, stirring a boiling pot. *Crap.* I'd hoped to be further along with dinner by the time he got back from school. "Why are you home already?"

"Basketball practice was preempted by the snow. In the Carpathians, we would call this the equivalent of 'a dusting.' A 'minor inconvenience.' Here, it seems to be cause for panic in the streets. Looting and rioting for the last loaf of 'Wonder Bread' at the grocery store, as though you couldn't get a pizza delivered if on the brink of starvation." Lucius sniffed the air. "I repeat: Why are you here? And what *is* that *smell*?"

"I knew you were tired of vegan casseroles, so I made you a rabbit," I said. "I saw them in your freezer when I was living out here."

He caught up short for a second. "You did *what*?"

"I cooked a rabbit."

"Actually, it's referred to as 'hare,'" Lucius corrected, joining me in the kitchenette. "And if you don't know what to properly *call* it, how did you know what to *do* with it?"

"I found this cookbook on your shelves." I held out the battered, stained reference. "See?"

Lucius frowned, reading. "*Cooking the Romanian Way.* In English! I'd forgotten I brought this." He glanced at me and smiled wryly. "Our cook sent this for your parents, anticipating that they would adjust their menus to meet my tastes—certainly never expecting that I'd find myself in the home of vegans who would never deign to accommodate even a royal Romanian's passion for flesh."

"Well, there's plenty of 'flesh' on the menu tonight," I promised. "I'm making the sour lamb soup, too." I took the book from him, opened it, and jabbed my finger at the page I'd marked. "This recipe."

Lucius perused. "How in the world did you secure 'minced levistan,' in Lebanon County, Pennsylvania?"

"I checked on Transylvaniancooking.com. You can substitute tarragon."

"The 'sour lamb' must be the smell," Lucius said, wrinkling his nose. "*That* will linger. And if your parents learn you cooked meat, woe to you."

"Hey, I'm trying to be nice here!"

Lucius laughed. "Yes. By providing me a nice case of trichinosis. Hare are notorious carriers. The inexperienced should *not* dabble with game." He lifted the lid on the potted hare, which was stewing away, then glanced at me, one eyebrow arched. "You did clean this little beast, correct?"

"Like . . . wash it in the sink?"

"Remove the innards. I see something floating in there . . ."

"There were *innards*?"

Lucius grabbed a slotted spoon and stirred around in the pot. "*Now* I believe we've identified the source of the odor. I would say this is a spleen," he announced, fishing out something that looked slippery. "Nasty little organ. Not the most palatable part of anything. Even starving cats won't ingest spleen."

"I guess we should just dump the hare," I said glumly. The dinner wasn't turning out as well as I'd hoped.

"Actually, Jessica, as much as I appreciate the effort . . ."

There was a knock on the door.

"Excuse me," Lucius said, heading to answer it.

"Um, sure." I peeked in the pot. There were other slippery things starting to bubble around in there, too, as the hare broke down. *Yikes. Who knew?*

The door squeaked open.

"Luc! Hey!"

Feeling something like a kick to my gut, I slammed down the lid of the pot. I knew that falsely chipper voice.

Faith Crosse.

What is she doing here?

"Did you have any trouble with the snow?" Lucius inquired.

I smelled pizza over the stench of the spleen.

"No, it's no big deal to me." Faith laughed. "I borrowed

my dad's Hummer. If I was in an accident, *I* wouldn't be the one killed."

What a humanitarian. I moved to the entrance to the kitchenette, leaning against the doorway, arms crossed, watching them.

"Finally, a Lebanon Countian who understands how to handle a scattering of frozen precipitation," Lucius said, approvingly. "And might I add that you're looking lovely, as usual. Although it really goes without saying."

Ugh. I was going to throw up and not from eating organ meats.

"Oh, Luc." Faith balanced the pizza box like a waitress, freeing one hand to clasp his forearm flirtatiously. "You always say the right thing."

"And you have *brought* the right thing," he said, unburdening her of the pizza. "This is one local delicacy that I have honestly come to appreciate."

"It sure smells better than whatever's cooking in here." Faith glanced around, seeking the source of the odor, and noticed me. "Oh, hi." She wrinkled her nose. "I was just saying *something* stinks in here."

"It sure does," I agreed.

Lucius brushed past me, carrying the pizza into the kitchenette.

"As I was about to say, Jessica, dinner would be somewhat inconvenient this evening, as I've invited Faith over to study."

"Study?" I felt more stewed than my rabbit. More sour than the lamb soup.

"Yes," Faith said. "Lucius asked me to be his partner in English lit."

Partner? For what? And if there is any partnering to do, why wasn't I asked? I looked to Lucius, knowing there was betrayal in my eyes. Wanting him to see it. But he was avoiding me.

"Yes, recall how I volunteered to do my 'mandatory oral book report' on *Wuthering Heights*?" he asked. "Well, after sitting through endlessly stultifying—and seldom edifying—presentations by our classmates, I thought it might be interesting to condense the novel into a small play. Highlight the dramatic parts."

"I'm going to be Catherine," Faith noted.

"I guess that makes you Heathcliff," I said to Lucius, barely masking the unhappiness in my voice.

"Precisely."

I switched off the burners. *Maybe the stench I caused will fade in a year or so.* "I guess I'll get going, then. Don't want to interrupt you."

"You could stay for pizza," Lucius offered. "You must not have eaten. At least, I hope you didn't taste the hare. It may not have boiled long enough to kill the parasites . . ."

"You're boiling hair?" Faith interjected. "Is *that* how you get it that way, Jenn?"

I glared at Faith for a long time, wishing I had a really great comeback. But nothing came to mind. Nothing. "I'll just head back to the house," I said, trying to exit with a little dignity. Trying to get out without crying. It had turned out all wrong. The whole thing was a disaster.

Lucius must have seen my disappointment, the humiliation on my face, because he said, "Excuse us for a moment, Faith."

"Sure, Luc," she offered, removing herself to the other side of the small space. "I'll just check out your weapons over here. I love the diabolical decor."

Lucius took my arm, leading me toward the door. "Jessica," he said softly, "I'm sorry."

"For what?" I hardly bothered to lower my voice. Tears really were welling in my eyes. Jealous tears. Embarrassed tears. I was so stupid. I'd tried to cook a *rabbit* for him, and he had a *girl* coming over. Not just any girl. Faith Crosse.

"It was kind of you to try . . . a sweet gesture . . ." There was pity in Lucius's eyes as he pushed a stray curl behind my ear, as if I were a hurt child. "But perhaps not the best idea. Not now."

"Yes," I agreed, shoving his hand away from my face. "It was a mistake."

"Faith is a friend," he explained calmly. "I find that I need a friend right now. Someone who understands me."

That really stung. *Who could understand him better?* "*I* understand you."

"No. Not in the same way . . ." He glanced at Faith, who had removed a sword from the wall and was testing the point. "I can't explain it right now."

"Oh, you don't have to."

His voice hardened a bit, as did his grip on my arm. "Jessica, you have Jake. You *chose* Jake. And you have Melinda, too. Must *I* be isolated?"

"No. Of course not. Whatever." I tore my arm from his grasp, flung open the door, and ran out of the apartment, not bothering to grab my jacket.

As I stomped down the stairs, the tears really started to spill, and I heard Lucius step out onto the landing. "Jessica, please . . ."

I ignored him and kept going, and he didn't call again. Before I had even reached the bottom, I heard the door to the apartment thud shut.

Chapter 32

I'D SUFFERED THROUGH the dream every now and then since childhood, and it had always shaken me, lingering in my mind even after I awoke. I would force it out of my brain the moment I jolted to alertness, inevitably in a cold sweat, twisted in my sheets. Always I dismissed it with *real* things. *The square root of any positive, real number can be determined using Newton's formula. . . .* That was how I coped. By clinging to reality. To the concrete.

But that night in mid-December, the dream, more vivid than ever, would not be dislodged.

"Antanasia . . . Antanasia . . ."

She was calling me. At first like a lullaby, a soothing singsong.

It was dark and snowy there, in unfamiliar, steep, and rugged mountains. The black, wet, rocky outcroppings that poked through the drifts were like jagged teeth. Like fangs. The snow fell somehow harder, deeper, in a way that seemed almost menacing. As if the storm was animated and out for blood.

"Antanasia!"

She would always call me three times, and the last time was always different. Like a sudden cry. The wail of someone falling away, off one of the mountain cliffs . . .

Then silence.

Just the sound of wind and the swirling of the snow, whipping around the mountain peaks, which receded farther and farther in the distance . . .

My eyes snapped open.

I lay in bed for a few minutes, for once allowing the dream to saturate my mind. To settle in and become familiar.

Gradually, I accepted it.

And then I kicked free of the snarled covers, swung my feet out to touch the cold wooden floor, and padded quietly to my dresser, pulling open the bottom drawer, trying to keep it from squeaking. Feeling blindly in a pile of T-shirts I no longer wore, my fingers located what I sought. The book Lucius had given me. I took it out and crept to my desk, switching on the lamp.

In the circle of light, I read the now-familiar title. With surprisingly steady fingers, I riffled through the pages, searching for the waxy envelope still tucked near the back, about forty pages from Lucius's heavy silver bookmark.

When I found the slender packet, I lifted it out, carefully— it seemed so delicate, or maybe just too precious to handle. Reaching inside with two fingers, I slipped out the contents. The photograph.

My breath caught as I stared down at a woman in a crimson silk dress, posed formally, her posture regally but comfortably straight, her shoulders back, her curly black hair piled atop her head, circled in a silver coronet. Her nose was a bit blunt, her mouth a shadow too wide to be conventionally beautiful. A hint of smile played at the corners of her lips, as if someone had told her a joke that she wanted to laugh at, although she'd been advised to be stern. To appear queenly.

A small, dark gemstone appeared to float just where her

breastbone met her throat, the chain too fine to be perceived in the image.

My mother.

I peered more closely. Her eyes . . . her eyes were definitely mine.

So was her nose. Her bemused mouth.

I recognized every plane of Mihaela Dragomir's face, as if I had seen her earlier that day . . . maybe because I had, in the mirror.

And yet the woman in the photograph was different from me. She had a special quality that was better than traditional beauty. She had . . . a presence.

Lucius's words from weeks ago came back to me. *"American women. Why do you all want to be nearly invisible? Why not have a* physical presence *in the world?"*

Even in an old photograph, my mother had that. Presence. Mihaela Dragomir was captivating. The type of woman who would draw all eyes to her as she entered a room.

I turned the photo over to see if it was dated, but nothing was written there, so I looked at her again, studying her face for many minutes, hearing the dream voice in my head. Savoring my birth mother's long-silenced lullaby and forcing myself to endure the scream of her loss. Again and again and again. Did she scream to lose her own life? Or for the loss of me? For our eternal separation from each other?

When I felt the weight of our mutual past beginning to bear down on me too hard, I slipped the photo back into the envelope. It met with resistance, as though there was something else inside, blocking it. I carefully placed the photo on my desk, turned the envelope over, and shook it gently. A small slip of nearly translucent paper fluttered into my palm.

I recognized the same script I'd seen scrawled across the whiteboard in Mrs. Wilhelm's class back in September: VLADESCU. The same script that was on the inside cover of my vampire manual.

> *Is she not beautiful, Antanasia?*
> *Is she not powerful?*
> *Is she not regal?*
> *Is she not exactly like YOU?*

It was almost like a poem. An ode. To me.

I read it again, although I had memorized it the very first time, then slid Lucius's note back into the envelope, followed by the picture, and replaced them both in the guide, which I laid on my desk. Then I turned around in my chair, catching my reflection in the full-length mirror that hung on the back of my bedroom door. In the soft light, I could have *been* Mihaela Dragomir, my flannel nightshirt a silken evening gown. . . .

On impulse, I piled my hair on my head and straightened my shoulders.

> *Is she not beautiful?*
> *Is she not powerful?*
> *Is she not regal?*
> *Is she not YOU?*

Releasing my hair, I snapped off the light and climbed back in bed, not certain whether I wanted to rejoice or sob or both.

> *Is she not YOU?*

Chapter 33

LUCIUS AND FAITH were late to English lit on the day of their big presentation, arriving five minutes after the bell rang— the better to surprise us all by appearing in costume. At least, Faith wore a faded dress that looked to be from the Victorian era—and which pinched her waist and strained across her boobs so tightly that Frank Dormand, in front of me, nearly fell off his chair when she swept into the room. Lucius, for his part as Heathcliff, simply resurrected the velvet coat and black trousers he'd worn on a regular basis just a month or so before.

"Oh, goodness" was all Mrs. Wilhelm could muster at the sight. I suspect that she was a little worried about Faith's boobs popping out at an inopportune time, which would definitely violate the school's dress code.

It was Lucius, though, who immediately commanded center stage, introducing his little play, lecturing with more authority than Mrs. Wilhelm had ever managed.

"Heathcliff is a wild thing—a damned man," Lucius reminded us. "Catherine is damned, too. Damned to love Heathcliff, who *must* destroy her and her progeny. It is in his nature to take what he wants. And what he desires is vengeance, above all. And Catherine, she is an admirable savage. Theirs is a heartless, cruel, bitter, evil love."

"Oh, goodness," Mrs. Wilhelm fluttered again from the seat she'd taken in the back corner. This time, I think she was swooning a bit over Lucius.

"I do so appreciate this story," Lucius added in an aside. "It resonates."

I twisted my pen in my fingers, nearly snapping it, confused and sick at heart. *Heartless, cruel, evil love. Is that what he wants? Is that what he always expected with me? Did Lucius ever expect any kind of "love" with me?*

I glanced back at Jake, who shrugged and rolled his blue eyes, like he thought the whole production was a bit over the top. I smiled at him but weakly. *Why, why can't I feel more for Jake? He's handsome, popular, without a cruel or dangerous bone in his muscle-bound body. Why am I so drawn to turn back around and watch Lucius? A guy who is totally wrong for me? An arrogant, enigmatic, potentially dangerous VAMPIRE?*

Jake—Jake was the sensible, sweet, predictable choice.

Yet I spun back around, eager to watch Lucius.

When I rejoined the drama, he was facing Faith, and their play began. Somehow, they had condensed the first half of the book, grabbing quotes here and there, making some up, I suppose, and stitching them together into an intense twenty-five-minute scene that took Heathcliff and Catherine from their gleefully negligent childhood on the moors to Catherine's careless discard of Heathcliff for the milder, blander Mr. Linton.

At least, I think that's what they acted out. All I could focus on were the rough and tender movements of their bodies. The way Lucius snatched Faith's wrist, yanking her to his chest. The way Faith's eyes snapped as she tore herself away. The passion almost looked . . . real.

My plastic pen really did crack under the pressure of my fingers, ink staining my hand and spattering my cheek. *No, Lucius. No.*

No one even noticed. The whole class was spellbound as Faith, blue eyes locked with Lucius's black ones, whispered, voice hot with what I desperately feared was *not* feigned ardor, "Whatever our souls are made of, yours and mine are the same."

They stood there, frozen, face to face, until someone realized it was time to applaud. And applaud they did. Mindy knelt on her seat, jammed her fingers in her mouth and whistled, which I hadn't even known she could do.

As if awakened by that shrill alarm, Lucius and Faith broke character, smiled, clasped hands, and bowed deeply toward their audience. Somehow, Faith's boobs stayed in place, although the way Frank Dormand was craning his neck, I think he at least got a nice view down her dress.

I had to admit, it was the best book report I'd ever seen. Probably the best book report ever delivered at Woodrow Wilson High School.

I despised every moment of it.

Lucius was *my* betrothed. It should have been me up there. Something had been stolen from me. And not just a few seconds of glory in front of a classroom. I knew, at that moment, that I'd squandered my chance at a *lifetime* of glory at the side of the most compelling, infuriating, charismatic, terrifying man I'd ever met. A part of me knew that I should feel relieved. Shaking free of Lucius Vladescu was all I'd longed for, for months. And yet, all I felt was empty and defeated and desperate to figure out how to bring him back to me. Then I remembered the pact. Lucius would never dishonor the pact. *Would he?*

As the applause died, Faith bounced down the aisle to take her seat behind me, followed by Lucius, who didn't even acknowledge me as he walked past.

It struck me, then. Did I even want him if he was only bound to me by obligation? What sort of victory would that be?

I glanced around at Lucius, but he was leaning forward, whispering with Faith.

A heartless, cruel, bitter, evil love . . . Did Lucius really want that? Did he honestly want *Faith*? If so, had I ever really had a chance? Should I even consider *wanting* a chance?

Chapter 34

"I'VE GOT YOUR laundry," I called, kicking at the door to Lucius's apartment.

He swung open the door. "Why, thank you, Jessica." He accepted the heaping basket of jumbled clothes from my arms with a frown. "What is *this*?"

"Mom said you can start folding your own clothes."

"But—"

"The free ride is over, Lucius," I advised him, following him into the apartment. I hadn't been inside since I'd tried to cook the disastrous Romanian dinner a week ago. The apartment still smelled a little bit like spleen.

Lucius dumped his clothes onto the bed and stepped back, surveying the tangled mess. "I suppose it's too late to hire a washerwoman . . ."

"Oh, for crying out loud. Don't be such a baby. I do this twice a week. And I don't think there are any 'washerwomen' around."

"That is *your* regional misfortune, not mine." He picked

up a sock, holding it out like it he'd never seen one before. "Where does one even *begin*?"

I snatched the sock from his fingers. "You say you can lead a vampire nation, but you can't match socks?"

"We are all skilled differently," Lucius pointed out, unable to suppress a grin. "Fortunately, my skills fall under the heading of leadership, not 'base chores.'"

I reluctantly smiled, too. *How can arrogance grow on a person?* "I'll help you—once."

"Thank you, Jessica." Lucius plopped into his deep leather chair.

"I said 'help,' not 'do it for you.'"

He made no effort to move. On the contrary, Lucius smirked, slid lower in the chair and laced his fingers behind his head. "I believe I would be best served by a demonstration."

"You jerk," I cried, tossing the sock back on the pile and grabbing his arm, tugging him upright. Of course, Lucius was far too strong for me, and when he pulled back, I ended up tumbling onto his chest, both of us laughing.

Gradually the laughter faded, and our eyes really connected for the first time since that awful night I'd tried to stew a hare. Suddenly, we weren't joking at all.

"Jessica," he said softly, circling my wrist with his fingers.

"Yes, Lucius?" I leaned more heavily against his chest, my heart starting to beat harder.

Maybe I hadn't been bested by Faith . . . His eyes had that same look I'd seen on Halloween, but without the anger and frustration. Instead, there was a gentler kind of desire there. A less fearsome, but almost as frightening, desire. Yet I didn't move from him. I knew, this time, that I didn't want to move. I could handle what happened. I *would* handle it.

Releasing my wrist, Lucius tugged gently on one of my shiny curls, letting it spring back into place. "You've changed your hair. Embraced your beautiful curls."

"Do you like it?"

"You know I do . . ." He twined another lock around his finger. "This . . . this is true to you."

I shifted slightly, and my hand rested on the hard curve of his bicep. He was wearing a T-shirt, and I could feel the jagged scar that ripped across his arm. My confidence wavered for a moment. *Honor. Discipline. Force. He was raised differently from you, Jessica. . . . The Vladescus are ruthless. . . .* "How . . . how did you get this?" I asked, tracing the scar with my fingertips.

Something changed in his eyes. The glimmer in the blackness dimmed slightly. "An accident. Not a story worth telling."

He was lying.

I kept tracing the scar. It was wide, and I couldn't imagine what could tear flesh like that . . . until I thought of the weapons on his wall. But who would do that to him? To anyone?

"You can tell me what happened," I urged. *I understand you. . . . Or I can try to. . . . Why are you drawing out this side of him, Jess? Why can't you leave well enough alone? Because I want to know about him. That's why.* I wanted to know the truth about Lucius. His stories. His past. What he wanted.

"Jessica." He groaned, encircling my waist. "If we could only not talk, right at this moment. If we could just *be.*"

No. Whatever happened . . . it had to be on my terms, too. I'd seen him with Faith. I wouldn't be a fool. I wouldn't fall for his

*charm, his experience . . . not if what he really wanted was some-
one different or something I couldn't provide. . . .*

I traced the other scar, on his jaw, and he caught my hand, pulling away slightly. "Jessica . . ."

"Do you really want that?" I whispered.

He kept hold of my hand, moving it to his mouth, brushing his rough lips across my palm. "Want what, Jessica?"

"What you said in class?"

He seemed uncertain. "In class . . . ?"

"A 'bitter, cruel, evil love'? Is that what you really want?"

When I said that, it was like I'd cut a cord that bound us, and Lucius, still holding my hand, sat upright, pulling me to my feet, gently but very firmly pushing me away. He stood, too.

"Lucius?"

He smiled at me then, grimly, like we hadn't just shared what we'd shared. "We loiter, wasting time, and the laundry waits on the bed," he said, the old, distancing mockery in his voice. He leaned over the mattress and grabbed a pair of his boxers. "At this rate, every wrinkle will be set. And a Vladescu may fold, under duress, but we do not iron."

"Lucius?" I touched his arm. I didn't want to know, but I *had* to know. "What, exactly is going on with you and Faith?"

Lucius shook out the underwear, studiously avoiding my eyes. "Faith?"

I sat down on the edge of the bed. "Yes. Faith."

"She intrigues me," he admitted, managing somehow to fold his own undergarments.

"Why? Why do you like her?"

As if I didn't know. Lucius Vladescu could talk all he wanted about the beauty of curves and curls and the importance of having a presence, but in the end, he was just like every other man—every *boy*—who fell for the blond, size 0 cheerleader with the flat abs, the perky little breasts, and the skinny butt that played peekaboo from under that stupid short skirt.

"Oh, Jessica," Lucius said, sounding somewhat exasperated. "I've asked you for months how you can favor a peasant, and you've never provided me a satisfactory response. Perhaps these things just can't be easily explained away."

"So you do *like* Faith?"

He looked at me then. "I *appreciate* her."

The flat-out admission made me queasy, even though I'd already known the answer. "Is there a difference?"

Lucius sighed and sat down next to me on the bed, staring at the wall. "Perhaps, Jessica. Does it really matter at this point?"

"What does that mean? Why do you keep saying things like 'at this point'? Like the pact is over? And what about the war?"

"You don't even believe in the pact or the war."

"I do now," I insisted.

Lucius ignored this revelation, even though I'd thought it was all he'd ever wanted to hear from me. A small smile crossed his face. "This upcoming Christmas dance. It's a much anticipated social event, is it not?" he mused. "Girls want to go, correct? Squatty will don his best 'overalls' and take you, yes?"

"About Jake . . ." *What am I going to do about Jake?* Ever since that day in the gym when I'd confided my doubts about our relationship to Mindy, I'd been distancing myself from him. And when I'd turned too eagerly away from Jake to watch Lucius perform his drama in English lit, I'd known I was turning my back on a great guy . . . a guy who genuinely liked me. Someone sweet who didn't drink blood or bear dangerous scars. And yet I'd done it. "I don't know if Jake and I are going to the formal," I said. "We're sort of . . . drifting apart."

Shrugging, Lucius stood and resumed folding laundry. "You two must do what makes you both happy, Jessica. Do what is right for you."

"And you'll do what's 'right for you,' I guess," I said glumly.

"This is America, as I am constantly reminded in social studies," Lucius pointed out. "We all have a choice in everything here." He mimicked a scale with his hands. "Pepsi or Coke? Big Mac or Whopper? The old boyfriend or the new?"

"Yeah, what about Ethan?" I asked. "He and Faith have been together forever."

"I just told you, Jessica. We all have a choice. Faith has a choice. Ethan has no claim on her. I've seen no ring on her finger."

Of course Faith had a choice. And she'd already chosen Lucius. I'd seen it back in the gym and in English lit class. Hell, I'd seen it back at the 4-H competition, when she'd absently gripped my arm, watching Lucius tear up the course on his doomed mare. I just hadn't wanted to admit it to myself. The whole thing had unfolded before my face, and I'd forced myself to be blind.

Lucius smiled at me then, although there was something like sadness in his eyes. "You are fortunate, Jessica," he said. "You are not bound so tightly by tradition, by the weight of the past. You are free here. Not only to choose a soft drink but your destiny. Rather exhilarating feeling, isn't it?"

I guess I'd lived so long with my possibilities that I didn't find them quite as "exhilarating" as Lucius did. In fact, I really wished, at that moment, to be bound a bit more tightly by the past. Yet, at the same time, a sudden anger lurched through me. Anger at Lucius.

"If you're so into Faith, then what the hell was that?" I pointed to the leather chair, where we'd just been tangled up together like the laundry on the bed. Where I'd sworn Lucius was about to kiss me—at the very least. "Back in the chair? When you had your arm around me?" I demanded. "What was that, Lucius?"

Lucius lowered the T-shirt he'd been folding, arms dropping to his sides. "That, Jessica," he said sadly, "was very nearly a mistake."

A mistake? Had he really just said, *"A mistake"*?

Rising to my full five foot four inches, and mustering a strength that I never knew I possessed, fueled by an indignation I hadn't known I was capable of, I drew back my open hand and slapped Lucius Vladescu so hard across the face that his head snapped sideways.

He was still rubbing his jaw when I slammed the door.

Stupid Romanian bloodsucker. He was lucky I hadn't bestowed another exalted scar on his imperial body. If he ever messed with Jessica Packwood—Antanasia Dragomir—again, he'd *really* get the royal treatment. Lucius Vladescu could take *that* to the Bucharest Federal Savings and Loan and bank it—right into his damned trust fund.

Chapter 35

"FOCUS, JESS, FOCUS," I urged myself.

But the more I tried to force myself to concentrate, the further concentration slipped away from me. It was like I was grasping at soap bubbles floating on air. Bubbles filled with meaningless numbers and mathematical ciphers. Plus signs, minuses, square root symbols swirling around my head. They all popped the second I grasped them. Popped and disappeared.

Somehow, in spite of skipping several practices, I'd made it to the countdown round of the Lebanon Regional Math Olympics, where the top students competed. No pens. No paper. Not even a chance to reread the questions. Just the moderator firing off oral problems and ten of us standing there trying to answer first.

I wanted to win so badly. This was one arena where *I* could shine. You didn't have to be beautiful, or blond, or rich, like Faith. . . .

Stop it, Jess. You can get to the state level if you get your head on straight.

Glancing at the modest crowd lined against the cafeteria walls, I saw Mr. Jaegerman sweating in today's polyester suit selection—a hideous taupe number—watching me. He smiled and offered a thumbs-up. Mike Danneker was sidelined, too, having been knocked out during the sprint round, when he got inexplicably panicked by some routine polynomials.

Mike cupped his hands around his mouth. "Don't blow it," he stage-whispered. Like that was helping.

The moderator finished shuffling her papers. "Question number two. A distracted bank teller transposed the dollars and cents when she cashed Mrs. Jones's paycheck, handing her dollars instead of cents, and cents instead of dollars. After buying a cup of coffee for fifty cents, Mrs. Jones realizes that she has exactly three times as much as the original check left. What was the true amount of the check?"

I could do this. A Diophantine equation. That's what it was. So why wouldn't my brain function?

I thought harder and harder, and the harder I thought, the more the whole language of equations seemed foreign to me. It was as if a part of my mind was just shutting off. Dying. It had started weeks ago, when I'd begun drifting away from Jake and toward Lucius. Away from regular humanity and toward a world where blood smelled delicious. Calculus had begun to make my mind wander. Algebra had slowly lost its appeal. And now I was standing in a room full of top mathletes, where I should have been a dominant force, and instead all I could think was *Dollars? Cents? Coffee sounds good. . . . Where can you get a cup of coffee for fifty cents?* But I didn't want coffee. I wanted to go to the state level. *Think, Jessica. . . .* But no thoughts came. Not the right kind, at least. *Would coffee really help?*

"No!" I hollered, not even realizing I'd said the word out loud until the already quiet room went completely silent, and all heads swiveled toward me.

I started sweating like Mr. Jaegerman on a June day getting excited about a word problem involving a high wall and the angle of the sun. Humiliated. I'd been humiliated.

"Sorry," I said, addressing everyone and no one in particular. They were all still staring—my competitors, my teammates, the spectators—and so I left my designated spot on the cafeteria floor and walked, with what I hoped was a little dignity, toward the door.

Out in the hallway, I leaned against the cool, tiled wall. What was happening to the left side of my brain? The part meant to control analysis and objectivity felt numb. And tingly. Like it was being chewed away by the right side, the random, intuitive, non-logical side. I pressed my fingertips against my temples, massaging them, trying to ease an ache that I knew wasn't really physical.

"Jessica, are you okay?" Mr. Jaegerman burst through the door and jogged to my side, puffing a little, dabbing at his forehead with a handkerchief. I knew what he was thinking. His prize racehorse had just broken a leg in the last furlong. He'd invested four years in me, and I had come up lame.

"Math just seems . . . hard lately," I tried to explain, staring at Mr. Jaegerman with no small degree of desperation. "I don't know what's happening. I can't concentrate."

"Are . . . are things okay at home?" Mr. Jaegerman attempted to ask. The effort to forge a real human connection between us—one not bridged by numbers—made the sweat pool above his upper lip and cascade around the corners of his mouth. He used his tie to dab his chin. "Not . . . boy trouble?" he ventured gamely, sputtering. He seemed on the verge of some sort of spasm. Like he'd wandered too far into a deep cave only to realize that there was no oxygen there.

If I'd actually started to unload, he might have passed out right there in the hall. I had to save him, let him breathe.

"No, it's not a guy," I lied, sparing Mr. Jaegerman a heart attack.

"Oh, thank God," he cried, clutching his chest. He immediately realized what he'd said. "I mean . . . of course, if it was a boy, you could tell me . . ."

"It's fine," I insisted. "It's nothing like that."

But it *was* something "like that." Actually, it was that exactly. Only Lucius wasn't a boy, really. He was a man. And I wanted him back. Too late, I wanted him back. But I knew it was hopeless. He wanted Faith.

"I'll do better next time, Mr. Jaegerman," I promised. "I'll hit the books tomorrow. Focus."

"Good girl, Jess," Mr. Jaegerman said. He reached out to pat my shoulder, hesitated, then withdrew his hand.

"Let's go back inside," I said gamely. "I can at least listen from the sidelines, try to solve the problems for fun."

"Yes, yes," Mr. Jaegerman agreed, clearly relieved that our too-personal moment was over. "That's an excellent idea."

I followed my coach back toward the cafeteria. But to be honest, solving problems didn't sound fun or excellent at all. It sounded like the most miserable activity I could imagine.

Chapter 36

DEAR VASILE,

Were you aware that here in the United States, "choices" are so abundant that some feckless, feeble-minded individuals actu-

ally find themselves overwhelmed and in need of psychological counseling (I know—we laugh!), all because they are unable to navigate the seemingly infinite options inherent in literally every small act?

Here, even ordering a pizza (at last, I stumbled upon something edible) requires multiple decisions. Large? Extra large? Miniature meatballs and pepperoni? Some sort of vegetable? More cheese? Less cheese? Cheese concealed, like a stringy surprise, within the crust? And speaking of crust . . . Thick? Thin? Hand-tossed? Or should one reconsider the entire order and opt for "Chicago-style deep dish"? Or "Sicilian," even?

Really, Vasile, calling for "delivery" (I have also finally discovered that I command a virtual army of erstwhile servants, all patrolling about in battered "Ford Escorts") requires as much strategizing as some generals devote to a battle in which actual blood, not just tomato sauce, will be spilled.

Speaking of which, I was sorry to learn that the Dragomirs grow weary of waiting for the return of their princess and the completion of the pact.

They always are an impulsive, impatient lot, are they not? But really, to accuse me of not "doing my best" to fulfill my obligation—and then attempting to stake a Vladescu in a fit of ire . . . That sort of thing can precipitate a nasty skirmish, Vasile. And I find the whole prospect, suddenly, so tiresome.

Must we vampires always resort so quickly to violence? Could we not all sit down over a "refreshing Bud Light" and "just chill," as my television and my teammates relentlessly urge me to do? (You would be amazed to see the effort that American teenagers put into securing any quantity of beer, which is verboten until age twenty-one. It's astonishing, really, Vasile, all for a bit of fermented hops. One would think it was blood.)

But returning to the minor flare-up of tensions between the Dragomirs and Vladescus. Please advise both sides to remain patient, reminding them that we are vampires. What is the hurry when we have eternity?

And while we are on the subject of impetuous Dragomirs and violence . . . Our princess-in-waiting dealt me quite an impressive blow across the side of the face the other day. You, of all vampires, know how difficult it is to make my head snap sideways with an open hand. I must say, I rather admired the force behind the slap. Very authoritative. And the way her eyes flashed, very regal.

As for the cause of my humbling at the palm of Antanasia's hand . . . Perhaps that is best reserved for another missive.

In the meantime, might I impose upon you to ship, posthaste, some of my formal wear? Say, perhaps, the Brioni "tux" I secured in Milan. And dispatch a discreet set of cuff links, too. I trust your judgment. Keep in mind that most of my fellow partygoers will be attired in "rental" tuxedos. (Were you even aware that one could rent clothes, Vasile? Does it not seem a bit . . . cringe inducing? Slipping into trousers worn by a succession of predecessors of dubious pedigree and uncertain hygiene? But it is true.) My point is, I desire, of course, to present myself in a manner befitting my station—without unduly upstaging others. Deliberate sartorial one-upsmanship is just crass, don't you think?

Thank you in advance for your assistance,
Your nephew,
Lucius

P.S. What the hell. Why not sign off with the traditional American greeting? "Merry Christmas," Uncle Vasile. "Happy holidays to you."

P.P.S. Really—"counseling"!

Chapter 37

"JESSICA, THE PHONE is for you," Dad said, poking his head into my room. "It's Jake."

"I didn't even hear it ring," I admitted, sitting up and accepting the cordless from his hand. I'd been lying in bed, staring at the ceiling, thinking as usual about faithless vampires and the fact that my brain seemed to be disintegrating, and wishing that my life was just normal again. "Hey, Jake," I said into the receiver with less enthusiasm than I knew I should have. "What's up?"

I should break up with Jake. I knew it, and yet I hadn't done it. *Why? What am I waiting for?*

"Hey, Jess," Jake said. "I was just calling . . . well, I was wondering if we're still on for the Christmas formal. I haven't seen much of you at school . . ."

"Yeah, I guess I've been busy," I said. "I've been thinking we should get together and talk, though . . ."

Outside, I heard the sound of a loud squeal, then laughter. I pulled aside the curtain. Lucius and Faith were in the yard, having a very vigorous snow fight. As I watched, Lucius swept up Faith and plunged her into a pile left by our plow, rubbing snow onto her pink wool hat. "Oh, Lucius," she screamed, kicking at him. "You are such a jerk!"

Yes, Lucius . . . yes, you are.

"Jess—are you there?"

"Oh, sorry, Jake." I let the curtain drop. "I'm here."

"I was asking about the formal, because I have to rent a tux . . ."

Outside, more delighted, horrified squeals.

Jake added, a little uncertainly, "I really hope you still want to go, Jess."

What a nice guy. A nice, nice guy . . .

Beneath my window, Faith shrieked, "Don't touch me!" It sounded as though she wanted quite the opposite.

I clutched the phone, forcing myself to pay attention to Jake. Was I *really* sure I wanted to break up with him? Was I going to stop living just because I'd been thrown over by an overbearing foreign exchange student who'd tried to seduce me in his apartment only to admit that it would have been a "mistake"? Was I going to waste my entire senior year lying in bed, worrying about being a vampire, for god's sake?

No, I would not.

"Of course I want to go, Jake," I said, forcing my voice to sound far more cheerful than I felt. "I'm looking forward to it."

Relief flooded his voice. "Great, Jess. I'm going to get my tux tomorrow, then. If you're sure . . ."

Will Faith Crosse never stop shrieking in my yard?

"Of course I'm sure, Jake," I said, adding just before we hung up, "It's going to be great."

I stretched back out on my bed, pulling my pillow over my face, covering my ears to shut out how much fun my former blood-pact betrothed and Faith were having outside.

As I lay there hating them both, my teeth began to ache. At

first, it was just a small, dull pain, but every time the sound of Faith and Lucius's mock battle carried to my ears, the hurt grew sharper, until it was almost like my teeth were too tightly wedged in my mouth, straining against my gums, and I wanted to claw at them, to pull them out, to find some way, the key, that would release them to become what they so desperately wanted to become.

Rolling off my bed, I rooted in my dresser, searching for my vampire manual, running my finger down the table of contents. There it was: Chapter 9, "Finding Your Way to Fangs!"

I flipped to the proper page.

"Girls will begin to feel their incisors ache as they approach age eighteen, although some 'early bloomers' may notice changes as young as age sixteen! The sensation often, although not exclusively, occurs during times of emotional stress, not unlike your initial thirst for blood. Try to be patient and accept the 'dental discomfort' as part of vampiric maturation, just as you learn to accept menstrual cramps as part of your concurrent growth into womanhood. Remember, when you are first bitten, your fangs will be released to expand and blossom, and you will soon forget the temporary twinges that carried you into full vampiredom!"

My fangs could be released by a bite from a vampire. Of course. Lucius had told me about that during our shopping trip. Women couldn't grow fangs until they were bitten. I stashed my guide away.

The good news was, I had a vampire handy in my backyard. The bad news was, I wanted to run a stake through his heart before he had any chance to come near me—not to mention the fact that he didn't seem to give a damn about me anymore. What was a "blossoming" young vampire to do?

Chapter 38

"YOU ARE SO LUCKY that at least one of us reads *Cosmo* and *Vogue*," Mindy chided me, clomping into my room burdened by at least ten shoe boxes. The pile was so high she couldn't even see around it. "Mindy and her shoe collection to the rescue!"

My best friend dropped the boxes to the floor in a tumbling pile, and her eyes grew wide when she saw me. *"Holy shit, Jessica!"*

"Is that . . . good?"

Mindy ran over, grabbed my bare arms, and spun me around, looking me up and down. "You look . . . you look gorgeous."

"Okay," I calmed her down, prying off her fingers one by one. "Take it easy, because this dress cost me practically every penny I earned at the diner over the course of the whole summer."

"It was worth every cent," Mindy said, nodding. "Every freakin' cent."

I glanced in the mirror that hung on the back of my bedroom door. "It is beautiful, isn't it?"

"You are beautiful," Mindy corrected. "The dress just lets the rest of us know. Where did you get it? Because that is *not* some polyester job from the mall."

"I went back to that snooty store where I got my dress for Halloween," I said. This time, it had been up to me to boss Leigh Ann around. But I had learned a lot from Lucius. Who knew, just a few months ago, how much could be accomplished simply by holding your chin high and talking down your nose?

"This is, like, real velvet," Mindy said, rubbing the fabric with awe in her voice.

"Yes, the top—the bodice, as Lucius would say—is velvet, and the skirt is hand-loomed Japanese silk." I smoothed my hands over the pure black dress. It was as dark and soft as an August night sky just before a storm. Strapless, the dress was cut straight and hugged my size ten body like the world's best, custom-fitted glove. Not too tight, but just close enough to show off every arc and hollow of my form. Looking in the mirror, I was glad I wasn't too skinny. This wasn't a dress made for a boyish figure.

"I have the perfect shoes," Mindy squealed, digging amid her boxes. She held up a pair of strappy heels, very subdued for Mindy, but just right for the dress. "These will go great."

"Are you sure it's okay if I borrow them . . . ?"

"Yeah," Mindy said, with only the slightest hint of regret or jealousy in her voice. "It's not like I go anywhere. They might as well get some use."

Taking the shoes, I hugged her. "Thanks, Min. You're the best."

"Oh, don't get all sappy," she said. "We still have to do your hair, and it's almost seven o'clock."

"Do you think you could help me with, like, an updo?" I requested. "I want it to be perfect. Even better than at Halloween."

"Do I not read *Cosmo*, *Vogue*, and *Celebrity Hairstyle*?" Mindy pointed out, reaching for my hairbrush. "You're in good hands, Jessica Packwood."

I hesitated, then reached for the photograph of my birth mother, which I had moved to a small silver frame that I kept on my desk. "Do you think you could make me look a little like . . . her?"

I handed Mindy the picture, and she gawked at it, jaw actually dropping. "Jess . . . this is . . . this has to be . . ." She glanced up at me, clearly astonished. "Was she like a *princess* or something?"

"It's a long story," I said, taking the photo back. I gazed at Mihaela Dragomir. "But she was special. Yes."

"What the hell aren't you telling me here?" Mindy demanded, curious and a little wary. "Something's going on."

"It's just a memento I was given," I explained vaguely, setting the photo on my desk. "Something I couldn't face before . . ."

"Jess, she looks exactly like you. It's almost eerie."

I flushed with pleasure. *Is she not beautiful . . . powerful . . . regal . . . like YOU?* "Thanks, Mindy, but can we talk about it later? Right now, I'm just desperate for help with my hair."

At the mention of hair, Mindy snapped back to the present and scooped up a big handful of my glossy curls. "I am all over it, Jessica. When I'm done with you, every girl at Woodrow Wilson is going to wish she was you."

About fifteen minutes and a complete pump bottle of hairspray later, Mindy held up a mirror. My curls were artfully, but chaotically, arranged on my head, like a glorious, lustrous crown, and she'd taken a thick handful and twisted it around the updo, not unlike the silver coronet in the photo of my birth mother. Mindy had done very well. "I will never laugh about *Celebrity Hairstyles* again," I promised.

Downstairs the doorbell rang.

"Jess?" Mindy asked, giving me one last spritz.

"What?" I was still admiring myself in the mirror.

"Is all this for Jake . . . or does this have something to do with the fact that Lucius is taking Faith? I know you always say you don't like him. But it still sucks sometimes when somebody who's been into you has a change of heart . . ."

"It's all for me," I interrupted her, squaring my shoulders. The dress, the hair, the shoes . . . they were all about me taking pride in myself. Believing that I was beautiful. Believing that I was worthwhile.

Forget Lucius and Faith Crosse. I intended to have a *presence.*

"Well, knock 'em dead," Mindy said, giving me a careful hug, so as not to muss my hair. "You look amazing."

I caught my reflection one last time as I went down to greet Jake. *Amazing.* That was one word for my transformation. I would have added, perhaps, *royal,* too.

In spite of being more than a little sad, and more than a little hurt, and completely confused by the state of my life, the young woman in the mirror managed a smile.

Chapter 39

"YOU LOOK REALLY pretty, Jess," Jake said, handing me some punch.

"You look nice, too, Jake." *Nice.*

"It's too bad you've been so swamped lately," he added. "I've kind of missed hanging out with you."

"You know, senior year." I shrugged, sipping my punch.

"I hear ya," Jake agreed. "It's totally busting my butt."

I flinched a little at the crude expression. It seemed like something a . . . a . . . peasant might say.

"I mean, if I don't get a wrestling scholarship, I'll be stuck at community college for two years," he continued. "That's gonna suck. I guess your applications are all out there already."

"I have to go to Grantley," I said. "You know, where my mom teaches. I go for free."

"Cool. Free."

I sipped my punch again, wishing Jake and I had more in common. Maybe it had been a mistake to come with him. Maybe I should have just stayed home. . . .

"Whoa." Jake's eyes widened, and he pointed over my shoulder. "Check that out."

"What?" I turned, and my heart seized up for a second.

Lucius had arrived with Faith's hand tucked in the crook of his arm. She was shimmering in a silver gown, with thin straps that slithered down her shoulders and gloves that snaked up to her elbows, her fair hair seized within a sparkling tiara, like some sort of ice princess. A harshly glittering snow queen.

And Lucius . . . Lucius was her dark counterpart in a perfectly fitting tuxedo. Even from across the gym it was easy to see that his suit was no rental like Jake's. Lucius's tuxedo was expertly custom-tailored for his tall, lean body, the pants cut perfectly to break at the top of shoes as impeccably polished as his manners.

I glanced at Jake. His tux was appropriate. Conservative black. Nothing obnoxious or embarrassing. But it strained across his bulging shoulders, and his bow tie was just the slightest bit askew.

It was completely unfair to compare the two—I mean, Jake couldn't afford a custom tux—but compare them I did. My blood-pact partner had never looked so good. And Faith glistened like a tall, cool icicle dripping from his arm. She leaned close, pulling Lucius down, whispering in his ear. He laughed, flashing teeth as pure white as his crisp shirt.

"Ethan is not going to like this," Jake muttered, grinning.

Glancing around the dark gym, I easily located Ethan Strausser, with his pudgy goon partner Frank Dormand at his side. Ethan was shooting daggers at Lucius and Faith, his chest actually heaving with rage. He clenched his paper cup, and punch shot out onto his shirt, which only angered him more. He brushed at the stain, and I could see his lips forming a stream of curses.

"Oh yeah, he's pissed," Jake noted. "Luc better watch himself in the parking lot. I heard Ethan wants to annihilate him. Go nuclear on his ass for going after Faith."

I looked back to Lucius. He was leading Faith onto the dance floor, and she sort of tumbled into his arms, her gloved hands creeping up his chest, circling his neck. He slipped his hand onto the small of her back, resting it in the curve of her spine.

I'd seen enough. "Come on," I said, grabbing Jake's hand. "Let's dance."

"Sure, if you're not afraid of me stepping on your shoes," Jake joked. "I'm not too good."

"It's okay, Jake," I assured him, suddenly feeling a tender

spot in my heart for the guy who led me across the gym, my hand clutched in his stubby, work-calloused fingers. Of course Jake couldn't dance, and he didn't own a tux, or know how to pay a suave compliment. He was a farm kid, not Romanian royalty. I slipped into his arms, and we made slow circles under the twinkle lights.

"This feels nice," Jake said, holding me close.

"Yes," I agreed, trying to focus on that feeling of tenderness. *He's nice, Jess. Try to feel something. Try to just enjoy being with a nice, normal guy. . . . Try to forget Lucius and vampires and pacts. . . .*

Jake leaned his forehead against mine. We were nearly the same height. "Jess . . ." He pulled me closer. "It's been a while since I've kissed you."

"Yes, it has been," I agreed, not sure what else I could say. *Just try, Jess. . . .*

Jake nuzzled closer. His lips were just about to meet mine, when he was yanked away. "Hey, what the . . . ?"

"May I cut in?"

Lucius was looming over us, smiling, but not in a happy way.

Jake twined his arm back around my waist. "Luc, we're kind of dancing here."

"And I'm cutting in. That's how dancing works where I come from."

"We're not in . . . wherever you come from," Jake said.

"Lucius!" I hissed through gritted teeth, glaring at him. *No.* He had no right.

Lucius put a hand on Jake's shoulder. "My apologies, if I

misunderstood your customs. But please, indulge me. I will not keep her from you long."

Jake looked to me, uncertain.

"Just give us a second, Jake," I said, looking daggers at Lucius. "I'll handle it."

Jake shot Lucius a dark look, too. "Just one dance." Then he stomped off through the crowd, clearly not pleased.

"What do you want?" I demanded. "We were just about—"

"Yes, I saw what you were 'just about.'"

"That's none of your business."

The song ended, and I crossed my arms over my chest, as though shielding myself against him. Because even when I hated Lucius, I felt vulnerable to him. "The song is over, Lucius. Go back to Faith."

"There will be a new song," he said. "That is how these events work, yes?"

And, of course, another song started.

"Shall we?" Lucius asked, slipping his arm around my waist, drawing me to himself.

"You won't stop until you get your way, will you?"

"No."

"Just one song, then," I grumbled, allowing myself to be pulled into his arms, hating the traitorous flutter in my stomach.

"Do you dance, Jessica?" he asked, smiling down at me. "Waltz? Quadrille?"

"You know I don't."

"Ah, but with your grace, you should. I could have . . ." Lucius seemed to catch himself, and trailed off. "For now, like this," he instructed, guiding my left hand to his shoulder and taking my right hand into his own, holding it close to his chest. His palm felt cool against the small of my back. That familiar coolness. Part of who he was. *No, Jess . . . don't buy into it. . . . He's with Faith. . . . You're just a potential "mistake."*

"Just follow my lead," Lucius advised. "I shall guide you. Just trust me."

Yeah. Trust you. . . . Yet I allowed myself to be led, my body echoing his.

"Yes, Jessica," Lucius said, looking down at me with admiration in his eyes. "You are a natural, as I would expect."

As soon as he said that, I stumbled against him, stepping on those impeccable shoes.

"Sorry," I apologized as he steadied me, drawing me even closer.

"It's all right," Lucius said. I realized that we had slowed, almost imperceptibly, but enough to put us out of synch with the music, moving to our own quieter rhythm. "Everyone stumbles now and then," he added. "As you well know." He guided my hand to his cheek, placing my fingertips against the place I'd smacked. "I still sting here when I shave. But it was deserved."

"If you're trying to apologize . . ."

"I'm trying to compliment you," he said. "It is the rare individual who can strike *me* and walk away unscathed."

The song was a long one, and we swayed together, still slightly out of time, but my heart had begun beating its own quick rhythm, the longer we held each other. God, I didn't want to feel this way. I wanted to hate Lucius with even greater fervor for thrusting himself into my date, interrupting my attempt at a *nice* evening. I tried to keep Faith in mind. *Faith, Faith, Faith. Jake, Jake, Jake. Mistake, mistake, mistake.*

Lucius placed his fingers under my chin, tilting my head so he could see my eyes again. "I had no right to barge in like that . . . but I suppose old habits die hard."

For some reason, when he said that, I wanted to cry. I wanted the song to end right then, or maybe go on forever. And I wanted to cry.

"You just look so beautiful tonight," he continued. "When I saw you in that gown . . . God, Jessica. I thought you were gorgeous before—and yet you outdo yourself this evening." His fingertips stroked the back of my gown, feeling the rich fabric. "Black velvet and silk are perfect upon you. You are like a living Chopin nocturne. A soft, yet stirring harmony meant to be enjoyed at night . . ."

"Don't, Lucius . . ."

"I just couldn't allow that *boy*—"

"You're with Faith," I reminded him, a bit sharply. "Not me."

A fleeting pain flashed in his eyes, almost as if I'd slapped him again. "Yes, of course. Of course you are right. I won't interfere again, Antanasia. I promise."

My fingers tightened on his shoulder at the sound of my old name. The name I'd noticed he'd *stopped* using. "You called me by my name. My old name."

Lucius squeezed my hand, pressing his thumb against my palm. "Old habits. Old names. Old souls."

"Is that what we are?" I searched his dark eyes. *We had a connection. . . . Dark mountains, blood pacts . . . He couldn't deny it. . . .*

But he did. "These are new times."

Still, Lucius let go of my hand in order to embrace me more completely, draw me even closer, until I almost felt like I was a part of him, hardly dancing anymore, just standing together in the middle of the room.

"How you do vex me," he finally whispered, bending close to my ear. "How you do test my resolve."

And before I could even question what he meant—*me*, the vexing one?—he rested his forehead against mine, as Jake had just done. Only Lucius didn't move his mouth toward mine. He simply drew his lips gently across my cheek, down along my jaw . . . down to my throat.

A ferociously wonderful and terrifying sensation shuddered through me, and in the split second his lips crossed my jugular the whole gym disappeared. We were alone, I swore, in a candlelit stone room, our bare feet on a thick Persian rug, a fireplace blazing at my back. I'd been there; I knew it.

Lucius opened his mouth slightly, and I felt the faintest touch of his fangs caressing my skin, just above the spot where my blood pulsed strongest.

His fangs . . .

I didn't care if it was irrational. I didn't care if it was impossible. I just wanted to *feel* them. I needed them, like I'd never needed anything in my life. In my own mouth, my own teeth began to ache. That delicious, delirious agony of something struggling so hard to be born.

"Lucius . . . please . . ." I bent my head back, exposing my throat to him, longing to wrap my hands around the back of his neck, shove my fingers up into his long, dark hair, and pull those fangs deep into my veins. The longing was so intense that it was pain, too. Pain and pleasure intermingled in the most inconceivably marvelous way possible . . .

"Oh, Antanasia," he whispered, voice rough in my ear, moving against me, testing my flesh with those razor-sharp incisors. . . .

Now . . . now . . . please make it now. . . .

"Excuse me! Hello!"

The image shattered. My eyes popped open, and I was back in the Woodrow Wilson gym, under the red and green streamers, bombarded by too many twinkle lights. We stepped apart abruptly, and Lucius raked his hand through his black hair, licking his lips, his fangs gone. He seemed genuinely shaken.

"Have you forgotten me completely, silly?" Faith Crosse was standing next to us, hands on hips, shaking her head. "If I didn't know better, I'd swear you were getting a little too close to your housemate here." Her tone was light, but she jabbed a finger at me, and there was anger and disbelief in her eyes. Her expression said, very clearly, "There is no way that you abandoned me for *that*."

"Lucius and I were just dancing," I said, voice even, immediately regaining control of myself. I would not panic. I would not be flustered. And I would not act like she was *superior* to me, or deserved Lucius more. I turned away from Faith. "I have to find Jake," I told Lucius.

"Wait," Lucius insisted, reaching for me. But Faith intervened, grabbing his hand.

"I'm sure Jenn wants to get back to her date. And I'm positive you do, too."

"Jess—"

A scene was brewing. Other couples were starting to stare.

"Thank you for the dance." I smiled, backing away. "He's all yours, Faith."

"Oh, I know that," she said, her own smile as glitteringly frosty as her dress. She swung into Lucius's arms. But he was looking at me. I think there was pity in his eyes. Or apology. Maybe he really just couldn't help himself. Maybe he really was like every teenage boy. Any throat would do in a pinch. Once again, I'd nearly been used—a mistake—just like that day in his apartment. Why was I so powerless to see through him? What hold did he have over me that I fell for him again and again and again?

God, he almost bit my throat. . . .

I met his eyes for a good long time across the dance floor, then I slowly turned my back on Lucius Vladescu and walked, head high and shoulders back, directly through the crowd. People stepped aside, making way for me. I refused to look back. But I hoped he was watching me. Watching me and realizing that he had made a terrible mistake, abandoning me for Faith Crosse.

Pity me? I don't think so. I pity you, Lucius.

Jake, of course, was nowhere to be found. I wasn't surprised. I'd completely humiliated us both. Anyone who had paid any attention must have thought Lucius and I were way too close. We were probably just lucky no one had seen his fangs.

I ended up calling my mom for a ride and sat in silence the whole way home, hating vampires. Meddling, heartbreaking, hormone-raging, throat-biting vampires.

Chapter 40

VASILE—

Is this how you planned it all along?

But of course it is.

I was such a fool not to see the scheme in its entirety. Or—I must be honest with myself—perhaps I did know the truth. I just wanted the power so badly, too. . . .

This evening, however, as I placed my fangs against Antanasia's throat, the whole future became so clear to me. The scent of her blood was like a truth serum injected into my veins, a cracked mirror into my own hellish self.

You knew all along that an American girl not raised as a vampire would be easily destroyed should she take the throne. The letter I wrote warning you that Jessica was not ready, that she would be vulnerable to attack from power-hungry females . . . those were not revelations to you. You have always prized her weakness. You counted upon it. Oh, god, Vasile, did we count upon it?

I would have married her, thus completing the pact, brought her into our world in Romania, where she would have been almost utterly defenseless, and then abandoned her to her dark destiny. When? How long would it have taken? A year? Less? But by then, the clans would have been legitimately united, and all the power in our hands. In your hands.

Would you have forced fate, Vasile? Would you have taken her down yourself? Secretly, of course, by the gloved hand of one of your minions . . . or would you have tried to force my hand?

With Antanasia hidden high in our castle, who better to attend to her "unfortunate" destruction than the man who shared her bed?

Was that the cruelest thrust, Vasile? To make me feel as I do—and then rip her away? Was that to be your greatest attempt at hardening me? Even for you, that seems too vicious. Too vile. Or perhaps, even after all these years, I underestimate you—which is always a dangerous mistake.

And if I had not done as you directed me—if I had not destroyed her—would you have dispatched me, too, on the grounds of insubordination? Eliminated the inconvenient heir? Who among the Vladescu Elders—and I assume they all know of and applaud your intentions regarding Jessica—who would have blamed you?

Damn. The power you would have wielded then: absolute control over the two greatest vampire clans, with no successor nipping at your heels.

Did you know all along that I would grow to feel so deeply for her?

Is it not appropriately cruel, Vasile, that now to have her, I must not have her?

Set us both free, Vasile. Release Antanasia from me, and release me, as well, if only for a short time. Just a few months. That is all I ask. Just let me be. I want not to think about pacts and power and all that I, like you, am capable of. . . .

Because the most sickeningly thrilling part is, I grudgingly admire your strategy. It gives me a twisted pleasure to see the plan in its entirety. To know that in your place I no doubt would have done the same thing: sacrificed an inconsequential American teenager without second thought, in the interest of lording over so many damn vampire legions. I can almost feel the power in my hands.

But of course, I am who I am: the product of your hand.

Thus I remain, as ever,

Yours,

Always, irrevocably, and irredeemably,

Lucius

P.S. Antanasia may have surprised all of us, Vasile. She really may have. She may have gone down with a hell of a fight. But I will not be the instrument of her inevitable destruction.

P.P.S. In case you have not inferred my meaning from all that I've written above, let me be perfectly clear: I choose to defy the pact.

Choice, Vasile . . . is it not a wondrous thing? No wonder the Americans prize it so.

Chapter 41

"JESSICA?"

My eyes popped open. I was in my room, lying in bed in the dark, but someone was there. I jolted straight up, fumbling for the light.

Someone else switched it on. I started to scream, but a firm hand over my mouth stopped me, pushing me back down on my pillow.

"Don't scream, please," Lucius whispered as I wriggled beneath him. I lay still, and he removed his hand. "My apologies for frightening you, and the rough treatment. But I needed to speak with you."

For a moment I was almost thrilled to find him in my room. *He is here for me.* . . . Then all the events of the evening came rushing back.

Propping myself up again, I clutched my sheets around my chest. "What do you want?" I spat at him, glancing at the clock. "It's three A.M.!"

"I was unable to sleep after what happened this evening." He sat down on the edge of the bed, uninvited. He was still wearing his tux, but the tie and jacket were gone and the shirt was untucked and rumpled. "I can't rest until we talk."

Lifting the sheet, I glanced down at myself, not sure what I'd worn to sleep in. *Am I even decent?*

"Everything is covered," Lucius reassured me, the smallest smile on his lips. "Your sleep attire reveals nothing but your insistent love of Arabians."

"You are on such thin ice right now that I can't believe you even tried a joke," I said. "You are so out of line!"

Lucius's face fell. "Indeed. I made the jest only in hopes of pretending that our relationship had not changed as of this evening."

"You nearly bit me, Lucius. And then you ran off with Faith. I would definitely say things have changed."

"What I did tonight—what I almost did tonight—it was unforgivable," he agreed, clearly miserable. "Reprehensible. Not only to come so close to biting you, but in public, too. And with Faith—the woman I was accompanying, for god's sake—looking on, no less. I don't know what came over me. I don't even know how to begin to ask for your forgiveness."

Everything about that apology stung. Being close to me was "reprehensible"? It was "unforgivable"? He couldn't imagine "what came over him," finding himself attracted to a disgusting creature like me. Especially since it might have upset his precious priority, Faith Crosse.

Lucius sighed, correctly interpreting my silence. "You despise me even more than usual, don't you?"

"Yes."

"You left. I suppose Jake was upset."

"We'll all live."

My cold tone seemed to take him aback. "Yes. I suppose we will." He waited. "I thought you would have more to say."

"What do you want me to say, Lucius?" I intended to stonewall him, but suddenly it all came spilling out. "You show up on my doorstep, you hound me for months, and when you finally convince me that I'm special—when I finally felt something for you—you turn everything around on me and fall for the same cookie-cutter blond girl every guy likes. You're such a typical guy—"

"You really did, didn't you? Begin to feel something for me?" His voice was bittersweet. More bitter than sweet.

"Felt, Lucius. Felt. It was just for a moment," I said. My anger drained away, settling into a sullen sadness. "It seems like a bad dream now. A 'mistake,' to use your word. A terrible mistake."

Lucius rubbed tired eyes. "Oh, Jessica . . . Do not think you know the whole truth about anything I do or say," he said cryptically. "Sometimes . . . sometimes I do not even know myself. If I seem inconsistent, it is only me struggling with myself."

He leaned forward, wringing his hands. "Damn, I've made a mess of everything."

"Yeah. I guess so."

He looked at me with misery in his eyes. "You will never understand how it is to be seduced by the normal."

I nearly snorted. "You? Normal?"

"Yes, me. Normal."

"The last thing *you've* ever cared about is being *normal*."

"No, Jessica. That is not entirely true. Not lately." Lucius rose and began pacing my small room, talking softly, almost to himself. "You have no idea what it was like, being raised in solitude. Being raised for a purpose. Your parents, Jessica, they have no *agenda* for you. You are not their *tool*. You simply exist to be loved by them. Do you know how foreign that is to me?"

I watched him pace, not sure what to say. Not wanting to interrupt him.

He paused and smiled at me, a sad smile. "I came here and suddenly, there was a whole new world. Our classmates. They're allowed to be so . . . so frivolous."

"You hate frivolity."

"But frivolity is so easy." The smile faded. "I used to think American teenagers so ridiculously self-absorbed. But it's addictive, for lack of a better word. I find myself drawn to your world, if only for a brief time. It is like a fleeting holiday to be among you. The first holiday of my life. If one discounts the pressures inherent in fulfilling the pact, there are no expectations for me, beyond making a three-point shot just before the buzzer."

"Lucius, what are you trying to say?"

He sank back down on the bed. "I find that I am reluctant to give all of that up quite yet."

"Give all of what up?"

"The dances with the cheap crepe paper. The jeans. The basketball. Being with a young woman without the weight of generations upon my shoulders, watching . . ."

"Faith. You don't want to give up Faith."

He reared back. "For a girl who blocked my every attempt at courting, you are suddenly rather proprietary."

"You're the one who kept talking about how important it was for us to get *married*, for crying out loud."

Lucius raked his fingers through his ebony hair. "If I had bitten you tonight . . . there would have been no turning back. You know that, don't you? Eternity. Those are the stakes when we are together. Eternity. Are you ready for that? And Jessica, a partnership with me . . . that is something you should not desire. Eternity may come more quickly than you anticipated if you are joined to me."

"I don't understand."

He took my hand, lacing our fingers together. "And that, Jessica Packwood, is precisely why I have set you free."

"What?"

"I have dissolved the pact."

"For Faith," I repeated, pulling my hand away. I hated the jealousy that tore at me like a physical force. "You want to bite Faith. That's what this is all about."

Lucius shook his head. "No. I would not bite Faith. Although I am not sure if I am reluctant to foist vampiredom on Faith—or to unleash Faith upon vampiredom."

I didn't believe him. I knew he wanted Faith. "Lucius, under the pact, you have to bite *me*. We're pledged to each other. If you don't, you violate the treaty, and the war will start . . ."

"I'm trying to tell you, Jessica. The pact is no longer in effect."

There was a finality in his voice that frightened me, and my jealousy was replaced by an even sicker, stronger trepidation. "What exactly did you do, Lucius?"

"I have written to the Elders. I have advised them that I will not participate in this ridiculous game anymore."

"You what?" It came out almost as a shout. "You what?" I repeated more softly.

There was a flicker of fear, but also determination, in Lucius's eyes. "I have written to my uncle Vasile. I have called off the entire affair."

"I thought you couldn't do that."

"And yet I did it."

My trepidation intensified to dread, which prickled up the back of my neck. The last thing I'd ever expected to see on Lucius's face was fear, even the smallest hint, and I knew he was in deep, deep trouble. "What will happen?"

"I don't know," Lucius admitted. "But you will be safe. You must not worry. I am the one who made the decision. They will not harm you." He took my hand again, and I allowed him to re-entangle our fingers. "If it costs me my existence, Antanasia, you will be safe. I owe you that much, for reasons you will never need to know or understand."

Real terror clutched at me, and I gripped his fingers. "What is going to happen, Lucius?"

"That's not your concern."

"Lucius . . ." I thought of the terrible scar on his arm. Of his words. *"Of course they hit me. Time and again. They were making a warrior. . . ."* "Will they punish you?"

He laughed harshly. "Oh, Antanasia. Punishment is hardly the word for what I face at the hands of the Elders."

"We could try to reason with them . . . ," I said, knowing I was grasping futilely at straws.

Lucius smiled at me, and there was a tenderness in it. "You have a kind heart, and you are blessed with a sometimes dangerous naïveté. But the world is full of creatures like my poor, doomed Hell's Belle. And me. Creatures who've seen monstrous things and become monsters themselves. Creatures who perhaps *should be* put down."

"Stop it, Lucius," I demanded. "Stop talking like that!"

"It is true, Antanasia. You can't even conceive of the things in *my* dreams and schemes and imaginings . . ."

I swallowed hard. "Is that what you meant on Halloween when you said you could show me 'not-nice things'?"

Lucius's fingers tightened around mine. "Oh, no, Antanasia. Not violence against you. No matter what you believe of me—what you recall of me in the future—please believe that in the end, I would not—could not—have hurt you. Perhaps there was a time before I knew you, if you had stood in my path to power . . . but not now." He hesitated and looked away, and I heard him mutter, "God, I hope not . . ."

"It's okay, Lucius," I soothed him. "I know you wouldn't hurt me." Still, his admission unnerved me. *Was there a time when he could have hurt me? Why did he add that caveat at the end . . . ?*

But Lucius wasn't listening to me. He was staring at the pink walls he so hated. "For my family—for my children—it could have been different. I really have seen a new way here, for all the times I mock this place and its conventions."

"What if you just stayed here?" I suggested, growing suddenly hopeful. "You could just live like a regular person . . ."

As soon as I blurted the words, I realized how foolish they sounded. Still, Lucius surprised me by saying, "Perhaps for a few more weeks, if I am fortunate."

"Or longer?"

"No. Not longer. I know where I belong, and it would eventually pull me back." Lucius disentangled our fingers, standing. "The important thing is, you know that you are liberated from the pact. Absolved. You are free to . . . well . . ." A touch of his mocking laughter crept back into his voice. "Free to do whatever it is that you intend to do with your life. College. Some sort of split-level house in the suburbs. Little fairhaired, agriculturally inclined children running around in the yard. Your fate is your own. I promise you that."

"What if I don't want those things anymore?"

"Trust me, Antanasia—*Jessica*—someday you will look back upon these few months as nothing more than a strange dream. A potential nightmare. And you will be very, very happy that it never came true."

Lucius kissed the top of my head, then, and I knew that the weight of our shared destiny would never be lifted from his shoulders. He could play at being a normal teenager, but it was just a short reprieve. Lucius Vladescu's fate was tied up in scrolls and bound in genealogies and meted out with fists or worse. And I shuddered for him.

I heard his footsteps move toward the door in the darkness, but he paused before leaving. "You really were the most beautiful creature I'd ever seen tonight," he said softly. "When I danced with you . . . and the sight of you leaving me, head held high, not looking back, as the crowd parted before you . . . No matter where you live or whom you choose to wed, Antanasia, you will always be royalty. And I will always recall the image of you this evening, just as I will always remember the way you wept for me as I lay broken downstairs. Those are two gifts you have given me, and I will carry them with me, for as long as I am able."

Lucius shut the door behind himself, then, and in spite of the sweetness and warmth of his words, I shivered in the darkness.

Chapter 42

IT TOOK LESS THAN a week for all hell to break loose after Lucius's letter made its way to the countryside outside of Sighişoara, Romania.

In the meantime, Lucius sucked deeply on typical American teenage life like it was a rich, red vein. He played hours and hours of pickup basketball, skipped school, and threw a party in his garage apartment that ended in a raid by the cops and a threat from my parents to deport him on the next flight to Bucharest. Faith was constantly clamped to his side like they'd been super-glued at the hip.

And then Lucius, Mom, Dad, and I were all summoned to a meeting of the Elders, to be held in Lebanon County. They were all deigning to meet here, so serious was the crisis. There was no choice but to attend. At least, it didn't seem like there was a choice.

"I can't believe they are meeting in a steak house," my mother complained, reluctantly entering the Western Sizzlin' on New Year's Eve at the appointed time. "It's like a slap in the face. They know we're vegans."

"It's a power play," Dad agreed.

"Please, just go along with it," I begged. I sensed that things were going to be bad enough without Mom and Dad worrying about the menu. "They have a salad bar."

"Sulfites." My father sniffed. "Preservatives."

Sometimes Dad missed the big picture.

"We're here for a meeting," Mom told the hostess.

"With a bunch of older . . . men," I added. "They said they reserved a room."

Fear as raw as the steak in one of their freezers crossed the hostess's face, but she managed a smile as she located three menus. "Come this way, please."

"Oh, shit." I couldn't help saying it as we entered the room. My mom clutched my hand. "It's all right, Jessica."

But it didn't look "all right" at all.

For in the middle of a paneled chamber merrily festooned with cardboard cutouts of Santa Claus and elves and reindeer with glowing noses, thirteen of the most funereal old guys I'd ever seen were hovering over a circular table, stabbing at a massive platter loaded down with bloody, barely seared steaks. They were slapping bright red cow flesh onto their plates and not eating the meat. Just . . . slurping. At the juice. The blood that seeped out. Although the heat was cranked in that restaurant, the air was cold with their presence. And the smell of the blood . . . it prickled at my nostrils, seeped in through my pores, tickled my stomach.

My parents clutched their own stomachs, and my dad started gagging a little into his fist.

The oldest, scariest vampire glanced up from his feast reluctantly. He gestured to three empty chairs. "Please, sit. And forgive us for starting without you. We are famished from the journey."

Vasile. He had to be Lucius's uncle Vasile. There was the vaguest resemblance in the facial features, and the same sense of controlled power. But the older Vladescu vampire lacked Lucius's charm and grace and the wonderful glimmer of mischief in his eyes. Indeed, Vasile was like a tormented, deformed version of his nephew. Whereas Lucius's power was beautiful to witness, tempered as it was with humor and even joy, Vasile's was bitter and hideous. It made me half sick to think of Lucius—wonderful, funny Lucius—under this man's control, feeling his fist. . . .

"Sit," Vasile ordered again. Even the arrogance—which had become one of Lucius's most endearing traits—sat all wrong on the uncle's hunched shoulders.

Still, we obeyed and sat. The hostess handed us menus. She looked at us with pity, like we were hostages.

"Will you be having . . . ?" She gestured toward the meat pile, clearly not certain what to say. "Or should I get a waitress?"

"Just three salad bars," Mom ordered for us all, handing back her menu. I could tell she was struggling to maintain her composure in the face of the carnage.

I glanced around the table.

There was one empty chair. I wondered if Lucius would even show. And then the door opened, and he entered. I had half expected him to wear his old clothes—the velvet coat and black pants—but he wore jeans and his Grantley sweatshirt. I kind of sensed he was drawing a line in the sand early. A defiant line. But he moved around the table, politely shaking hands, one by one. "Uncle Vasile. Uncle Teodor."

Each vampire would pause in his consumption of blood just long enough to shake hands before falling back upon the feast. Lucius sat down, winking at us. But I could tell he was nervous.

"He's scared of them," Mom whispered in my ear.

"Me, too," I agreed. "Do you recognize any of them from Romania?"

Mom nodded, just slightly. "I seem to recall one or two . . . but it was long ago."

"Eat," Vasile urged, jabbing his fork toward us. "Then we'll talk."

My parents decamped for the salad bar, and I followed. But not without looking back over my shoulder at those steaks with more than a little awful desire. The odor of the blood . . . it was so heady in there. In spite of my fears for Lucius—and for all of us, really—that smell drew me. I felt guilty, feeling desire at such a dreadful moment.

When we returned, it was quite obvious that we had interrupted an intense, if quiet, discussion. The platter was heaped with sucked-dry steaks, the individual plates pushed away. All heads were turned toward Lucius, who sat stock-still. His eyes darted toward us. "Must the Packwoods be here?"

228

We stood clutching our salad bowls, waiting for the verdict. I don't know what we would have done if Vasile had told us to leave. But he didn't.

"Yes," he said. "They must remain."

We put our bowls at our place settings, and the sound of their thumping echoed in the suddenly silent room. Pulling out our chairs, we sat.

"Eat," Vasile directed again.

Even the salad dressing seemed to stick in my throat, so I took a few token bites and pushed my bowl away.

The vampire on my right leaned toward me. No longer hunched over a bloody steak, he could have been any businessman out for dinner. And yet, there was something different about him. Something menacing in his eyes. *So these are the Elders. . . .* "Are you not hungry?" he asked in a thickly accented voice.

"No," I said, forcing myself to meet his black eyes. I would not flinch or show fear. *Are these really my people? My kind?*

"They are done," Vasile announced, standing, after my parents had pushed their bowls away, too. "I will do the introductions."

He went around the table, but I immediately forgot all the names. I was too busy watching Lucius. He looked like a condemned man waiting for the electric chair in the company of his executioners and wouldn't meet my gaze.

Vasile sat, folding his long body into the chair like some sort of human accordion. He tented skeletal, knobby fingers, tapping the fingertips together. "What are we to do with these young people?"

"Not young people," Lucius interrupted. "Just me. This is about me."

"Silence," Vasile hissed, head swiveling toward Lucius.

"Of course, sir," Lucius conceded.

Vasile glared at my parents. "You know that Lucius has decided, in some sort of fit of *independence*"—he spat the word—"that he will no longer abide by the pact."

We all nodded.

"Lucius has advised of us of his decision," Dad spoke up. "And we support his choice. He is also invited to stay with us for as long as he wants."

"You *support his choice*?" Vasile thundered, incredulous. "You support his *insubordination*?"

"Look, Vasile," my father began. His voice cracked, and he had some spinach stuck in his teeth, but I was proud of him nonetheless. "They're just kids."

"I don't know that term," Vasile said.

"Kids. Young people. Teenagers. Why not just let them be . . ."

Vasile pounded the table, and a few dry steaks tumbled off the pile. "Let them be?"

My mom laid a hand on my arm. "Yes," she added, bravely. "If Lucius has decided that he wants out of the pact . . . Well, it was all very long ago, and he's a young man. You must see that it was ridiculous to expect these two teenagers to fall in love and marry just because of a decree."

I glanced toward Lucius. His eyes were on Vasile.

"Love?" Vasile barked. "Who said anything about love? This is about power."

"It's about kids," my father contradicted. "Lucius is seeing a young woman, and Jess is getting ready for college . . ."

Clearly, my dad had spilled a ton of beans. At the phrase "seeing a young woman," Vasile popped out of his chair and spun around on Lucius like a snapped whip. Lucius flinched, as if the whip had caught him a good one across the cheek.

"Courting?" Vasile roared. "Outside of the pact?"

"It's my choice," Lucius said calmly, using his favorite new word. "Jessica was amenable to the pact, but I have chosen otherwise."

Somehow, even though I knew he was protecting me, the words stung. Still Lucius didn't look at me.

At some silent cue that I missed completely, four senior vampires rose and the next thing I knew, Lucius was standing, being ushered away. One of the older vampires had draped his arm around his younger relative's shoulders, but I knew that Lucius was not about to get a kindly lecture from a well-meaning uncle.

"Where are you taking him?" Mom demanded.

"It's fine, Dr. Packwood," Lucius reassured her. He shook off his relative's containing arm, as though he preferred to go to his doom with dignity. "Please. Don't become involved in a family affair."

"Lucius, wait," I cried, rising from my chair.

He turned to me, just for a second. "No, Jessica."

A huge lump clogged my throat as they grabbed him again and shoved him toward the door. *Four against one . . . cowards.*

I tried to follow him, but Mom pulled me back. "I don't think so, Jessica. Not now."

"Sit down, please," Vasile added, voice oily. "Even if you were to follow . . . well, you couldn't find him. He is perfectly safe with the family."

"I think we should go," Dad said, rising. My mom and I followed his lead.

"This is not over," Vasile said, pointing a skeletal finger at all three of us. "Lucius will return with a different mind-set. And you will not go back on your promise."

Mom bristled. "My daughter will not do anything against her will."

"Her will is to marry him. She is destined for him. She knows it. To use your parlance, she *loves* him."

Dad looked at me. "What is he talking about, Jessica?"

"I don't know," I stammered.

"I saw her, when Lucius was led away." Vasile laughed. "Being raised among humans has made her so transparent."

"We're leaving." Dad grabbed my arm.

"Good night, for now," Vasile said. He bowed slightly to me.

As we made our way past the vampire clan, edging around the circle of the table, I felt something pressed into my palm. The move was so quick, it was like a magic trick. Somehow I had the good sense not to yelp. Glancing back, I caught the eye of a vampire I hadn't really noticed before. He was a little heavier than the others, and a little shorter, and his skin was a shade pinker. His eyes harbored a hint of amusement, and when I met his gaze, he placed a finger to his lips, clearly signaling that we now shared some secret, and winked at me. I didn't wink back.

I held on to the slip of paper until I got all the way to my bedroom, and opened it with fingers that fumbled with impatience. It was a note:

DON'T LOOK SO SCARED YET. ALL IS NOT LOST. YOU SEEM LIKE A NICE GIRL. VASILE IS JUST OVERBEARING. ALWAYS FULL OF HIMSELF. MEET ME TOMORROW AT THAT NICE PARK WITH THE STREAM. SAY TENISH? I'LL BE IN THE GAZEBO. AND LET'S KEEP THIS BETWEEN OURSELVES, EH?

YOURS, Dorin

Chapter 43

MY MOM CAME INTO my room around midnight. "His light hasn't come on yet."

"You're watching, too?" I'd been staring out the window, watching the garage.

"Of course."

I tore my eyes away for just a moment. "Do you think he'll be okay?"

"I honestly don't know."

"You knew about how they beat him, didn't you?"

Mom pulled the curtain back farther, joining my vigil. "I didn't know for sure, but I suspected . . ."

"Lucius said they hit him again, and again, and again."

When I said those words out loud, my already intense fear spiked close to panic.

"I told you that the Vladescus had a reputation for ruthlessness, and Lucius was raised to be their prince," Mom said, releasing the curtain. "I'm not surprised to learn that his childhood was not happy." She sat down next to me on the bed and kissed my forehead like she used to do when I was a kid scared of thunderstorms. "But Lucius is strong," she reminded me. "Try not to let your fears run away with you."

I could tell she was jumping to conclusions, though. Just like me. "What if he doesn't come back?"

"He will." She hesitated. "Jess . . . do you really love him?"

I was spared having to answer when a light flicked on in the apartment above the garage. Air came whooshing out of my lungs, and it felt like I had been holding my breath for hours. I didn't wait for Mom. I just tore out of the room, my bare feet flying through the frozen yard. I didn't care how cold it was.

I found Lucius in the cramped garage bathroom. He was shirtless, bending over the sink, washing his face. He heard me enter but didn't turn around. "Go away."

"Lucius, what is it?"

He remained bent over. "Leave me alone."

I edged closer. "No. Turn around."

"No."

Footsteps sounded on the stairs, and Mom padded up behind me. She patted my arm, then moved toward Lucius in the same quiet, nonthreatening way I'd moved toward Hell's Belle on that awful day.

"Lucius," she soothed, placing a hand on his back. I recognized that gesture from when I was a child throwing up. Lucius's muscles rippled, shuddering.

It struck me that maybe, just maybe, he was crying. Or trying not to. Really hard.

My mom bent down near Lucius, pushing back his black hair. She straightened, addressing me. "Jess, go get the first aid kit, under the kitchen sink."

"Mom . . . is he okay?"

"Just go, Jess," she said calmly.

I didn't want to go. I wanted to stay with Lucius.

"Now," she urged.

"Yes, Mom." I paused at the door, looking back, and saw that my mom had folded Lucius to herself, her arms wrapped around him. He was shaking. Convulsing. She was stroking his hair, talking to him softly. That's why my mom had sent me. She knew Lucius wouldn't want me to see him breaking down, perhaps under the pressure of the first motherly touch he'd ever known. Closing the door quietly, I obeyed her and ran back to the house.

I returned with the first aid kit, followed by my groggy father, who was still struggling to tie his robe around his waist, even as he was halfway up the stairs.

By this time, Lucius was lying on his bed, my mom sitting beside him. She snapped on the bedside lamp as I handed her the first aid kit. Lucius turned his face to the wall, but I could see that he was badly battered. His lip was split, and dark bruises were forming beneath his eye and across his cheek. His nose looked a little crooked.

"I'll get a cold washcloth," Dad offered, making himself useful.

"I'm fine," Lucius insisted. But he winced when Mom dabbed at his broken lip with alcohol.

"You are not fine," Mom said.

"Not my best year, eh?" Lucius joked bitterly. "At least the horse didn't know what she was doing."

Dad sat down, too, at the foot of the bed. He absently clutched the washcloth like he didn't know what to do with it now that he'd brought it. "Lucius, what happened?"

Lucius didn't respond.

"Lucius," Dad prompted again. "Tell us."

"Jessica should go to bed," Lucius finally said, face still to the wall. "It's late."

"I want to stay."

"You're a child," Lucius said. His voice was rough. Distant. "You don't need to be privy to all this."

My parents glanced at each other, and I realized that at that very moment, they would judge whether I really was still a child.

"Jess can stay if she likes," Dad finally said. "This affects her, too."

"I'll be gone in the morning," Lucius promised. "It won't affect any of you any longer."

"You will not go anywhere," Mom said, taking the washcloth from Dad and cleaning some blood from Lucius's cheek. She gently turned his face toward her, and I saw the damage full-on, for the first time. Although the room was dim, I could tell that the horse had spared the rod, to use Lucius's term, compared to his "uncles." My stomach tightened with anger and sadness.

"This is between me and my family," Lucius said. He sat up a little. He still hadn't looked at me. "I shall go home and deal with it."

We all knew what that meant. More pain. More scars.

"This is your home now," Dad said, voice firm. "You'll stay here."

As Dad extended that invitation, and as I watched my mother tend to Lucius's wounds, I saw, finally, the people who had stolen a child away from Romania, saving her life. It occurred to me, suddenly, that they had no doubt risked their own lives for me. It seemed odd and selfish that I'd never realized that before. Of course, they'd always downplayed their own risks.

"Home." Lucius spat the word with contempt.

"Yes. Home," Mom said.

"In fact," Dad added, placing his hand on Lucius's arm. "You've been out here in this garage for too long. I never realized how cold it is out here. Tonight you'll move back into the house. Permanently. We'll make room."

"I could not impose more than I have." Lucius addressed Dad. "And you need not fear for me. The Elders do not plan to stay. Trust me. They are confident that their message has been delivered. That I will obey."

"Still, I want you to move inside," Dad said, overriding Lucius. "Can you get up?"

Lucius seemed too battered, too exhausted to protest further. He swung his legs around, slowly, and paused on the edge of the bed. "Damn," he said, clutching his ribs. "They memorize every place that has been broken in me—the better to break me again, more efficiently."

Mom put her arm around Lucius's bare shoulders, comforting him, and I wished it could have been me in her place. Lucius leaned into her, again allowing to some weakness, and she held him for a moment, looking at my dad over Lucius's bowed head. There was a deep, deep sadness in her eyes.

"Try to stand," Dad said, taking Lucius by the arm.

"Thank you," Lucius replied. Even badly beaten, he retained a regal air once on his feet. "Thank you for everything. I'm sorry to be such trouble."

"It's not a problem, son," Dad promised, helping to steady Lucius with an arm around the waist. "No trouble at all."

Lucius flinched again as Mom slipped her arm around his waist, too. They began to walk, slowly, but Lucius stopped after a few steps. "Dr. Packwood . . . Mr. Packwood . . . in the past, I have not always been kind. I fear that I may have called you . . . weak. You are so different from my family, you know."

"It's okay, Lucius," Mom promised, urging him along. "You don't have to say more."

"No," he objected. "No, I do. I was wrong to insult you, and not only because you are my hosts. I am afraid that I mistook kindness for weakness. My apologies. I stand—only with your aid—profoundly corrected."

"Come on, Lucius." Dad patted Lucius's back. "Apology accepted. Now let's get you to bed."

We made a pathetic, slow, shuffling little parade through the frozen yard, Mom, Dad, and Lucius trudging together through the snow with me trailing behind. My mom made up a bed for Lucius in her office, a little cubby of a room between our two bedrooms, and pretended to go to bed herself. But I knew my parents would be alert all night. I knew they wouldn't trust Lucius's assertion that his brutal relatives were headed home. And they would worry that he would disappear into the darkness. I was worried, too. Soon, though, I heard Lucius's deep, steady breathing from next door. He had to be sleeping. Certainly he was exhausted. As I pulled up the covers, back in my warm bed, I recalled that it was New Year's Eve, and realized that the new year had already begun. I would be eighteen soon. Technically old enough to marry.

In the room next to mine, the man I'd been engaged to practically since birth, right up until just a few days ago, turned over and gave a muffled grunt of pain. How many times, I wondered, had he been "efficiently" broken and cried out like that, suffering even in his sleep? And did he carry other injuries deep inside? Pain even worse than broken bones and cuts and bruises?

Chapter 44

I APPROACHED THE GAZEBO in the park at "tenish," as the note had advised, and the vampire waiting there waved, clutching his coat around his throat with his other hand. It was a bitterly cold day, with the threat of snow.

"I was afraid you wouldn't come," he said, smiling.

In spite of the smile, I approached warily. "Lucius said you'd all gone home."

"Indeed," he confirmed. "The rest have already returned to Romania. I linger behind in hopes of helping the situation."

I relaxed a little, glad to hear that most of Lucius's uncles had departed. The farther away, the better.

"I'm Dorin," he added, holding out a gloved hand. Actually, it was a mittened hand. He must have seen me staring at the bright wool. Yellow and orange stripes. "Nifty, huh?" he said, flipping his hands back and forth. "I got them at the mall."

I shook his hand. "You shopped at the mall?"

"Oh, sure. American culture. It's all about the fun here. I was so jealous when Lucius was dispatched here for several months' stay. Of course, it was good to get him away from old Vasile for a while." He sucked in his cheeks, making them cadaverous, in imitation. "Seemed a healthy move."

I studied Dorin's face. His cheeks were rosy in the cold, and his eyes were black, like I'd come to expect from vampires, but they had a merry little crinkle around the edges. "Sit, sit," he said, gesturing to a bench, brushing off a dusting of snow.

The seat still didn't look very inviting. "Do you think we could go to a coffee shop or something?" I suggested, blowing on my hands. I cast a longing glance at his mittens.

Dorin mused on this, head waggling back and forth. "Sure. Why not? I suppose I got a little cloak-and-dagger with the whole empty park. I'm a fan of the spy novel, you know."

"Me, too," I said, smiling.

"Well, I'm not surprised," he said, ushering me out of the gazebo. "Being related and all. We probably have lots in common."

"We're related?"

"Yes, yes. I should have put that in the note. Less scary for you then, maybe."

"How?"

"I'm your uncle," he informed me. "Your mother's brother."

I stopped short and stared at him, searching for anything familiar in his face. Any resemblance to my birth mother or me. "You don't look quite like her . . . or me."

Dorin's rosy cheeks blanched a little. "Well, I'm more of a half brother, really. Your grandfather had a dalliance out of wedlock . . ." He grinned sheepishly. "I'm the product!"

"But you can tell me about my birth parents, right?"

"Of course, of course," he promised. "But first, let's get you inside. You're shivering."

Yes, I was. From the cold and from anticipation. The vampire at my side was my uncle. He had known my birth parents. . . . Finally, after nearly eighteen years, I was about to learn who they really were. Finally I was ready.

Dorin offered me his arm, and I tucked my hand in the crook of his elbow. "Come along then, Antanasia. We have much to discuss."

Together we strolled across the frozen park toward The Bean Counter, the closest coffee shop. Dorin paused before entering, reading the sign. A smile broke across his face. "I get it. I really do. Funny stuff. Americans and their puns. In Bucharest, it would be called 'Coffee Shop.' The communists messed up everything."

We ordered—decaf for me and a double latte with whipped cream and sprinkles for Dorin—and took our drinks to a corner table. Dorin sucked off the cream like it was blood from a steak.

"Before we get on to family stories," he began, "that was bad stuff back there last night, eh?" He dabbed at his foam mustache with a napkin. "But that's Vasile for you. Loves drama more than a common villager. Everything's about staging."

My initial warm feelings for my uncle frosted over. "So what happened to Lucius, that was just for some sort of effect? Because his broken nose looked awfully real."

Dorin paused in midsip, lowering his mug. "No? Really?"

"Yes."

"Oh, goodness. I thought they were beyond all that. Not good. Not good, indeed. I never thought they'd really lay a hand on him again. Never thought they'd have the nerve to fight *that* one. Wouldn't risk it, myself."

"It was four against one," I reminded him.

"Still." Dorin appeared to be weighing the odds. "I wouldn't risk it. How is the boy? How did he fare?"

How could I put it into words?

"That bad, eh?" Dorin looked honestly pained. "Vasile never had much interest in children. But Lucius turned out well, in spite, didn't he? He's a fine young man. Outstanding vampire. The whole Vladescu clan is justifiably proud. Of course, it's not surprising that Lucius would rebel, given the tight rein Vasile kept on him growing up."

I traced the rim of my mug with my finger. "What's going to happen to Lucius?"

"Well, that letter surprised all the Elders. We thought you'd be the one who might be difficult to draw in, in spite of the pact. Americans: not so much on blood pacts. More of a European thing. I tried to point that out. No one listens to me, though. They were fairly certain you'd come around."

"That I'd 'come around'?"

"Well, look at Lucius. We just assumed he'd make any teenage girl swoon. He's very popular in Bucharest among certain debutantes who enjoy the dark side . . ."

I didn't want to hear about Lucius's old conquests. "So you figured eventually I'd fall for him, and he'd put up with whatever he got."

Dorin cocked his head, considering. "Yes. I guess that's about it. And you did fall, didn't you? You do love him, right?"

I flushed. "I don't know about *love* . . ."

"We all saw how you looked at Lucius. And Vasile, for all his faults, is very adept at reading other vampires' thoughts. Better than most. He's so damn old. What skill hasn't he perfected?"

"I'm not a vampire yet," I corrected.

"But you do thirst, no?" Dorin asked, hopeful. "By now, you must . . ."

I glanced around the coffee shop, making sure it was empty. "Yes," I confessed, whispering so the barista behind the counter wouldn't hear. "Sometimes."

Dorin nodded approval. "You have much to look forward to, Antanasia. Your first taste of Siberian Red—especially Type O, vintage 1972 . . ." His gaze drifted off, and he smacked his lips. "Oh, it's something else. Indeed it is."

"Not if I never become a full vampire. Not if I'm never bitten."

Dorin came back around. "Oh, yes, the pact. And our way-ward boy, Lucius. We—meaning you—must be the one to bring him around and ensure that the pact is fulfilled."

"How can *I* do that?"

"You love him. You can bring him back to his senses. It's fairly simple, really."

"It's not simple at all. Lucius is done with the pact. And he's got this girlfriend . . ."

"Lucius is rebelling. He's being a teenager. He'll come back. He'll come back to *you*."

I finished my coffee. "You are so wrong." Dorin hadn't seen how Lucius was with me now. At breakfast, he'd been com-pletely aloof. Entirely shut off. Something had happened with him when they'd beaten him. The laugh, the sarcasm, the light-ness . . . they were all gone. Snuffed. Lucius was different now. Intense. Frightening.

"We need to try," Dorin said. I wondered if he could read my mind, like Vasile. "You can do it. You are Mihaela Dragomir's daughter. And damn, that woman could do any-thing she put her mind to."

Across the table, my uncle squinted at me.

"What?"

"Certain ways I look at you, you look exactly like her. Spit-ting image, to use the disgusting English colloquialism." He shook his head, sighing. "Beautiful, beautiful woman. Such a waste."

"Dorin, why can't you take over as leader of our clan?" I suggested. "You're an Elder. Can't you fix this mess for us? Change the pact somehow?"

"I told you. My blood isn't pure. You are the last pure Dragomir heir to the throne. It has to be you. We are all counting on you. Counting on the blood that runs in your veins. Your mother, Mihaela—she was leadership material. Same with your father. Very kingly, that one. You are pure stock. Pure stock, indeed."

"If the pact isn't fulfilled, would there really be war?"

"The Dragomirs and the Vladescus already grow impatient. There are rumblings of distrust on both sides. Your marriage is intended to provide stability—to make sure power is equally shared between clans that have battled for generations, fighting for supremacy. But as rumors that the pact may not be fulfilled begin to spread, the old instability reasserts itself stronger than ever. Already, the situation grows volatile."

"Could vampires actually *die*?"

"Vampires don't die," Dorin pointed out. "But they can be destroyed—and that is much worse than death. To answer your question, though. Yes. Vampires would be destroyed. The old war, which halted with your betrothal to Lucius, would resume."

An actual war. *Over me.*

"Your parents achieved the first peace," Dorin pointed out. "You will achieve the lasting one."

"Tell me about them," I urged Dorin. "I want to hear everything."

He smiled broadly, warmly, and signaled to the barista at the counter. "I think we'll need a whole pot over here." He turned back to me. "There is so, so much to tell, my future princess."

Chapter 45

"WHAT ARE YOU doing here?" Jake asked, looking unhappy to see me waiting by his locker.

I stepped aside so he could spin the combination. It seemed like ages ago that I'd seen him struggling with the lock on the first day of school. So much had happened since then.

"I wanted to see you," I said. "To talk about what happened at the formal."

"You made me look like an idiot." Jake snapped open the door, banging it against the other lockers.

"I was the one who looked awful," I said. "I was the one who—"

"You don't have to describe it," Jake said, shoving his books into the locker. "I saw you and Luc. I was there—in case you forgot like you did that night."

"I deserved that," I admitted. "And I just want to say I'm sorry."

"Why did you even want to go with me?" Jake asked. "Was I a consolation prize, since Luc asked Faith? Because he might have had his hands all over you at the formal, but it seems to me like he has a girlfriend."

Jake wanted to hurt me, and he had. Then again, I'd hurt him. "Jake, you're nobody's consolation prize," I promised. "You're one of the nicest guys I know, and I wish I hadn't treated you like I did."

"Yeah, me, too," Jake said, slamming the locker shut. "But don't feel sorry for me, Jess. I'm the one who feels sorry for you, because that guy might be a hotshot from Europe, but he'll never treat you as nice as I would have."

The sad thing was, I knew Jake was right. "Nice" was not in Lucius Vladescu's vocabulary. Intense. Chivalrous. Funny. Arrogant. Dangerous. Honorable. Passionate. Those were the words that Lucius lived by. But nice? Never.

"I see how you look at him," Jake added. "Hell, I knew we were going to break up that day you came to wrestling practice. You weren't watching me. You were watching him."

I had nothing to say. No way to defend myself.

"He's gonna break your heart, Jessica. That guy is gonna *destroy* you."

And with that, my first boyfriend turned and walked out of my life—with a very un-peasantlike dignity.

I stood there, watching Jake leave and thinking how curious it was that he'd used that very vampire-centric word for what Lucius would do to me.

Destroy.

How odd that of all the expressions Jake could have selected—*crush, hurt, wreck, screw you over*—he would choose that particular term. It shook me a little, almost like a premonition.

But why?

You know, Jess. . . . In the back of your mind you know you have good reason to fear Lucius. . . .

I was the pure-blooded heir to leadership of a clan that had warred with Lucius's for generations. I was set to inherit power that his family had always wanted to seize. *If I was out of the way* . . . I recalled Lucius's strange comment right after the Christmas formal.

*"Please believe that in the end, I would not—could not—
have hurt you. Perhaps there was a time before I knew you, if you
had stood in my path to power. But now . . . God, I hope not . . ."*

No. Lucius would never hurt me, even in the interest of
smoothing a path to power. I clung to the first part of his
curious declaration. *"In the end, I would not—could not—have
hurt you."*

Then I thought of the changed Lucius. The distant, angry,
bruised young man who wouldn't even meet my eyes. Could *he*
do me harm?

I wouldn't believe it. If there was one certainty I had to hold
tight to in my new topsy-turvy life, it was Lucius's promise to
protect me, even at the cost of his own existence.

And yet I couldn't stop feeling uneasy—almost queasy—
about Jake's uncharacteristic, and very dire, warning.

Chapter 46

"LUCIUS, I BROUGHT you some hot chocolate." I poked
my head into his new room, carrying a tray. "It's the vegan
kind, but not too bad."

He was lying flat on his back on his makeshift bed, which
was an air mattress on the floor, his eyes closed, listening to
headphones. The desk lamp provided the only light in the
room, casting shadows all around him. I took a second to study
him before he realized I was there and turned away, like he always did now. His bruises had healed some, and the swelling
around his eye had gone down. I set down the tray and tapped
his shoulder.

He started, tearing off the headphones and bolting upright. "Don't startle me like that. Don't you know that's unwise? Don't you know by now?"

"Sorry." I stepped backward, seeing how flinty his eyes were. "I just made some hot chocolate, and I thought—"

"I don't like chocolate."

"You just finished another carton of Dad's carob tofu ice cream," I said. "So don't pretend you don't like chocolate. Just have some."

Lucius pushed my hand away, spilling some on the floor. "Jessica, it's late. Go to bed."

I ignored him and sat down cross-legged next to him, sipping the cocoa. "What are you listening to?"

"German metal. Richthofen."

Setting down the mug, I waved for the headphones. "Can I listen, please?"

He ground his teeth, but agreed. "As you wish."

Clamping the headphones over my ears, my heart sank. It sounded like elevator music for tormented souls on the way to hell. Guttural German lyrics, synthesizers growling, no melody. Just howling and groaning. Scary stuff. "What happened to the Black Eyed Peas?" I made an effort at a joke, removing the headphones.

"I find this is more in tune with my psyche."

"Lucius—"

"Jess, go."

"Stop pushing me away."

"Stop trying to pull me close!"

I hugged my knees to my chest. "I'm worried about you."

"The time for worry is past."

"No, that's not true. We can still fix things."

"Jessica, in a few weeks, I will return to Romania to face the punishment for my defiance. Just leave me in peace for a short time. The time I have left. That's all I ask."

"But Lucius, I want to help you."

He laughed, a short, bitter laugh. "You? You want to help me?"

"It's not funny. I can help you. I might be the only person who can help you."

"How?"

"I can marry you, that's how."

His eyes softened for just a second, and then he rubbed them with his palms, grinding against the bruises, as if he was punishing himself. "Jessica . . ."

I leaned forward, taking advantage, grabbing his hand. "We could do it. I would do it."

Lucius yanked his hand away. "You don't even know what you offer, Jessica. All you know is that you feel sorry for me. I will not be married out of pity. To be saved like an ailing mongrel about to be euthanized who is adopted at the pound by some too-kind soul. I would rather be destroyed with dignity."

"I don't pity you."

"No?"

"No." Tears pricked at my eyes. "I love you, Lucius."

I couldn't believe the words had slipped out of my mouth. I had always thought the first time I said them, the moment would be perfect. Not desperate and sick, like this.

There was a long silence, and Lucius's eyes grew hard again.

"More's the pity, Jess," he replied. Then he lay back down, rolling onto his side, as if to sleep.

I ran out of the room, smack into my mom, crashing into her arms. She led me into her bedroom and closed the door with a soft click.

"What were you doing with Lucius?" she asked, pulling some tissues from a box and handing them to me.

"Just talking." I wiped at my eyes, but the tears wouldn't stop.

"And what did he say to you? Why are you crying?"

"I told Lucius that I love him," I admitted, clutching the soggy tissues. "That I want to marry him."

My mother's eyes flew open. Her usual calm demeanor cracked completely. "And what did he say?" she asked. Her voice was low, deliberately even, but scared.

"He said no. That he'd rather be destroyed than have me marry him out of what he believes is pity."

My mom exhaled visibly. She closed her eyes, clasped her hands, raising her fingertips to her lips, and I heard her whisper, "Good man, Lucius. Good man."

Chapter 47

"JESS, WE'RE GOING to be late for calculus," Mindy said, practically dragging me down the hall.

I tugged back. "I'm not going. I think I'll just skip."

"Again?" There was concern in Mindy's voice. "Jess, you never used to skip class. Now you hardly ever go. And this is *math*, Jess. Your favorite!"

"I just don't feel like it, Min."

"What is up with you, Jessica?" she demanded. "Is it Lucius? Because you two have *both* changed. And he had those bruises . . . What is going on at your house?"

"It's nothing, Mindy. I swear."

"You're cutting classes, Jake is history, Lucius looks like he's always on the edge of committing murder and nothing's going on?"

I wandered toward the restroom. "Just go to class, okay? I'm going to hang out in here until the halls clear so I can get out of here."

"I'm worried about you, Jess," Mindy said, clutching her books to her chest. "Really worried."

"It's nothing," I promised her. *Nothing but a broken heart and a broken pact and a looming war.* How could I concentrate on dull textbooks and pointless homework and tedious lectures when everything was falling apart? When lives were at stake? "I'll call you later, all right?"

Mindy was still standing there looking scared when I slipped into the restroom and ducked into a stall. But misery couldn't even leave me alone in the bathroom. As I stood there next to the rust-ringed toilet, waiting for the bell to ring, Faith Crosse came in with her friend Lisa Clay. Through the crack between the wall and the stall door, I watched as they assumed their places at the altar of the mirror, ready for some self-worship.

"So what's with you and Luscious Lucius?" Lisa asked, rummaging in her purse and pulling out some lip gloss. She slicked a slimy trail across her lips. "And who gave him the black eye?"

"He won't say." Faith shrugged, brushing her hair. "You know Lucius. He keeps his secrets. But ever since it happened, he's been, like, totally crazy."

Lisa dabbed some cream blush on her cheeks. "Crazy good or crazy bad?"

"Crazy *after* me," Faith complained, rolling her big blue eyes. "It's like he won't leave me alone. He just wants to fool around, all the time. And it's so intense."

Lisa turned her head to and fro, checking her cheeks for streaks. "Guys. They're so horny."

"Yeah, but this is, like, extra horny. Like he can't get enough. We go up to his apartment behind the Packwoods' place, and he practically drags me to the bed."

He is having sex with Faith.

My teeth ached so sharply, so jarringly, that I thought for a second my fangs really might pierce right through my gums, and I stifled a cry, clapping my hand over my mouth, bending double in pain. And my thirst . . . I needed blood, so desperately . . . I had to have it. *Lucius is having sex with Faith Crosse behind my house. My betrothed betraying me, his princess . . .*

"But I keep telling him," Faith continued, oblivious to my silent torment in the corner stall, "I'm not throwing away my whole future to have sex—not until my mom lets me get on the pill. I mean, I'm not getting knocked up before Stanford."

So it isn't sex. It isn't full-blown intercourse. I tried to quell my jealousy and rage. But still my teeth pulsed with pain at the thought of Lucius on the velvet blanket with Faith. I placed one hand against the cool tile wall, shaken and suffering, trying to steady myself.

"Yeah," Lisa agreed. "I don't know why guys can't just be content with a . . ." She cupped a hand around Faith's ear and whispered something I couldn't hear. But I could guess from the giggles.

"I know." Faith laughed. "I mean, that's practically the same as going all the way. And then there's this thing that Lucius does that's almost better than—" She paused like she realized she'd revealed too much.

My heart stopped, and I became oblivious even to my throbbing mouth, my desperate craving.

What thing? WHAT THING?

"Well, don't leave me hanging," Lisa cried, shaking her friend's arm. "What does he do?"

"It's just . . ." Faith hesitated one more second, and then couldn't bear to keep it to herself one minute longer. She turned to Lisa. "This thing with his mouth. On my neck."

My heart didn't just stop. It seized up, like a huge hand had clenched the muscle in my chest, trying to rip it out. *No, Lucius. Don't do it. Don't betray us any more than you already have. And don't risk more punishment by* irreparably *breaking the pact. Not yet. I need time to fix things.*

"What?" Lisa squealed. "Like a hickey? That's so junior high. Who cares about a hickey?"

"No." Faith shook her head, turning back to her reflection. She got a little thoughtful, staring into her own eyes. "It's not a hickey. It's . . . I can't describe it. It feels amazing, though. Like, dangerous, or something. Like we're doing something really *bad*." Digging in her purse, she located a hair band and swept her blond cascade of hair into a high ponytail. "Like, I like it, but I know I shouldn't."

"God, I wish Lucius could teach my boyfriend. Allen has *no* moves."

"I don't know if this is something you can teach. It's just something Luc *does.*"

Lisa pointed to her friend's neck, frowning. "Well, whatever it is, it leaves scratches. You want some makeup for that?"

Faith twisted to look at the side of her neck, close to her ear. She ran her fingers along fine red marks, smiling, remembering. "Oh, Lees . . . you should feel it when he's doing it."

"You are so lucky to have a European guy," Lisa pouted. "So, so lucky."

When they left, I collapsed against the stall wall, breathing hard, waiting for the aches and appetites inside me to subside. Waiting for the vampire side of myself, so desperate to fully emerge, to calm down and hide again.

Lucius . . . What are you doing?

Chapter 48

"HE'S GOING TO BITE Faith Crosse," I informed Dorin.

"No, no, no," Dorin objected. He stirred cinnamon into his cappuccino. "That wouldn't do. I just don't think our boy would do it."

"Dorin, I saw his girlfriend, Faith, in the bathroom at school. She said Lucius is doing weird things to her neck. With his mouth. And she had scratches."

Dorin set down his cappuccino, his crinkly eyes clouding. "Big scratches?"

"I don't know. I wasn't close enough to tell. Does it matter?"

"Not really, I guess. As long as he doesn't really sink in there, you know?" Dorin curved his hand, arching two fingers like fangs, and swiped at the air. "That kind of thing—that would be bad news."

"For Lucius or for Faith?"

"Hard to say for the girl, really. I mean, of course, if he didn't suck this Faith person dry—kill her on the spot—well, she'd be undead then. Now, that's something some girls really regret if they do it on the spur of the moment. Not something to rush into. And girls who don't have a vampire lineage, like you . . . they're the ones who get all nasty, after about a hundred years. Don't like drinking the blood. Can't embrace the lifestyle. Wish they'd just married a regular human, bought a minivan and had kids. Whiners. Troublemakers. They make you wish you had a stake through the heart, just to spend a few minutes with them. Lucius might very well be sorry he indulged in a moment of passion, after a few millennia."

"So you're saying *they'd* get married if he bit her?" I hated the envy—the Biblically proportioned, sinful coveting—that consumed me. A twinge pricked my gums, and I rubbed my jaw.

"Hurts, eh?" Dorin asked, noticing.

I rubbed harder. "It's that obvious?"

"If you know the signs. But trust me, it's a good thing. If your fangs didn't ache—that's when a young vampire needs to worry."

"I know," I said. "I read the book."

"Lucius gave you a copy of *Growing Up Undead*?" Dorin grinned. "It is a classic!"

"Yes, it's very helpful," I agreed. "But about Lucius and Faith—"

"Oh, yes," Dorin said. "If Lucius did the honorable thing—as I suspect he would—they would wed. You can't just bite an unsuspecting virgin and go your merry way. It's not done."

The ache roared to life, and my gums throbbed. "I can't believe Lucius would be linked to *her* for eternity."

Dorin shook his head, avoiding my eyes, dumping more cinnamon in his mug. "No. No, he wouldn't."

"But you just said Lucius would do the honorable thing—"

"Honor, schmonor. If Lucius ultimately does break the pact, it won't matter who he bites. Vasile won't stand for insubordination. The whole reason vampires have survived so long is harsh justice. Something like breaking a treaty between clans—that's grounds for immediate destruction."

Jealousy was banished by raw fear. "What?"

"Destruction. With a capital D."

I'd known they would punish him, and severely. Even Lucius had been afraid of what they'd do. But I hadn't really thought they would *destroy* him. "But he's their prince . . ."

"And princes are expendable. It's not like they're *kings* yet."

My voice seemed stuck in my throat. "How much time will Vasile give him to obey?"

"He's already hanging by a thread," Dorin admitted. "Vasile is determined to make Lucius obey, but he won't wait forever." My uncle mimicked jabbing his chest with what I assumed was a stake, then lighting a match. "And then . . . poof."

The steamy, chicory-scented air in the coffee shop suddenly seemed raw and icy. "Is that really how it happens? With a stake?"

"That is, indeed, the surest way." Dorin confirmed Lucius's earlier assertion. "Time tested."

The image of Lucius being stabbed through the heart—of Vasile, giving a quick upward thrust just below the ribs that had been broken too often—flashed through my mind, and I swore, it was almost like I could feel the sharp wood piercing my own flesh. I actually clutched my chest. Had my parents done the same, in their final moments?

"What will happen to Lucius then?" I said, willing the horrible images out of my brain.

"What do you mean?"

"Like . . . his soul."

"Oh, that. His soul belongs to the clan. It's not the typical heaven-hell stuff, like you're used to. A vampire's soul is a different thing. The clan giveth, and the clan taketh away. Well, sometimes angry mobs taketh away." Dorin shrugged. "We'd just go to hell, anyway. Might as well just be gone."

The thought of a universe without Lucius—Lucius just *not existing*—was too much to bear. And yet I felt helpless. "He still refuses to honor the pact, even though I told him that I love him. That I want to marry him."

Dorin brightened. "You *really do* love him, don't you? You can admit it to me."

"Yes, I do," I said.

"Then don't let him bite Faith Crosse, even if it means sticking by his side twenty-four hours a day," Dorin advised, sipping his cappuccino. "Because the second he bites her, the clock will strike midnight for Lucius Vladescu. I can guarantee you that."

Lucius destroyed. A universe without him. I couldn't imagine it. And yet I had no idea how to prevent it, either.

All that night I tossed and turned in bed, remembering how I'd felt when I'd thought Lucius had died. That cold wind, tearing through my hollow chest—ripping me open like a stake.

If he didn't honor the pact, I feared it wouldn't just destroy him. It would destroy me, too.

Chapter 49

"OH, DAMMIT," I muttered, watching out my window as Lucius and Faith Crosse crept across the yard under cover of darkness, headed toward his old apartment. I hated spying on him, but I didn't know what else to do. I had to keep him from biting Faith. And so I waited just a few minutes and followed them.

"Hey, you guys," I said, barging in without knocking. "What are you up to?"

As if I can't tell.

Faith practically leapt away from Lucius, smoothing at her hair, tugging at her disheveled shirt. "God, Jenn. Don't you knock? *Some* people have sex lives."

Lucius didn't make any effort to disentangle himself. He just sat there on the bed, keeping his arm loosely around Faith's waist, idly stroking her hip. "What do you want, Jess?" His voice was low, menacing.

"Maybe she wants her pots and pans," Faith smirked. "You know, to do her hair."

"I can't smell the hare anymore," I shot back. "The stench

of *peroxide* is so strong. You'd better ease up on the bleach, Faith, or you'll wind up bald."

"I could do worse." She sniffed, staring pointedly at my head. "Better bald than a Brillo head."

"Better a Brillo head than a bitch."

I don't think anyone had ever spoken to Faith Crosse like that. I could hardly believe I'd done it. But damn, it felt good.

Faith sat in stunned silence, curled up against Lucius, eyes wide. Then she pulled away from him, jabbing her finger at his chest. "Did you hear what she just said to me, Luc? Are you going to let her call me a bitch?"

Lucius laughed, a mirthless sound, and drew her closer. "Oh, Faith. Accept the compliment."

She shoved his chest. "Watch it, Luc."

Lucius ignored the warning, addressing me. "I repeat: What do you want, Jessica?"

"I need some help with Belle in the barn," I lied. "I think she's favoring a leg, but I want your opinion. You know horses better than me."

"Call a veterinarian," Lucius said. "I'm no horse healer."

"Come on, Lucius," I urged. "It will just take a minute." *Anything to get you away from Faith . . .*

"It is nearly ten o'clock," Lucius noted. "The horse will live until morning. And we are rather preoccupied here." His face was obscured by the gloom in the room, but I thought I caught a flash of fangs.

"Lucius, be reasonable," I urged, abandoning my story about Belle.

"I am so done with the pointless banter," Faith said, sliding out of Lucius's embrace. "Later, Luc."

"Don't go," Lucius said, pulling her back.

But Faith tore her wrist away. "It's getting kind of late anyway, Lucius. And my parents are going to kill me if I break curfew again." She snatched her red leather purse off the floor and gave Lucius a peck on the lips. "Bye."

As she flounced by me, I grabbed her by the arm. "The name is *Jess*, by the way. Remember it next time."

Faith twisted out of my grasp with a sneer. "Oh, I will. And you'll be sorry I do."

She left the door hanging open, and I slammed it as she marched down the stairs.

"What do you see in her?" I demanded of Lucius. My voice was petulant, too angry, but I couldn't control myself. "She's the most evil person I've ever known."

"You know worse, Jessica. Trust me." Lucius stood, crossing his arms. "Why are you really here?"

"To save you, you idiot," I said. "You are going to bite Faith! You're totally out of control!"

Lucius groaned. A groan that spiked to a growl. He balled his fists and ground them against his forehead. "Jessica—do not meddle in this."

"Even if you don't care about me, or yourself, or the pact, have you thought about what will happen to Faith if you two get carried away? You're messing around with her soul, too. I might hate her, but what you're doing—it's not right."

Lucius scoffed. "Faith's soul. Faith is already as corrupt a soul as you can imagine. Don't worry about Faith. She lies, cheats, steals, and would probably kill to get what she wants. I've seen into Faith's soul, and it's just as dark as mine. That's why we're so good together. We are one and the same."

But they weren't one and the same. I knew it. "You can't base your life on a novel," I said.

"What are you talking about?"

"She's not Catherine, and you're not Heathcliff. You don't have to destroy each other."

"You read too much into a small drama. A high school diversion," Lucius said.

"You don't think it's a diversion. I know you, Lucius."

"You do not know me!"

The rafters fairly shook as Lucius really raised his voice, for the first time I could recall. The sound was fearsome.

But I would not back down. "I do know you. You are an honorable vampire. You are *royalty*. And Faith is not your equal," I shot back. "She's not even a vampire."

"Oh, neither are you." He drew closer and clutched a fistful of my curls. "You've changed your hair, you've changed your clothes, you've read the guide, but you don't know anything about being a vampire. You saw my uncles. Are you ready for that world?"

"I was born to *rule* that world. You know it! You taught me that!"

But Lucius laughed at me, releasing my hair. "Indeed? You can barely utter the words, let alone take the throne."

"You're just hurt, Lucius," I pleaded. "Don't throw away your"—*Life? Undeath?*—"existence over a fight with your uncle."

"Get out." He bared his teeth like an animal, breathing heavily, and I saw his fangs.

But I wasn't afraid. My own teeth ached. My throat felt parched, too. "No."

"Don't push me," Lucius snarled, grabbing my shoulders. "You have no idea what I'm capable of. Didn't you see what they did to me? That blood is in me."

"You won't hurt me." Wrenching free, I raked the room with my gaze, searching for something. How could I prove that I was the one not just to save him, but to seal our destiny? And then I saw it. The cup. The cup from Orange Julius that I knew would have warm, crimson liquid inside. It was on his nightstand, and I darted for it, knowing that he was quicker than me. But I had the element of surprise on my side, and I snatched it up, tearing off the lid, half disgusted, half mad with craving.

"Jessica, don't," Lucius yelled, lunging for me.

I sidestepped and tipped the cup to my lips, pouring the thick, slippery, clotted blood into my mouth. It slid over my tongue, down my throat, and I poured so fast that it drenched my chin and my neck and seeped across my shirt. It was sticky and salty and sweet and tasted like life, on the brink of death. I drank it all, overcome by the taste, the smell . . . the pungent smell, now inside me, filling me, satisfying me.

Lucius stood transfixed as I finished, dragging my arm across my mouth. He said nothing as I shoved the cup against his chest, forcing him to accept it.

"There," I growled, feeling more powerful than I'd ever felt in my life. Powerful and sated and half sick. "Don't ever tell me that I'm not ready to rule."

Still, Lucius didn't say a word. He just stood, still and rigid as a corpse, clutching the bloodied cup against his chest. I marched past him and made it down the stairs and out the door before I started shaking. I stood in the small circle of light at the entrance to the garage, letting the cold wind calm me. My shirt was sodden, but the blood, in the frozen winter air, was already clotting, freezing, hardening into scarlet ice. I wiped my chin again with a sticky arm. I wanted to throw up—and drink again. So I just waited a moment, trying to calm down, to figure out what to do. What if my parents saw me covered in blood?

I glanced toward the house. And that's when I saw Faith Crosse, standing about five feet away from me, staring.

"I was just coming back . . . I forgot my cell phone," she stammered, clutching her red purse to her chest, so we looked a little like mirror images. Except her torso was covered by red leather, and mine was covered in gore. Her blue eyes were huge. "What . . . what the hell happened to you?"

I started to say something—anything—but I couldn't think of a single lie. As if a lie could explain why my face and throat and chest were covered with coagulating blood.

It didn't matter. Faith turned on her heel and ran to her car. I was still standing there, shaking with the cold and with emotion, when the sound of her squealing tires disappeared into the night.

I knew that I had done something I could never undo. I had altered not just myself but the future. Something had been set in motion the instant I'd tilted that cup to my lips, and I was sharply aware that Lucius and I didn't have just angry old undead Elders to fear anymore. I had poured bloody grist into an American high school rumor mill—the only thing perhaps more dangerous than legions of warring vampires lusting for power.

Chapter 50

"JESS, WHAT HAPPENED to you in the apartment?" Mindy asked, clutching my arm, holding me back as I started up the stairs, headed for advanced chemistry. Her eyes were wide, imploring me to reassure her that everything was okay. "You can tell me. I'm your best friend."

"Nothing happened," I lied.

I wanted to tell Mindy everything. The whole crazy story. I was so tired of carrying the entire burden myself. But I couldn't. She would never believe it, and if she did, what would she think of me if I told her I drank blood? That I wanted to drink *more* blood? I resumed climbing the steps. "We're going to be late for class."

Mindy kept her hand on my arm, still holding me back. "I don't care about class. I just need to know what's up with you. There's a rumor going around that you had *blood* on your *mouth,* Jess. That you were coming out of Lucius's apartment, and you were covered in blood."

"That's the stupidest thing I ever heard," I said. *Lies piling upon lies.*

Mindy slid her hand down my arm, grasping my hand, squeezing it. "Is it Lucius, Jess? Is he abusing you? You can tell me. We could get help!"

Oh, god . . . that's what she thinks. . . . "No, Min. I swear. If that was it, I'd tell you. I promise. Lucius has never laid a hand on me." *Not in a way I didn't want . . . didn't long for. . . .* "It's not what you think."

She stared at me, and I realized I'd said too much. "But it is *something*, Jess. You just admitted it."

"It's nothing," I insisted, trying to smile. "You're getting carried away."

Mindy released my hand abruptly, as if I'd betrayed her. Which I had. I'd lied to my best friend, and she knew it. "I don't believe you, Jess. And I can't believe you don't trust me." There was a catch in her voice as she said that, and she ran up the stairs, away from me.

I sank down in the empty stairwell, lonelier than I'd ever been in my life. I'd lost Lucius, and Jake, and now Mindy. Even my parents seemed almost like strangers living in a simpler world that I'd left behind. My only friend was an old vampire who loved cappuccino.

And, of course, I was gaining enemies.

"Well, well, well. The Packrat."

The vile voice came from above me. I glanced up and over my shoulder to see Frank Dormand and Ethan Strausser standing on the landing.

"Get lost," I said.

They stomped down the stairs, looming over me. "Whatcha doin,' freak?" Frank sneered, kicking my shin.

I stood, ready, almost eager to confront them. "What do you want?"

"We want to know what's going on in that garage at your parents' freak farm," Ethan said. I'd never noticed how literally thick his skull looked under his fuzzy, fair buzz cut.

"You two use the word 'freak' a lot," I noted. "You should check out a thesaurus. They have one in the library. You do know where the library is, right?"

"Ooh, the Packrat has a smart mouth today," Frank mocked me.

I tried to push past them, but they blocked my way.

"Not so fast," Frank said.

"Yeah," Ethan grunted. "We want to know what the freak—"

"Seriously, find a synonym."

"What the freak who lives at your house is doing to my girlfriend."

His girlfriend? That was a laugh. "I think Faith has a new boyfriend. In case you haven't noticed."

Ethan scowled. His pinkish face was downright ugly when he got angry. "That guy . . . he did something to Faith. He's not normal. He . . . he, like, hypnotized her."

"I don't know what you're talking about. And don't be a sore loser. Didn't football teach you anything?"

Frank flicked my ear. "Don't talk to Ethan like that."

I gave Frank a warning shove. "I'll talk to him any way I want. And don't *you* ever touch *me* again."

"Or what? You'll sic your bodyguard on me?" Frank taunted. "Because I say bring it on."

"We know about him," Ethan added ominously.

"You don't know anything."

"We know about the blood on you," Frank said. "And we know about Vladescu. We checked him out on the Internet. That dude thinks he's a vampire."

It was the first time I'd heard anyone, outside of Lucius and my immediate family, use the V-word. My blood froze. "What?"

"A vampire," Ethan repeated.

"And you know about it," Frank added, twisting a finger into my shoulder.

"You two are crazy. Do you even hear yourselves?"

"There's a whole website about Luc's family—the ones in Romania," Ethan said.

Frank smirked. "And do you know what they do in Romania? To vampires?"

I swallowed thickly. *Yes, I know.*

Frank made a motion like jamming a stake into his chest. "They've done it. For real. They've done it to old Luc's family. His *parents*."

"We don't like weird people around here, either," Dormand added.

There was something really menacing in the way he said that. I forced myself to laugh. But my laugh sounded hollow and frightened. "You're both nuts."

"Oh, I don't think so—"

Frank was interrupted by the slam of a door above us, and the rapid clip-clop of shoes against steps. "There you are," Faith Crosse cried, throwing herself into Ethan's arms, nearly knocking me down the last few stairs.

She started sobbing, clutching Ethan. He held her loosely, confusion on his bland, dumb face. "What's wrong, babe?"

"He broke up with me," she wailed. "That freak—"

Okay, I was seriously buying them all thesauri for graduation.

"He dumped me." She pulled away, jabbing a finger at her chest. "Me! Faith Crosse!"

She suddenly realized I was there, and turned her wrath on me, stabbing the finger in my direction. "You . . . you two . . . you're both . . ."

"Freaks?" I ventured.

"Yes! I hate you two." She turned back to Ethan, clutching him. "I don't know why I ever broke up with you. It's like he put me under a spell. But now it all seems so weird."

She started crying, clinging to Ethan. It seemed a little over the top to me, but Ethan was buying the act. He patted her back with his beefy hand.

"I just missed you so much." Faith sobbed. "Why did I ever go out with that guy?"

A part of me was hugely relieved. Lucius had sobered up. He had ditched Faith. *Maybe, just maybe, he's going to honor the pact. . . .*

My exultation was short-lived. Loosening her grip on Ethan, Faith whipped back around to face me, eyes narrowed to slits, mouth twisted with rage. She stabbed that finger at me again, talking through gritted teeth and tears. "You tell your precious Lucius Vladescu that nobody—nobody—dumps Faith Crosse. He *will* be sorry."

Faith was still glaring up at me when I reached the top of the stairs and looked down on her. "He'll pay," she called to me.

I believed her.

Everything I'd set in motion with that one cup of spilled blood . . . It was spinning out of control even faster than I'd ever imagined it could.

I had never really believed that Frank Dormand would actually manage to link Lucius to the word *vampire*. But he had. And now Faith was furious at Lucius.

Frank, stupid as he was, had stumbled upon the damning knowledge. And Faith was just the person to use it, ruthlessly.

I had underestimated my enemies.

Lucius would have called it a rookie mistake on my part. The error of a girl not ready to rule vampire legions. I had so much to learn and not enough time to learn it.

Chapter 51

"LUCIUS?" MY VOICE echoed in the near-empty gym, sounding small.

The cavernous room was practically dark, with only one bank of lights turned on. At the far end of the court, Lucius practiced layups alone in that repetitive, ritualistic way I'd seen before: dribble, slam, retrieve . . . again and again and again, never missing a shot. Never faltering. He didn't turn at the sound of my voice, and uncertain if he'd heard me, I walked toward him across the long expanse of hardwood.

"Lucius?" I tried again when I reached the top of the key.

He crashed the ball through the hoop and let it bounce away, turning to face me, puzzled. Not pleased. "Jessica . . . how did you find me?"

"I saw you leave with the ball, and it's too cold to play outside." I glanced around the empty gym. "I decided to see if you were here."

"How did you get in? The school is locked."

"The same way you did. I knocked on the window where the custodian was working. He told me where to find you."

"He usually just leaves the door nearest the gymnasium propped open for me," Lucius said. "I have made it worth his while, of course, to break the rules."

Some of the anger seemed to have faded from Lucius, as if it had healed along with his bruises. And yet the old Lucius wasn't back, either. The vampire before me seemed like a brand-new incarnation.

"Are you okay?" I asked. "I heard about Faith. That you broke up with her."

"Yes. That had run its course, as such things must."

I realized that Lucius and I were standing very close to where we'd danced, back at the Christmas formal, which seemed a lifetime away, although it had only been a few weeks. As close as we'd briefly been that night—our blood nearly commingling—that's how far apart we seemed in the empty gymnasium. I might as well have been standing at the other end of the massive room. I might as well have been standing on another planet.

"I made a mistake, Lucius. Drinking the blood. Letting Faith see it."

"I have made worse errors, Jessica. Don't worry yourself unnecessarily."

"But now Frank is talking about you being a vampire, and Faith is furious, and everyone is gossiping. Even Mindy is pulling away from me, scared by the rumors."

"Yes, quite a few things seem to be converging, do they not?" Lucius didn't smile wryly, as I'd expected. He was strangely quiet. Almost preternaturally calm.

"What are you going to do, Lucius?"

He turned his back on me and scooped up the ball, palming it easily. "Play basketball, Jessica. And wait."

"Lucius—"

"Good night, Jessica," he said, drowning out any reply I could have offered with the sound of the basketball smacking the hardwood, the squeak of his shoes on the court, and the swoosh of the shot through the rim. Again and again and again.

Chapter 52

"HEY." RESTING MY BACK against the tiled gym wall, I sank down next to Mindy, who had been eliminated right before me. "That looked like it hurt."

Mindy avoided my eyes. She kept staring at the dodgeball game like she had a million-dollar bet riding on the outcome.

"It's just a ball."

"But that idiot, Dane, aimed right for your head . . ."

Mindy edged away, just a little, on the gym floor. She still didn't look at me. "It didn't hurt so bad."

"Are you still mad at me? Or just freaked out?" I finally asked.

Mindy shrugged. "A little of both, I guess."

"Oh. Because at first it was like you always had an excuse for why we couldn't eat lunch, and then you got really bad about returning phone calls . . . You've been avoiding me for *two weeks*, Min."

Mindy fiddled with her shoelaces, retying them with the sort of focus usually associated with five-year-olds. "I'm just busy, that's all."

"You're not *that* busy."

Mindy finally looked at me. "I'm sorry, Jess, but . . ."

"But what?"

"It just got too weird for me."

"So you believe the rumors."

She stared back out at the dodgeball game. "I don't know what to believe. And you won't tell me."

"It's complicated," I said. "But if you can just trust me for a while until I sort it out—"

Mindy turned to me again, and this time there was fear in her eyes. "It's not just about you, Jess."

"Then what?"

"It's . . . him. He's the one who changed you. He did something to you. And he did something to Faith. She showed people the scratches . . ."

Mindy didn't have to clarify who "him" was: Lucius.

"Everything was normal until he came here, and he changed you," Mindy said, misery in her voice, as if Lucius had actually stolen something from her. And I suppose, in her view, he had.

"It's not Lucius's fault," I said. "I mean, it's nobody's fault, because everything's fine."

"It's not fine, Jess." Mindy's composure was cracking. "You know I like Lukey—I *liked* Lukey. But people are saying he's not right. People are *scared*."

"There's nothing to be scared of."

Mindy tried to smile but couldn't quite manage it. "If you say so, Jess."

"You're still coming over for my birthday, right?" I asked. "For dinner?"

My eighteenth birthday was a few weeks away. Mindy and I had always celebrated our birthdays together. We had exchanged presents and eaten cake and made wishes, side-by-side since we'd been four years old. I gave her hand a shake. "You'll be there, right?"

But the force with which Mindy pulled away and the way she glanced around to see if anyone had noticed me touching her told me that the tradition was over.

"I'm sorry, Jess," she said. It sounded like her throat was tight. "I just can't. Not if *he's* there."

"Please, Mindy . . ."

But I didn't get a chance to finish convincing her, because an errant dodgeball smacked the wall right above my head. My inadvertent yelp alerted Coach Larson to the fact that Mindy and I were just sitting around, and she blew her whistle. "Get your butts back in here or do some laps," she hollered, clapping fiercely. "Don't just sit there getting fat and lazy!"

I slid slowly up the wall with my usual goal of wasting as much gym time as possible, but Mindy was on her feet like a shot, tearing into the fray, grabbing up a ball and hurling it at our classmates with a vengeance that astonished me. I'd never seen Mindy Stankowicz actually participate in gym class. She always did her best either to be the first person retired from any game or to fake an injury. And she was the most believable actress I'd ever known when it came to cramps. One month she'd managed to have her period for three straight weeks. But now . . . now Mindy was rocketing around the gym floor, scooping up every stray ball she could get her hands on, firing like a Gatling gun in a gangster movie. Maybe she was imagining me out there, cowering against the wall.

"Get in here, too, Packwood." Coach Larson blew her whistle again. "Now!"

But I ignored her. I just watched Mindy for a few moments, then walked to the locker room, excusing myself with a resolute dignity that my gym teacher seemed powerless to counter, because she didn't even attempt to order me again.

Chapter 53

"MRS. WILHELM?"

I glanced up from an elaborate doodle I'd been sketching in my notebook to see Frank Dormand waving his fat hand around, trying to get our teacher's attention. I'd never seen Frank raise his hand for anything, so I figured he either had diarrhea and needed a hall pass or . . . actually, I couldn't think of any other reason a moron like Frank would call attention to himself in an academic setting. Therefore, what he said next greatly surprised me.

"Yes, Frank?" Mrs. Wilhelm seemed puzzled, too.

"I did a book report."

What?

"Oh. Dear." Mrs. Wilhelm clearly didn't know whether to be delighted, terrified, or both. "You did? Because you weren't assigned . . ."

"I know," Frank said. "But I was so interested in the books that I read ahead . . ."

I could see Mrs. Wilhelm getting a little intrigued in spite of her obvious misgivings. To hear that a student—especially a dismal scholar like Frank—had read ahead . . . well, it must have seemed like she'd won the lottery and found true love all on the same day. "You did?" she repeated, eyes getting a little starry.

Something about the whole situation struck me as very, very wrong. I glanced back at Lucius, slightly alarmed, but he was merely watching, eyes neutral with that new strange calm he'd cultivated.

"And what did you read?" Mrs. Wilhelm inquired.

"*Dracula,*" Frank announced. "And I'm ready to talk about it."

Oh, no. Oh, please, no. I swung back around in my seat. We were on some sort of dangerous ground now. Frank and Faith had cooked up something. *Please, Mrs. Wilhelm. Tell him just to shut up.*

"Well, Frank, we are still weeks away from reading Bram Stoker," Mrs. Wilhelm mused.

"I know, but I really got excited about this great book," Frank said. "It gave me lots to think about. I really want to tell the class about it."

Mrs. Wilhelm wavered for one more second, but the idea that a lackluster student was actually excited about a book— had found things to *think about . . .* it was just too much for her. "Please, then, Franklin. Do share your report." She took a seat as Frank squeezed out from behind his desk and lumbered to the front of the class.

My heart was racing. I glanced at Mindy, but she kept her gaze locked straight forward. I knew she was aware of me looking at her, but she would not meet my eyes. *What the hell was about to happen? Did my former best friend know?*

Frank rattled a sheet of notebook paper and cleared his

throat. Then he read, in his awkward, flat way, "The thing about Bram Stoker's *Dracula* that is very surprising is that it is based on a real story of a vampire that actually lived in Romania. That vampire's name was Vlad the Impaler, which is sort of like the name Vladescu."

Shut up, Frank. . . .

Behind me, Faith laughed softly and whispered, "Uh-oh!" Just loud enough to make sure Lucius and I heard.

"Some people say that vampires still exist," Frank continued. "If you look on the Internet, there is a lot of information about people who drink blood—*human blood*—and call themselves vampires. Many of these freaks live in Romania, where they are often killed because normal people shouldn't have to live with them."

He paused and stared pointedly past me. At Lucius. *No, no, no.*

"Franklin, I'm not sure this is appropriate," Mrs. Wilhelm sputtered, standing up.

But Frank returned to reading, more quickly, before anyone could stop him. "There are even names of blood-drinking people on the Internet. Lots of people who say they are vampires have the last name Vladescu, just like Lucius. That is a weird coincidence."

"Frank, sit down now!" Mrs. Wilhelm ordered.

But it was too late. The murmurs had started, and everyone turned to gawk at Lucius. Everyone but me. I just kept staring straight ahead, maybe because my heart had stopped and I was technically dead. My fingers, clutching my desk, felt cold and stiff.

"You can check it out online," Frank concluded, ignoring

our teacher. "Vampires. Just like in the book." He paused. "And that is my report."

Frank folded his paper and jammed it in his back pocket, a smug smile on his face. A smile that faded about the same time a shadow was cast across my desk.

Lucius, don't go up there.

But of course a vampire prince would not sit still and be toyed with. Lucius stalked to the front of the class, and the smile on Frank's face disappeared completely.

"Did you wish to make a point with your awkward and ill-conceived 'report,' Mr. Dormand?" Lucius demanded, squaring off in front of Frank. His back was to the class, but you could see the tension in his broad shoulders. Like a muscular cat about to pounce on a fat rat.

"Lucius." Mrs. Wilhelm rushed forward.

Lucius ignored her. He leaned over Frank, jabbing his index finger into the bully's chest, pushing him against the whiteboard. "Because if you have something to say, you should be less oblique. You are not clever enough to be subtle."

"Get security," Mrs. Wilhelm ordered Dirk Bryce, who sat closest to the door. "Run!"

Dirk hesitated for a second, like he was afraid to miss the action that was clearly brewing, then took off like a shot down the hall.

Edging out from under Lucius's finger, Frank swallowed hard, glancing at his classmates. He seemed to draw some courage from their presence. "What I'm saying is, your parents were killed because they were bloodsucking vampires. Is that clear enough?"

"Franklin Dormand, stop this now!" Mrs. Wilhelm shrieked, tugging at Frank's shoulders, pulling him farther away from Lucius.

"Are you accusing me of being a vampire?" Lucius demanded, matching Frank's retreat step for step. "Because I am indeed—"

"No!" I yelled, bolting from my seat and rushing at Lucius. I grabbed his arm and yanked as hard as I could. "Don't let Frank bait you."

Lucius spun around, furious, as though he was about to shake me off physically, but our eyes met, and he regained control of himself. The new calm resignation glazed his eyes again. He peeled my fingers gently off his arm. I started to grab him again, as if I could silence him with my hands, but at the last second, I let my hand drop to my side. There was nothing I could do at that point.

The whole classroom grew eerily quiet as Lucius and I stared at each other. Me, silently begging him not to say anything more to damn himself. Not to provoke a real fight. Lucius challenging me with an unspoken, *Why the hell not at this point? Why not let the end begin?*

You could hear Frank, Lucius, and Mrs. Wilhelm breathing hard as we all waited for what might happen next. It was the flash point. We teetered on the edge of chaos—or of calm.

Lucius found it in himself, somehow, to choose calm.

He turned slowly back to Frank. "The next time you have something to say to me, say it directly. And be prepared for a response that will leave you wishing you'd had the good sense to stay silent."

"Is that a threat?" Frank spun around to Mrs. Wilhelm. "He can't make threats! That's grounds for getting kicked out of school!"

"Stop, Frank," Mrs. Wilhelm said. "Stop now."

Security arrived then, storming into the room only to find us all standing, tense but in control. "What's happening here?" the school cop demanded, clearly eager to abuse some authority.

I waited for the hammer to drop, but to my surprise, Mrs. Wilhelm didn't blurt the whole story. Her voice was a little shaky, but she was steady on her feet as she said, "Nothing's happening. It was just a small misunderstanding. Everything's fine now."

Frank's eyes widened, and he pointed at Lucius. "But he just threatened—"

"SILENCE," Mrs. Wilhelm thundered, with more force than I'd ever heard her use before. "SILENCE, FRANK."

It took me a few seconds to figure out what she was doing. Protecting Lucius. Her pet student. The one pupil who actually loved literature as much as she did. He might be a bloodsucker, but to Mrs. Wilhelm, Lucius Vladescu would always be the guy in the back row who understood hidden metaphors, obscure symbolism, and the shadowy passions that consumed a fictional character named Heathcliff. Good old Mrs. Wilhelm: She would protect Lucius from the wuthering gusts as long as he was in her classroom. I thanked her silently in my heart.

Unfortunately, Lucius couldn't live his whole life in English lit.

As the class filed out of the room, I glanced at Faith Crosse. The faintest trace of a smug, bemused, satisfied smile shimmered—or slithered?—across her cotton-candy pink, high-gloss lips.

Chapter 54

"JESS, BLOW OUT the candles."

My eighteenth birthday. It should have been one of the highlights of my life, but it was just awful. Depressing. I had no friends and so no party. My only guest was, of course, Uncle Dorin, whose continued presence we had finally revealed to Lucius and my parents.

My uncle sat at the table, watching everything with his bright little eyes. "This is just lovely," he kept saying. "Top notch."

"The wax is dripping," Mom said, prodding me. She had concocted a vegan cake out of rice syrup, soy milk, and unsweetened applesauce. A real crowd-pleaser. Still, I blew, to make her happy. The candles sputtered, died. I didn't bother to make a wish.

"Hooray," Mom said, trying to rally the little party.

Lucius stared at me from across the table as Mom cut the faux cake. If there is one thing worse than an angry vampire, it is the inscrutable version. Nobody can do blank eyes like a vampire. I stared back, trying not to miss the person who was right there in front of me. It didn't work. I missed him, anyway. If only he would just talk to me. . . . He had to be lonely.

Everyone was sidestepping him at school, whispering behind his back, as the story of Frank's book report spread through the halls, adding more force to the rumors already circulating. The fact that Lucius had pretty much admitted he was undead, right in front of Mrs. Wilhelm's class, hadn't helped to calm things down.

Suddenly it wasn't uncommon to hear the word "vampire" whispered in the halls of Woodrow Wilson High School.

"Hey, this is great," Dad said, digging into his slice of cake. *Does he really believe that?*

"We got you a gift." Mom smiled, handing me a box wrapped in the cheerful, crinkled pink-and-yellow paper we'd been recycling since I was about ten years old.

"Oh, gifts," Dorin cried, clapping his hands together. "I do love presents."

I carefully removed the wrapping so Mom could put it away for yet another year. Inside the box were a new, high-tech calculator and a card announcing that I had a renewed subscription to *Math Whiz* magazine. I gave my parents a puzzled glance. They knew I'd quit the math team.

"You might regain your interest someday," Mom said.

I knew what she really meant: You might become yourself again. You will get over Lucius and your life will go on.

"Thanks, Mom and Dad. It's a great gift."

"Lucius, don't you have a gift for Antanasia, too?" Dorin nudged.

Lucius snapped back from some private reverie. "Yes, yes. Of course."

"Really, Lucius?" He'd been so detached, so drawn into

himself, that I certainly hadn't expected him to go shopping on my behalf.

I watched with anticipation as he reached into the pocket of his jeans, pulling out a box. A tiny case. Red velvet. Like the kind of box rings come in. Engagement rings.

Both my parents sucked in their breaths. You could hear the sound of air whistling past their lips. With the exhale, a few crumbs of the hideous cake dripped out of Dad's open mouth.

Suddenly my own heart was racing, too.

Lucius slid the box across the table. "Here. Happy birthday. Many happy returns."

"Oh, goodness," Mom was saying. "I'm not sure . . ."

I willed my fingers not to shake as I reached for the box and flipped open the lid. *Is this going to be it? Did Lucius change his mind? Are we going through with the pact?*

But no.

Inside, lying on a small square of pure white velvet, was not a ring, but a necklace, with a stone so deeply crimson as to be almost black.

It was beautiful.

I loathed it.

I nearly reeled from the disappointment that squeezed my chest, making it difficult to breathe. At the sight of the ring-sized container, I'd really believed that Lucius had changed his mind about fulfilling the pact. For the briefest moment, I'd pictured us together. Our whole future had flashed before me. Me. Lucius. Peace among vampires. Safety in each other's arms, no matter what the Elders or our fellow students threatened. For the briefest moment, I'd believed the small box had held the promise of all that.

But of course, looking across the table at Lucius, I realized that my hopes had been absurd. His was not the posture of a man proposing marriage. He sat upright, eyes neutral, self-contained in his new, serenely disinterested state. Lucius Vladescu wasn't a suitor about to marry. He was a vampire about to be destroyed. Waiting for what would converge upon him.

I wanted to scream and hurl the necklace across the room, like a petulant child who didn't get the toy she desired. But I wasn't a petulant child. I was a devastated young woman, and I had to at least exhibit a grace I didn't feel.

"Thank you," I managed to say. "It's lovely." Then I snapped the lid shut and set the box aside. "I'm rather tired. If you don't mind, I think I'll go upstairs."

My parents both looked sad and drained, and I realized that they were also being dragged down by my too-apparent suffering and their concerns for me and Lucius. Pushing back my chair, I went over to Mom and hugged her tightly. "Thank you so much for a wonderful birthday. You're the best mother ever." I moved to my dad. "And you're the best dad. Of all time."

"You're a beautiful young woman, Jessica," Dad said, voice catching in his throat. "We're both proud of you."

Pulling free of Dad's embrace, I nodded to Dorin and Lucius. "Good night, and thank you," I said.

"Good night, Antanasia," Dorin chirped. "Many happy returns!"

Lucius didn't say a word. He just sat there, staring at the rejected gift.

I maintained my composure all the way up to my bedroom, even after I was out of earshot of my family. Even as I undressed and pulled on my nightgown, I didn't yield to my tears. I saved my sobs until I'd climbed into bed, buried my face in my pillow, and smothered them, so no one would hear. I would not make my parents worry even more than they already did.

"Jessica."

His voice came from my door.

I rolled over to see, through my tears, the wavering shape of Lucius standing in my doorway. I swiped at my eyes, embarrassed to have been caught weeping.

He entered the room, quietly closing the door behind him, and came over to me, sitting down on the bed.

"Please, don't cry," he soothed. "There is nothing worth crying over. It is your birthday."

"Everything is wrong," I protested, grinding away my tears with the heels of my palms.

"No, Jessica," Lucius soothed, pulling away my hands. He gently drew his thumb beneath my eyes, first one then the other, wiping the tears. "For you, things will be right. This is a happy day for you. Your eighteenth birthday is an important milestone. Please, I cannot bear your tears."

"A happy day?" I was incredulous.

"The box . . . you thought it was something else," Lucius said. "I saw your face. You were disappointed. You thought I had undergone a change of heart . . ."

"Yes," I said, still sniffling.

"No, Jessica." He shook his head. "Never. You must forget all that."

"I can't," I said, reaching out for him. But Lucius stood, rising quickly, almost like he was scared to touch me, and I knew that for all his cool detachment, a part of him still felt drawn to me. That he had always felt drawn to me, as I had—and did—to him.

"You did not give me the opportunity to explain my gift," he said, reaching into his pocket and again retrieving the box. He held it out to me. "It is better than a ring, for you. Better than a promise of . . . what? Eternity with a doomed vampire?"

"Nothing could have made me happier than your agreement to the pact," I said, refusing to take the box.

"Oh, Jessica, abandon those notions in favor of what I *can* offer." He extended his hand again, the box on his palm. "Did you not recognize the contents?"

I was confused, but stood up, curious, reaching for the box. "Recognize it?"

"From the photograph. I know you've looked at her, Jessica. I knew you would, in your own time. When you were ready."

My mother. It was the necklace from the photograph he'd tucked in my book. I snapped open the lid again. "Oh, Lucius. Where did you get it?"

"It was held for you, in Romania. To be given to you on this occasion. It was your mother's favorite possession, and it is my honor to deliver such an important keepsake to you. I hope you wear it many years in good health, with good fortune."

I went to my desk and picked up the photograph in the silver frame, looking at the bloodstone that graced my mother's throat. The bloodstone that I now held in my other hand, tangible evidence of Mihaela Dragomir's existence. A real link to her. The stone lay on the velvet, deep red, like a real heart. A heart transplanted from my mother to me.

Lucius came up behind me, resting his hands upon my shoulders. "Is she not beautiful, powerful, regal . . . just like you?" he asked.

"Do you really believe that?"

"Yes," Lucius said. "And I think you have come to believe it, too."

"Then—"

"No." Lucius didn't even allow me to bring up the pact.

I replaced the photograph on the desk and turned to face my mirror. Removing the necklace from the box, I held it up to my throat.

Lucius followed me, watching my reflection. "Allow me. Please." He again stepped behind me, taking the delicate chain from my fingers. I swept my hair off my neck, and Lucius slipped the necklace around my throat and sealed the clasp.

The stone was cool against my skin, much as my vampire mother's touch would have been. As I watched myself in the mirror, the power I'd felt growing inside of me—her power—surged with even greater strength. The connection I'd been forging with Mihaela Dragomir was finally welded tight with the clasping of that fragile chain, and I could almost hear her whispering in my ear. *"Do not give him up for lost yet, Antanasia. That is not our way. Your will is as strong as his, and his love as strong as yours."*

I turned to face Lucius, and I didn't wait for him to pull

away, or draw me close, or make any movement. I placed my hands on his chest, slipped them upward, and wrapped my arms around his neck.

"Antanasia, this cannot be. . . ." Lucius clasped my wrists in his strong hands, as though to push me away.

"It can be," I promised him, holding firm, my fingers linking behind his neck, lacing into his black hair.

"Why can I not do as I should?" He groaned, giving up easily, not only accepting my embrace, but answering it. "I should have gone by now . . . I waste time, just to be near you, I fear. And for what? A few more moments before I am nothing but one of your memories? A tragic entry in a young woman's diary?"

"You stayed for this moment," I said, allowing him, then, to take control, as I knew he would want. I had wielded all the power I'd needed. I had drawn him back from the cold distance. Now I wanted *Lucius* to kiss *me*. To bite my throat. To fulfill what we'd both wanted for so long. Ever since he'd leaned over me in the kitchen on the first day he'd arrived at our house, his hand brushing my cheek. Ever since he'd met my eyes and asked, *"Would it be so repugnant, really, Antanasia? To be with me?"*

Even then, I'd known, deep inside, that it would be far from repugnant. That it would be something miles and miles beyond *nice*. That it might just be bliss.

Lucius hesitated just one more moment, staring into my eyes. "I am no less dangerous to you, Antanasia," he whispered. "Whatever we do . . . it is only for tonight. It changes nothing. I will leave to meet my destiny, and you will stay here to carry out yours."

288

"Don't think about that now," I begged. Because I did not believe that what we did that night would change nothing. I believed it could change everything. "Just forget the future for now."

"As you wish, my princess," Lucius said, closing his eyes, giving in to me. He leaned down to brush his cool, rough lips against mine, first gently, then more insistently.

I snaked my fingers deeper into his hair, pulling him against me, and when I did that, Lucius made a hungry little sound, slipping his hands up into my dark tangle of curls, and we kissed harder, like we were famished for each other. Like we were devouring each other.

And as we kissed, really kissed, something inside of me was smashed, like a splitting atom, erupting with all the force of a shattering nucleus. And yet I was strangely at peace, too. It was like I'd found my place in the universe, in the chaos, and Lucius and I could go along locked together throughout time without end, like pi, existing infinitely, irrationally, spinning through time.

His lips moved down to my throat, and my incisors began to ache at the touch of his fangs, which brushed my skin, sharp against me. He traced his teeth along the length of my neck, down to where the bloodstone rested in the hollow, close to my breastbone.

"Lucius, yes," I urged him, opening my throat as far as I could, offering and begging. "Don't stop . . . please don't stop this time . . ."

If he bites me, he would be mine. . . . Always . . .

"No, Antanasia." He fought himself, but I pressed him to myself again, feeling his fangs prick at my flesh, almost enough to pierce the skin, and my own teeth sharpened against my gums, nearly ripping through.

"Yes, Lucius . . . my fangs . . . I can feel them . . ."

"No." Lucius regained control of himself then, but it was a tenuous control, and he slid his hands around to cup my face, pulling away, again staring into my eyes.

"We came too close, Antanasia . . . The kiss must be enough between us. I will not be the one to damn you, no matter how much I desire it. I will not drag *you* to destruction, too."

"I don't understand . . ." *We were so close. . . .*

"Please don't ever regret this, Antanasia," he implored me, and his eyes were the opposite of cool and detached. He seemed fevered, shaken, almost desperate, suddenly. "Don't be angry, when I am gone or changed. Please, just remember this for what it was, which was everything to me. To the man I am right now."

"You won't change, Lucius," I promised, grasping his wrists, not understanding. What we had just shared . . . surely the two of us, together, could seal pacts and stop wars and answer any challenge. We were vampire royalty. And we were together. "You're not going anywhere," I reassured him. "It's fine now. It will be fine."

"No, Antanasia. No, it is not fine. It will not be fine."

I had not noticed, until that moment, that my bedroom window had been pierced by a flashing red light, which spattered a crazy blood pattern against the walls.

"Lucius? What's happening?"

He didn't answer. But he was still holding me when Dad burst into the room.

"Lucius, the police are here," Dad said. He was strangely composed. "A girl claims to have been bitten by a vampire, and she's identified you."

"Lucius?" I stared up at him, desperate for an answer.

But Lucius just kissed me once more, lightly on the lips, and turned to my father. "It's best that I face this alone, Mr. Packwood," he said. "Please—let me deal with this without your help this time."

Dad hesitated, then stepped aside and allowed Lucius to go, capturing me in his arms as I tried to follow.

Chapter 55

"SHE'S SETTING LUCIUS up," I told my parents. "Faith swore she'd get back at him for breaking up with her. She made it all up."

They shot each other looks that said they were uncertain.

"Lucius broke up with Faith days ago," I added, pleading his case. "And I'm pretty sure it was because he was afraid he was going to bite her. He knew he was getting out of control, but he stopped himself."

Mom was clearing plates from my dismal party. "Jessica, Lucius has been going through something very difficult, struggling within himself. We can't be sure what happened."

"Nothing happened!"

"And was 'nothing' happening in your room?" Dad asked. "You are too involved with Lucius to be objective, Jessica."

"He's a Vladescu," Mom added, dumping plates in the

sink. She seemed very upset. "He wants not to be, but perhaps he couldn't fight that side of himself. Perhaps it was even dangerous to allow him to live here. I'm not even sure we did the right thing anymore."

"You're not being fair. Just because his uncles are terrible doesn't mean Lucius is a monster! He *didn't* bite Faith. Please, let's go to the police station!"

My parents shared another uncertain look. Then Dad said, "Jessica, no matter how we feel, Lucius asked us to let him handle this alone. We are going to respect his wishes. And so are you."

"I'm eighteen now," I pointed out. "I don't need your permission to do anything."

"But you do need a car," Mom noted.

I hurried to the hook by the back door where my parents kept the keys. Gone. "Where are the keys?"

"This is for your own good, Jess," Dad said. "You've gotten in way too deep with Lucius. You need to step back."

"And it is our responsibility to protect you," Mom added. "We want to help Lucius, too, of course. But you are our first priority."

I stared at them, betrayed.

"He doesn't want us right now, Jessica. We've done all we can," Dad said.

The phone rang, and I snatched up the receiver. "Lucius?"

"No, it's Mindy."

"I can't talk now—"

"It's about Lucius," Mindy said. There was panic in her voice.

292

"What is it? What's going on?"

"I don't know if I should tell you."

"Just say it, Mindy. Please."

"They're out of control," she said. "They're talking about beating him up for what he did to Faith. Frank has them all worked up, with all that vampire stuff. They're crazy!"

My fingers clutched at the receiver. "What exactly did you hear?"

"Some of the guys . . . They're waiting for Lucius. They're going to take him out to Jake Zinn's barn and 'teach him a lesson.'" She paused. "I'm scared for him, Jess. I don't know what he did to you—"

"Nothing!"

"But I'm scared for him. They're talking about the blood on you, and the scratches on Faith, and how his leg healed so fast . . . and all that stuff they found on the website about Lucius's family, Jess." She paused. "Faith heard you call him a vampire, too. In the barn."

That day in the barn so long ago. Again I made things worse for Lucius. Me . . . I'm the dangerous one. . . .

"They keep talking about vampires and stakes," Mindy cried.

"Stakes?" The receiver nearly slipped from my grasp.

"Yes, Jess. They're taking *stakes,* like it's the Middle Ages or something! In case he's really a vampire! They're crazy!"

Stakes. Out-of-control people. Mobs. My birth parents were destroyed that way. . . .

I struggled to remain calm. "Did they say when this is all happening?"

"Tonight. Later tonight. They're going to get Luc when he comes out of the police station . . . Everybody heard about him getting arrested . . ."

Of course. The rumor mill was probably going berserk. "Thanks, Mindy."

"I . . . I know we haven't been friends lately . . . but this— this is crazy. I thought you should know."

"I gotta go."

"And Jess?"

"What?"

"Happy birthday."

"Bye, Mindy." I hung up the receiver, tore out the door before my parents could stop me, and ran for our barn to saddle up Belle.

Chapter 56

DEAR VASILE,

Pardon the Mount Gretna Police Station letterhead on the admittedly cheap stationery. I am fortunate to have even this with which to write you.

It appears that I am accused of "attacking" a local girl here, Faith Crosse, and biting her in the neck. They will finish "processing" me soon (like the region's famous bologna!), so I shall try to keep this "short and sweet," as the Americans say. Most importantly, I did NOT sink my fangs into that insufferable girl. She completely fabricated the injury. The police officers slid a series of "shocking" photographs under my nose, watching my face.

I could but laugh. Bite marks, yes. But from a vampire? No. A clever fakery, though. Faith is nothing if not clever. And apparently admirably inured to pain. The marks appeared rather deep. She had a few good bruises, too. Bravo. Excellent work.

During a particularly dark time, I rather enjoyed Faith's devious nature. Now my dalliance comes back to bite me. Almost deliciously ironic, isn't it?

Regardless. I sense that the mood in this little village is rather unforgiving at present. Although I am to be released "upon my own recognizance" until formally charged, I have a strong suspicion—vampire's intuition—that "the jig is up." (You must sample some of the old American crime dramas available on DVD. They have a certain grimly humorous sensibility that connects with a vampire.)

Or, to put it in terms you are more likely to understand, the mob is gathering, as I have anticipated for some time now.

I write because I know that you had longed for the pleasure of destroying me yourself for defying you. For breaking the pact and ruining your plan. Oh, how you no doubt thirsted to thrust the stake deep. But now the much-yearned-for task will fall to a gang of ridiculous American teenagers. In a sense, they have bested you, Vasile. Is it cruel of me to feel so happy to deprive you of that which you so desired? And yet I do feel a certain joy to know that you will always wish it had been you. . . .

Thus, I go willingly to my fate in humble Lebanon County, Pennsylvania. Thus, history repeats itself. Yet another Vladescu destroyed. I shall strive to go as bravely and stoically as my parents. To uphold the honor of the clan—which is more than you have done, Vasile, in my view.

I also write on behalf of Jessica. I never bit her, Vasile. She remains an American teenager. Leave her be. The dream of a Dragomir princess is over.

Is there more to say? It seems odd, given my penchant for rambling missives, that my final letter is so brief. But, in truth, I am done—in more ways than one. (Who can resist gallows humor? Is it not a mark of courage to laugh at one's own demise?)

I entrust this now to the United States Postal Service. Very reliable organization. It is the rare bureaucracy that one would trust to deliver one's last words. And yet I feel confident this will reach you expeditiously.

Your nephew in blood and memory,
Lucius

Chapter 57

BELLE'S HOOVES THUNDERED in the rainy night. I was freezing on her back. It was late winter, and the night was still icy cold, the sleet pelting against my face, melting through my thin shirt. There had been no time to grab a coat.

"Come on, Belle," I urged, slamming my heels into her flanks, willing my mare to go faster. It seemed like she understood my urgency, for she flew across the frozen field. I prayed she wouldn't hit a groundhog hole and snap a leg, the night was so dark and we tore so recklessly across the uneven terrain.

Save Lucius . . . Save Lucius . . . That's what I heard pounding in my ears with every hoofbeat.

Ahead of me, finally, the Zinns' barn loomed, pale gray and

arched like a tombstone against the sky. A little cry escaped my lips. There were cars there. Already. *But I can't be too late. I just can't.* As I leapt from Belle's back before she even reined to a stop, I heard raised voices from inside the barn. Angry, male voices, and the sound of a scuffle. Running to the barn, I tore open the heavy door, hauling it back on its rusty track.

Inside: pandemonium. The struggle was already underway. The mob was loosed.

"Jake, no," I cried, seeing my ex-boyfriend there in the middle of the melee. But he didn't pay any attention. No one did. No one even noticed me running into the fight, trying to drag the boys off of Lucius. The crowd was in a lather. There was blood everywhere, fists flying, and Lucius struggling alone against them. He was so strong, but not strong enough for this. . . .

"I'll kill you for what you did to her," Ethan Strausser was screaming, pounding on Lucius. I tried to grasp Ethan's fists, but someone pushed me away, flinging me against a wall. I came back, yelling at them to stop, but no one paid attention. They were drunk on revenge and fear and hatred, hatred of someone different than themselves.

"Stop it," I begged. "Leave him alone!"

Lucius must have heard my voice, because he turned toward me, just for a second, and I saw surprise in his eyes. Surprise and resignation.

"Lucius, no," I begged, knowing what he was about to do. Get himself destroyed.

But he made the fatal move, anyway. He turned back to the already furious boys and bared his fangs.

Macho bravado was abandoned among the attackers.

"Vampire!" Ethan cried, terror and shock mingling in his voice.

"Son of a bitch . . ." Frank Dormand backed away, looking petrified, as if he'd suddenly realized that it wasn't just a terrible game anymore. He'd unleashed a power he had never really expected to loose, for all his talk of vampires and websites and stakes.

Ethan scrambled backward on the hay-covered floor, too, but he was reaching blindly behind him for something.

I saw it before he located it. The stake. Homemade. Crude. But lethal. Half buried in the hay. I dove for it—but Jake saw it, too, and he was faster. He snatched it up and stalked toward Lucius, who was fighting his way to his feet, squaring off against the shorter but still powerful wrestler.

"No, Jake!" I wailed, scrambling to my knees, scrambling to grab Jake's legs, missing them as Jake gained speed. Lucius growled, advanced, too.

And then, as if in slow motion, I saw my ex-boyfriend raise his arm, lunge forward, and plunge the stake into Lucius's chest.

"Jake—no!" I screamed the words. Or I thought I screamed the words. I don't remember actually hearing them come out of my mouth.

And in a split second, it was over.

Jake—the *nice* boy—was standing over Lucius's body. Lucius's too-still body.

"What have you done?" I cried into the sudden silence.

Jake stepped back, the heavy, sharp, and bloody chunk of wood in his hand. "It had to be me," he said, looking at me with miserable eyes. "I'm sorry."

I didn't know what he meant. I didn't care.

"Lucius," I moaned, stumbling through the hay. I collapsed at his side, feeling for his pulse. It was there, but fainter than usual. Blood seeped from a hole in his shirt. A gaping hole. I glanced up at the circle of faces. Familiar faces. Guys I knew from school. The anger was gone now, and the realization of what they'd actually done seemed to be settling in. How *could* they have done this? "Get help," I begged them.

"No, Antanasia," Lucius said softly.

I bent over him, gently pressing my hands over the hole in his chest, as if I could stop the blood. "Lucius . . ."

"It is over, Jessica," he managed to say, voice soft. "Just leave it be."

A commanding voice came from the darkest corner of the barn. "Get out. All of you. And never speak of this. Never. Nothing ever happened here."

Dorin. My uncle had shed his usual merry demeanor, and he spoke with an unfamiliar authority as he emerged from the shadows, striding in, taking control.

Feet shuffled quickly in hay as the cluster of teenagers obeyed and dispersed, running as though the vampire's words had been a slingshot releasing them into the night.

Where had Dorin come from? Why hadn't he been here in time? I rose and ran at him, pounding my stained fists against his chest. "You let this happen. You should have protected him!"

"Leave, Jessica," Dorin insisted, grabbing my fists. He was surprisingly strong. Sadness suffused his eyes. "This is Lucius's destiny. It's what he wishes."

No. That can't be. We just kissed. . . . "What do you mean, 'what he wishes'?" I wailed, running back to Lucius, falling to my knees. "Our destiny is together, right? Say it, Lucius."

"No, Antanasia," he said, voice weak and fading. "You belong here. Live a happy life. A long life. A human life."

"No, Lucius." I sobbed, begging him to live. He couldn't just give up. "I want to live with you."

"It is not to be, Antanasia."

I swore I saw tears in his black eyes, just before he closed them, and I started screaming, and the next thing I remembered was my dad's hands lifting me, pulling me away, carrying me, fighting against nothing and everything, to the van. I didn't know when they had arrived or how they had found me.

It didn't matter.

Lucius was gone.

Destroyed.

The body disappeared, and Dorin disappeared, and, as per Dorin's instruction, nobody ever spoke of it again. It was like the whole thing had been a dream. If not for the necklace around my throat, the way the clasp kind of burned where his fingers had sealed it, maybe I wouldn't have believed it myself.

Chapter 58

"AND THE WOODROW WILSON School Spirit Award goes to . . . Faith Crosse."

My fingers clutched the chain-link fence as the girl responsible, in large part, for Lucius's destruction strode to the temporary riser like some sort of hero, mounting the steps to a chorus of whistles and cheers from a sea of graduates in navy blue caps and gowns. Beneath her cap, Faith's blond hair flapped like a flag in the brisk wind as she accepted her award and waved to the crowd.

The numbness I'd carefully nurtured as a way of dealing with my pain and rage and loss nearly shattered to see Faith applauded, and I'm not sure how I kept from shrieking out loud.

Why did I come to watch graduation? I had refused to participate in the ceremony, but something perverse in me had drawn me to the football field to witness my classmates, many of whom I'd known since kindergarten—and a few of whom had participated in the slaughter of the one person I'd loved most in this world—receive their diplomas. I suppose I wanted to see their faces. Was there any hint of the evil deed they'd committed in that barn? Or had they convinced themselves that nothing had ever happened, as Dorin had advised? Or— and this was the possibility that made me sickest—did one or two of them believe they had done something good? Did Jake feel that way? He'd said to me that night, "It had to be me." What did that even mean?

"Antanasia." The voice was soft but clear. "It does no good to torture yourself. Although dreaming of revenge is a very typical vampire behavior."

Turning, I saw him.

A slightly pudgy, balding vampire, just a few feet from me, leaning against the wall of the field's concession stand under a sign urging us to contribute to the Woodrow Wilson Band Boosters. He wore a navy T-shirt with the Wilson mascot—a tough-looking, jowly dog dubbed "Woody"—embroidered on the chest.

Catching my eye, Dorin waved.

Just seeing him—someone connected to Lucius and that night—made me want to vomit, for just a second. When my stomach stopped lurching, I started walking like some sort of zombie.

Behind me, I heard more cheers as Ethan Strausser won an award for outstanding achievement in athletics.

The applause seemed to come from a million miles away as I made my way across the grass toward Dorin. Toward a brief but intense past that still consumed me.

"Well, well, well. Don't you look pale and serious." Dorin clucked as I approached him. "Almost like a proper vampire." He hugged me, but I stiffened in his embrace, still believing he'd failed to protect Lucius. "Why aren't you graduating today with the rest of them?" he asked.

"They don't mean anything to me," I said, stepping back from him.

"And yet you're here!"

"Dorin—forget about me. What are *you* doing here?"

"Hmm." Dorin frowned. "It's very complicated stuff. Very difficult to explain."

I really wasn't up for anything challenging, but I asked anyway. "What kind of complicated stuff?"

"It seems that there's a bit of a dustup in Romania." Dorin sighed, avoiding my eyes. "Something of a mess, really. You're not supposed to know about it, of course. But I got to thinking . . . it's not really fair to keep you in the dark. We've probably done so for too long. That was Lucius's idea, of course. Don't blame me. If he knew I was here . . ."

My knees nearly buckled, and Dorin lunged to catch my elbow. "Steady there!"

"Did you just say . . . Lucius?" I demanded. "If *Lucius* knew you were here?" *But that's impossible. . . . Lucius had been destroyed. . . .*

Dorin cleared his throat, looking guilty and nervous. "He thought it was best to do it his way. But he's just miserable, and things are falling apart back home."

I grabbed Dorin by the shoulders, shaking him harder than I'd ever shaken anything in my life. "IS. LUCIUS. ALIVE?"

"Oh, yes, quite," Dorin admitted, trying to wrench out of my grasp. "But at this rate . . ."

It is weird how relief and joy—the most intense joy imaginable—and fury—the most intense fury imaginable—can get all mixed up, and the next thing you know, you are sobbing and laughing and pounding your fists against a vampire's chest, driving him backward against a high school concession stand.

When I regained the smallest measure of my composure, we went home to get my passport. I was going to Romania. I was going home to find Lucius.

Chapter 59

"SO JAKE ROSE to the occasion, so to speak. Agreed to be in on the whole stunt. Said he sort of admired Lucius, in spite of everything. Something about Lucius standing up for you against that bully Frank Dormand."

"And that was enough to convince him to thrust a stake into Lucius's chest?" I was skeptical.

"Well, I may have threatened him, too. Just a little," Dorin confirmed. "But he's a nice boy, that Jake. It's a good thing Lucius had mentioned him in letters home."

"Lucius had mentioned him?"

"Oh, of course," Dorin said. "He was always complaining about the 'squatty, nice' boy who was messing up the whole courtship."

Nice. There was that word again. This time, it made me smile. "Yes, Jake is a nice guy." If I ever made it back to Lebanon County, I would thank him.

"Pretzel?"

"No, thanks." We were flying at about 35,000 feet, zooming toward Romania, back to the land of my birth, and Dorin was filling me in on the whole story. How he'd enlisted Jake in a last-minute scheme to stab Lucius, making sure Ethan Strausser or some other zealot didn't get the chance to plunge the stake in too deeply.

As it was, Jake had nearly gone too far. "The boy doesn't know his own strength." Dorin sighed, shaking pretzels into his hand. Somehow he'd gotten about a dozen packs from the flight attendant. "Young Mr. Zinn was rather concerned about the whole thing for quite a while. But it had to be realistic. I told him not to worry, not to worry. Everything went just fine."

"Why didn't Lucius just run away?" As soon as I asked the question, I realized how absurd it was. A vampire prince turn tail? Not likely.

"Don't be ridiculous," Dorin said, echoing my thoughts. "Lucius wouldn't have even liked my enlisting Jacob. He really did want to be destroyed that night. He was quite surprised—and a little peeved—to wake up still alive. He got over it, though."

I stared out at the passing clouds. "But how could Lucius do that to me? Let me think he was gone? Why didn't he contact me?"

Dorin patted my arm. "He really thought it was best for you to believe he was gone. Lucius—he sees his dark side. Very clearly."

"Lucius can control that side of himself. He just won't believe it."

"Yes," Dorin agreed. "You and I are certain that Lucius is honorable. Anyone who knows him can see that. Indeed, Lucius's endless struggle with his conscience is evidence of the strength of his good side. But Vasile tried to twist him, to make Lucius a pawn in his cruel schemes. And so Lucius never seems to know his true nature. Noble prince or vicious fiend? Both? He is a vampire at war with himself."

Dorin added, "Buying that horse, Hell's Belle, didn't help, either. Lucius got a bit obsessed with that animal. He felt a kinship with it, and started thinking maybe he was just too damaged to live, too. That eventually, he would harm . . ."

"Me."

"Yes. He didn't want you to suffer eternity with a monster—in the more technical sense of the term. You know, someone capable of terrible cruelty . . ." Dorin trailed off. "But now *he* suffers."

I looked at my traveling companion. "What do you mean?"

"Lucius needs you. He mourns you. He *loves* you. It's very unusual for a vampire to truly love. Some hold that real love between vampires is a myth. That we are too vicious by nature. But Lucius does. He loves you—as you love him."

I wanted, more than anything, for Lucius to love me. But I was still hurt. "Didn't he realize that the cruelest thing he could do was leave me?"

"He thought you would recover quickly, get on with your life. That's what teenagers do, right? 'Bounce back'?"

"But I'm not a normal teenager."

"Of course not." Dorin paused. "Lucius thought he did you a favor, though. At great cost to his own heart. Tremendous cost."

My eyes filled with tears, like they always did when I thought of Lucius. "I miss him so much."

"Of course. But you must be prepared when you see him. His dark side really does grow more powerful every day. He destroyed Vasile, you know."

"What?" I didn't think I'd heard right.

"Oh, yes," Dorin confirmed. "When Vasile found out Lucius was still with us, and in Romania, he ordered him destroyed for disobedience. For abandoning the pact he was sent to fulfill. Well, Lucius marched right into the castle and said, 'Do it yourself, old man,' or something to that effect. And Vasile said, 'You impertinent chit,' and set upon Lucius like a wolf on a hind—that's a deer in your country."

Lucius fighting Vasile? It hardly seemed fair. Lucius was strong, but Vasile was beyond strong. He was like a force of nature. "What happened?"

"Lucius won. And in a fight to the finish . . . well, someone gets 'finished.'"

"Oh." Even though Vasile had been unspeakably cruel, it was hard to imagine Lucius plunging a stake into anyone's chest. . . .

Dorin correctly read my silence. "Lucius had no choice. But he was nearly shattered when it was all over. Wouldn't eat for days. Still, what could he have done? Stand there and let Vasile destroy *him*? If you ask me, the boy had endured far too much already. The world's a better place with Vasile out of the way."

"But Lucius can't accept that, can he?"

"No. Of course not. Lucius was raised—indoctrinated—to honor family above all else. He was taught since infancy to re-spect—and protect—Vasile as his mentor and superior. Of course Lucius sees disobeying and ultimately destroying Vasile as just more evidence that he is irredeemable. And so he *acts* irredeemably."

"What exactly is he doing?" I was truly scared to hear the answer.

"He is precipitating a war; that is what he is doing."

"How?"

"Our people, the Dragomirs, are furious about the pact. They think Lucius left you behind deliberately, for the express purpose of denying us our princess. Of denying us shared power. Lucius not only allows this misperception to fester, he fuels it. He taunts us toward war. Already, there are skirmishes between the Vladescus and the Dragomirs. Vampires have been destroyed in anger. Militias are being formed. Soon it will be all-out war."

"Vampires have been destroyed because *I* didn't come back with Lucius? While I was wasting time mucking stalls, my relatives have been getting *staked*? Why didn't you come get me?"

Dorin fidgeted. "I am not strong, Antanasia, like you . . . I feared Lucius's wrath . . . He told me that you were not to come to Romania, not to know that he lived. But the situation has gone too far. I cannot allow more Dragomirs to be lost, just because I am afraid to defy his decree. I had to come for you."

I squeezed my uncle's hand, almost as though I was the older, more experienced vampire. "Well, at least you did the right thing in the end. I promise I'll do my best to protect you from Lucius's 'wrath.'"

"Indeed, I trust that you are the one force capable of bringing back the benevolent side of Lucius. I stake my existence on it—and the fate of our people. For in a war with the Vladescus . . . well, in the time of peace, which began with your betrothal ceremony, we Dragomirs have allowed ourselves to soften. If this war cannot be averted, I fear that the Dragomirs, for all our current outrage, will be no match for the Vladescus."

"How bad might it be for our family?"

"Obliterated," Dorin said glumly.

"So if I can't convince Lucius, in a last ditch effort, to admit that he loves me and honor the pact . . . ?"

"The Dragomirs, I fear, will soon be no more. Lucius, as he is now, cannot be counted upon to show much mercy, I fear."

I leaned my head against the seat back, letting it all sink in. My new to-do list: Control angry Dragomir vampires. Win back no-longer-destroyed, reluctant, rampaging fiancé. Stop imminent war.

I fingered the bloodstone at my throat. I was up for the challenge. I had no choice.

The plane hit some turbulence, and we jolted sharply, several times. So sharply that several passengers yelped.

Dorin grabbed my hand and smiled. "Welcome back to Romania, Princess Antanasia."

Chapter 60

GIVEN ALL THAT Lucius had told me about living in castles and eating the finest foods and having his clothes tailor-made, I was a bit surprised to find myself bumping along the rutted roads of rural Romania in a battered Fiat "Panda," which huffed and puffed along on only three of its four cylinders.

"Um, Dorin," I said, clutching the dashboard as my uncle once again ground the gears into submission. "I thought we were vampire royalty."

Dorin nodded to me. "Indeed. Excellent bloodline."

"Then . . . what's with the car?"

"Oh. That. Do not think this vehicle representative of our heritage. It is just a temporary manifestation of our somewhat . . . er, reduced circumstances." He wrestled with the non-power steering, trying to avoid a rut as we climbed into the Carpathians.

The mountains stood in sharp contrast to the Appalachians that rolled gently across Pennsylvania. Indeed, the Carpathians, steep, rocky, and jagged, shamed the Appalachians' claim to mountain-hood. From time to time, the road would veer out over sheer, breath-snatching drops, then snake back into dense, shadowy forests, where Dorin assured me bears and wolves still prowled, only to emerge in brightness, cutting through small towns that seemed carved out of stone and fixed in the Middle Ages. Crooked cottages, snug little chapels, and busy taverns hugged narrow streets. I would glimpse these things, then, in the blink of an eye, we would plunge back into the wilderness.

I could see why Lucius had missed his homeland: the fairy-tale villages; the sense of time stopped; the pervasive impression that one was within a hidden mystery; a secret, wild enclave forgotten in a modern world.

"Hold on," Dorin advised, turning off the main road from Bucharest and bumping onto an even narrower lane.

We jerked along, and my head thumped the Panda's low ceiling. "Ouch." I rubbed my curls. "Is this really the best we can afford?"

"Well, I've told you. The clan has hit some hard times in recent years. We sold the Mercedes years ago. The Fiat's very reliable, though. I have no complaints. None at all."

I had a few complaints. How was I supposed to assume my proper place as a vampire princess when my mode of transportation was the size of a golf cart, with an engine that sounded like it belonged to a tabletop fan?

We rode in silence for quite some time, until we crested a rise that revealed, below us in the distance, a large cluster of terra-cotta-colored roofs glowing in the sunset. "Sighişoara," Dorin announced.

I leaned forward, staring out the windshield with eager eyes. So we had arrived, finally, in Lucius's home territory. This was where he had grown up, become the man I'd grown to love. "Will we drive through?"

"Yes," Dorin said. "Anything you wish."

I had noticed that my uncle's demeanor toward me had changed subtly since we'd landed in Bucharest. He had become more formal. More deferential. I considered telling him that he didn't have to treat me like a princess just because we weren't in the United States anymore. Then I realized, no, I would assume my rank. I would need deference; I would need to project authority if I was to achieve what I meant to achieve. I was in a Fiat Panda, but I was still a princess. "Please, show me," I urged.

"Of course." Dorin drove us into the heart of the city, and I gazed, enchanted, at arched stone passageways leading to twisting alleys, at cramped and crowded stores whose specialties—breads and cheeses and fruits and vegetables—spilled out onto the sidewalks, and at the seventeenth-century clock tower that served as the city's heartbeat, striking the hour as we passed. Six o'clock.

At each spot that captured my notice, I wondered. Had Lucius strode this street? Made a purchase at that store? Listened to the deep tolling of the clock, realizing that he needed to be somewhere, ducking his tall frame beneath one of those stone arches to keep an appointment in a hidden byway? This—this was a place where Lucius would not seem out of place, even in his velvet coat, his fitted trousers.

"Are you hungry?" Dorin asked. "We could stop for a moment, before all of the merchants close for the day."

"It's just six," I noted. "Is it, like, the local custom to shut down so early?"

Dorin pulled the car to the curb. "No. It is not always this way. But the people of this region have lived in the company of vampires for many generations. They keep the pulse of the clans. They have heard rumors of a coming war, and know that there will be thirsty, angry vampires about, seeking the fuel of blood—and recruits for our undead armies . . . They will not linger in the streets after dark without good reason."

A shiver shook through me, too. Although I was now a member of the vampire clans myself, I could definitely sympathize with the local people's fears. "So even the regular people are affected by the tension . . ."

"Indeed," Dorin said. "They mourn the passing of nearly two decades of peace. For a time, we seemed to have reached a détente with the humans, too. That was largely the doing of Lucius. He was a good ambassador for us. So charming . . . Even those who would cross themselves at the name Vladescu could hardly dislike him. But now, of course, they know that he is changed . . ."

Dorin led me toward a small restaurant, opening the door and ushering me into a cramped, narrow room. The décor was simple—a few scarred old tables scattered about a wooden floor—but the smell was amazing. "Here. We will buy *papanași*: cheese dumplings rolled in sugar. A local delicacy."

"Sugared cheese?" I was skeptical.

"I ate the vegan birthday cake," Dorin noted. "Trust me, this will be a treat by any comparison."

I couldn't argue with that.

We stepped up to the counter, and the elderly proprietor rose from a stool with effort, greeting Dorin. *"Bună."*

"Bună." Dorin nodded. He held up two fingers. *"Doi papanași."*

"Da, da," the old man said, beginning to shuffle away.

Then he noticed me and stopped abruptly, his swarthy, weathered face growing visibly pale. He pointed at me with a shaking hand, wide eyes darting to Dorin. *"Ea e o fantoma . . ."*

"Nu e!" Dorin shook his head. "Not a ghost!"

"Ea e Dragomir!" the old man insisted. "Mihaela!"

I understood the words Mihaela Dragomir—and the gist of the conversation, however unfamiliar the language.

"Da, da," Dorin agreed, seeming to grow impatient with the man, waving him off. *"Comanda, vă rog.* Our food, please."

The man hobbled away, but continued to glance over his shoulder at me as he prepared our *papanași.*

"He recalls your mother," Dorin whispered to me. "He thinks you are her ghost. Her *fantoma.* You should get used to that."

I was both flattered and vaguely uneasy to be mistaken for my birth mother. I realized, with a jolt, that this man believed, beyond a doubt, that I was a vampire. He had been raised with the reality of vampires. He had been alive when my parents had been destroyed. Perhaps he had taken part. . . . Now, standing in his shop, I knew from the old man's suspicious eyes that I was not just a curiosity; I was a potential threat. I felt vulnerable suddenly, high in the Carpathians, beyond the protection of Mom and Dad, alone in a claustrophobic shop with an uncle I barely knew and a stranger who considered me a bloodsucking fiend, possibly fit for destruction.

The old man handed Dorin our food, and my uncle paid,

handing over a few coins. The proprietor continued to eye me warily.

"Come along," Dorin said, guiding me toward the door. "Try not to be shaken by this. Of course some of the older people will recognize you. You look exactly like her. It will take a while for them to understand that you are her daughter and have returned home."

We left the shop, and I stared at the street, trying to think of this unfamiliar place as "home."

"We should go," Dorin gently urged. "It is growing dark, and the road is dangerous."

I folded myself into the little car and tried the *papanaşi*, biting down on the crisp sugared dumpling to release the warm, gooey cheese. "Mmm . . ." I closed my eyes and savored the treat, braver and comforted with warm food in my stomach.

"Good?" Dorin seemed pleased. He put the car in gear and pulled out into the street, which was nearly empty now.

"Very good," I said, reaching into the paper sack for another. "Much better than vegan cake."

"That is Lucius's favorite, you know," Dorin said. "He likes them from that particular shop best."

I slowly licked the sugar from my fingers, watching the city pass by my window. *Lucius could have been there. I could have walked into that shop and seen the man I'd been mourning alive and well.* "Does Lucius live very near here?" I ventured. "How close are we, exactly? Minutes? A half hour?"

"Very close," Dorin said, glancing at me. He sounded a bit nervous. "You . . . you're not thinking of swinging by, are you?"

"Just to see his home . . ." A sudden apprehension gripped me. Apprehension and excitement. "Will he be there, do you think?" *Do I want him to be there? Am I ready?*

"I don't believe so," Dorin guessed, and I felt a little wave of relief. As much as I desperately wanted to see Lucius, I knew I should get ready first. Not only did I need to clean up from the plane ride, but I had to prepare mentally. To brace myself to face the Lucius whom Dorin had described on the plane. The Lucius who had destroyed his uncle, who was precipitating a war and scaring the local townspeople. The Lucius who was believed capable of "obliterating" my family, without mercy.

"He's been out with his troops a lot lately," Dorin added. "In the field."

"Are *we* preparing?" I asked, concerned by this latest revelation.

"Somewhat . . ." Dorin drifted off. "No, not really. Not in an organized way like Lucius. He is a warrior creating an army. We are more like your American colonists: earnest, if ill-prepared, vampires forming informal militias."

I gazed out at the rugged landscape. The deeper we drew into the Carpathians, the more profoundly I recognized the mountains as my dreamscape. I could hear my birth mother's voice in my mind, singing to me. Being silenced. This was a beautiful place. But a severe, untamed place, too. "We will need more than 'informal militias,'" I muttered, staring out the passenger side window into the gathering darkness. "We will need to prepare, too." If only I knew what that meant. If only I'd been raised as a warrior, not a vegan in a farm overrun with stray kittens. *Can I really help my Dragomir kin?*

"Look this way," Dorin urged, letting the Fiat drift to a halt on the side of the road.

I turned in my seat and sucked in my breath, confronted—assaulted—by a towering stone building. The phantasmagoric edifice where Lucius had been raised, schooled with violence, reared on tales of his vampire lineage, and made fiercely aware of the Vladescus' proud place in the world.

"Wow."

We were parked on the edge of a precipice, overlooking a valley so steep, deep, and narrow that it looked as if a giant had created it with one sharp whack from a mile-long cleaver. Lucius's castle, black against the orange sunset, clung to the far escarpment, rising out of the hillside and seeming to claw up at the sky. Sharply pitched eaves, turrets like enormous spikes to jab the clouds, pinched and vaulted Gothic windows. It was an angry house. A house at war with the universe.

Did Lucius really live *there*?

We parked the car and stepped out to the very edge of the cliff, the better to examine this snaggle-toothed architectural expression of rage.

"Impressive, eh?" Dorin asked.

"Yes." But the word was thick in my throat. Looking at that house, I was scared. It was ridiculous to be scared of a building, and yet the sight of that castle struck a chord of raw fear in me.

Am I scared of the house—or the person who can stand to inhabit it?

As Dorin and I watched, a light went on behind one of the windows. One single light, in a high window.

My uncle and I exchanged glances.

"Could be the servants," Dorin surmised. "Or, then again, maybe the boy came home for the night."

"Let's go," I urged, grabbing my uncle's arm. Go, before I did something stupid. Like run right up to that castle and bang on the doors. Or run right home to Lebanon County and never look back. "Please. I want to go."

"Right behind you," Dorin agreed, hurrying for the car.

Chapter 61

THE GOOD NEWS was the Dragomir clan actually did have its own fairly impressive estate. The bad news was it was open to tourists four days a week. This was yet another manifestation of our "reduced circumstances," as Dorin liked to call what was, quite apparently, real economic distress.

"The tours don't start until ten A.M.," Dorin reassured me, helping me lug my suitcase into our musty mansion. He sidestepped a metal sign that instructed visitors: "NO SMOKING! NO FLASH PHOTOGRAPHY!" in about seven languages. "We're very popular this year," Dorin added, like that was a great thing. "The Romanian tourism authority really stepped up the advertising. Motor coach traffic is up sixty-seven percent."

Good grief.

"Of course, there are private living areas," Dorin added, seeing my disappointment. "The bedrooms and bathrooms are mostly off-limits. Although the occasional American finds his way to the private toilets. I suppose it's the unfamiliar foods. . . . At any rate, don't be alarmed if you open a door and find one

of your countrymen perched there. It's embarrassing for everyone, yes. But not harmful, really. It's hardly an inconvenience,
even. They're very good about flushing. For the most part."

*Tourists? Pooping in my castle? I bet nobody pooped, unau-
thorized, at the Vladescu estate. . . .*

"Dorin?"

"Hmm?" He was dragging my suitcase up a tall, curving,
stone staircase. The bulb in a fake, electrified torch flickered
on the wall, a cheap imitation of the actual fire that I was fairly
certain blazed in Lucius's home. He would suffer no less than
the real thing. I once again stroked the bloodstone at my throat,
and the word *unacceptable* flashed through my mind. This
was unacceptable. If things went as I hoped, and I really did
come to lead this family, I would reclaim our castle for the
Dragomirs—not tourists. The idea excited me to a surprising
degree. As we reached the highest landing, I surveyed the
vaulted ceilings, the once majestic corridors. Yes, we could do
better.

"What happens next?" I asked Dorin, following him down
the hallway and into a cavernous bedroom.

Dorin dropped the suitcase with a thud. "Why, you need
to meet the family. Everyone's very excited to dine with you.
They'll be here soon."

Images of Lucius's "family" flashed through my mind.

"How many are coming?" I asked, hoping that I wouldn't
have to confront too many of my vampire kin all at once.

"Oh, just twenty or so of our closest kin. We did not think
it wise to overwhelm you on your first day here, but of course
everyone is curious to see our long-awaited heiress. I suppose
you'll want to clean up a little? Change clothes?" Dorin hinted.

"Yes," I said, grasping the opportunity to be alone for a moment. To reflect. To pull myself together. This was all happening so fast. I needed to think.

Dorin moved through the room, snapping on lights. The space was dusty, dated, and drafty, but livable. It was not too far gone from its former glory. Yet. "I hope you are comfortable here," Dorin said, tossing my bag on the four-poster bed. "I'll come back for you in about an hour. Take a nap if you like."

"Thanks."

"Oh! I almost forgot." Dorin trotted to a large wardrobe, opened the door, and pulled down a gown on a hanger. It was a bit faded but still beautiful. Silk that had no doubt once blazed bright crimson had mellowed to a richer, deeper red. "This was your mother's. I thought you might want to wear it for dinner. It *is* a big occasion, and I'm afraid we left so hurriedly that I gave you no chance to pack something formal."

As if in a trance, I moved to Dorin and ran my fingertips across the fabric. "I recognize this. From her photograph."

"Ah, yes, her portrait." Dorin smiled. "Mihaela had many gowns, but this was her favorite. She loved the intense color— so like her personality. She wore this to so many lovely gatherings, in a different time, before the purge . . ." He looked for a moment as if he might cry, then brightened. "You will do it justice, Antanasia, and usher in a new era for us. Perhaps we will all be happy again soon. Perhaps your mother's fondest dream—peace for the Vladescus and Dragomirs—will be made manifest after all."

I stroked the fabric again. "Are you sure it's okay? To wear it?"

"Not just 'okay,'" Dorin promised. "Appropriate. Perfect."

He left me alone then, and I gently laid the dress on the bed. I wore her necklace, I was about to slip into her gown, and I stood in her home. But could I live up to the legacy of Mihaela Dragomir? Was I a real princess, as I hoped, or just a ghost—a pale, insubstantial shadow of her—like the old man in the restaurant had believed?

Doubts won't help now, Jess. Lucius believed you were just like her, in every way. . . .

Locating the bathroom, I stripped off the jeans and shirt I'd worn on the plane and took a long, hot shower. Toweling off, I carefully removed the dress from the hanger, undid a row of seed-pearl buttons that ran down the back, and stepped into the gown, drawing it up around my body like an embrace from the past. A leftover hug from my mother.

It fit perfectly. As if it had been designed for me.

I gazed into a gilt mirror that stood in the corner of the room, watching my reflection by the light of a full, clear moon that shone like a quavery searchlight through a long bank of warped, leaded windows.

Is this how Mihaela had regarded herself? By the light of this moon? In this same mirror?

The collar of the dress was high, rising almost to brush my jaw, but the neckline plunged deep, showcasing the bloodstone at my throat. The gown curved over my breasts, then fell as sharply and abruptly as a waterfall cascading over a Carpathian cliff, ending in a sweep of silken train that swished like a whisper when I walked. Like the whispers that no doubt followed any woman who dared to wear this spellbinding dress.

This was a gown that made a statement about the woman

who wore it. It told everyone who saw her, "I am powerful, and beautiful, and just *try* to look away from me. I *will* be noticed."

I had no silver coronet, so I gathered my curls loosely behind my neck and allowed them to tumble freely down my back, glossy black hair upon glossy red fabric, staking my own more youthful, but still dramatic, claim to the gown.

The young woman I saw reflected in the mirror, her dark eyes glittering in the moonlight, really did look like a princess.

Strong. Determined. Unafraid.

There was a knock on the door, and Dorin called in to me, "Your guests have arrived. Are you ready?"

"Come in," I urged him.

Dorin poked his head in the room, and his merry, crinkled eyes snapped wide open. For a long moment, he simply stared at me, finally saying, "Yes. You are ready, indeed." Then he stepped aside, allowing me to walk through the door before him. I noted that he bowed to me, just slightly, as I passed.

Chapter 62

THEY WERE WAITING for me at the foot of the curved staircase, every face turned in my direction as I descended, and I watched as their looks changed from skepticism and concern to appreciation and wonder—and hope. And the fact that they were beginning to believe in me gave me confidence, even as it terrified me, too.

Who am I to be anyone's savior? Anyone's princess?

You are your mother's daughter . . . beautiful, powerful,

regal . . . Dorin's reassurances and Lucius's ode echoed again in my mind, giving me courage.

One by one, my vampire relations approached to meet me as I paused at the foot of the staircase. Dorin introduced them, and as each of my Dragomir kin—cousins close and distant— came near to bow or curtsy, I saw echoes of myself in the curve of a nose, the arch of an eyebrow, the slant of a cheekbone. They were attired in good clothes, but I noted that the dresses were a bit outdated, the suits sometimes ill-fitting. *What has become of us since my parents' destruction?*

"Come," said Dorin when we had all been introduced. "Let us dine."

I led a small procession into a long and lofty dining room, chilly in spite of a fire that blazed in a cavernous fireplace, and, at Dorin's indication, claimed my seat at the head of a table glittering with silver and candlelight. We Dragomirs were in difficult financial straits, but all the stops seemed to have been pulled out for my return.

"Sit, sit," Dorin said quietly, pulling out my chair. "I am afraid I must serve . . . We are short on servants right now, and it is difficult to draw anyone from the village, anyhow, given the current state of things. No one wants to be working late at the Dragomir estate . . ."

"It's fine," I reassured him, taking my seat.

Toasts were raised to me, in Romanian, and Dorin translated for me. *To my health . . . to my return . . . to the pact . . . to peace.*

A murmur went around the table as the last toast was concluded, and Dorin bent to speak to me. "They wish to hear from you. They are too eager to eat. You must tell them your plans."

For the first time since I'd donned the red silk dress and begun to settle into my new royal role, I felt a flash of genuine panic. *I didn't prepare a speech. I should have prepared a speech. What can I tell them? God, what do I even plan to do?* "I can't do it," I whispered to Dorin, leaning close to him. "I don't know what to say."

"You must, Antanasia," Dorin begged me. "They will expect it. They will lose confidence if you do not."

Confidence. I cannot afford to lose their confidence. And so I rose, facing my family, and began, "It is my honor to be among you tonight, back in our ancestral home . . ." *What can I say?* "It has been too long."

Dorin translated for those who didn't speak English, glancing at me now and then with more than a little dismay in his eyes. He knew I was struggling, and looking at my relatives ringed around the table, I saw uncertainty creeping back into their minds, too. I was losing their trust as quickly as I'd gained it.

"I intend to ensure that the pact is honored," I added. "As your princess, I promise I will not let you down."

"Tell me, *Jessica*," someone began. A deep voice.

Oh, thank goodness . . . a question.

"Yes?" I searched the faces, trying to find the speaker in the dim, candlelit room.

"How *do* you intend to keep the bargain? Stop the war? Because I understand the Vladescus have no interest in the pact anymore."

The voice came from behind me. The familiar voice.

I spun around, knocking over my chair, to see Lucius Vladescu standing in the doorway, leaning against the door frame, arms crossed over his chest, a bitter smile on his face.

"Lucius." My heart stopped in my chest, and all the blood drained from my face. It was *Lucius*. Alive. Standing not twenty feet from me. How many times had I dreamed of seeing him again? Dreamed of touching him? How many times had those dreams nearly devastated me with their futility? But now, he was so close. . . .

His smile faded, as if he couldn't maintain his coolly ironic demeanor at the sight of me, and I heard him murmur, just faintly, "Antanasia . . ." In that one word, I perceived longing, relief, tenderness, eagerness. The same emotions I was experiencing. He hesitated, uncertain, one hand extended as though he might approach me.

"Lucius," I repeated, blinking at him, as the reality of his existence slowly sank in. "It's really you."

When I said that, Lucius's hand dropped to his side, and he regained his ironic smile. "Indeed, there is only one," he joked bitterly, all traces of tenderness fading. "And the world is better for it."

I began to run for him, then, nearly tripping over the train of my gown, wanted to hurl myself at him, tackle him, and kiss him again and again for the joy of seeing him. And then scream at him for lying to me and abandoning me. But then I saw his face up close, and I stopped short, in midstride.

"Lucius?"

It seemed as though he'd aged years in the few months we'd been apart. All vestiges of the American teenager were gone—

and not just because he'd resumed wearing his tailored pants, his velvet jacket. His black hair was longer, drawn into a careless ponytail. His mouth was set more firmly. His shoulders had broadened. Stubble shadowed his usually clean-shaven jaw. And his eyes were blacker than ever, almost as if they had no soul behind them, animating them.

Behind me, the Dragomirs seemed frozen in place, to find their enemy in their midst.

"Security's a tad lax," Lucius noted. He pushed off from the door frame and strode past me into the room, not meeting my eyes, assessing the obviously timeworn furnishings with the same disdain he'd exhibited months ago in our farmhouse kitchen. Only this time, he seemed not just arrogant, in the innocent way of someone who's known nothing but privilege, but deliberately dismissive. "I was going to sign up for the tour," he added. "But I couldn't wait until ten A.M. to see you, Jessica."

I stared at him with a mixture of dismay and fury. He knew that using my American name was an insult in this place. And he was being so cold. "Don't speak to me like that," I told him. "It's cruel, and I know you are not cruel."

He still refused to meet my eyes, deliberately averting his gaze. "Am I not?"

"No." I moved toward him, refusing to let him control every moment of our meeting. This wasn't a high school dance, where he could assume the lead. He was in my family's home. Shaken as I was to see him so unexpectedly, to find him so altered, I would not be cowed, like my relatives behind me, quaking in their chairs. "You are not cruel, Lucius."

We were standing close to each other now, near enough that I could smell that aromatic, exotic cologne he'd gotten away from wearing sometime during his transformation into an American student. Lucius the warrior prince was back, in every aspect. Or so he wanted me to believe.

"Why did you come here?" Lucius asked me, softly so that my relatives would not hear. He still didn't meet my gaze. "You must leave, Jessica."

"No. No, Lucius, I won't."

He turned to me then, and there was a flash of misery—of humanity—in his eyes, but it was momentary, and he stepped around me, putting physical and emotional distance between us again. I could tell that he was struggling to keep his emotions in check. To keep me at arm's length. At least, I hoped he was struggling. The coldness, the distance: They seemed so real.

"You were watching my house," he noted, circling the table like a hawk looking for the rabbit that didn't have the good sense to stay still. As he passed behind each of my vampire relatives, they cowered visibly. I wished, desperately, that they'd stop doing that.

"How did you know?"

"It's wise, on the eve of a conflict, to stay alert," Lucius advised, voice growing even flintier as he talked of war, slipping into his role as a general. Slipping away from me. "Of course I have guards on the perimeter of my property. Your family pesters me endlessly, whining about the unfulfilled pact, claiming that I never wanted to share power . . . And the more they say that, the more I realize, Why share what I can take by force? I am not averse to a little spilled blood, if it achieves my ends."

"Lucius, you don't mean that."

"Yes, I do," Lucius said, placing his hands on the back of Dorin's chair. My uncle locked up with a full-body spasm. I knew he was terrified that Lucius would destroy him, right then and there, for bringing me to Romania. "Have you ever known me to jest about power, Dorin?"

My uncle said nothing.

Lucius leaned close, speaking right into Dorin's ear. "I shall deal with you later for defying me and bringing her here."

"Step away from him," I ordered. "You're here to see me. Don't torment my family in our own home."

Lucius surveyed the room again. "When all this is mine, I shall have to make some serious changes. Giving tours. It shames all of vampiredom!"

I stared at him, refusing to become visibly upset or tearful, even, over just how callous he was acting. The Lucius before me was even icier and more inaccessible than he'd been after Vasile had ordered him beaten so severely. *Lucius . . . where is* my *Lucius?*

"I want you to leave now, Lucius," I told him, deliberately calm. "I won't talk with you when you're like this."

He arched his eyebrows. "Is this not the reunion you hoped for, Jessica? Is this not what you came thousands of miles for? Are you disappointed to find your family weak—and your former betrothed more despicable than ever?"

"You can't make me hate you," I said. "No matter how hard you try. I know what you're doing. I know you're trying to drive me away from you. You think you're beyond redemption because you destroyed Vasile. You're convinced that you're just like him—or worse because you betrayed your family. But you're not like Vasile." I dared to stroke his arm. "I know you."

Lucius pulled away. "Do not touch me like that, Antanasia!"

"Why not?" I asked, dropping my voice so my family would not hear. "Because you're afraid that you'll lose control, like you did in my bedroom back home?"

"No," he countered. "Because I fear that I shall lose control as I did with my uncle."

"Lucius, you had to do that."

When I said that, his eyes shifted, and he glanced at my relatives, still sitting in unsettled silence, staring at our exchange. "Come with me." He clasped my elbow in his firm hand and led me across the room, out of earshot of my family. "We speak of private things in front of others. It is not right."

We stopped in front of the fireplace, and the firelight cast soft, flickering shadows across Lucius's face, making him look younger again. I nearly reached out to touch his cheek. But his eyes were still too distant. Too black. "I shall tell you this, and then you shall pack your bags and go home, Jessica."

"I'm not going—"

"You think you know me," he spoke over my objection, still clutching my arm, fingers digging in. "For some reason, although I clearly abandoned you, although I obviously wanted you to think that I was gone . . . in spite of this, you cling to some desperate hope that there is a future for us. It is time I disavow you of that, once and for all, because we are no longer in civilized Pennsylvania, attending high school, playing at war on a basketball court. This *is* a war, Jessica."

"It doesn't have to be, Lucius. I know you love me."

"The Vladescus never acted in good faith, Jessica," Lucius continued, his mouth a grim line. "We had a plan. For you."

"A . . . plan?"

"Yes. I was to win you over, marry you—innocent as you were, an American teenager ignorant of vampire culture—and bring you back to Romania. The pact fulfilled, we would have waited a reasonable time, until none could accuse the Vladescus of violating our part of the obligation—"

"And then?" *I already know.*

Lucius stared deep into my eyes. "And then we would have discreetly dispatched you. In secret. Acting as though we mourned your loss, but quietly pleased to have the last, inconvenient Dragomir princess out of the way."

"No, Lucius." I shook my head, horrified. I wouldn't believe it. "You wouldn't have done that."

"Oh, Antanasia. You are still so absurdly innocent. Do you think the Vladescus ever intended to share their sovereignty with an enemy?"

No. Of course they hadn't. "How . . . how was it supposed to happen?"

"I was not privy to those details," Lucius said. "But perhaps by my hand . . . I would have had so many opportunities, alone with you in our castle."

No, Lucius, not you.

He gazed into the fire. "It was so perfect for us, that you had been raised in America. In their attempt to keep you safe, the Dragomirs actually doomed you. A true vampire princess would have understood the risks of marrying me. She could have protected herself, remained always alert. But you, you would have come with me willingly, never even suspecting . . ."

I took a ragged breath, forcing myself not to cry out, cognizant of my family not far away. They were watching. I had to maintain my composure, although betrayal ripped through me. "You knew all this when you came to my parents' home? When you *lived* with us? When you *kissed* me?"

Lucius, too, was aware of our audience. The misery that had seeped into his eyes was not reflected in his regal posture. "Oh, Antanasia . . . when did I know? From the beginning? Only toward the end? I am not sure. Perhaps I was innocent myself at first. Or perhaps I just deceived myself, not wanting to see the truth. But there came a time, yes, before I kissed you, when I knew that I was complicit."

I choked back a sob, swallowing it down hard, keeping my shoulders straight. "I don't believe you."

"Does it not make sense, Antanasia?" He glanced to my family. "Look at them. The Dragomirs are diminished. Vasile could have duped them easily and controlled them without the loss of a single Vladescu. Without a war. The only blood shed would have been yours. You were to be sacrificed in the interest of Vasile's little coup."

"That was Vasile's idea," I pointed out, desperate not to believe Lucius capable of destroying *me*. *He cared for me. I felt it in his kiss, seen it in his eyes. But he's dangerous, Jessica. He doesn't want to be a Vladescu, but perhaps he always will be.* "This was *Vasile's* plan," I repeated. "Not yours."

"And when I saw the whole scheme in its entirety, I was thrilled by its simple brilliance. Does that sicken you, Jessica? Because it should."

"You wouldn't have destroyed me, Lucius," I insisted. "You love me. I know you do."

Lucius shook his head. "Only enough to tell you that I

330

would have destroyed you. That is as much as I can give. Now go home, Jessica. Go home and despise me. I had hoped to leave you with a happier memory of me. But you have come here, and now I cannot even do that."

"I won't leave, Lucius. If only for my family. The Dragomirs need me."

"No, Antanasia. You give them nothing but false hope. Look at you." His gaze traveled up and down the length of my body, and again his eyes came to life, this time with deep admiration. Admiration I'd seen there before. "You are beautiful. Amazing. *Inspiring.* They will fight harder, to think that they do so for their returned princess. To think, foolishly, that you have been wronged by the failure of the pact—when in fact I saved your life by breaking the pact. They will go on believing that they have been cheated out of peace and shared power, and they will rally to fight for you. But in the end, the Vladescus will prevail. Do not prolong their agony or increase their losses."

"They are already angry," I pointed out. "I can't change that. They want a war, too, unless the pact is fulfilled."

"If you tell them to yield to me, they will," Lucius pointed out. "You are their leader. Tell them to submit to me, and then go home."

I hesitated for a moment, considering his one-sided bargain. If I told my family to yield, perhaps they really would. I *was* their leader. I could save lives. I fingered the bloodstone at my throat, hearing my birth mother. *Don't do it, Antanasia. . . . Don't make your first act one of submission, even to Lucius. Especially, now, to Lucius . . .*

"No," I said firmly. "You *did* destroy the pact, you are to blame for ruining the peace, and the Dragomirs will not kneel before a . . . a bully."

Lucius smiled at that, a small shadow of his old mocking smile. "Is that what you think me to be, Jessica? That I am a bully, like pathetic Frank Dormand?"

"You're worse," I said.

His smile grew sad. "Indeed I am. Frank, for all his faults, for all his small cruelties, never even dreamed of *destroying* a woman as magnificent as you."

I was still struggling to find the right words to reply when Lucius turned on his heel and left us.

Chapter 63

AFTER MY FAMILY departed, none of us having even touched the feast that had been carefully prepared to celebrate my return, I retreated to my room, where I sat for several hours, pulling a chair up to the leaded windows, just staring into the darkness. I couldn't even think about sleeping.

What can I do to save my family? To save Lucius? Can I still save Lucius—or is he really beyond redemption, as he believed?

Outside, a wolf howled in the mountains. I had never heard a live wolf cry out before, only in movies or on TV, and the sound, carrying across the wilderness, was so mournful that it nearly made me cry. Everything about my trip was summed up by that miserable, beautiful, poignant sound. Lucius was alive—but he might as well have been gone. My heart still ached, perhaps more, because I had entertained such high hopes for our reunion. Lucius had been right. It had not gone as planned. I was devastated to find him so changed.

And the revelation about the plot to destroy me . . . that had shaken me to the core. Yet I didn't believe that Lucius had been complicit, as he'd said. The plan was Vasile's strategy. Perhaps there had been a time when Lucius, twisted and nearly crushed under Vasile's thumb, would have been capable of entertaining the possibility of such a dark act. But he'd changed in the United States. As he'd said himself, he'd seen a new way. He had told me, *"For my children, it could have been different . . ."*

I also recalled his words earlier that very evening. *"I saved your life by breaking the pact."*

By refusing to honor the clans' agreement, Lucius had actively striven to save me from Vasile's scheme, willingly risking his own life. He had known that Vasile would try to destroy him for insubordination.

Lucius would always protect me.

For all my parents' warnings about the Vladescus' ruthlessness, for all Lucius's own vehement assertions that he was dangerous to me, I knew differently.

But how could I make *Lucius* believe that he would never do me harm? That we still belonged—and would always belong—together?

There were no answers in the blackness outside the window, so I rose from my seat and opened my suitcase to unpack. *At the very least, I will not run home, as Lucius desired.*

As I unfolded my clothes, my copy of *Growing Up Undead*, which I'd tucked in at the last minute, tumbled to the floor.

Picking it up, I thought back to the day I'd discovered the manual near my bedroom door, Lucius's bookmark gleaming in the morning sun. I'd hated the gift, then. But Lucius had been right. In spite of its cloying tone, the book had been a good guide through a confusing time. An accurate resource. Almost like a confidante, when there'd been no one else with whom I could discuss the changes taking place in my body, my life. Sitting on the bed, I opened to the final chapter, which I'd purposely overlooked as my feelings for Lucius had grown stronger and stronger.

Chapter 13: "Love Among Vampires: Myth or Reality?"

Of course vampires can love. Dorin believed Lucius was capable of loving me.

Yet my heart sank as I began to read the guide's sobering advice.

"It is best not to harbor unrealistic notions about love among vampires. Vampires are romantic, even affectionate, on occasion. But in the end, we are a ruthless race! Try to accept that vampire relationships are based upon power and, yes, passion—but not the human concept of 'love.' To begin trusting in 'love'—as many young vampires are foolishly wont to do—is to put yourself at risk of serious peril!"

No.

I slammed the book shut and tossed it aside, knowing that it had served its purpose. I no longer needed its advice. Because this time, the guide—however well respected, however venerable—was wrong. I knew the truth. Lucius loved me.

I realized, in a moment of vivid clarity, that I was willing to stake my life on that conviction. That I *would* stake my life on it, that very night.

Chapter 64

UNABLE TO LOCATE more appropriately majestic stationery in the middle of the night, I inked my abdication note on the back of a tourist pamphlet describing our ancestral home's amenities—SEE A REAL DUNGEON! EXPLORE THREE PARAPETS!—that I found near the front door.

I wrote,

Dear family,

It is futile to wage war against the Vladescus. I have decided that it is in our best interests for me to return to the United States—to step down as your princess. But my final act as your sovereign is to order every Dragomir to submit without struggle to Vladescu rule. I am bringing our clan under Lucius Vladescu's power so that we may have peace. Henceforth, you will be his subjects.

This is my command, issued at midnight, June 9, and effective at 6:30 A.M. this same day, just before my official abdication at 7:00 A.M.

Antanasia Dragomir

I placed the note on the long dining room table, still littered with plates and goblets from my aborted feast, where I felt fairly certain Dorin would find it at breakfast. The pamphlet looked ridiculous propped against a tarnished silver candlestick, and I hoped that at least my words sounded official.

Then again, if anyone ever read my directive, I was dead, anyway. The fate of the clans would no longer be my problem.

That won't happen, Jessica. . . .

I had kept my gown on, wanting to present myself before Lucius as regal and powerful, which made it difficult to shift gears in the cramped Panda. The dress's train kept getting caught in the clutch, but I managed to maneuver out of the parking lot and onto the skinny, convoluted road that twined like a poisonous vine toward Lucius's castle.

I was glad that I had been so acutely aware of Lucius's home—its proximity to my ancestral estate, its horrible grandeur—when I had ridden with Dorin, because I was able to retrace the route, even though the way was confusing in the pitch-black mountains. Or maybe I got lost a few times, because the trip seemed to take forever. But eventually, I saw the castle's jutting spires stabbing at the full moon, and I turned up the lane, which was nearly vertical, interrupted by hairpin turns that sprang up in the darkness like jack-in-the-boxes, forcing me to hit the brakes again and again, so as not to fly off the sharp drops that appeared to my left and right at gaps in the thick forest.

"Come on," I repeatedly encouraged the Panda, patting its steering wheel, willing its struggling engine onward, certain that it was about to give up.

The pavement ended, dropping off into dirt, and still we climbed.

Finally, just as I had begun to believe that the mountain could go on forever, a stone-and-iron gate loomed before me, standing at least eight feet tall. *Why didn't I count on that?* I stopped the car and yanked the emergency brake as hard as I could, with visions of the poor Panda disappearing down the vertical road and plunging driverless into the ravine, never to be seen again. Hiking up my dress so my train would not drag on the dirt road, I strode to the gate and ventured to tug on the heavy iron ring that served as a handle, certain that the exercise was futile.

To my surprise, though, the gate swung back an inch or so. I tugged harder, struggling against its weight, and managed to pry it open just enough to slip inside. So much for Lucius's much-vaunted security system.

I ventured a few steps onto Vladescu land, and the gate swung shut behind me with a loud, metallic clang like an ominous gong in the silent forest. I glanced behind myself, immediately feeling vulnerable, closed off from my car—and closed in with what? Vampires, definitely . . . and maybe scarier things? I remembered the howl of the wolf. And dogs. What if Lucius kept guard dogs on patrol?

Should I push the gate again, try to open it, get back in the car?

But I had a terrible feeling that I was sealed inside. Besides, I had no real intention of turning back.

Before me, I could barely discern the footpath, even in the moonlight that filtered through thick trees. I had no choice but to go forward, though, so I squared my shoulders and began walking. With each step, I became more aware of the sounds of the forest. The snap of twigs in the distance, the rustle of leaves as some animal—*Please, let it be some Romanian rodent*—darted away, startled by my footsteps.

There were bigger things out there, too. I could hear them near me, and I picked up my pace, at first just walking faster, and then breaking into a trot, which was as fast as I could manage on the uneven dirt-and-stone path. *Please, please, let the castle come into sight.* My breath started coming so raggedly that the other sounds were shut out, but monsters were so active in my imagination that I didn't need to hear them to know that they were there, nipping at my heels. And then I stumbled.

But before I could fall to my knees, two pairs of hands gripped my arms and yanked me upright, hauling me roughly to my feet.

I didn't even have time to scream out loud. As my head snapped up to see who held me, I saw before me, bathed in moonlight, Lucius. Standing a few feet ahead of me, arms crossed, blocking the path. My own arms were still tightly contained, and I glanced to my sides. Two young men—vampires, I presumed—pinioned me. "Let me go," I cried, trying to shake them off.

"Eliberați-o!" Lucius ordered them in Romanian. "Release her!"

My arms were freed, and I stood on my own, brushing myself off, as though they'd soiled me with their touch.

The young vampires waited for Lucius's instruction, crowding me, clearly ready—eager—to recapture me.

But they were destined to be disappointed, much to my relief.

"Mergeți. Lăsați-ne în pace," Lucius said, apparently dismissing his guards, because they disappeared into the night.

Hearing him speak in a tongue familiar to him but so strange to my ears—he had almost never used Romanian while at our farm—long past midnight, in a remote and gloomy forest, only emphasized how foreign to me Lucius had become, and some of my resolve wavered.

We stood facing each other in silence, his body closing off the path to his castle, and his guards, presumably, alert for my retreat. "How long were you following me?" I finally asked him.

"The headlights on your toy car are dim, but still visible from many miles away. Few people travel this way at night. The road is too perilous—and the destination far too treacherous."

"So that's why the gate was open. You knew I was coming."

"Indeed. I wanted to see how far you would take this ill-advised visit." He paced toward me, hands clasped behind his back. "I must admit, you came much farther than I ever anticipated. You are nearly at my home."

"I'm not afraid of the dark," I lied.

Lucius advanced closer, looming before me. "There are wolves in *these* woods," he advised, leaning in to watch my face. "And they would find it difficult to resist one as tempting as you, I fear. Especially in that magnificent bloodred gown."

I glanced down at my dress as Lucius circled around me, surveying me, in a parody of what he'd done months ago in my parents' barn, the day we'd met. He had changed since then—but I had, too. Gone were my dirty boots, my ragged T-shirt. Red silk glistened in the moonlight.

"Did you never read 'Little Red Riding Hood,' Jessica?" Lucius asked, still circling slowly, crowding and confining me. "Do you not know what happens to innocents who wander alone in dark forests?"

A weird thrill of terror mixed with anticipation shivered through me. Lucius was too close—and not close enough. I couldn't quite see his black eyes in the darkness. I couldn't quite gauge his mood. Was he toying with me as prelude to a kiss—or the thrust of a stake?

You're betting your life on the former, Jess.

"I forget the story, Lucius," I said. "It's just a tale for little kids."

"Oh, it is one of my favorite fables," he said, pausing behind me. I tensed, feeling vulnerable with him at my back. "The origins are lost in time," he continued. "And there are many adaptations. In some, the little girl is saved. But I particularly love the ending just the way Perrault related it in the classic version."

"How . . . how does that end?" I inquired, not moving.

"'Grandmother, what big TEETH you have got!'" Lucius recited, leaning so close over my shoulder that his lips brushed my ear, almost nipping at me. "'All the better to eat you up with.' And, saying these words, this wicked wolf fell upon Little Red Riding Hood—and ate her all up.'"

I shivered as he told the story, half from his nearness, half from the clear relish with which he related the awful conclusion.

"Is that not a simple, satisfying ending, Jessica?" He laughed softly.

"I like happier endings myself."

Lucius laughed harder. "What could be happier—for the wolf? Why do humans always look at these things from the wrong perspective? Predators deserve our sympathy, too."

"I didn't come here to talk about fairy tales," I said, breaking the sinister spell. He was genuinely starting to unnerve me.

"Run along home then, Riding Hood," Lucius said, taking my shoulders and steering me back toward the car. "It is late, and you are in danger of becoming wolf fodder. What would I write to your parents then? That I allowed Jessica to be devoured, torn limb from limb, after they were so hospitable to me?"

I shuddered again, this time mainly from the cold, and turned around, shaking free of his grasp. "I want to go inside to talk. I came here to strike a bargain with you."

Lucius paused, head cocked, bemused. "A bargain? With me? But you have nothing with which to bargain." I could tell that he was nevertheless intrigued. "Do you?"

"Yes. I think so."

"And this bargain . . . does it end with you returning to Pennsylvania, where you belong?"

"It could end with me leaving," I said. *This world. Forever.*

"You capture my interest," Lucius admitted, touching my shoulder again. "And you tremble with the cold. I am a rude host, to taunt you in the frigid air, when you are unused to a Carpathian Mountain spring. Let us go inside, where I can infuriate and inspire loathing in comfort."

We began to walk side-by-side down the path, Lucius's feet sure on ground familiar to him, me unsteady and ill-dressed for a late-night hike. I wobbled slightly, and Lucius reached out to steady me. After I regained my footing, he kept his hand at my elbow, and I felt that with that simple gesture, I had come one step closer to winning the Vladescu-Dragomir war.

Or perhaps not. Because when the massive wooden door to his castle swung shut behind us, sealing us in an imposing Gothic stone foyer that disappeared above me into blackness too high to be penetrated by a circle of twenty actual, flaming torches, Lucius noted, "You know that you effectively declared war this evening. And now you are my first prisoner."

I spun around just in time to see him slam a long iron dead bolt home, locking us into his monstrous mansion.

"You're joking, right, Lucius?"

It was the wrong thing to say. His eyes were flinty when they met mine. "The sad thing is, Jessica, I had almost thought you had finally learned not to trust me tonight."

As I watched in horror, Lucius reached behind his back and withdrew something that had apparently been concealed, tucked in his belt, the whole time we'd been together alone in a dark Carpathian forest.

A stained, sharpened stake.

Chapter 65

LUCIUS TAPPED the rudimentary, but nonetheless potentially deadly, instrument against his palm. "I have done all that I could to keep us from this moment, but you refuse to cooperate. I will offer you one last chance, Antanasia. *I* will slip the bolt, *you* will slip into the night, and my guards will ensure your safe return to your car. From there, you will fly home and forget this entire episode. That is *my* offer, on the table."

As Lucius spoke, his eyes had become completely black, the irises consuming the whites, as if he were some exotic nocturnal animal. The transformation was just as captivating and terrifying as it had been the first time I'd seen it back in my parents' dining room, when Lucius had thirsted for the blood that would heal him. It took every ounce of my courage not to beg him to pull back the bolt, allowing me to run for safety. But

I couldn't do that. Our short, intense, confusing relationship would come to its climax, for better or for worse, that night. I would not wait one day longer.

I mastered my voice with effort. "I'm not interested in your offer of flight," I said. I pointed at the stake. "*That* is precisely why I am here. That in your hand is the crux of *my* bargain, too."

Lucius watched me carefully, clearly caught off-guard.

"Did you expect me to be afraid, Lucius?" I asked, hoping my eyes or my voice didn't betray just how scared I really was.

"Yes," he said. "As you should be."

"Maybe, for once, you were the one who was naïve. Who underestimated just what *I'm* capable of."

Lucius hesitated, and the silence in the tomblike foyer was deafening, except for the occasional hiss and pop of the torches. "Let us talk," he said finally.

Walking ahead of me, not waiting to see if I followed, Lucius led me through a maze of passageways that opened into wider chambers, like a series of tunnels linking caves, sometimes ducking beneath stone lintels built at a time when men were much shorter than Lucius Vladescu, sometimes mounting quick flights of steps that seemed to have no purpose. This was a castle designed not to welcome visitors, but to confound enemies. It wasn't a home. It was a lair. A stone spiderweb. As we traveled deeper into the edifice, the turns seemed to become tighter, the hallways more narrow, the steps steeper. I realized, with more than a bit of alarm, that I was completely lost. Completely at Lucius's mercy. If things did not go as I hoped, I would never escape. My body would never even be found.

He stopped so abruptly that I bumped into his shoulder as he reached to open a portal I hadn't even noticed in the wall. Twisting the knob and giving the door a push, Lucius stepped back. "After you."

I eyed him warily. His eyes were no longer pure black, but they were still cold. I stepped past him. "Thank you."

As Lucius pulled the door shut behind him, I gazed around the chamber, then at Lucius. "Lucius . . . this is beautiful."

At the heart of the Vladescu labyrinth was a richly appointed study, a truly magnificent version of the stage set that Lucius had cobbled together in our garage. A gargantuan, antique Turkish carpet smothered the stone floor, and the walls were lined with overflowing bookshelves—as I would have expected from Lucius. Deep leather couches were cracked and worn, testament to the hours he'd no doubt spent poring over the works of Brontë and Shakespeare and Melville. Tucked among the books was one red trophy, with a basketball player arcing a ball that tripped off his gilt fingertips. Lucius's award for winning a free-throw contest back in December. I turned to him, smiling, heartened that he'd retained a bit of his life as an American teenager. "You brought your trophy home."

Lucius smiled, too, but in a caustic way. "That? Dorin rescued that. I keep it to remind me never to be an idiot again—indulging in ridiculous games when there is business to attend to."

I didn't believe him, but I let it go.

Shrugging out of his coat, Lucius bent to pick up a log, tossing it into a guttering fireplace. Sparks rose in a shower, and the fire fluttered back to life. He had tucked the stake back into his belt, and I could have snatched it at that moment while he had his back to me and hurled it into the flames. . . .

"Do not even think you would be fast enough," Lucius advised without even turning around, nudging at the logs with his booted foot, urging them to life.

"It never crossed my mind," I said.

Lucius turned around, a knowing smile on his face. "Of course not." He retrieved the stake again, running his hand along it, testing its point on his fingertip.

"Lucius—you don't really think you're going to destroy me tonight, do you?"

Instead of answering, Lucius came over to me, taking me by the wrist, and pulled me to the very center of the room, where the complicated design of the carpet culminated in a pale, worn circle. "Look down," he ordered, voice suddenly very rough, his grip on my arm too tight for comfort.

I did as I was told and saw a dark stain that spread across the fibers. Blood . . . It didn't even look as though anyone had tried to clean it up. "Is that . . . ?"

"Vasile. This is where I did it. This is where I destroy."

When I looked up again, tearing my gaze away from that stain to search Lucius's face, I saw that his eyes were narrowed—and pure black again. We were so close that I could peer deep, deep into the wide irises, almost as if I could see his actual thoughts, read his mind directly through his eyes, as true vampires were supposedly able. . . . And the thoughts spinning through Lucius's brain were so, so dark that I flinched. In his eyes, I could read my destruction.

"Lucius, don't," I started to urge him, but in a split second, he was behind me, one arm firmly across my chest, my hands trapped in his, and the spike he'd been clutching in his hand upthrust under my breastbone, nearly piercing my skin, pricking the red silk of my gown. Stopping just in time. I held my breath, afraid to move.

"You said you had a bargain to strike," he growled. "Speak now."

"This is it," I managed to say, pressing myself against his chest, away from that spike. "I left a note telling my family that I've abdicated. But my last act was to order them to submit to your leadership without a struggle."

"That is not a bargain." Lucius laughed. "That is submission."

"No." I shook my head, feeling my curls graze his stubbled chin. His arm was heavy and tense across my chest. In another time, under different circumstances, it would have been heaven to be held so tightly by him, in a way that could have felt protective. If not for the stake at my breastbone. "If you don't destroy me tonight, as you seem intent upon doing, I'll go home before Dorin wakes up and throw away the note. The war will go on."

Lucius paused, clearly thinking. "You know I have no qualms about continuing the war."

"And you say you have no qualms about destroying me. About sacrificing me," I countered. "So just do it. Do it and prevent the war. I am sacrificing *myself*, Lucius." I heard my voice rising in tandem with my emotions. "Just do it, if you're so goddamn hardened! So goddamn vicious! Do what you claim you were going to do all along!"

Fear and frustration and anger at his obstinance and changeability and refusal to accept our love for each other—

feelings that had been harnessed in me for so long now—erupted to make me suddenly reckless, and I found myself pushing him hard, even though I knew the risks were tremendous. "Go ahead, Lucius! Do it!"

"I will do it," he swore, vehemence in his voice, and I felt him breathing hard, his chest heaving against my back. The stake pressed a touch more closely to my flesh, sharply, and I arched away from it. "Do not test me!" he cried.

"That is exactly what I'm doing," I said, gasping. When I spoke, the stake pricked at me, making my breath come short and ragged. I cried out a little and twisted my head against his shoulder, writhing away from the weapon, and he relented, slightly.

"I am *testing* you, Lucius," I continued, struggling to reach him while he showed the faintest bit of vulnerability. "I am risking my life to prove that you are not Vasile. That you are not damaged. That you love me too much to have ever destroyed me, let alone now. I am betting everything that you will spare me."

"I can't spare anyone!" Lucius roared, his composure gone, abruptly and completely. His hand beneath my rib cage shook. "All of my options are cruel, Antanasia! I destroyed my own uncle, for god's sake. I imperiled your parents—even as they tried to save me. My horse, destroyed. My mother, destroyed. My father, destroyed. You—no matter what I do, you are destroyed. I can't leave you behind—you won't let me. And I can't drag you into this . . . this world of mine, either. Everything—everything around me gets destroyed!"

He buried his face in my hair then, clearly spent, and his hand dropped away from my chest, the stake falling to the floor, rolling across the carpet, and I knew that I had won. I had gambled and won.

I turned around slowly, still trapped against Lucius by his arm, and I wrapped my arms around his neck, pulling his head to my shoulder, comforting him. He allowed me to hold him that way, stroking his black hair, caressing his stubbled jaw, tracing the scar that no longer frightened me.

"Antanasia," he said, voice unsteady. "What if I could have done it . . ."

"But you couldn't. I knew you couldn't."

"What if someday . . ."

"Never, Lucius."

"No, never," he agreed, lifting his head from my shoulder and cradling my face in his hands, wiping at my eyes with his fingers. I hadn't even realized I'd been crying. I had no idea how long I'd been crying. "Not to you."

"I know, Lucius."

He drew me in again, resting his head back on my shoulder, as we both composed ourselves. We stood that way for a long time, until Lucius whispered, "There will always be a part of me that is treacherous, Antanasia. That will never change. I am a vampire, and a prince at that. A ruler of a dangerous race. If you are to do this, you will have to understand that . . ."

"I don't want you to change, Lucius," I promised him, drawing back so I could look into his eyes.

"And this world," he said. "I worry about you in this world. You will have enemies . . . a princess does. And a vampire princess faces ruthless foes. Others will want your power and will not hesitate to do what I could not."

"You'll protect me. And I'm stronger than you think."

"Indeed, stronger than me," Lucius admitted, managing a grudging half-smile, although he was clearly still shaken, just like me. "I did all that I could to have my way—to keep you safe from me and our kind—but you would have your way, like a true princess."

"I wanted you, Lucius. I had to have my way."

We clung to each other in the center of the room, standing above the bloodstain that marked the passing of the vampire who'd tried to create in Lucius a real monster. Behind us, the fire crackled, and I thought back to the Christmas dance, when I'd been transported to this very scene, as we'd held each other. This—this had been the place I'd imagined.

Lucius bent his head and touched his lips to mine, still cradling my face, and in the very heart of that stone labyrinth we kissed, tenderly at first, our lips barely meeting, again and again. Then Lucius drew one hand up behind my head and another down to the small of my back, a gesture both protective and possessive, and kissed me more fiercely, and I knew that he was finally taking me for himself as his destined partner, for all time. That we would fulfill the pact.

He drew away, searching my face. All the softness was back in his eyes. I knew that I would see the warrior prince again, many times. He was still Lucius Vladescu. But the hardness, the harshness, that was inside him would never again be directed at me. It never had been, really. Only in his imaginings and fears.

"This is eternity, Antanasia," he said, both warning and imploring. "Eternity."

He was giving me one last chance to leave—and begging me not to.

I had no intention of going anywhere beyond that room or outside of his embrace. I bent my head back, wordlessly acquiescing, and closed my eyes as Lucius again found the point where my pulse beat strongest in my throat, and this time there was no hesitation, beyond the briefest few breaths during which we both savored the moment that would bring us together forever. Then his fangs pierced my throat, and I cried out softly, feeling him plunge, with sure force but infinite gentleness, into the vein, drinking me in.

"I love you, Lucius." I gasped, feeling myself drawn into his body, becoming a part of him. "I always have."

My own fangs were liberated, the ache ending, and when Lucius was done, my throat burning with an unimaginable, stinging pleasure, he drew me to one of the couches, pulling me onto him so I could reach his throat easily, and it seemed so natural to press my own mouth against him.

"Here, Antanasia," Lucius whispered, softly placing his fingertips beneath my chin, guiding me to the proper spot, and the moment I felt it, his pulse pounding just below the skin, I couldn't wait any longer, and I sank my own fangs deep into him, tasting him, making *him* a part of *me*.

Lucius groaned, pressing me closer, so my fangs punctured more deeply and the blood flowed more swiftly, coursing cool and rich into my mouth. His blood tasted like power and passion touched by sweetness . . . just like Lucius.

"Oh, Antanasia," he whispered, caressing my face and helping me to ease out my still-unfamiliar fangs as I finished drinking, reluctantly. "I have always loved you, too."

We slept in each other's arms on the couch in front of the fire, exhausted, completely satisfied, completely happy. At least I slept through the night. Lucius, at some point, arose and slipped away, because when I woke up just before dawn, realizing that I needed to hurry back to my home to destroy the note—before I accidentally abdicated—Lucius advised me that the young vampire guards had already been dispatched in the wee hours to ensure that my reign did not end unexpectedly early.

And as I lay curled up next to Lucius, my head on his chest, protected in the circle of his strong arms, fingers testing the tender puncture wounds on my throat, I realized that he had done more than order his minions to do his bidding.

The stake that had fallen to the carpet was gone.

Lucius never told me what became of it. Whether he'd tossed the reminder of his most violent deed and our darkest moment into the fire, which had been fed during the night, or hid the stake away somewhere in the castle, in case he should ever choose to use it again. And I never asked.

Acknowledgments

Writing seems like a solitary act—until you sit down in the aftermath of creation and think about all the people who *really* made "your" book possible.

Special thanks, of course, to my agent, Helen Breitweiser, a force of nature who not only initially promoted the book, but held my hand throughout its entire production. I couldn't ask for a better advocate.

I am also indebted to my editor, Gretchen Hirsch, both for her incredible insights into the story and her adept handling of a new author with countless questions. I was lucky to have such a great partner in the process.

And thanks, too, to Liz Van Doren, who was the first to give me guidance.

Finally on the editorial side, I'm grateful to Kathy Dawson for stepping in at the last minute and seeing it through.

As for the "home" team . . . I would never have even *started* a novel without the support of my fantastic husband, Dave, who not only offered moral backing, but kept our wacky kids occupied and out of my office so I could work. My parents and my in-laws, George and Elaine Kaszuba, also stepped up repeatedly to serve as babysitters, always with an encouraging word for me. Thank you.

And speaking of wacky kids—thanks to Paige and Julia, preschoolers who have absolutely no clue what I'm doing sitting all those hours at a computer, but think it's cool, nonetheless. Now *that's* support.

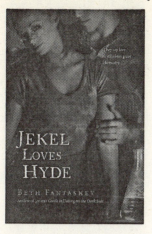

Prologue

Jill

I BURIED MY FATHER the day after my seventeenth birthday.

Even the sun was cruel that morning, an obscenely bright but cold January day. The snow that smothered the cemetery glared harshly white, blinding those mourners who couldn't squeeze under the tent that covered Dad's open grave. And the tent itself gleamed crisply, relentlessly white, so it hurt a little to look at that, too.

Hurt a lot, actually.

Against this inappropriately immaculate backdrop, splashes of black stood in stark relief, like spatters of ink on fresh paper: the polished hearse that glittered at the head of the procession, the minister's perfectly ironed shirt, and the sober coats worn by my father's many friends and colleagues, who came up one by one after the service to offer Mom and me their condolences.

Maybe I saw it all in terms of color because I'm an artist. Or maybe I was just too overwhelmed to deal with anything but extremes. Maybe my grief was so raw that the whole world seemed severe and discordant and clashing.

I don't remember a word the minister said, but he seemed to talk forever. And as the gathering began to break up, I, yesterday's birthday girl, stood there under that tent fidgeting in my own uncomfortable, new black dress and heavy wool coat, on stage like some perverse debutante at the world's worst coming-out party.

I looked to my mother for support, for help, but her eyes seemed to yawn as vacant as Dad's waiting grave. I swear, meeting Mom's gaze was almost as painful as looking at the snow, or the casket, or watching the endless news reports about my father's murder. Mom was disappearing, too . . .

Feeling something close to panic, I searched the crowd.

Who would help me now?

I wasn't ready to be an adult . . .

Was I really . . . alone?

Even my only friend, Becca Wright, had begged off from the funeral, protesting that she had a big civics test, which she'd already rescheduled twice because of travel for cheerleading. And, more to the point, she just "couldn't handle" seeing my poor, murdered father actually shoved in the ground.

I looked around for my chemistry teacher, Mr. Messerschmidt, whom I'd seen earlier lingering on the fringes of the mourners, looking nervous and out of place, but I couldn't find him, and I assumed that he'd returned to school, without a word to me.

Alone.

I was alone.

Or maybe I was worse than alone, because just when I thought things couldn't get more awful, my classmate Darcy Gray emerged from the crowd, strode up, and thrust her chilly hand into mine, air-kissing my cheek. And even this gesture, which I knew Darcy offered more out of obligation than compassion, came across like the victor's condescending acknowledgment of the vanquished. When Darcy said, "So sorry for your loss, Jill," I swore it was almost like she was congratulating herself for *still having* parents. Like she'd bested me once more, as she had time and again since kindergarten.

"Thanks," I said stupidly, like I genuinely appreciated being worthy of pity.

"Call me if you need anything," Darcy offered. Yet I noticed that she didn't jot down her cell number. Didn't even reach into her purse and feign looking for a pen.

"Thanks," I said again.

Why was I always acting grateful for nothing?

"Sure," Darcy said, already looking around for an escape route.

As she walked away, I watched her blond hair gleaming like a golden trophy in that too-brilliant sun, and the loneliness and despair that had been building in me rose to a crescendo that was so powerful I wasn't quite sure how I managed to keep my knees from buckling. Not one real friend there for me . . .

That's when I noticed Tristen Hyde standing at the edge of the tent. He wore a very adult, tailored overcoat, unbuttoned, and I could see that he had donned a tie, too, for this occasion. He had his hands buried in his pockets, a gesture that I first took as signaling discomfort, unease. I mean, what teenage guy wouldn't be uncomfortable at a funeral? And I hardly knew Tristen. It wasn't like we were friends. He'd certainly never met my father.

Yet there he was, when almost nobody else had shown up for me. Why? Why had he come?

When Tristen saw that I'd noticed him, he pulled his hands from his pockets, and I realized that he wasn't uneasy at all. In fact, as he walked toward me, I got the impression that he'd just been waiting, patiently, for his turn. For the right time to approach me.

And what a time he picked. It couldn't have been more dead on.

"It's going to be okay," he promised as he came up to me, reaching out to take my arm, like he realized that I was folding up inside, on the verge of breaking down.

I looked up at him, mutely shaking my head in the negative.

No, it was not going to be okay.

He could not promise that.

Nobody could. Certainly not some kid from my high school, even a tall one dressed convincingly like a full-fledged man.

I shook my head more vehemently, tears welling in my eyes.

"Trust me," he said softly, his British accent soothing. He squeezed my arm harder. "I know what I'm talking about."

I didn't know at the time that Tristen had vast experience with this "grief" thing. All I knew was that I let him, a boy I barely knew, wrap his arms around me and pull me to his chest. And suddenly, as he smoothed my hair, I really started weeping. Letting out all the tears that I'd bottled up, from the moment that the police officer had knocked on the door of our house to say that my father had been found butchered in a parking lot and all through planning the funeral, as my mother fell to pieces, forcing me to do absurd, impossible things like select a coffin and write insanely large checks to the undertaker. Suddenly I was burying myself under Tristen's overcoat, nearly knocking off my eyeglasses as I pressed against him, and sobbing so hard that I must have soaked his shirt and tie.

When I was done, drained of tears, I pulled away from him, adjusting my glasses and wiping my eyes, sort of embarrassed. But Tristen didn't seem bothered by my show of emotion.

"It does get better, hurt less," he assured me, repeating, "Trust me, Jill."

Such an innocuous little comment at the time, but one that would become central to my very existence in the months to come. *Trust me, Jill . . .*

"I'll see you at school," Tristen added, pressing my arm again. Then he bent down, and in a gesture I found incredibly mature, kissed my cheek. Only I shifted a little, caught off-guard, not used to being that near to a guy, and the corners of our lips brushed.

"Sorry," I murmured, even more embarrassed—and kind of appalled with myself. I'd never even come close to kissing a guy on the lips under any circumstances, let alone on such a terrible day. Not that I'd really *felt* anything, of course, and yet . . . It just seemed wrong to even *consider* anything but death at that moment. How could I even think about how some guy felt, how he smelled, how it had been just to give up and be held by somebody stronger than me? My father was DEAD. "Sorry," I muttered again, and I think I was kind of apologizing to Dad, too.

"It's okay," Tristen reassured me, smiling a little. He was the first person who'd dared to smile at me since the murder. I didn't know what to make of that, either. When should people smile again? "See you, okay?" he said, releasing my arm.

I hugged myself, and it seemed a poor substitute for the embrace I'd just been offered. "Sure. See you. Thanks for coming."

I followed his progress as Tristen wandered off through the graves, bending over now and then to brush some snow off the tombstones, read an inscription, or maybe check a date, not hurrying, like graveyards were his natural habitat. Familiar territory.

Tristen Hyde had come for . . . me.

Why?

But there was no more time to reflect on whatever motives had driven this one particular classmate to attend a stranger's burial, because suddenly the funeral director was tapping my shoulder, telling me that it was time to say any final goodbyes before the procession of black cars pulled away from the too-white tent and the discreetly positioned backhoe hurried in to do its job because there was more snow in the forecast.

"Okay," I said, retrieving my mother and guiding her by the hand, forcing us both to bow our heads one last time.

We sealed my father's grave on a day of stark contrasts, of black against white, and it was the last time I'd ever find myself in a place of such extremes. Because in the months after the dirt fell on the coffin, my life began to shift to shades of gray, almost like the universe had taken a big stick and stirred up the whole scene at that cemetery, mixing up everything and repainting my world.

As it turned out, my father wasn't quite the man we'd all thought he was.

Correction.

Nothing and no one, as I would come to learn, would turn out to be quite what they'd seemed back on that day.

Not even me.

And Tristen . . . He would prove to be the trickiest, the most complicated, the most compelling of all the mysteries that were about to unravel.

Chapter 1

Jill

THE FIRST PERIOD of the first day of my senior year kicked off with an academic ritual that I'd dreaded since my earliest days in school.

The choosing of partners.

"Come up and get your get new lab manuals, a copy of the text, and then pair up at the lab stations," our advanced chemistry teacher, Mr. Messerschmidt, said, directing our attention to the front of the room, where his long desk held neat stacks of books and papers waiting for us. He did a quick head count, lips moving as he pointed at us, one by one. "We're *supposed* to have an odd number," he said, frowning, like the tally hadn't turned out as planned. "So somebody'll have to work alone this year, if everyone shows."

No . . . not an odd number . . .

I felt my heart race, the way it always did when there was a chance that I might end up alone. One year in gym class, I'd been the odd girl out for square dancing two weeks in a row, standing in solitary shame against the wall until the teacher forced somebody else to switch out so I could have a turn. And even though chemistry was my best subject, that was no guarantee that Jill Jekel would find a partner here, either.

As I moved to get my manual and book, I tried not to look desperate, even as I made vague attempts at eye contact.

Becca was in the class, but she was so popular . . . I looked in her direction, but Seth Lanier was telling her some joke, making her laugh. She'd probably team with Seth . . .

Tucking my stick-straight, brown hair, that was forever escaping from my ponytail behind my ear, I reached for the lab manual, trying to look relaxed and nonchalant. I could always act like I *wanted* to work alone, if worse came to worse.

"Hey, Jill."

I glanced over to see Darcy Gray edging in next to me, snapping up a manual, and I felt a surge of hope, albeit one tempered with skepticism.

Darcy seemed to be winding up to tell me something. Or *ask* me something. Was there a chance that *Darcy Gray* was going to ask me to partner? Because we were the two best students in the room . . . It made sense . . .

"What's up?" I greeted her, hoisting the heavy book Mr. Messerschmidt had picked for us. Sterne and Anwar's *Foundations of the Chemical World, 17th Edition.* A classic, trustworthy text. My father had kept an earlier edition in his office at home. It was, of course, still there, if we ever unlocked the door to that sacred, forbidden space.

"I just wanted to tell you that station three sucks," Darcy said, taking her own copy from the pile. She scowled at the cover, like she disapproved, not even looking at me as she spoke. "I had three last year, and the Bunsen burners don't work right. It totally screwed me over, and Messerschmidt wouldn't let me change."

"Oh." So that was it. Darcy was tipping me off about a faulty lab station. Which was nice, I guessed. But not what I'd hoped for. Not by a long shot. I felt my cheeks warming, wondering if Darcy had any clue that I'd sort of expected her to ask me to be her partner. "Thanks."

"No problem," she said, still not looking at me as she headed for station one—and her boyfriend, Todd Flick. Gorgeous Todd, not a brain in his head, but he'd take Darcy's directions without complaint or question. He was probably the perfect partner for somebody as domineering as Darcy.

But why had she bothered to warn me about the lab? We were competing for valedictorian, and she could have just let it go. Could have let fate take its course, maybe to my detriment. Was Darcy that confident that she'd take first place?

Probably.

Hugging my books, I took a deep breath and turned around to face the whole class. As I'd expected, most of my classmates already seemed to be pairing up as surely as the animals on Noah's ark. It was like watching that square dance all over again as students moved around the room, coalescing into teams, gravitating toward desks. A few stragglers were still coming up for books, but in general, it appeared that the world was, as usual, operating two by two, with me as the odd girl out.

The odd, odd girl.

Just try to have some dignity, I told myself, squaring my shoulders and starting my solitary march toward the back of the room, eyes fixed on the farthest station, in the corner. I figured I might as well take the last table if I was going to work alone. At least I wouldn't have people staring at the back of my head, thinking about the empty chair at my side.

But just as I was about to put my books down, Becca grabbed my arm, laughing her easy laugh. "Jill, where are you going? Get over here!"

I blinked at her with surprise. "What?"

"Our station," Becca said, pointing to lab three. "I grabbed one for us."

"Us?"

Becca looked at me like I'd lost my mind. "Duh, Jill. We're partnering, right? I mean, you have to save my butt! You're the one who understands this stuff!"

"I . . . I . . ." I stammered for a second, still uncertain. Becca Wright had picked me not necessarily because we were friends— she had too many friends to count—but because I was *serviceable* for her. Which, I supposed, in her eyes was a pretty darn good reason for us to link up. Not insulting at all to a person who would never imagine worrying about having a partner.

So why was I little hurt to be seen mainly as a human study aid?

And Becca had set us up at station three, which Darcy claimed didn't work right. "We should switch to lab ten," I suggested, pointing to the back of the room. "I heard lab three . . ."

"No way," Becca interrupted, still smiling. "I want to be near Seth, and he's on five, right behind us."

I hesitated for one more second, knowing that if Becca had her heart set on being near Seth, she wouldn't budge, even if the malfunctioning burner threatened to set us both on fire.

I gave one last glance to the empty table at the far end of the class.

Then I went with Becca to lab three, awkwardly climbing onto the high stool. Hearing somebody behind her, Darcy turned around to see who was getting stuck with the misfiring burners and gave me a surprised, incredulous look like, "Didn't I just warn you about that lab?"

I smiled weakly and shrugged, and Darcy rolled her blue eyes before twisting back around to face front.

"Okay, everyone," Mr. Messerschmidt announced, clapping his hands to summon our attention. "Are we all set? All partnered?" He counted heads a second time, then consulted a sheet of paper in his hand, frowning again. "We still seem to be missing someone . . ."

Just then the door opened and in walked Tristen Hyde. Late. And not seeming to care that the whole class was already assembled. He strolled right in front of Mr. Messerschmidt and picked up the textbook, checking the cover and nodding like I'd done. Like he recognized the book as a good one, too.

Mr. Messerschmidt watched this performance in silence, mouth set in a firm line. "You're late, Mr. Hyde," he finally said when Tristen took his sweet time collecting the lab manual.

"Sorry," Tristen said absently, more focused on trying to jam the manual into his battered messenger bag, like he had no intention of looking at the rules and regulations.

I noticed that he'd gotten a light tan over the summer, and the sun had highlighted his thick, dirty-blond hair, and I wondered for a second where he'd been, what he'd done over the last few months. Tristen was a cross-country runner, a track star. Maybe he'd just been . . . running? Or had he traveled back to England? I'd heard that his dad was a psychiatrist, here for some kind of visiting professorship. Maybe they'd gone home for the summer break?

I definitely couldn't recall seeing Tristen around town. Then again, I hadn't really seen anybody around town. I'd worked in the basement of Carson Pharmaceuticals cleaning equipment and inventorying stock. A pity job that my dad's old boss had wrangled for me. Although I'd hated the work, it had been really nice of Mr. Layne to look out for me, given what my dad had been accused of doing at Carson.

We were fortunate, too, that Mercy Hospital was desperate for nurses, so Mom hadn't lost her job when she'd had her breakdown right after Dad's funeral.

Yes, things could have been worse. So why didn't I feel luckier?

Still standing at the front of the room, Tristen took some time to survey the lab stations, looking for a spot. He didn't seem panicked or desperate, even though it must have been obvious that everybody was already paired up.

"Do you have a pass or an excuse?" Mr. Messerschmidt asked, holding out his hand.

"No," Tristen said, still coolly appraising the class.

"Oh." Mr. Messerschmidt didn't seem to know what to make of Tristen's total lack of justification or concern. My teacher's hand flopped to his side. "Well . . . take a seat, please."

"Sure," Tristen agreed, starting to make his way down the center aisle.

"We have an odd number this year," Mr. Messerschmidt began to point out.

"That's fine," Tristen said, heading toward the empty table at the back of the room. Lab station ten, where I'd nearly ended up.

"I *suppose* we could have one team of three," Mr. Messerschmidt suggested as we all followed Tristen's solitary progress. "You could join—"

"No, I'm good," Tristen interrupted, thudding his messenger

bag on the table, claiming the space. He slid onto the stool and began to leaf through the textbook, sort of shutting Mr. Messerschmidt—and all of us—out.

There was a weird moment of silence, during which we all stayed swiveled toward the back of the class, looking in Tristen's direction. He continued reading.

"Well, then," Mr. Messerschmidt finally said, clapping his hands again, ending the interruption and regaining control of the situation, which Tristen had somehow hijacked with nothing more than a casual disregard for . . . everything.

Over the course of the next half hour, our teacher proceeded to guide us, page by laborious page, through the contents of the lab manual, advising us of all the ways we could inconvenience the local emergency crews, the school district, and the Commonwealth of Pennsylvania by variously scalding, searing, asphyxiating, and blowing each other up if things were mishandled.

I'd had Mr. Messerschmidt for basic chem the year before, and I knew all the proper procedures, but I turned the pages anyway, as directed.

But now and then, for some reason, my mind would wander back to the far end of the classroom. To Tristen.

Did he even remember that day in the graveyard? Should I tell him, someday, that he'd been right—and wrong—back then? That some things had gotten better . . . but some had gotten much, much worse as the police had delved into my dad's activities, exposing a double life? Late nights at Carson labs. Murky images on security cameras. Unexplained thefts of chemicals that seemed innocuous enough, but which Dad had stolen, nonetheless.

And then there was Mom, who still seemed to be hanging on by her fingernails.

My grief had softened a little as Tristen had promised on that day he'd held me. But I wouldn't say life was "better."

Would I tell Tristen all that someday?

Of course, I knew I wouldn't. We hadn't even talked again, except to say hi in the halls now and then. I wouldn't go bare my soul to him just because we'd shared one close moment in a cemetery.

Yet I found myself glancing over my shoulder at him. And when I did, I saw that Tristen wasn't following along with his lab manual. It wasn't even on his desk. He was still reading the textbook, which was spread open before him, and his mouth was drawn down in concentration, like he was engrossed in some concept or theory that challenged him.

I watched his face, his mouth, thinking, *Those lips have brushed against mine.*

How weird that touch seemed in retrospect. Tristen was like a million miles away from me although we were in the same room. How was it that he'd ever held me, stroked my hair?

Like the rest of that whole period of my life, it all seemed part of some crazy dream. A crazy *nightmare*.

I must have stared at Tristen so long that he sensed me watching, because he glanced up from his book, caught me observing him, arched his eyebrows . . . and smiled. A smile that was at once surprised, questioning, and maybe a little teasing. A grin that managed to say, "Me? Really? I'm flattered, I guess!"

NO!

I whipped back around, face flaming. Why had I been studying him?

Becca had noticed the whole thing, too. She elbowed me and whispered, "What was *that* about?"

"Nothing," I told her, meaning it. "Nothing!"

Then the bell rang, rescuing me, and I gathered up my books, refusing to look in Tristen's direction again. Fortunately Becca was immediately shanghaied by Seth—or maybe it was vice versa—so I was spared more questions.

But I wasn't quite in the clear. As I made my way toward the door, Mr. Messerschmidt called out above the din of chattering students. "Jill! Darcy! Hyde! Come here! I have something for you three."

Turning to see what our teacher wanted, I noticed that he held a few folded sheets of lime green paper. "I'm coming," I said as Mr. Messerschmidt began waving the papers, using them to summon us.

Under the room's fluorescent lights those colorful flyers *looked* like a cheerful enough invitation. But in truth, the bright leaflet with my name on it would turn out to be the ticket to a lot of dark places.

Dark places in my school.

Dark places in my home.

Dark places in *myself.*

Standing shoulder-to-shoulder with Tristen and Darcy, who would take the wild ride with me, I opened the flyer and read.